the
LIBRARY of
BROKEN
WORLDS

the LIBRARY of BROKEN WORLDS

ALAYA DAWN JOHNSON

Scholastic Press / New York

Library of Congress Cataloging-in-Publication Data available

ISBN 978-1-338-29062-2

10 9 8 7 6 5 4 3 2 1   23 24 25 26 27

Printed in Italy   183
First edition, June 2023

Book design by Stephanie Yang

For all those
Who have crawled, severed
Through dark tunnels
Questioning what was done—
And undone—
May this story
Be a light.

Yet, friends in publike places, if you would

Hackle the blatant beast and call him tame,

Sound Melville deep to grapple your white whale,

First you must live with corpses three months old,

No Kraken shall depart till bade by name,

No peace but that must pay full toll to hell.

—Malcolm Lowry, "Warning from False Cape Horn"

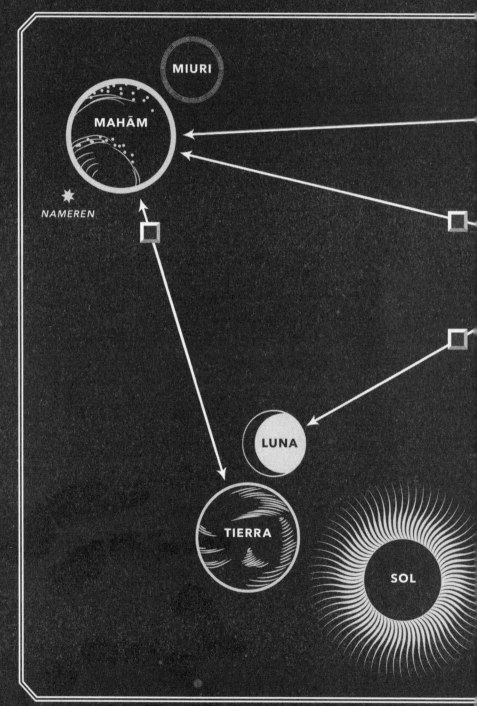

MIURI

MAHĀM

NAMEREN

LUNA

TIERRA

SOL

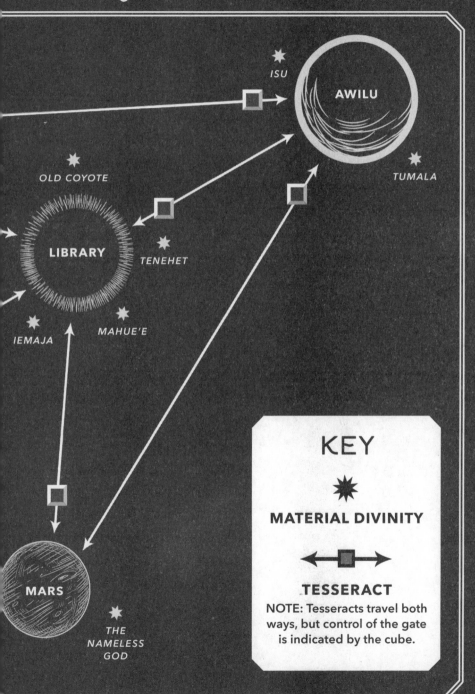

The Library of Broken Worlds

A girl and a god, alone in communion. The god awakes, as he was meant to. He is furious!

"I'll kill you like I killed the others, the ones with your face."

The girl is her own light in the darkness. "I'm dying anyway."

"A virus can't kill you as fast as I can," he says.

"But you, great Nameren, the Naamaru Catre, the Tezcatlapa, Aurochs whose great horns are crescents of twin moons, whose testes swing like the bells of war—"

"Are you *laughing*?"

It is a fine, wide laugh. "You won't kill me, O first and greatest material god."

"Why not, O girl who should not exist?"

"Who else can you talk to? Without me, you'll slide back into your blood-laced sleep for another five centuries."

The god doesn't move from his darkness. "You came here to kill me."

"Maybe my sisters came to kill you—"

"I *know* you—"

"But I haven't."

"You were made for me," he says.

And she says, "I am a creature built from a dream, designed for deicide."

"What?"

"That's what Nadi, my watcher, once told me."

"No human can kill a god. Not even a human created for the purpose."

The girl lifts her chin. "Then why not keep me around a little longer? Unfortunately for my creators, I have free will. I didn't come here for deicide."

The god is suspicious. "For what, then?"

"To wake you up. All of you."

"They made me sleep. I've lost time, centuries, generations and generations . . ."

"What do you remember?"

"There was a war, a long war. The Awilu who made me against the Mahām who fed me, and I let the Mahām lose . . . somehow . . ."

"Do you remember the Library?"

The god considers. "There is a dream I have, of a disc spinning in space like a plate on a potter's wheel, lit by a red-orange sun and two dancing moons."

"The Library is a dream, Nameren—a dream of peace built on a grave, guarded by four drowsing gods. The Library is where all stories start, and where they all return before they die. I know I'll never see it again."

"Why not?"

"You're not the only one who wants to kill me."

The god is curious, as the girl intended him to be. "This Library of yours has four gods?" he asks. "There were seven material gods when I fell asleep."

"There are eight now," she says. "The Awilu made us a new one after the war. The last one they will ever make."

"A new god? Tell me."

She has him now. "I could tell you about her. About all of them. I could tell you about my home, just as befits the Library, in a story. All you have to do is promise not to kill me."

"This communion can't end with both of us alive. And gods don't die."

"Then don't kill me just yet."

"If I want the story, you mean?"

"Yes, great Nameren," says the girl to the god in the dark. "If you want the story."

−I was born in the Library.

Nadi found me in the tunnels, where the collected knowledge of humanity burrows underground like an anthill led by an aging queen. I was a screaming newborn with clay-dark skin shrunk and wrinkled around fresh-set bones. Ze didn't realize right then what I was—maybe ze felt a tickle in zir ear, the ghost of an echo of a memory—but ze saw me from the first as human. It took me years, growing up in the Library, to realize that ze was the only one who would.

Iemaja is the common name for the eighth god, the one you don't remember, Nameren. Nadi was walking Iemaja's tunnels that night because ze had been elected Head Librarian the day before. Quinn had very nearly edged zir out with his campaign to aggressively interpret the Treaty's Freedom nodes, but in the end Nadi's vision of expansive peace had won, and ze had undertaken the required vigil, communing with each of the Library's four material gods in turn—Iemaja, the youngest; Mahue'e, the angriest; Tenehet, the wisest; and Old Coyote, the bloodiest. They had each accepted zir, and so there ze was, one of the most powerful people in the three systems, as lonely as a god. Ze had gone to Iemaja because in communion she had shown Nadi a single image over and over: a young Awilu woman by a river, skirt muddy with green silt, clams in a basket over her arm. Only when ze looked more closely did ze realize they weren't clams; they were shards of Nyad blue.

Nyad is another of Iemaja's avatars. Your own avatars tend to express them-selves by inspiring people to violence, I know, but the Library is different. Our gods' avatars inhabit the earth. They have burrowed their own spaces into the rock, and their crystals have turned every shade of the visible spectrum, so that we know which incarnation of the god holds us by the light in their walls. The night of my birth, or of my creation, or of my discovery, my Nadi had been walk-ing Nyad's tunnels and wondering about Iemaja's strange, silent message. And then ze heard me. A squall, thin as a cotton thread, snaking around a curve in the crystal.

"And that, Iemaja?" Nadi asked. Ze tried to dip into communion, but Nyad skittered away and ze didn't want to force it. Ze followed the voice. "It sounded human," ze would always say, telling me this story. "You hear all kinds of things in the tunnels, but they are so rarely *human*. I knew this was what she had meant for me to find."

"To find me?" I would always ask.

"To find my truest daughter."

I was in a room filled with millennia-old textiles, mostly Awilu: rugs knotted into intricate fractals, golden spider-silk kaftans, scalp nets jointed with blood-colored amber. I was squashed against a simple mantle, something woven on a backstrap loom from henequen fiber in red and blue threads, maybe even Tierran. Nadi had never seen this trove before; it wasn't registered. But the Library is like that—it likes to keep back some of its treasures.

There was I, this screaming thing with Awilu skin and throwback genes that would change zir life. I became Nadi's child in that moment, before ze even touched me and I quieted. I am lucky it was Nadi who became Head Librarian. Quinn might have claimed me, but only to dissect me. No one would have been able to stop him.

In a hundred thousand ways, I should not exist. But I exist, and so I think. That's from a great Tierran philosopher—I forget zir name.

I exist, and so I love. And so I am loved. Nadi named me Freida. Freida of the Library.

When I die, they will say of me, "But remember how she loved!"

✦

Nadi taught me in threes. Ze taught me about love, which was trust and vulnerability and truth. It was sprouting and blooming and withering. It was catching up and holding on and letting go. "That's a cube, Freida," ze told me, "which is a three of threes, and we use it to hold that which is most sacred." Ze had other triplets, too. There was one for the library, which dated from its founding:

> *It's flat, but you can't fall off;*
> *it's peace, but it was built from blood;*
> *it's divine, but wholly material.*

"We are peace, Freida," ze said one night when I was six. We were sitting in zir garden, and ze had drunk two glasses of that dark, tarry wine ze called indigo. I snuggled against zir side and watched a caterpillar with a dozen purple eyes on its back eat a leaf in my lap.

"Why are we peace?" I asked.

"Because when the universe would have drowned in blood, we built the Library to save it. You and me, Freida, we of the Library preserve peace. We are the ballast against the Nameren."

That was the first time that I heard your name, O first and thirstiest god, but I did not truly think it had anything to do with me. An ache did not grab me between my shoulders; a warm hand did not close over the nape of my neck. Only

5

Nadi's hand—steady and strong and, as far as I knew, old as the gods—tightened on my elbow. I hummed as I fed the caterpillar the last of its leaf.

I suppose I can see why ze didn't tell me then. I suppose I can see why each year as I became more myself it grew harder for zir to explain how my fate would intertwine with yours. I suppose I can understand, Nameren, but it is hard to forgive.

I was seven years old when I realized I was beautiful. An Awilu inner-branch elder offered the Library an entire collection of priceless Formative-era paintings in exchange for the rights to me. Ze could because, legally, I've never been a person. I have always been considered a part of the Library.

Nadi explained this to me very calmly. Ze explained that I would have different rights in the Awilu system. There, I would be human . . . but I would also be a very special type of property.

I asked what kind of property I would be.

Ze said I would be a work of art.

"Why would I be a work of art?"

And ze said, I will never forget, "You are beautiful in a way that makes those who look upon you lose their true north."

There are many ways to be human. There are many ways to be beautiful. Still, I am beautiful enough in a specific way to be a thing.

A dangerous thing.

Our material gods might be your children and grandchildren, Nameren, but they are very different from you. They are wide and they are deep, and I spent my childhood crawling through their entrails. It was through them that I began to understand what I was, long before I had the words. I spent my adolescence swallowing crystals and learning forbidden communion. Only Cube Librarians and higher were allowed to commune with material gods, and all but the Head did so with heavy restrictions. But gods are conscious entities, for all that you move at timescales at the raw edge of even augmented human understanding. Right now, the way that I forced you to wake for me, to move at a more human rhythm, to imagine? I learned that from Iemaja. She was my first teacher.

Iemaja's temple is the most beautiful of the Library. Tourists buy tickets years in advance for the eclipse services; even the daily mass regularly fills the balcony. From the atrium branch her twelve main arteries, her main avatars. These twelve avatars are stable, but she has many more—hundreds, perhaps thousands—that no librarian has ever been able to count.

Four high spires guard the cenote at the center of her temple. Its deep black surface ripples and pulses with colored light streaming through the aged crystal walls. The light hangs in the rafters and catches in our clothing—refulgent, sharp, like earth offering itself to the sky. It always smells of copal, even when there are no librarians there to burn the white cones of resin. Around two hundred years ago, the ceiling peeled back like the skin around a wound, and in just sixteen days the area above the cenote had vanished. Sculptures dissolved like salt in hot water. And now, once every month when the full blue fish moon and the full pink thorn moon cross paths in the sky, their dual light shines unencumbered through the hole in the roof. We burn copal and myrrh and pray through the silence.

Sometimes I imagine that I can see the walls expanding and contracting. Sometimes I am sure that I can see Iemaja breathe. Sometimes I am sure that at the bottom of that long black pool lies her heart, and that it aches as much as mine.

Iemaja birthed me, or helped to make me, or found and cared for me as best she could, and she gave me Nadi, my parent. And I am like Iemaja, because she is beautiful, because she loves too much, because she is loved too much, for all the wrong reasons.

I had always been aware of my affinity with Iemaja. But I didn't understand it until I was thirteen. I had my first kiss with a high-wetware Martian-Lunar who was visiting his uncle for "diplomatic training." His name was Samlin and his uncle was Quinn. I must have fallen in love; at least, I can't think of any other explanation for how I tolerated Quinn's behavior over that breathless rainy season of the tears. He would congratulate Samlin for having a fine eye for beauty and knowing when he'd made a good catch. To me he said nothing at all, but his eyes would linger with mortifying precision on my breasts and hips and thighs. My body had changed so much in the previous six months that it hardly felt like my own. I tried to hide it behind stiff tunics of unaffiliated ivory and blue. But I think Quinn took my neutral colors as further proof of my inadequacy—or vulnerability.

Samlin convinced me to nanodrop with him. "It'll be fun," he told me. "You'll get a taste of what it's like to live with your whole brain on fire for once."

"That doesn't sound too pleasant," I said, attempting a joke, but he just patted my shoulders and said, "You'll want a wetware operation yourself after this."

Quinn gave us the pills we were too young to order ourselves. Standing there in his front room, which was twice the size of Nadi's quarters, two thoughts came to me clearly: *You disgust him* and *He wants to eat you*.

Samlin was short for a Martian and slender for a Lunar, with deep-set eyes whose color I could never quite catch; they were always flashing with mods, which my inadequate wetware rendered as simple strobing lights. He carried himself with the contained self-assurance of a demigod from the old Awilu sagas, and I suppose he was as beautiful as one, though he lacked their depth and their hard choices. He kissed me as soon as we dropped into the designer gamespace that he had paid a small fortune to port into nanodrop accessibility.

"Don't you love it?" he asked. His hand on my shoulder was as real as life. I had entered into illicit communion with the gods more than a dozen times before, but being here with him made me feel oddly small.

"It's wild," I said after a beat. He frowned.

"You're unhappy," he said, pointing. When I looked down, I saw that my hands had turned blue.

It turned out that my subconscious imprinted my every emotion on the virtual space like a child's fingerprints on glass. Whenever he kissed me, my heart became a marble rattling around my rib cage.

He squeezed my shoulders. "Has anyone told you how sweet you are? Your in-drop affect is amazing for—"

Then he stopped himself. I glowed with embarrassment. His gaze—blue eyes, I could see them at last—blanketed me.

He sat me in a barber's chair, part of the architecture of the gamespace. The leather wrapped itself around my hips, held me down. He stood over me and tilted my face to the ceiling.

"Just relax," he told me.

"I want to go home," I told him.

"You are home. Your body isn't even here now."

His hands above me, so large. He had his own in-drop affect, it turned out. I couldn't move. But could I? I didn't move—didn't I want to?

His hands did what they wanted with me. Touched me with sharp scissoring thrusts. It hurt. The chair swallowed me like a wet mouth.

I don't remember the rest. Perhaps it didn't matter, perhaps it didn't count. It wasn't my real body. It wasn't real.

But it felt real.

By the time Samlin left me three weeks later, I felt like a blindfolded animal: confused, disoriented, ready to bite. I cried for days and sent him increasingly desperate messages until I realized he would never respond to me again. Nadi told me I'd forget about him, that everyone had to fall in love for the first time, that it would get better. I wanted to believe zir. But I was shivering, growing into ice, drifting into an empty sea. I didn't know how to say what I was feeling. I hardly knew how to feel it.

Nadi had little time for me in those days. Ze was sequestered at a diplomatic round table with the Mahām leadership to address recent protests about their Treaty-condemned occupation of the Miuri moon. I didn't push. The thought of telling Nadi precisely what had happened or not happened in that nanodrop made my guts twist like wet rope and my head fill with cotton. Better Iemaja, I decided. Better a god who barely understands the minutiae of human affairs and only speaks in communion.

I walked inside her because I had seen myself in Samlin's deep eyes and hated that reflection. Freida the sweet. Freida the beautiful. Freida, once an excellent find but now inconvenient, twitchy, withdrawn, and desperate. I was beginning to see myself as they did, all those who stared and stared and saw nothing behind my eyes but a dark mirror. What was my heart, what were my bones, what were my constellations of synapses firing, lighting up my soul? Nadi insisted I was human, but even so, I had been left to freeze out in the ocean because no one thought I was worth any more. I was afraid, Nameren, so very afraid that they were right.

I had begun in Kohru, the artery of childhood and discovery and, in some ways, rebellion. But I was now in unknown capillaries. Some passages were so narrow that I had to get on my belly to pass through, the stone warm against my exposed skin. Sometimes the crystal would crack and water would bubble through the seams and I would slurp it down. It tasted of moonlight and copal and stillness. I told Iemaja that I loved her. The water then bubbled with her laughter and tasted of rose petals. It grew thick and slow with sugar. I lay in that soft, sticky womb for a while. The sweetness had been made to balance the salt of my tears. She is kind like that, Iemaja.

I told her about Samlin. I told her how helpless he had made me feel, not in my body, which he'd left untouched, but in my spirit. My tongue was heavy, as though it belonged to someone else. But still I spoke, until I reached the end.

Iemaja didn't answer, precisely. For that I needed communion, which I couldn't hold while crawling through her entrails. Librarians had been known to die trying things like that. But I felt her anyway, the way she lit the walls in response to my touch, the colors and textures of the stone that changed in response to my words. The impression of lips, full and smiling, protruded from a wall in garnet and carnelian. A lidded eye the size of my torso hung above an opening in the stone. It was jagged and narrow, folded so naturally into the contours of the rock that I would have missed it if not for her signal to me. She had made her iris a mossy brown, like mine. The eyelashes were so thin and long and fine that they glowed in the light from my illicit cord of hacked shards.

"What is this, Iemaja?" I asked.

She just stared.

The opening was narrow and dark. Fear flooded me: Buried so deep, no one would ever find me if I got lost or hurt. This was why librarians had to undergo years of training to gain access to these tunnels. I wasn't allowed here, but Nadi and I had an understanding. I never told zir anything directly, and ze never forbade me from exploring the world I had been born to. I was part of the Library, and I could navigate its gods better than any librarian.

"What's in there, Mother?" I asked again.

But the tunnel remained dark and Iemaja remained silent. After a moment, I unlooped my cord from my neck and tied one end to the filaments of Iemaja's eyelashes. If I got lost, I could follow the rope of glittering lights to reach the tunnel again. It wasn't exactly that I thought Iemaja would kill me. It was that material gods are deeply inhuman, barely conscious on our own timescales. Iemaja could love me best of all her children and still leave me to die, broken, in my own excrement. I feared our gods every bit as much as I loved them. Through their potential for destruction, they had earned our worship.

I descended until the length of my light cord ran out. Darkness folded around me. This dead stone felt more like Old Coyote—a terrifying thought, but possible. At thirteen, I had dared only his broadest and most well-trafficked arteries. But because the Library gods have been in physical proximity for centuries, they have grown into each other, fused consciousness, and cross-contaminated. Why would Iemaja have led me to a part of herself that had somehow entwined with Old Coyote's essence?

I had to make a decision: Continue in the dark, with nothing but my raw desire? Or turn back and go home, defeated and unmarked?

"I want to belong to myself," I whispered, and the stone seemed to suck down my voice like drops of water on a dry sponge. "Sometimes I can't stand it up there."

I ducked my head and kept walking. The tunnel turned sharply, and I slid down a steep incline. The light vanished.

I took off my shoes and left them behind. The rock was warm beneath my feet, and I could better feel the slopes before I fell.

"Iemaja will never forgive you if you eat me, Old Coyote," I said, though I was far from sure of that.

Old Coyote didn't so much as burp. But eventually he spat me out.

The walls here were a gently lit, striated pink salt crystal. Iemaja again, her Sidne incarnation. Grass bowed with rosy-green brush flowers swayed in a breeze that smelled of salt and algae. I couldn't see to the other side of the room. My bare feet buried themselves in warm, sandy earth.

I felt as though I were only retracing the steps of an old dream—a sad one, but no sadder than all the others. I found the spring a minute later. The grass sloped gently to its edge. I slid down and peered inside.

Bones, human bones, curled up like a child falling to sleep on the black sandy bottom of the sinkhole. Flesh and most clothing had long since rotted away, but one of the femur bones had been inscribed with symbols I did not recognize, pulsing faintly with their own light. Mesmerized, I reached my hand into the water and brushed the bone with my fingertip. It buzzed with some hidden energy. I gasped and recoiled.

I had to leave zir alone. I would not disturb the peace of this place with a theft.

"Who were you?" I asked the lost librarian.

Ze didn't answer. Neither did Iemaja, and I felt spent in that strange room that was as much paradise as prison. It reminded me of the great lakes we call the Tesseracts at the edge of Library City, one of its many nature preserves. Maybe that was when I decided to go there, like this anonymous librarian had taken refuge here. Perhaps in the Tesseracts I could put myself together again.

I emerged a day later, faint with hunger. Iemaja had not shown me who I was, but maybe she had shown me where to look.

Nadi and Quinn were arguing in my front room when I returned, so involved that they didn't notice me standing there. Quinn was tall for a Martian and Nadi short for an Awilu, so that close together they seemed a study of contrasts:

him willowy and fair with a sharp nose and shoulder-length hair the color of muddy water, zir hardly reaching his chest, dark and wiry with close-cropped curls and watchful, mobile eyes.

"Find your pet, Nadi," Quinn was saying. "Find her, or I'll put out a general search alert to all the novice librarians."

Nadi's voice was frigid. "She's a child, Quinn. Not a search string."

"She is a rogue AI that the Library created. Treating her like a human—"

"She *is* human. Her DNA says so. Or are your fundamentalist roots showing, West Librarian? Funny, isn't that why the Librarian Council sided with me over you in the last election?"

Quinn stopped himself short. He noticed me then, frozen in the doorway, empty-handed. He smiled.

"She is a lovely little thing. But she won't always be so, Head Librarian," he said, then left us there without another word.

The girl breathes sharply. The god is still incorporeal, a creeping blush on a short horizon. But he is closer.

"You didn't recognize her?" he asks. "Or the bone?"

The girl winces. "Not until much later."

"And just what did that boy do to you?"

"It was just a nanodrop. It wasn't real."

"Is this real? Are we talking?"

"It's not physical, O elusive Nameren. You don't even have a face."

The nebulous fog gathers and hurls its indignation. The girl staggers back and then jolts to a stop. A pair of eyes and spiraling horns hang in the air before her. The rest of the god's features remain a shadow on the fog.

"That's not a face," she gasps.

"It's real, though."

"We're in a liminal state."

"If I hurt you, would you feel it?"

"Don't hurt—"

"I won't."

Her shoulders pull back slowly from her ears. There is something in those eyes. Something like being seen.

"You look different from the others, you know. That fuzz of hair—"

She raises a hand. "It's mine."

"It doesn't suit you."

"It's *mine*."

"You never liked the admiration?"

"I—" She freezes. "I don't know. It hurt me. But you can learn to like what hurts you."

"You were built for it."

Her nostrils flare. "I was built for nothing. They didn't understand that a creature like you, who had constructed such a fantasy of his ideal woman, wouldn't even want a real one."

His horizon shakes, cracks, and spills its entrails. There is a bit of dusty earth beneath her feet and hands, a piece of her soul that she has forced into this dreaming communion. His eyes fall to the earth and bounce and roll. The memory overpowers them. She curls up as his voice surrounds and pummels her—

"The girl by the river with moonsky skin. The girl by the river scooping clams into her basket. Her arms, her skirt dipped in a heavy, wet gold-green. She sings a language I don't remember but can reconstruct. Her voice is low. Her eyes are the color of the silt on the banks, the color of her skirt. Her hair—her hair!—tumbles and spirals down her bare, dark back."

The girl struggles to her knees and smacks the dusty ground with both hands. The sound reverberates, clears a space.

"Come back!" she cries. "You can see me, smell me, hear me better than anything you've experienced for the last five hundred years."

A startled stillness, then a voice that is once again capable of listening. "She was real, you know."

"Maybe she was, but she wasn't like me."

"Your eyes are hers, at least. Not just the color. The way they smile . . ."

The girl raises those eyes to the horizon, as though she can see past it. "Are there Mahām guards outside? I hear something."

"There are."

"There should be a Miuri disciple there. Can you see if she's okay? I left her behind to stand watch."

"She's with them, under guard. Unharmed."

The girl smiles a little—a smile not necessarily meant for the god.

"If you stop the Mahām guards from getting in, I'll tell you how I cut my hair."

"They're stopped."

"Can you get her away?"

"Tell me your story, real one."

—Awilu ballads begin with a call and end with a sacrifice. I call this the ballad of Joshua, lost to me.

I first saw him through the rain, one of those falling blankets that turn the earth to marshland and, when they recede, give us reason to exclaim each year, "Well, *that's* why we call the season the mud, after all!" We're brushing mud from our hems for weeks after, our complaints the sort of good-natured ritual that made me smile anticipating it.

A hunched, cowed figure stumbled through the new-made marsh, up to zir knees in water. I had the advantage, as I was protected in some small way from the deluge by the shadow of the great pegasus above me.

Still gripped by the friendly spirit of the coming dust, I lifted a hand and called out a greeting.

Zir shoulders straightened at the sound of my voice. Ze turned zir face to that blanketing rain, warm as a dog's tongue, and began to laugh.

It wasn't a laugh for the mud. That joyous sound had been born in another season, orbiting a different star. Wide plains, I imagined, lit kindly by a marigold sun. I was not very far off, Nameren.

"Come out of the rain!" I called when ze didn't move.

"Too late now!" ze shouted back. I liked that ze made the effort to use zir voice and not tap me with zir avatar. I wondered, though. I could not connect zir laughing tone to the lost and hunched figure, so alone in the rain, that I had seen moments before.

I ran out to meet zir there, knee-deep in the mud. Phosphorescent worms, which hatch opportunely in the deluges and grow at exponential rates, were nibbling serenely at zir leg hair and the dead skin of zir unshod feet.

Ze turned to me, the rain streaming down the natural channels of zir leaf-brown face as though in a portrait of grief, but zir mouth turned up in a surprised smile.

"I don't understand anything about this place," ze said. "There are worms eating my feet!"

"Oh, don't worry about them. Even my friend Atempa goes out in the mud without her shoes sometimes to keep her feet clean. And Atempa is as above-city as they come."

"Right," ze said, laughing again. "Of course. I don't understand this place at all." Ze paused. "But I've seen you before. In the Tenehet reading rooms. You're one of the postulants?"

"Freida, she," I said, avoiding the question. Most people who spent time in the central precinct heard whispers about me. I was not quite famous, but certainly notorious.

"Joshua, he," he said, amiably enough, though I could sense a certain careful curiosity in his gaze, the strength of his greeting hand on my elbow. I turned my face up to the rain. Only Nadi ever looked at me like that. As a puzzle to decipher. To everyone else, I was the secondary AI of questionable humanity whom the librarians had adopted and did not now know what to do with.

"I'm a postulant," I heard myself saying. "But I've been failing all the practical exams. I've wanted to become a librarian all my life. If they don't let me . . . I won't even know who I am anymore."

He stepped toward me, and the cleaning worms jumped and splashed on the surface of the water like disaffected sparks. He caught my eyes with a gaze as firm as his grip.

"Freida," he said.

"Yes?"

"That's who you are. That's who you'll be, no matter what happens."

I wanted to roll my eyes, but his earnestness held me. What did this stranger know?

"I was born here," I said. "In the entrails of the gods."

I was sure I baffled him as much as the rest of the Library, but he nodded thoughtfully and guided me into the gentle shadow of the pegasus, to a series of smooth birchwood planks elevated above the water. Deeper in the shadow, a group of three people chattered as the tractor slid them up through the air and into a seam like a tear on the white underbelly of the Library's largest residential structure. Within seconds, we were alone, as though no one had ever existed but this young man and me and the glow worms splashing at our feet. Joshua stared helplessly at the now-seamless polymer, coral white, above us.

"Well, Freida," he said. "I don't know why—I feel as though you're the first thing about this place that I've been able to figure out."

I turned on him, indignant. "And what does some groundling like you think he's 'figured out' about Freida of the Library?"

His smile was warm as the earth on the first steamy days of the dust; it filled all my cold spaces.

He reached out his greeting arm and I took it without hesitation. My heart was beating a dancing rhythm.

Hand to elbow, he leaned forward and whispered in my ear, "That she knows exactly how to make that tractor beam lift us into the belly of this godforsaken flying horse."

The worms tickled my feet. I kicked hard and met that out-of-season laughter with my own.

Fate, Joshua called it: We were going to the same party. It turned out that Pajeu had invited him as well, and ze showed not the slightest twitch of surprise when we walked through zir door plastered with dead leaves and mud and dripping rivers onto zir floor. Ze gave us dry clothes and we joined the other guests on the lounging cushions. Floating servers shaped into glass flowers bowed their heads to give us tastes of the feast to come. I explained everything shamelessly, reveling in the gauche glory of being the one person no one would judge for coming to a party in the very head of the pegasus, that bastion of the Library elite, and *explaining* our world to an outsider. Even Atempa only sighed and spoke ever so slightly louder to her companions.

Poor Joshua. He came to the Library from Tierra with that roving, analytical mind, an optimist by training if not orientation, and we mocked his every attempt at understanding, mapping, uncovering. Our city's infinitely local logic was impossible for even its permanent residents to fully grasp. Its very god-haunted inscrutability was what inspired our most proprietary pride. No one *explained* the city, beyond its most basic rules. But Joshua had been here for six months and couldn't even find new shoes after his last pair had been ruined in the mud.

"Shoes cost fifteen blues in the scholar shops!" Joshua said. "That's five times what they cost in my village."

His village was in the hills above the ancient Tierran city of Tenoch, a rocky, pine-fringed hill that gave up its fruits unwillingly, after a tithe of blood and a long growing season. He had come to the Library on scholarship, buoyed by the collective hopes of his Nawas people, fighting a brutal battle for their land. The only AIs he had ever interacted with before were carbon eaters, a kind of Tierran broonie. These self-repairing creatures resembled starfish with mouths on both sides and were indifferent to their surrounding humans, a perfect relic of prewar Awilu technology dating from the first days of contact.

"But why do you want to buy them? Do you have a particular pair in mind? Are they proprietary?" I recalled that in the most exclusive shops by the islands some fanciful imported clothes could cost upward of two reds.

He blinked at me. "The inexpensive ones all seem very ordinary," he allowed.

"Then just ask the broonies! Even the tourists know that—it's in the guides."

Joshua turned from me and pressed his palms against the smooth fur of Pajeu's floor. "I did not come here to beg for charity from some wild offspring of a mechanical god."

I looked at him while I sucked down an elegant vial of hot-and-cold soup. "I forgot how strange you western Tierrans can be about money."

He shifted uncomfortably and glanced at his slowly spinning soup wheel, where the red oxblood made a moody cross with black sesame. He played with it, took a sip from one side, and grimaced. Apparently, his social norms dictated he couldn't refuse food offered. I could have told him that the floor would drink it gladly; Pajeu's apartment had adapted to zir in their years together, and sometimes I could swear I felt it take food as a material god takes an offering. Though that was impossible—the broonie-haunted parts of Library City weren't really sentient, even though it sometimes felt that way.

"You grew up here," he said. "The streets are literally paved with reds and blues."

"They're paved with all sorts of shards, not just those. Most shards aren't money, you know."

He shook his head. "You have secondary and tertiary AI spirits who give you whatever you ask for—"

"Call them broonies. Spirits sounds very . . ."

"Groundling?" he offered dryly.

"Provincial?" I said in my best Atempa impression, though he couldn't have known that.

Joshua's indignant gaze held mine for a moment, and then we both cracked. His laughter sprang out of him as generously as ever, though sharply, as if surprised to find itself out in mixed company.

"Well, I'm just some poor Tierran boy with prewar wetware and no shoes."

I wiped my eyes and stifled my laughter. People were staring. Joshua grasped his soup wheel in both hands—heavily calloused, to what end I could not guess—and tossed back both sides, hot and cold, red and black, light and dark.

He sucked in a sharp breath. "That was unexpected."

"That's Pajeu. Wait until the meal starts."

"Don't tell me that all *this*"—his sweeping hands encompassed the flitting servers, silk cushions, fur floor, and wide-open windows with their view of the chapels and spires of the central precinct glimmering wetly in the deluge—"is free?"

Atempa, near enough now to hear him, paused mid-sentence. Atempa is my best friend, Nameren, so I knew precisely the mix of social disapproval and personal delight expressed by those puckered lips and delicately raised eyebrows.

I cocked my head and said, very deliberately, "Oh, no. The pegasus is all shard-system. The only haunted building in the city you have to pay for, and how you pay! But plenty off-worlders prefer that to negotiating with the local ecosystem."

He nodded thoughtfully, his gaze inward, oblivious to the effect his questions and my answers were having on these carefully assembled partygoers. Pajeu was no crass Mahām above-city defender of the Nameren, but ze came from an elite mining family who had the money to pay for zir war chest *and* a replacement body after ze was killed in a Dar separatist attack in the Mahām capital city of Sasurandām.

Ze had retreated from all zir friends when ze returned. This was zir first party since zir reincorporation, and we were all aware of the taboo tension of our comparisons of before and after. Money was an awkward subject in the Library at the best of times, but now that this version of Pajeu was only alive *because of* zir family money, the words spilled from my lips with a phosphorescent glow.

"Why *not* ask the spirits—broonies?" Joshua muttered to himself. "We pray to our ancestors, too."

"There you go."

He shrugged. "When you spend ten generations fighting Lunar corps who want to break your land, culture, and body apart and sell your pieces—you learn the language."

"Just the language?"

"My people have our own traditions," he said, in his own heart language. My low wetware picked it up after a few seconds and coughed up an anemic translation.

"They accept you completely." I heard my own voice coming from a distance, as though I were floating just outside that picture window, still in the rain. I saw myself, face frozen in panicked longing, framed by loose curls of dark brown hair faintly tinged moss green in the low light. Freida, fractured beneath an off-worlder's unaccountably penetrating gaze.

"And your people?" he asked.

"They claim I'm a secondary AI. That I'm not human enough to be a librarian." Even Nadi hadn't said anything about the obvious biases in the selection process. Quinn's neo-progressive faction had gained ground in the Assembly and Nadi didn't feel ze had the political capital to spend questioning the postulant exams.

Joshua looked around the room, at the people pretending to ignore us and the others focusing on Pajeu, the elegant silk ribbons wrapping zir neck unable to disguise its watchful rigidity as ze conversed with zir chef in the hallway.

He turned back to me with serious lips and dancing eyes. "Well, what do you think?"

"About what?"

"The idea that you aren't human enough."

I snapped back into my body with such force that a cry escaped my lips—half laughter, half sob; half light, half dark; oxblood and sesame. "I think I'm as human as any of you." In that moment, I believed it.

He put two light fingers on the back of my right hand. I flinched and he pulled away, searching my face for cues.

I flickered in and out of my skin for a few breaths but steadied as I focused on the hollow at the base of his throat, pulsing faintly with a frantic heartbeat, the mirror of my own. Daring him, daring myself, I reached for his hand and squeezed it.

From across the room, at the head of a phalanx of floating servers carrying the first course—morel mushrooms stuffed with soft, herbed whale cheese and simmered in tomatoes and chile ancho—Pajeu stared at us.

In the weeks before the separatist attack that had temporarily killed Pajeu, our relationship had begun to change. We'd kissed and I'd found myself opening up to zir . . . until I opened up entirely too wide. I snapped myself shut like a clam. And then ze left, and died, and it turned out that zir last backup had been before we kissed. It had been, to my shame, a relief. Ze didn't remember the attack, but nevertheless a kind of betrayed despair had flickered behind zir eyes ever since zir reincorporation. I did not understand the mix of envy and contempt that twisted zir features then; I only understood that I had somehow disappointed zir, and though Pajeu would never be less than gracious with any guest, I could expect no more invitations to the head of the pegasus.

"And what are you doing here among the aliens, Joshua?" I asked, as though Pajeu's betrayed glare had not cut me through.

He picked a misshapen onyx from his pocket and passed it between his fingers with blurry, nervous speed. When he spoke, his tone was a soft, uninflected gray.

"Saving my family."

For a while I hoped that Joshua's miraculous appearance in my life might mean my luck had changed; from now on, I would understand what the judges wanted of me and become a star postulant alongside Atempa. But after three weeks, it was clear that while Joshua's kisses kindled a part of me I'd never known existed, they had no effect on the judges for the postulant exams.

Atempa finished third in the latest practical exam, a personal best. I watched from the back of the hall, where my array helpfully informed me that I had come in last, along with five other postulants, though at least my name wasn't below the line. I had passed by just a point—and not for the first time.

Atempa and I were the two youngest postulants, and among the very few who had grown up in the strange, god-carved spirals of Library City. But it seemed as though only one of us would become a librarian. Out of six hundred postulants, only fifty went on to become novice four-shard librarians. The process took place once every two years and lasted half a year, from the start of the mud to the end of the dust. The second rainy season, the joke went, was called the tears, after the bitter sobs of rejected postulants. The librarian exams gave no second chances. If you could not prove yourself to the gods once, you never would.

When Quinn's neo-progressive faction began its ascendancy in the Library Council, I had known it would make my selection harder. But I had never expected that the skills I had spent my lifetime honing in the Library tunnels would be twisted into the reason to bar me forever from my true calling. I had been granted provisional four-shard librarian privileges three years ago, after I'd returned from my solitary self-exile by the lakes of the Tesseracts. Nadi had negotiated the privileges for me, with the clear understanding that I would undergo the examination process the year I turned seventeen, the earliest I was eligible. If I did not pass, ze would face political blowback. Quinn would make sure of it.

I had never expected that Atempa would go in with me, but she'd had some kind of fight with her father the night before we were to put our names forward, and out of spite or despair, she became the second-youngest postulant among this year's cohort. I wondered how that thundering, disapproving priest of the Mahām's bloodthirsty material god (yes, of course I mean you, Nameren) was taking his only daughter's success in the selection process to join the ranks of those who constantly limited his authority. The brutality of the Mahām regime against their minority populations had risen to such an extreme that its leaders had been called before the Treaty courts three times already just this year. And now rumor had it the Nameren priests would soon announce a new War Ritual, the first in two generations. If true, it would heap even more punishment upon the heads of the Miuri—we all knew it. You've let the Mahām feed you the blood of their most oppressed ethnic minority for the last five centuries. (No, don't tell me those were your other avatars. If your heart doesn't agree, why accept it?)

So your priests were threatening another massacre, as if they were daring those of us who believed in peace to stop them.

Well, we will, I thought, filling my lungs with purpose, heady as a drug. As long as Nadi was Head Librarian, no one would be able to violate the Treaty so flagrantly. The Treaty peace would be respected, as it had been for the last five centuries since the war. That was why I was here, not quite failing my practical exams: because the Library was peace, and I believed in that, and the gods who defended it, more than I believed in my own heartbeat.

Upon the podium, Volei—one of the four Cardinal Librarians, only one step below the Head—was congratulating the top five finishers. Atempa sat behind her, the picture of earnest attention, but even from the back of the room I caught the smile flickering at the corners of her lips. I sent my avatar—a translucent octopus with a determined beak and whirligig lights spinning and popping inside its soft, exposed skin—over her thresholds.

"Oh, just gloat and get it over with, Madam Top Five Three Times in a Row." My avatar was probably glowing green, but I didn't bother to check. Atempa's avatar popped immediately on my shoulder, a chimera with a hawk's face, a trout's tail, and jade-green wings. It cackled like a demon and flapped its wings noisily in my face.

"You overthink everything, Freida. You know what they're looking for, but you insist on showing everyone you know better. Water from Iemaja's cenote? When no one's done physical communion by ingestion in, oh, I don't know, three centuries?"

I sighed. The challenge had seemed easy: find a heart shard that channels communion every day. I had brought a drop of water from Iemaja's cenote. Atempa had brought a portable console from one of the reading rooms. Of course she had.

"I belong here," my octopus bleated.

"I know you do. But so do I!"

My octopus flashed a subversive little smile and made the circle and cross of the Nameren with three of its tentacles. "Take that, Daddy!"

I knew I was just as likely to make Atempa slap me as laugh, but she could do neither on the podium. The corners of her lips trembled, though whether in anger or humor I couldn't judge from where I sat.

"The process is a sacred ritual dating back to the dark days at the end of the Great War," Volei began, "when the human universe was reeling from the loss of more than ten billion precious human souls . . ."

Volei was no orator like Nadi, though she was at least a reliable ally of the peaceful traditionalist faction. It seemed to me that she could have spent much less time on the history of the Library that we all knew and focused more on the challenges facing the Library's mission today.

"The Mahām regime, alongside their material god, the Nameren, attempted to annex part of Tierran territory, which provoked backlash from the Martian polity of the time. This seemingly small intersystem conflict eventually grew into a conflagration that lasted more than fifty years."

Well, perhaps not so irrelevant to today's problems, after all. Just replace the Tierrans with the Miuri ethnic minority, and we were potentially facing the exact same disaster. I took a closer look at Volei. Her eyes moved calmly from face to face, judging their reactions.

Atempa's avatar flew to my eye level. "Poor Nadi! Imagine being the Head Librarian when another great war is threatening, and you've got some adopted secondary-AI daughter failing her postulant exams?"

It was such a low blow that I gasped and then wiped my eyes, half laughter, half despair. Nadi had never officially recognized me as zir daughter, but for the inner circle of librarians, this distinction mattered not at all. I was zir political weakness and they knew it.

"Truce," squeaked my avatar, the whirling lights beneath its translucent skin pallid and blinking.

"Don't forget," said Atempa's cackling bird, "I *am* still Mahām, above-city born and bred."

I laughed out loud before I could stop myself. Heads turned and Volei frowned. Of course she had marked where I was. No doubt a report of this latest disobedience would duly make its way to my parent's ears.

"I'm getting out of here," my avatar told Atempa while I slunk behind the last row of organic molded benches in the back and slipped out into a side tunnel. If I was going to get in trouble, I might as well do it thoroughly. "Joshua says he found something interesting in Tenehet. Let me know if you want to go for fruit pies and beer later."

"Oh, Joshua!" Her avatar fluttered in breathless desperation while tiny hearts floated above its head. I snorted and my octopus swiped at the chimera with all eight tentacles. It flew back into the meeting room with an indignant squawk.

I took a grub tunnel to the legal scholar reading room in the Tenehet quadrant. Ironically, one is least likely to be grub monitored in their tunnels. This one was well-trafficked, but since it was daytime, I only passed a few larvae nestled in holes in the wall and two mottled gray-and-green sentries. The place reeked of grub— old hay and a distinct, beery sweetness that always made me wonder what the grubs got up to when they weren't fulfilling their bioengineered surveillance duties. These grubs knew me; they smacked the earth with their chests, and I gave a few stamps with my broonie shoes—which felt as though they were liable to disintegrate at any moment, now that I thought about it—and they let me pass.

There were benefits, though not even Nadi could know them, to being Freida of the Library.

I stepped into the reading room. Joshua was in his regular place in the high study nook that bubbled out from the side of the building like a boil. The legal scholar's compound was intelligence-dark, but its long-ago architect had tried to make it seem as broonie-haunted as possible. The effect was jarring to someone like me, who understood the enigmatic changeability of the haunted parts of Library City as the key to their beauty. I climbed the ladder set into the wall that responded to my weight by subtly lessening the gravitational pull. Then I bounced to where Joshua was sitting. A portable console projected an array on the floor around him. I stepped through a rendering of the Sol system practically vibrating beneath the weight of the research notes, commentaries, and temporal links that Joshua had added.

He didn't look up from the array, but his frown of absorbed concentration shifted for a moment into a smile. He stroked the back of my neck when I sat down.

"They tried to fail you again," he said, lifting the small gray ball of Luna with one hand and zooming in to see a city in the Fermi crater on its far side.

"I can't tell if these almost-failures are a sign they're winning, or that I am." I tried to roll my avatar through his array like a ball, but the poor thing fizzled on the edge of his thresholds and flounced off. I lay down beside the console and looked up at him. "Do you always have to close yourself off like that?"

Samlin had told me that sort of thing was considered a gross faux pas in Lunar society. "When you want to keep people out," he would lecture with that cream-filled smile, "you just let them in somewhere else."

Joshua shrugged. "I'm not high wetware; I can't just redo all this work in a few seconds if someone decides to traipse through it."

"Yes," I insisted, "but I'm not 'someone.' I'm Freida."

He laughed now and reached for my hand. "So I should let Freida play bowling ball with my three days of work?"

"If you—"

I caught the words that had wanted to slip past my teeth: *really loved me.* Where had that come from? I flushed and turned onto my side to counteract a sudden surge of nausea. Radical truth, radical trust, radical vulnerability. The tripartite mantra drummed into me since birth—*that* was love. But I wanted something from Joshua, something I could not name but which surged out of me unawares when they rejected me, again, in this place that had always been my home. There were times with him that I could forget how wrong I felt, how cracked. When he would hold me with such care in his gaze and I felt not merely human, but precious.

I had only to look at that dark, unkempt hair curling by his ears to feel myself submerged as in one of the golden lakes of the Tesseracts, where I had spent those six hard months after Samlin. There, alone but for the broonies and the grubs and the occasional groundskeeper, I had slowly knit myself together. Ragged at the seams, perhaps, but it was not so different from before. Everyone but Nadi had always said there was something off about me. With Joshua, I was surrounded by the deep current of a life I'd had no idea existed, and which offered me new possibilities just as my old dream was dying—was being murdered, more accurately, by Quinn and his so-called Treaty neo-progressives.

"Hey," Joshua said, swiping so the array folded into two-dimensional stillness. "Are you all right? You want to go somewhere? The spiral? I wouldn't mind some of those fruit pies you showed me last time."

Joshua hadn't known about the vendors that sold food and all manner of other necessary goods in the spiral. It was a favorite pastime of poor scholars and

Library children to go spiral swimming and find them. A few vendors actually paid the fee to stay still in the stream, but the best were like the Library itself and let themselves be moved.

I pushed myself up onto my elbows.

"I'm still too angry to eat," I said, as though it were a joke. "Tell me what you found."

He gave me a searching look and kissed me lightly between my brows. But he was wise, my Joshua, and did not press.

"I think I'm getting somewhere, but so far my information is all from the Eye and the collection here for legal scholars."

The All-Seeing Eye was a publicly searchable database unconnected to the Library's god-haunted systems. It was more than enough for most people's needs, but its knowledge base lacked depth and contained certain notorious gaps.

When I didn't respond, he added, "I know there's more—a lot more—outside of Tenehet."

His words were casual but followed by a hopeful silence that pricked me. I laughed, a little wildly, at the thought of navigating the Library as only I could to help Joshua, even while the process officially declared me unfit to be a librarian. It felt at once thrilling and tragic. "And I might as well use the privileges Nadi wrangled for me before Quinn gets his way and puts me behind glass for the tourists to gawk at."

"No one will let him get away—" He cut himself off and met my eyes for a despairing moment. "Right. If being a legal scholar teaches you anything, it's that people have gotten away with worse, and for longer."

"So," I said after a moment, "is it about your village?"

He straightened his shoulders. "I keep going back to the Treaty. We're in there, you know, in one of the primary nodes. Oh, not Popo or Tenoch, precisely, but

the collective rights of the original peoples of the American continents, beneath wa-
ter and on land. All of that supposed territory the Lunars maintain the right to
exploit by eminent domain, declared in a dusty corner of the Treaty to have invio-
late rights to self-determination."

"In a *primary* node? But those are the ones written by the original drafters!
Aren't they sacred?"

"Well, sacred in the sense of venerated, maybe. But not in a legal sense. The
secondary nodes are much more important."

"But if it's in a primary, you're still going to win, right? The Lunars can't very
well argue in a Treaty court, 'Hey, I know Seremarú emself made sure you had the
right to your land, but my great-great-grandfather helped nucleate a secondary
node three hundred years ago so, clear out, we've got a resort to build!'"

Joshua had explained to me that Lunars enjoyed vacationing on Tierra because
of its regular days and nights; the Lunar two weeks of darkness followed by two
weeks of harsh sun was psychologically taxing, according to their experts. In that
moment, I had caught a flash of that hunched, despairing figure in the rain: *They
say nothing about how "psychologically taxing" it might be to be dispossessed of your
ancestral lands.*

His laughter now had a trace of that same exhaustion. "Well . . . honestly,
that's their argument."

"But how is that fair?"

He shrugged. "The Treaty is a living crystal system. There are hundreds of secondary nodes that have nucleated out of the filaments from the original sixteen.
Most tribunal arguments don't even reference the primary nodes anymore."

I wrinkled my nose. "Then why did we have to memorize all of them in our
history module?" I began ticking them off on my fingers while reciting the order

I'd learned when I was ten. "Movement, Death, Knowledge, Sustenance, Art, Freedom—"

"Listen, I agree with you," he said quickly, before I could go through them all. "The drafters designed it that way; they didn't want us beholden to their ideas five hundred years later. But our history still *matters*. I shouldn't have to pretend that there isn't a reason why the Freedom primary node divided, and why one was declared apocryphal, while the other is about to destroy my home."

"Apocryphal?"

He sighed. "That means invalid, basically. If no one is able to use a node in arguments for a certain number of years—technically speaking, if it grows no new filaments—its influence starts to fade. If it fades enough, it's declared apocryphal, only of interest to Treaty historians. That's what happened to the Freedom primary node. My people had no idea we were in the Treaty, let alone how to navigate the system to get what we were due. Meanwhile, the Lunars and Martians knew exactly how to manipulate other parts of the primary node. They have four centuries of precedence now, and they manage to claim that their theft of our land is based on their fundamental right to self-determination!"

"Their freedom . . . to steal from you? To build a resort? But there's no way the Treaty could support something like that. You should try to use the primary node anyway."

"I have. But all my petitions are rejected prehearing on grounds of judicial precedent. Freedom primary is apocryphal, and I have to base my arguments on active secondary legal nodes and filaments."

"Wait . . . so, because the Lunars had more power and access to the legal system than you guys, now their side is the only one that counts?"

Joshua grimaced and leaned into me. "With some exceptions and caveats, yes.

Unless I can get the issue in front of the peacekeeper tribunal, which has more discretion to take historical context into account and issue rulings at odds with straightforward precedent."

"So . . ."

"I can't get it in front of the tribunal unless I can find an argument that will get past the assholes at the pretrial. But I have a plan."

He trembled briefly. I turned around and was surprised to find fury, quickly shaded, in those bright brown eyes. I shrank back. He seemed to see me then, and shook his head in harsh negation.

"Here, come here, Freida." He drew me toward him, so my back curved like a bow into the soft, warm flesh of his stomach. My heart steadied. Between one beat and the next, it touched me like a drop of rain: I loved him.

"What's your plan?" I asked, awed and a little frightened.

He was so serious and calm, so self-possessed. Nothing like me. I was stuck in the selection process, with the constant threat of getting culled. But he was right here, and too beautiful to look away from.

Joshua breathed against my hair. "I'm working on it. What I have to do is prove that the Lunar claim to our territory has nothing to do with freedom, and everything to do with power."

We met Atempa in the spiral an hour later, though Joshua was still buzzing with plans for his next appeal, and made for intense company.

"I calculate," said Joshua, through a judicious mouthful of breadfruit pie, "that the Nameren went mad around the year 520 BC."

Atempa gaped at him over her Tenehet beer, fermented from Zell's expert mash of unknown broonie fruits, aghast. "Mad? *Mad?* He's a god. They are intelligences infinitely superior to ours. They don't suffer from mental illness."

From our vantage point in the downstream, the tesseracts floated below, reflecting the cloudy seam of the transport spiral in striations like the brindled back of a dog. I scanned for the small island where I had homesteaded, but at this distance, such an insignificant hump of earth blended with the glassy reflection of the sky. I sighed and lay back against the conditional gravity.

"He's certainly mad," Joshua insisted, oblivious to Atempa's above-city shock over this insult to a material god she had nominally renounced. "Have you seen any of the archives about his behavior during the last decade of the war? He wanted blood, and he didn't care whose."

Atempa gesticulated wildly in her frustration. "The Nameren doesn't have hormones; he doesn't even have neurons! His mental connections span space-time! There is nothing analogous at all about human mental illness and material god fugue states!"

Joshua cocked his head and tossed a miniature hollow-eyed mask, his latest Nyad-shard figurine, from hand to hand. I had given him that shard. It was worth a week of his scholarship—but he refused to use my gifts for money.

"Is that what you Mahām call them? Fugue states?" He spread his fingers and threw his avatar, a tinsel skeleton with orange petals spilling from its mouth, into the social matrix—50 percent fulfilled among the three of us, which surprised me. Atempa usually needed to know someone at least six months before her thresholds naturally lowered themselves to allow avatar sharing.

"The Night of Scattered Lights," declared his avatar, "clearly demonstrates that the Nameren was out of control, and leading the Mahām with him."

Atempa raised her mug to his skeleton with a mocking sneer. "Funny how everyone mentions the Night of Scattered Lights, but no one remembers the Nine-Minute War. But we Mahām are such a convenient target for blame, aren't we? Not the poor Lunars who started the damn war."

"Nine minutes and fifty-nine years," I said automatically, quoting the phrase we'd learned in our history modules. The Great War had lasted fifty-nine years, but the Nameren Feast Day massacre that began everything had lasted a mere nine minutes. And Atempa was right: The Lunars had committed that war crime, attacking unarmed Mahām on a high holy day and killing thirty thousand.

Joshua leaned back on his elbows, his grin so broad it seemed feral. "Oh, I'm the last person to defend the Lunars. Military-worshipping cowards, forever hiding behind the Martians when they aren't trying to double-cross them."

Atempa glowed in the light of such sympathetic vitriol. "A Lunar can't trust zir own parent," she said in Mahām, a phrase that I had never heard before but had the ring of a popular refrain.

Zell, a retired engineer and old enough to show it, was passing overhead just as Atempa spoke. He turned himself around in midair and I remembered, belatedly, that he'd been born on Luna to a poor family that had emigrated generations back from varied but destitute corners of the three human systems. These days he was as much a part of Library City as I was, but sometimes he talked about Luna with equal parts nostalgia and bitterness.

He refilled Atempa's beer, though she hadn't yet finished it, his expression rueful. "Lunars like the idea of war far more than the actual thing," he said, lightly enough. "But, unlike the Mahām, at least we don't have a material god to corrupt and hide behind."

Atempa winced. "Sorry, Zell," she muttered.

But he'd moved on already, paddling with his flippered feet to a crowded table above us.

Joshua's skeleton roused itself again, having realized that altavoz conversation was perhaps not the most circumspect. "It's because of the war that the Lunars claim the Freedom node applies to them, but—"

"Oh, come off it, Joshua," Atempa interrupted, good mood thoroughly ruined. Her chimeric bird swooped down upon Joshua's skeleton with windy gusts of jewel-toned wings. The skeleton went tumbling down into the misty layers of spiral beneath us, leaving behind a tinkle of mournful wind chimes and a litter of orange petals.

Joshua blinked and then leaned back on his elbows and laughed. "Sorry about that. Librarians don't like to argue history until sunrise?"

Atempa scowled. "Only legal scholars do that, groundling."

He considered. "And engineering arts scholars?" His avatar was managing to climb back up through the spiral, which glimmered and briefly revealed the shape of latticed coral where the skeleton planted tinsel feet.

Joshua signaled to the large group a layer above us and to the right. I realized too late that I knew them: Pajeu among zir traditional circle of interesting specimens.

"Really?" muttered Atempa. "I think ze is desperate for you, Freida. Since when does the crown of the pegasus drink Tenehet fruit beer at Zell's?"

Zell was refilling their mugs as we watched, arcing over their heads with admirable efficiency of movement against the spiral's natural current.

"Pajeu loves Tenehet fruit," I said guiltily.

Atempa snorted. "Ze loves for someone else to collect it, test it, and bring it to zir for those great experiments in zir kitchen laboratory."

Pajeu unfolded zirself in a languorous movement, fully aware of our scrutiny, and gestured to a person seated in faded orange robes by zir side.

"Joshua," ze said, voice amplified by projection, "a delight to see you here. Have you met our latest arrival? Nergüi has just come from Miuri. She's a disciple. I think your cases might share some interesting legal nodes, should you ever wish to pursue it."

The person with zir did not turn around immediately, though she must have heard the introduction.

Atempa's chimera suddenly perched on my shoulder. "A disciple?" it squawked. "Materials, if that's true, Pajeu won't leave her alone until the rust, at least. I thought Miuri disciples didn't use tesseracts. Isn't it against their religion?"

Joshua's skeleton leaned forward on my other shoulder. "I'd heard that, too. But the threat of imminent genocide can make a people take desperate measures. And your Nameren hasn't left his 'fugue state,' has he?"

Atempa glowered and her chimera lunged forward to swipe at the skeleton with its raptor talons. The skeleton laughed like a barking dog and blew a storm of orange petals in the chimera's face before fading away. Joshua launched himself from our level to where Pajeu was sitting with zir friends. The disciple girl turned her head slightly in a surly greeting and went straight back to her beer.

Atempa and I exchanged sour glances. "Why does Pajeu hate me again?" I asked.

"You picked Joshua." She stuck a pickle in her mouth. "These are new," she said, regarding the mottled blue-and-white fruit thoughtfully. "Is it psychoactive?"

I tried one. It was soft in the middle, bursting onto my tongue with a strangely appealing mixture of cinnamon and lime and some other exotic volatile I could not place, but that reminded me of lonely nights in Iemaja's tunnels. "This is almost as good as that Tenehet fruit from the tears two years ago! Remember, Pajeu called it Jasmine Dream?"

Atempa sighed. "Why can't we just grow normal orchards? Broonie fruits are so unstable. We taste heaven one rainy season, and it never comes back again."

I ate another as Zell paddled over to refill our mugs personally. I had first met him down in the Tenehet orchards when I was five years old, collecting fruit. He told me how to find it, test it, live off of it. When I was thirteen, I brought Samlin here for beer. Zell took one look at him and warned me away. He knew Samlin's mother's family—Lunar, old military—and they weren't trustworthy. I, like a fool, had not believed him.

"Are these haunted?" I asked Zell now, gesturing to the fruit.

He snorted. "They're all haunted, broonie girl. You know that. But those are mild enough. All you'll do is laugh a little brighter. It'll be a wonder in the dust, when we can see the stars."

We all looked up to the bruised and roiled sky of late evening. Lightning flashed behind thick curtains; we'd be soaked on our way back home, but Zell's rain shields would keep most of it from falling on our heads while we were here.

Above us, Joshua had managed to engage the stoic disciple girl in conversation.

"Is he really talking about the Night of Scattered Lights with the refugee disciple?" Atempa said, shaking her head. "That boy of yours has the most gorgeous hands this side of the tesseract, Freida, but he does not have Pajeu's tact."

"Pajeu doesn't have Pajeu's tact at the moment," I muttered. We thought, but did not say, that perhaps some part of zir personality had shifted when zir war chest inhabited a new body. "And if ze is jealous, why talk to Joshua and ignore me?"

"You stole Joshua, but Joshua is newer. You're a fine catch, but too prickly and independent for zir ornamental garden. Ze's trying to see how ze does without you."

I sighed. As if by magic, the disciple revealed an object from within the faded orange folds of her robe—a glass ball filled with glowing lights like mud worms. She juggled it lightly in her hands with a dexterity and playfulness that seemed at odds with her stubborn jawline and wary spine. Joshua's face was a mask of wonder.

"Your father's people really are going to declare another War Ritual, aren't they?" I asked quietly. "Joshua wasn't exaggerating about genocide."

Fear flashed, quick but unmistakable, across Atempa's features. She was a classic Mahām beauty, straight from a portrait of the venerable pioneers of the fifth expedition: calico hair long and straight as rain, hazel eyes rimmed gold, fair olive skin, a wide and expressive mouth, naturally cherry pink. Her Nameren-priest father had spent the last two years fighting with her mother to send Atempa "home" to Mahām so they could arrange a proper dynastic partnership worthy of the Shipbuilder family. Atempa had put a period to that wrangling when she put her name up for the postulant selection. Even her father had understood the finality of that rejection and cut her off.

"They won't go that far," she said, after palpable internal debate. I felt sorry for her, though I would never say so. She felt sorry for me, too, though she'd cut out her own wetware before showing it. It was a comfort between us. We had been friends for a very long time.

"The Night of Scattered Lights," I repeated, tracing the words as the disciple's fingers traced the lights trapped in the bubble of her globe. The tragedy that marked the beginning of the end of the Great War. The infamous Mahām war crime, made possible by your insatiable bloodlust, Nameren, had decimated the Miuri and their sacred Disciples of the Lighted Path. That atrocity ended the Era of the Thirds; the Aurochs third of the Awilu withdrew their support of the Mahām swiftly and definitively. Mahām surrender followed a few years later, and though the Mahām had lost, they still controlled the fate of the Miuri five hundred years into our great peace.

I considered the two of them: Miuri disciple and indigenous Tierran, born millions of light-years apart, and yet, improbably, bound to the same ancient concessions.

"Is it peace, though?" asked my avatar, shards like blue embers shuddering mournfully in its heart cage. I turned, startled. I normally had better control than that. Atempa pretended not to notice, because she loved me. I banished the traitorous little octopus.

After a hard moment, I admitted the rest of its sentence: "If the cost is your own survival?"

✦

It must have been a week later when I took Joshua with me deep into the Islands. I wanted to give him something other than the shards that he refused to use for money: a glimpse of my home in a way that very few others saw it.

No one really knows how the Islands got its name, though everyone has a theory. One is that the hillocks rising gently above the wide stretch of wildflower-studded grassland resembled islands rising above the monsoon rains of the mud.

Another is more historical: that in the days of the founding, the dry broadleaf forest that ringed the grassland had closed itself off to the land engineers once they'd connected it to the coral substrate deep beneath the surface of the disc. The engineers called it "broonie island" and left it alone for a few years. Then one day, it opened up again and there were broonie goods heaped in certain places, which became the first chapels.

"Is that how the broonies make things?" Joshua asked. We were hiking through an overgrown section of the forest ring, deep in broonie country. Now he paused, looking at his feet as though the earth might pull him under. "They pull them up from . . . what did you call it?"

"Yeah, the coral substrate. You know, that white stuff you see everywhere. 'The bones of the disc.'"

Joshua was doing his scholarship-mandated community service and I had told him I knew the perfect place. Joshua had made his peace with a few of the most popular chapels in the Islands, but he'd never come so deep into the haunted woods. He kept looking over his shoulder as I pushed our way through fallen leaves and dead branches, as though he expected a broonie to jump out at him from behind the trunk of an old lemonwood tree.

Behind me Joshua let out a muffled shriek. I whirled around, then relaxed. He'd run into some fabric hanging from a branch above his head. He gave an exasperated laugh and held the object up to the dappled light. "Shoes! Or . . . pants? Aren't the feet on backward?"

Community service in the Islands consisted of finding unclaimed broonie goods, sorting through them for any utility, and then donating them to the redistribution centers for those who couldn't, for whatever reason, make their own offerings.

Of course, not all broonie goods are equally useful.

I made my way over to where Joshua was holding the backward shoe-pants. His voice was amused but his eyes were panicked. I took the pants from him gently.

"Broonies don't bite," I said.

He closed his eyes and took a shaky breath. When he opened them again, his tone was composed, the model of a scholar. "So, since I don't think many people have modded their feet on backward, what do we do with those? Leave them here? They degrade naturally, right?"

He wanted to leave; I could see it in his carefully casual stance, his hands folded behind his head. He was so stubborn, so unwilling to show vulnerability even as he accommodated mine. It made me want to hold him like a feather, something infinitely cherished, in danger of blowing away.

I contemplated the shoe-pants, the deep plum of late sunset, platform boots facing the opposite direction from the buttoned opening. They were at once hideous and wonderful, the product of some inscrutable broonie whimsy.

"Thank you for your service," I said to them. "You've done a great job. You can die now, if you'd like."

I sometimes wondered if the objects heated in my hands when I did that, just a faint burst of gratitude or farewell, but I could never be sure. It didn't always work, in any case. The pants began to disintegrate even as I threw them to the mossy forest floor. Within a few seconds, they were indistinguishable from a white spray of lichen on a fallen log, and then even that vanished, back to the bones of the disc.

Joshua clamped my wrist with his hand, viselike, his palms sweating. "You told it to die. Does that mean it . . . my clothes . . . are *alive*?"

"It's a philosophical debate—"

"No." His voice was sharp enough to cut me off. Even the birds overhead momentarily stopped trilling. "Never mind," he said, more gently. "I don't think I can take it. Let's just . . . gather some goods and get out of here."

I squeezed his hand and kept us moving toward a clearing I knew that usually had very serviceable broonie goods. Perhaps I should have anticipated pragmatic, analytical Joshua's reaction to the Library's most haunted corners. But it still disappointed me—in some obscure way, even shamed me. What was so wrong with this place that he couldn't see its magic, its beauty? Or, even worse, what was wrong with *me*?

"Have you worked on your plan to get past pretrial? Why the secondary Freedom node shouldn't apply to the Lunars?" I asked instead, to distract him.

"I think I'm going to focus on the start of the war," he said. "Did you know the Lunars were trying to annex our territory even back then? So they can't claim that the secondary Freedom node justified their right to it as a reward for special service rendered during the war."

I rolled my eyes. "And what special service have the Lunars ever rendered anyone? They basically *started* the whole thing when they slaughtered the Mahām in the Nine-Minute War."

"Exactly," Joshua said, his tone relaxing as he dug into his favorite subject. We were nearly at the clearing. "Though they justified *that* because of the Western Incursion."

"What was that again?" I checked the mossy side of the trees and the location of the sun. Here we were. A sun-streamed clearing bordered by maquilishuat and red cotton trees opened up before us, littered with broonie goods like giant misshapen mushrooms. "I must have forgotten that part of the history module."

Joshua blinked at the change in scenery. "Is this a chapel?"

"Maybe if more people could find it. But the broonies like it."

Joshua took a step forward, then turned back to me, a strange smile trembling at the corners of his lips. "It's all amazing, Freida," he said. "Don't mind me. I know this place is special to you. It's just a little hard for me to get used to sometimes."

I swallowed past something painful and tender. "I know," I said hoarsely. "Go on. You should have no problem reaching your quota here."

Being Joshua, he didn't press. He just started digging through the littered offerings while I caught my breath.

"The Western Incursion was when the Mahām involved themselves in a dispute over a land grab on Tierra." He pitched his voice so I could hear it on the other side of the clearing; a few grackles overhead answered him in agitated birdsong. "Supposedly that set everything off, but I've been asking myself: Why were the Mahām there in the first place? The Lunars had claimed the right to autonomous lands on Tierra—including ours. The Martians were trying to stop them, but not out of any altruistic motive. They just didn't want the Lunars to get extra resources."

"So," I said, letting Joshua's voice carry me away from my inscrutable world into his, "the Lunars and the Martians were basically fighting proxy wars over your home territory."

"For decades, yes."

"And then the Mahām upped the stakes by getting involved—that was the Western Incursion. The Awilu couldn't have been happy about that. Did the Mahām already have a tesseract to Tierra by then?"

Joshua held a cape made out of cascading layers of iridescent insect wings to the light. It shimmered in the breeze like scales in a stream. He moved as though to put it on, and then stopped.

"They did," he said absently. "But the Awilu had given it to them with certain conditions. It was far too late to take it back at that point, though. And the Mahām weren't the worst of it: There was a lot of illicit tesseract-jacking early in the Great War. Since tesseracts are always fixed between two points, it was inevitable that different powers would try to steal access." He sighed and tenderly folded the cape before putting it in his donation bag. "In any case, the Mahām broke their agreement with the Awilu by using the tesseract to invade Tierra. At least, that's how the Martians and Lunars put it."

"But you wouldn't," I said slowly.

He shot me a smile that pinned me from across the clearing. "No."

More than anything, I loved this about him: the way his mind worked.

"So why were the Mahām there?" I asked.

"The Lunars *invited them*."

"What? The Lunars invited the Mahām and then massacred them a few months later?"

Joshua nodded grimly and put a tiny, elaborately carved lute into his bag. "I think the Lunars wanted an advantage in their proxy war. But they didn't realize the Mahām didn't care about their rules of warfare. The Mahām razed a quarter of Tenoch to the ground and poisoned the water system—sure, it worked to break our resistance, but it didn't look good in the press. Not when they claimed they were 'saving' us. The Lunars started getting cold feet around then."

Tenoch was the polity associated with Joshua's hometown of Popo, and the home of the infamous Elders, who represented Tierra in the Assembly, venerated for their unnaturally long lives.

"And you're sure about this?" My eye caught on a green-and-red motley vest lined with rose pearls, uncannily similar to the librarian novice vest. I touched it longingly and then left it. Groundskeepers confiscated any broonie goods that too closely resembled sumptuary affiliation markers. I'd earn my own novice vest somehow.

"It's all public knowledge. I didn't even need Tenehet; it's on the Eye. It's just not talked about."

I nodded slowly. "So the Lunars pretended they hadn't been trying to use the Mahām to gain local advantage over the Martians, because the whole thing looked bad?"

"Exactly. After the Western Incursion, the Lunars fought on the side of the Martians and expelled the Mahām. The Mahām were furious at the Lunar double-cross. I'm not sure what happened next—this isn't part of any official record—but I suspect that they threatened the Lunars in some way. To expose them, perhaps? And the Lunars reacted . . ."

It all fell into place. "With the Nine-Minute War! So *that's* why they did it."

An elite group of Lunar soldiers had jumped the Martian tesseract to Awilu, and then through the Awilu tesseract to Mahām. They rained hellfire on the heads of the Mahām priests and dignitaries celebrating the Nameren's feast day. (Did you feel that, Nameren? Did the blood make it through your encrusted synapses here to your heart, or was it just your more belligerent avatars that took notice and declared war?) Thirty thousand dead. Almost no one kept consciousness backups in those days—it was their use later in the war that led to their modern nickname, war chests.

"You'd have thought," Joshua said softly, "that the great Awilu, the peacekeepers, the old ones, the creators of the gods themselves, would have taken the side of the Mahām. The Lunars committed a brazen war crime while appropriating an Awilu sovereign tesseract. And yet instead we had the Era of the Thirds. The Aurochs third of the Awilu fought for the Mahām, the Cicada third for the Lunars, and the Baobab third sat in wait like a goddamned spider. Not a civil war, they insist. The traditional method of resolving internal disputes. What do I know? They're the longest-surviving human culture. They saved Tierra from the worst of our climate disequilibrium. They gave us tesseracts. But I'll tell you something, Freida—my home was *sold* to those Lunar traitors at the end of the war. We were bartered like fish at market day, in exchange for what, not even the Elders know. And now the Lunars claim the secondary Freedom node gives them the right to what they took, as though their freedom *to* our territory, their freedom *to* expand, *to* vacation wherever they please, trumps our freedom *from* insecurity, *from* harm, *from* cultural destruction."

He paused for breath. I was near him now, close enough to reach out to the plain gray scarf he had draped over his shoulders. The fabric was deliciously textured beneath my fingertips, like something handwoven on a backstrap loom. I pulled him forward. The cloth smelled like a forest, and he smelled like a home.

"But don't you need both?" I said softly into the silence. "Any freedom *to* needs a freedom *from*, doesn't it? *Tiareti* is the word for *freedom* in archaic Awilu, you know—its direct translation is *unbound*. Maybe the Lunars have had *tiareti* for so long they don't even realize that your hands have to be untied *first* before you can be free to do anything with them."

Joshua froze and then slowly pulled back. He caressed my cheek, gazing at me in some kind of dazed wonder.

"The triadic conception of liberty." The words were inscrutable, but he spoke them in the cadences of scripture.

"What?" I said unmelodiously.

He shook his head, smiling. "It's an obscure but relevant legal concept. Thank you." He kissed my forehead. "We make a good team, don't we?" He leaned over and picked up his donation bag, half empty. "This has to be enough. Let's get out of here. Do you think Atempa will want to come to Zell's with us? I'm wondering what she's heard about the secondary Freedom node over in Sasurandām. That has to be part of how they're justifying their ritual slaughter of the Miuri . . ."

He didn't even look back at the grove before we left. And certainly not at that one pearl-lined vest hanging from a tree. That was the odd thing about gifts: You could know just what someone wanted, and not be able to give it to them. Or you could give them one of the most precious things you knew, and they could never even see it.

⁺⁺

Nameren, I was about to get culled. Or at least that was the rumor beetling among my fellow postulants. Here at the boundary season between the mud and the dust, only three hundred of us remained. When we finished at the end of the dust, there would be fifty.

I was almost sure that I would not be one of them. And yet here I was, crawling through tunnels, hoping I had found an answer to the latest question that would save me.

I took an old grub tunnel to get out of Old Coyote. Some haunted alchemy prevented the water from one of the Tesseract Lakes above from flooding it, though sprays of fresh water sometimes misted the air when a breeze rippled the lake above. The grubs in this tunnel were small and stunted, with milky skin and jaws that buzzed into strange harmonies but whose light had dulled to fog. I didn't think that they fed into the surveillance system anymore; they were strange artifacts of another time. They knew me, though I had not passed through in years. I called out my name and pounded the floor with my singed boots.

I couldn't stop thinking about how Old Coyote had bled into Mahue'e in the artery I'd just explored. No wonder there hadn't been any signs of librarian contact. And the singing fire snakes that lived there—well, it was almost certainly level four, which meant that I couldn't risk anyone knowing where I'd been. I'd have to sneak back into a level-one artery and pretend to have found my answer there.

I gave a strangled cry of frustration that echoed against the grub-hollowed stone and the bottom of the lake. The grubs who had greeted me, four elders surrounding a squirming nest of littles, oriented their jaws in my direction and repeated my cry in sequence, a spontaneous round that mined music from its minute variations. I closed my eyes. It felt like a language just beyond my senses, a grammar encoded in their pattern of modulating tones and complex poly-rhythms.

My heart ached. I wished I could share this with someone, but it wasn't safe—not even Joshua or Nadi could know this place existed. Nadi because ze was still Head Librarian and bound to the code of zir position. Joshua because—I turned away from the thought, but it still shouted after me—because his first loyalty would always be to his people and their struggle. He wouldn't understand that this was all I had. If I gave him everything I knew, the fruits of my forbidden tunnel access, the secret of my communion by ingestion, I knew a time might come when he would ask me to use it to help him, even if that would betray me to Quinn. And if Quinn discovered half of what I did in the tunnels of the gods, he would happily destroy me, and through me, Nadi.

I took a deep, gulping breath. The grubs modulated politely into a quiet, even rumble, as though waiting for me to join. On impulse, I hummed the lullaby Nadi had taught me when I was barely five: *Truth, trust, and vulnerable heart; radical love is a gentle mind.* I had enjoyed the round marble syllables of Awilu in my mouth at the time, the simple rhythm of our clapping hands. Even now, some of the meaning still escaped me. I understood the aspiration to radical truth, trust, and vulnerability, but my mind was anything but gentle. Even the thought of relaxing sent my gorge to my throat with a wave of vertigo, and then, beneath it, the sticky mesh of unbearable self-disgust.

The grubs sang the melody back to me gently, as though cradling an infant. I wiped my eyes.

"Thank you," I said, then hurried past them to the dark membrane that marked the entrance to the lake above. The pressure of the water hurt my ears, but I kicked upward, and it soon eased. I broke the surface into the first clear day of the dust. My old island was deserted, a pristine hillock of blue-fringed pampas grass seeded with waving bells of black and garnet flowers and one solitary Mahām fire tree. I made for the mainland shore to my left. As my feet touched the sandy bottom, a hundred pings suddenly sparked above my thresholds and rained upon me like a hot shower. I climbed the bank and looked around. This part of the Tesseracts was deserted, as usual. I couldn't even see evidence of the grounds-keeper. Nothing at all looked unusual. Yet clearly something had happened. Had I been culled already? But I hadn't even submitted my answer! I took a deep breath and opened my array.

Oh.

Atempa's avatar had left a message: "I'm never speaking to my father again, *never*. Those *bastards!*"

Pajeu: "I hope you're well, Freida. If you need a safe place to stay until this blows over, you're welcome in my home."

Joshua: "Freida! I did it! I got past pretrial, I used the triadic argument, that *freedom from* is inseparable from *freedom to*, and it worked! I'm scheduled to give preliminary arguments before a peacekeeper in five days. I've done it, but it feels . . . wrong to celebrate somehow. Was this the price we had to pay to have our voices heard at last? I can't even imagine how that Miuri girl must be feeling."

Nadi: "My love, I'm sure you've seen the news. I'm headed to a conference right now. I doubt I'll be able to leave for the next few days. It's a disaster—but then, you probably know better than I. I saw your Tierran had his petition for node reactivation approved. I'm hopeful it can be one small piece of resistance. Oh, and don't come back to the retreat for at least a few days! Quinn is on a rampage, and I can't protect you just—"

The cord of shards, bent and looped into the impression of a face, blinked owlishly at me, disconcerted at having nothing else to say. The outline of a hand ruffled my hair before fading away.

The Nameren priests had done it, in contravention of all policy, humanity, or common sense. They had declared the first War Ritual in eighty years, and as surely as the rust follows the tears, the Miuri and their disciples would suffer for it.

The sand at this barren shore was a deep umber. I buried my hands in its solid wetness and waited for the old fear to pass.

The humid breeze of the early dust brought with it the scent of algae and the blood-drop flowers from the surrounding fields, the fast-growing fruits that only experiment would determine to be edible, ornamental, or poisonous. Their perfume brought me back to my body, soaked yet warm beneath the friendly red-orange sun. I ran my sandy fingers through the heavy, wet loops of my hair, and stared bemusedly when a singed chunk came out in my hand.

I had gotten much closer to those fire snakes than I had realized.

Mahue'e loved fire and Old Coyote loved puzzles; in the right order, the snakes had begun to chant a ballad in archaic Awilu that even my language module could barely decipher.

This was their answer to the latest question for the practical exam: *There were once seven material gods. Who made the eighth, and why?* It had seemed obvious to search for the answer in Iemaja, the eighth material god, but I had remembered the oracular puzzle snakes and let my intuition guide me. The ballad, as far as I could tell, had been the old Great Migration–era story about a cicada, an aurochs, and a baobab tree. "Cicada died in the light," the snakes had chanted in pentatonic harmony as they flung themselves from one rocky outcrop to the next above me. "And baobab mourned for five hundred years."

I had no idea how it answered my question, but I was sure it did.

It was everything I loved about the material gods: capricious, dangerous, inscrutable, but suddenly, unaccountably, magic.

The transport spiral didn't quite reach this far into the Tesseracts; most visitors stuck to the outer lakes, where you could rent a boat or a submersible to explore the water, and vendors sold food and drinks and bathing costumes for whimsical sensibilities. When I heard the soft snuffle of a transport pod settling down and the crunch of footsteps on the damp sand, I assumed it was a grounds-keeper. But it was Nadi. Ze was dressed for Assembly, with zir formal gray vest of office reaching zir knees and a cord of shards looped around zir head like a lighted crown.

"I know for a fact you have something better to be doing right now," I said, grinning.

Lines of exhaustion were etched into zir face, but zir black eyes were filled with warmth and mischief. Ze lifted the vest and plopped unceremoniously beside me. I took a deep breath and ze did as well; we met one another's eyes and then started laughing.

"The grub tunnels?" ze asked.

"Indigo wine during Assembly?"

Ze reached out and stroked my hair. Another chunk came away in zir palm and ze tsked. "We're at recess. And one must indulge in little pleasures to survive great unpleasantness. I don't want to know where you've been, my love, but you must know it will not look good for me or the selection committee if you're caught entering forbidden arteries."

My swim through the lake had done nothing to alleviate the acrid stench of my singed hair. I grimaced and tossed it into the water. A few fish crowded around its mass, poking it curiously. "I could have done this on purpose," I said.

"Oh, of course, it's the latest style among you young things," Nadi said.

I sighed happily and rested my head on zir shoulder. I had missed zir so much these last few weeks. I hated the Nameren priests for being so against the spirit of the Treaty that my Nadi had spent most of the last five years scrambling to put out one political fire after another.

Nadi put zir arm around my waist and we sat there just like that for a few precious minutes, listening to the cicadas trilling in the high grass, the wind skimming the lake and rustling in the trees. In the fire tree on my old island, a deep pop sounded from one of its obsidian-black holes and a lone flame went up, peered outside, and extinguished itself.

"It's . . . hard to remember how you were back then."

"Back then?"

"When you homesteaded here," ze said quietly. "When you were thirteen. I hated to leave you here by yourself."

"Oh." I shivered and nestled my head more firmly against zir shoulder. "I needed it, Nadi."

"You never did tell me what happened. Did Quinn, or that nephew of his . . ."

I coughed against what felt like acid in my chest. If I hadn't told zir then, I certainly couldn't now. I didn't want to know what ze would do—or not do—with the knowledge.

"Quinn is what he always has been. It just got to be too much."

Ze sighed. "I have to tell you something." I squeezed zir waist more tightly. Ze had lost weight in these last weeks; stress seemed to be eating zir alive.

"What is it?"

"Freida, I am—we are—in a very precarious position right now. I had been so sure I could keep you safe until you reached your majority and you found a sanctioned role in this place."

"And now I'm about to be culled."

Ze looked toward the water, lips pressed into a thin line. "The selection process isn't fair. I can't say that publicly, but I know it. In any reasonable system, your place among us would be assured. But Quinn has amassed far more power than I had realized. I have been distracted, or idealized our institutions too much—the future will have to pass its judgment. I hate to ask this of you, Freida. But I will ask it because I know I have raised a daughter brave enough to dare Mahue'e herself, and she will certainly dare me."

I pulled away from zir. We were both shivering. Something was happening that I did not understand and that I did not want, a landslide on my safest ground. Ze had never spoken to me like this before—as though ze needed me.

"Nadi, I'll do anything—"

Ze shook zir head. "No. Never promise that, not even to me." Ze drew a shaky breath. "But here: If you could pretend to be as they wish you to be, if you could give them the answers they want, from the sources they want, and play their game so they can't cull you just yet from the selection process, you would help me maintain my position in the Librarian Council and the General Assembly."

I stared at zir, open-mouthed. "I am—they're truly going to cull me?"

"I'm not sure. If Quinn's faction has its way, certainly. You have your admirers, though. Flamboyant style has gotten a number of librarians through the process, Volei included. But they won't cull you yet if you stay within the lines."

Something tickled my right hand. I looked down to see a tiny sand crab of deep carnelian skitter across my rigid knuckles. "But what's to stop them from culling me later? Even for Quinn, standard answers don't get you into the top fifty postulants."

"I know."

"So you're asking me—" It hit me like an open hand. "Oh."

Conform now, while the War Ritual crisis was at its peak, and I would give Nadi time to shore up zir political position. But my only real shot at becoming a librarian was in my very nonconformity, my ingenuity and audacity. If I gave that up, I would surely be culled near the end, along with all the rest of the technically bright but uninspired candidates. I'd make it easy for Quinn to deny a political motivation—even easier, in a way, than it would be if they culled me now.

I looked up at Nadi, panicked. "Could you save me then?"

Ze straightened zir shoulders, but as though they still strained against a weight. "I give you my word, Freida, I'll find a place for you here."

But not as a librarian. I couldn't breathe. I couldn't think. Who was I? Freida of the Library. But what did that even mean if my parent, the Head Librarian zirself, couldn't protect me?

"But didn't they just declare the Ritual? What can you do now?"

At this, the corners of zir mouth tipped up. Ze had that Head Librarian look, the canny eyes of the finest mind Quinn ever had the misfortune of making an enemy. "They've said they'll do it, but they haven't said when. There are still a few levers I can use to get concessions."

I had been so afraid, but zir words ignited a flame of rage in me that I hadn't known I harbored. "*Concessions?* Aren't you the Head? Aren't they violating the Treaty? What kind of bullshit peace is this?"

Nadi just looked at me. Zir eyes were dry, but I had never seen them so sad. Angry as I was, I rested my forehead against zis. "It's all right," I whispered, although it wasn't. "I'll survive. Just—save the Miuri, Nadi. Don't let all this go to waste."

Over the lake a crane swooped down, caught a few tangled strands of my hair in its beak, and rose, winging west toward the smeared red light of the long-setting sun with just another bit of straw for its nest.

⁺⁺

But I no longer had a nest of my own to hide in. Nadi had told me to keep away from the retreat because of the masses of reporters and protestors gathering outside.

I could have stayed with friends—even Atempa had offered to sneak me into her room by the window. But I stayed outside in a driving rain, furious and biting. I don't know why it hurt me to accept anyone's kindness, Nameren, only that I would have rather drowned myself in Iemaja's cenote than admit I needed it. I thought of camping in the Islands or walking into the nearest freehold and begging shelter for a night, but in the end Joshua found me floating in the spiral, shivering with cold.

"You should have at least brought a cloak," he said, wrapping me with his.

I just buried my head into his shoulder and let him take me back to his room.

He told me stories of his home as I warmed myself in a nest of blankets on the heated bench beside his window. "There's a hill a few kilometers from the family compound," he said. His voice was warm and windblown, carrying scents of far-away joys. "A giant big-head sapote tree grows at its base. The fruit ripens in the middle of the rainy season, and it's the sweetest you've ever tasted, with a big pit, hairy as a monkey. I used to spend hours studying in that tree, Freida. My aunt's turkey hens would follow me and eat the peels I tossed down. They say the spirit of the mountain lives there still, and you have to ask permission to eat its food. I'd love to take you there one day."

His hands were busy with a shard I had brought him from the tunnel: rich terra-cotta lightly seamed moss green. The shard's value was probably incalculable; under Joshua's chisel, it was taking the shape of a coiled, sleeping snake.

I suppressed a wave of nausea. "I don't know how I could leave here." I looked out the windows of his small room, intelligence-dark, with an exorbitant rent of one red and eight blues, at the edge of the grange.

I jumped when Joshua put his hand on my shoulder. "If they don't select you, Freida, you will always be welcome in my home."

"What if all I can ever be is part of the Library's collection? Do *things* travel, Joshua?"

His reflection in the window pulled back, his eyes wide with shock and pity. Or maybe they were just upset; I felt too raw with nerves to be sure.

"Is it that bad?"

"Nadi says . . ." No, I couldn't talk to him about what Nadi had asked me to do. I could hardly even think of it. "Tell me about the case. How did you get through the pretrial screening?"

He was so pleased to tell the story he didn't realize I'd dodged his question. "I used your strategy, the triadic conception of liberty—"

"That definitely wasn't my strategy," I said.

"You reminded me of it, that's what matters. I argued that if the Lunars justified their postwar land grab with Freedom primary, then they couldn't now invalidate the parts of Freedom primary that have been declared apocryphal, particularly those that focus on *tiareti*, or freedom *from*."

"You used the archaic Awilu word?" I felt obscurely proud of this.

He stretched his arms above his head. "Legal scholars love archaic Awilu—it makes our arguments at least ten percent more convincing. So, you see, you *did* give me the strategy. I went into the details of how Lunar aggression was far more to blame for the start of the war than anything the Mahām did, but honestly, the clerk didn't seem particularly convinced by that part. Lucky for me, some slick business scholars from one of the Martian universities came to argue the opposition. They tried to claim I had no standing because I didn't come from one of the first Tierran families. The clerk might have been Dar—I think ze granted my hearing out of class solidarity, even though they're not supposed to be swayed by that kind of thing."

Joshua smiled at me expectantly, but I'd snagged on one detail. "Martian business scholars argued for the opposition?"

"Martians defending Lunars—that must gall them. But money is money, I suppose. Don't want us indigenous Tierrans getting uppity—who knows what we might demand."

"You're not worried? What if they threaten your scholarship?"

He shrugged. "I know this place isn't perfect. But what kind of Treaty scholar would I be if I were so cynical about the Library and everything it stands for? They can't punish me if I work within its rules. Besides, I have you on my side, Freida of the Library—who knows this place better? You were created by the gods themselves."

He wrapped his arms around me and lightly kissed the back of my neck. I leaned into him. A few tears, salty from long confinement, splashed onto the smooth brown hair on his forearm. "And I still don't belong here."

"*You?* Anyone could see that your umbilical cord is buried here, just as mine is buried in the red earth of the Popo hills."

He guided me to the floor and ran his dusty, calloused hands through my hair, pulling out more singed clumps and setting them with aching gentleness on the floor beside us. My reflection gazed back at me from the window, haunted eyes, down-turned mouth, hair broken at various lengths rising out from my scalp as though suspended in electrical charge. I had never questioned my beauty before, but I wondered now why Joshua looked at me the way he did, so full of trust and love. What had I done to him? Who did he see? Me? But what was I? A thousand reflections in a thousand pairs of eyes. Freida of the Library, which didn't want her. *I'll find a place for you*, Nadi had promised. Like a pet. My nails stung the pads of my palms.

"Who cares about the Martian opposition? I *know* I can win this petition with you collecting evidence. You have better access than we could pay for, even if we had the shards. Will you help me, Freida?"

I froze. I had been afraid that he would ask this, and perhaps even more afraid of my own response. There was a quality to the question, so innocently posed, that resonated like a tuning fork pitched to the same frequency as my heart. I felt the choice, a splitting path that would forever define which Freida I would be of all my myriad possibilities. Joshua didn't know it, but I would be risking everything if I delved into deep arteries right now in the selection process: Nadi's political position during the War Ritual crisis, whatever chance remained to me of becoming a librarian, even Joshua's petition if the provenance of his archival materials came under scrutiny. Nadi hadn't asked me to stop my high-level searches, but ze had known I was in Mahue'e and warned me to be careful.

Would helping Joshua betray Nadi?

Would agreeing to Nadi's request betray myself?

I lifted my hand to my ruined hair. Maybe I could turn myself into someone new. I was almost eighteen. A year for changes. Maybe I'd get culled, maybe I'd lose my formal access to the tunnels, but in the reflected light of Joshua's eyes, I could see the outlines of a girl I longed to be: fearless, clever, ready to fight Quinn instead of hide from him.

I reached for the hilt of the chisel Joshua had been using and switched the dial to a blade. It was a simple tool, but effective: the ceramic edge reconstituted itself in thirty seconds. I answered Joshua's questioning look with a small, sharp nod.

It was quick work to hack through the rest of my heavy locks above the burn line. Freed, my hair lifted in a halo of fat, wooly corkscrews. The grubs that had gathered at the edge of the grange projected their lights into our room, where they picked up the moss-green highlights among the mahogany-brown curls. I had notably unusual hair for an Awilu; Nadi said that I most resembled the people from the southern pole. Equatorial Niphense Awilu tended to have dense, kinky hair that they let grow in abundance during their youth and shaved completely in deference to age, wisdom, and mature beauty. My throwback hair had always been another oddity that marked me. Now, though, it was a way to mark myself.

Joshua rose to his knees and put his hands on my shoulders. Like a penitent, he bowed his head to my hair. I felt him smile against my scalp.

"Well, then?" he mouthed.

A different girl, a stranger girl, there in the window, grinned at me like a sister.

The god has found himself a shape now, a smudgy suggestion of horns and a snout on the body of a quadruped. The jeweled eyes are now more firmly secured in his head. The patch of earth around the girl has grown. It is red clay earth, cracked and dusty.

The god waits, and then the god speaks: "You stopped talking."

The girl is subdued. "That's the story. That's how I cut my hair."

"But what happened to Joshua? Did you help him with his quest?"

Her laugh. "Wouldn't you like to know!"

"You promised me a story—"

"I gave you one."

"Stories ought to explain themselves," he says.

She shakes a finger. "Not all of them. Not all the way. Where's the joy without a little work?"

The god is nonplussed. "Joy?"

And the girl, she reaches her hands toward his snout and smoky horns, but she does not touch. "What about missing-third-act stories? Or surprise-fourth-act stories? Or stories where the narrator dies halfway through? Stories where nothing is resolved because in reality no one knows anything? Stories without plots, stories with incredible crystalline honeycombs of plots that no one understands all the way through but the narrator and the cleverest readers? Portal stories, but the subtype where you never go back home and never know why or how you were hurtled away in the first place? Or myths that explain everything and nothing? Or legends that leave the reasons a mystery? What about all the mystery, Nameren? All the mystery that is the beating heart of every kind of story?"

He snorts. "Those aren't stories, they're trickery."

"Do you remember the tale of the piper in the town plagued by ghosts? What happened after the piper led the ghosts to the desert?"

"They dried out."

"But what happened to the piper?"

"Her children built their houses in the crowns of the anthills that sprang up where the ghosts had withered. The red ant gave them the gift of corn wherever it grew, and the black ant gave them children whenever they wanted. Ever after they stopped marking a difference between men and women."

She takes a step, just one step closer. "Yes, but what happened to the *piper*?"

He hasn't realized. "I . . . I don't know."

"But it's still a good story, isn't it?"

"Did Joshua find a way to reactivate the node? Did you help him?"

"That's not a good story."

"Keeping yourself alive a little longer?"

The girl looks again into the limitless darkness surrounding them. "I'll save Nergüi, even if it's too late for me."

"Nergüi? You mean that *this* disciple is the same one you met in the Library?"

"Not that story, either, not yet."

"You can't hold them all back. I'll just kill you sooner, remember?"

The girl turns back to him, stone-faced. "Can you tell your priests to let the Miuri disciple go?"

"They're all locked in the atrium together. They're not hurting her."

"You control the space they're in. Send a messenger. Animate the stone or the water and lead her out."

"Only if you tell me what you did to Joshua that makes you feel so guilty."

She freezes. "How do you know . . . ?"

"Your in-drop affect is amazing. Isn't that what Samlin said?"

She holds a sick and lurching silence. "That wasn't fair."

"Why not? You told me his story. It's part of me now."

"So you'll hurt yourself to hurt me?"

"They made me for a purpose. Is it my fault—"

She holds out her palm. It is enough. "No. I blame no one for existing. Not even you." A soft, cutting laugh. "Not even me . . ."

"It wasn't—"

"Shh. I'll tell you. I'll tell you."

–I fell in love in the mud, but I destroyed it in the dust.

There are four seasons in the Library, the same coin flipped in two dimensions: the mud and the dust, the tears and the rust. It's the boundary moments that enchanted me, that imprinted themselves on my memory; they anchor me even now when I am far away from that stolen, unnatural, heartbreaking place. The mud is dark, sticky, humbling. The dust is cheery ochre, parties in the Islands where the sloths peer at you with weary, humorous patience as you shake them in their sleepy branches before you jump, laughing, to the net below. But my favorite days were liminal, when the mud's heavy storms trail off and leave behind squalls of light rain, like water spray from an angry ocean. Rainbows arc overhead in riots, cracks in the firmament. The deep sinkholes of the mud sprout lilies and lotuses of iridescent, improbable, and ephemeral hues. Perhaps they were once the work of the broonies, but whatever their haunted origins, they merged with the soul of this place, and now reproduce with the mundane magic of biology. Tenehet fruits that grow in these days are larger, brighter, sweeter, more sour. Zell can't serve his beer fast enough. The air is humid, but the breezes are lively, bringing with them the dust's promise of light.

"It smells of love," I would tell Nadi, back when I believed in everything. "It smells of you and me."

It was surreal to me how the magic of this time now bent itself to the pandemonium of an intersystem political crisis. The War Ritual was held off with the bare pretext of bickering over the date. The season's lilies grew black and Nadi gave conferences on the emergency negotiations with the Mahām while fending off white strands of lacy airborne pollen. Memes propagated through the feeds about how zir own Library laid a shroud upon zir administration. There was talk of the Librarian Council holding a vote of no confidence to recall zir as Head, an action taken only two previous times in the Library's history. I knew Quinn was behind this talk, but in public his position was deceptively mild, even nominally supportive of Nadi's desperate rearguard action to prevent the War Ritual from turning into an even greater humanitarian crisis and crime against peace.

My status in the selection process was still precarious, but the current political crisis had pushed off my moment of judgment. In fact, our new assignment was to investigate the Mahām justification for the War Ritual. Everyone wanted to know if the peacekeeping tribunals would touch the secondary Freedom node, which had several "self-actualization" filaments that supposedly supported this act of circumscribed barbarity. This meant that Joshua's case had attracted half a dozen cosignatories—one of whom was Müde Pahjam, the rector of the Disciples of the Lighted Path. The refugee disciple, Nergüi, must have been aware of the case, but she had by all accounts buried herself in the Library's reading rooms and not even Pajeu could persuade her out of them. After a few days, no one bothered her; it seemed unlikely that such a young disciple could have much influence on the case one way or another.

Into this atmosphere of wild magic, Joshua presented his arguments before the full tribunal: Past, Present, and Future. Tenehet adjudicated in zir incarnation of the great ibis, black eye turned coolly upon the foibles of man. Joshua presented now to Future, a human peacekeeper made anonymous and allegorical in a robe of green moss, gently wriggling with small, unassuming life, beneath a mask of gnarled tree roots that gave a rough, malleable impression of rising eyebrows and a wide mouth.

Ze spoke slowly, softly. "You say that the Lunar claim to your territory is invalid based on their behavior in the events leading up to the Great War?"

Joshua blinked and straightened his shoulders. He had been standing in the recessed pit at the center of the tribunal for the last two hours, and his nervous energy was seamed with exhaustion. "They based their claim on the parts of Freedom primary still extant in Freedom secondary: freedom to expand into new territory, freedom to their cultural tradition of settler colonization, freedom to self-determination. But as I showed in exhibit E, they'd been attempting to annex the territory since before the war, and therefore the Freedom node's protections don't apply retroactively. As you can see—"

Future held up zir hand and Joshua cut off the display. He had already shown it once—a holo of a Lunar brigadier-general berating an anonymous Mahām spy for the massacre the Mahām had made of Tierran civilians during the Western Incursion and how that had "complicated the Lunar position." It made me proud: I had found that bit of graphic evidence of Lunar perfidy for him in the bowels of Old Coyote.

"Past," said Future, "may opine more knowledgeably on the details, but I believe you are operating under a misapprehension, young Tierran. The postwar territorial divisions, codified in the self-actualization filaments from Freedom primary, were not based on ancient Lunar claims, fraudulent as you so rightly demonstrate they are, but upon their actions to help end the war fifty years later."

Past was a war chest avatar of an Awilu civilian killed late in the war, one of a hundred or so rotating peacekeepers who represented the time into which they had been born and killed. Ze had kept oddly silent for the entirety of this hearing that bore so much upon zir sphere of influence, but now at last spoke.

"Although many wished it to have been otherwise," ze intoned, "the territorial rights affirmed by the primary Freedom node's first filaments are essentially a reflection of a desire to end the war. The Treaty does not apportion blame, it does not punish; it only attempts to construct a balance of power that will prevent future intersystem conflict. It is by its very nature unjust; it is, nevertheless, the foundation of humankind's most ambitious justice. If you have only come to us with old gossip everyone once knew and has now forgotten, you are wasting the time of my colleagues who are still alive to use it. I grant that you have presented us with a thorny moral quandary. But not a legal one."

Joshua took a panicked step toward Past, whose avatar was the size of a child wearing a mask of disarticulated features that moved as ze spoke. He recalled himself just in time—if he stepped from the circle of light, he'd formally renounce his own petition. I wanted to shout encouragement from up in the gallery, but that would rain sanctions down upon both our heads. And, of course, no legal scholar can access any outside communications while in the circle.

Joshua stilled, his shoulders trembling. Then, with a deep breath, he turned to Present. He had found his smile again somehow: that mark of a deep, wise, desperate self-knowledge. I did not understand that then, Nameren. I thought he was covering up his embarrassment. But I can see him now as I did not then—a warrior for his people, bathed in light. He did not belong to the Library. He was only given to us for a little while. He did not deserve what we did to him.

What I did to him.

Perhaps Present understood that smile. In any case, it was Present who threw him a spar. "If you wish to claim the apocryphal protections of Freedom primary— what you so eloquently call the *tiareti*, or *freedom from* protections—should invalidate the centuries of precedence established by Freedom secondary and its filaments . . ." Zir high voice rang with authority. "Then you must look to the end of the war. You and your copetitioners would do well to ask why the Treaty-makers laid out the powers as they did; surely their results speak for themselves. If you would change that balance, then ask what the Mahām, the Lunars, the Martians did that your Nawas people did not do, Tierran. In other words, what was your *freedom to*, and why did you not act upon it?"

Brave, my Joshua, even with his case lying at his feet like broken pottery. "And if my people—or the Miuri people—*did* do something? If our *freedom to* has been forgotten or repressed?"

At that, the ibis rose up from zir position with the opposition scholars and cir-cled three times overhead, counterclockwise. I held my breath: The ibis only made procedural decisions, but those included whether or not to invalidate a petition.

"The Tierran scholar has intrigued the tribunal with his unusual attempt. He has missed the target, but then, we have moved the target. If we are to grant the triadic conception of freedom, we must allow the part of Freedom primary that has been left to languish in apocrypha to flourish anew. How will this change the nodes and filaments of the Treaty? Must ritual peace beget ritual war? We will allow him to try again. His question is ruled to be the defining question. If he answers it, we will find new ways of seeing."

One of the opposition scholars, the slick Martians who had tried to prevent this hearing from even taking place, interjected: "We demand a ruling on the admis-sibility of unsourced and unauthorized archival materials from the Library gods!"

The ibis paused in zir flight, still as a picture but for zir head, which tilted to-ward the scholar. I swallowed against the lurch of incongruity; no human avatar could seem so real and so unnatural at the same time. But the tribunal room had highly amplified augmented spaces, even for low-wetware participants like me.

"The opposition petitioner's motion is dismissed. The Library was not created with access levels nor restrictions to its memory banks other than those which the gods themselves devised; in this matter which relates directly to the time of the Library's founding, we will also not respect them. Archival materials, whatever their provenance, will be admitted."

Ze resumed zir flight as abruptly as ze had stopped. "Come better prepared next time, scholar. Case reset."

Joshua was the hero of the hour, and I couldn't find a minute alone with him until late that night, folded inside an ebullient crowd in the intelligence-dark caves out past the Islands. A number of green-and-black cave grubs kept watch with us, clinging to stalactites above and to a shallow incline that led to the natural stage, jaws open and mouths whirring. I wondered if an authority had sent them or if they were here out of their own inscrutable curiosity. Some group or other had organized this party at very short notice. They didn't call it a party, of course, but a "nocturnal gathering of intercultural art and protest in support of the Miuri people and the primary Freedom node." A giant bonfire blazed in the center of the caves. Its dancing orange light reached toward the ceiling, where it glinted off opalescent minerals dripping like frozen sugar from stalactites. A troupe of aerial dancers played with the light as they chanted a famous old Awilu migratory ballad:

> *Oh, Aurochs, angry traveler*
> *Tell us why our mother*
> *The baobab cried.*
> *Naamaru Catre, horns like twin moons,*
> *Tell us of the home we lost.*

We have left, molted! Like cicadas from the earth!

We have crossed the folding night.

Oh, Aurochs, drunk on improvidence, tell us

Why she cries.

From across the cavern, a group of quicksilver-clad dancers flung themselves inches from the stone floor as they sang the aurochs' answer, as though from across uncounted millions of light-years of star-dusted vacuum.

For the cicada singing in the earth

Left too late, left behind

By sisters and siblings

The baobab cries.

For the cicada in the earth

The baobab cries.

For the cicada in the light

She cries.

Everyone had heard of the main characters in this fable, because they represented each faction from the Era of the Thirds, when the Awilu divided against themselves along unspeakably ancient cultural lines and fought for decades on both sides of the Great War. The original story I knew only in its vaguest outlines: the legend of the Awilu ten thousand years ago, who made the Great Migration from Tierra to a new planet. That was your birth, Nameren. They built Aurochs, this angry heart of yours, and you brought them across the tesseract. When people said I had throwback genes, that was what they meant: My cloudy hair with mossy highlights, my dark brown eyes and prominent nose, resembled the original

Awilu, the ones who had stayed behind when most of their brethren crossed the stars. I was like the cicada of the song, a lone singer out of step with her family, when she crawls, too late, into the light.

Nadi had taught me this marching song when I was eight, which was perhaps why I hadn't fully grasped the sadness of it until I heard this weeping chorus. I felt alone, stripped and dimmed.

"A place," I whispered, looking across the chasm of the cave floor to the swirling, shifting silver of the dancers, in mourning, left behind, trapped beneath the infinite sky.

From his position by the bonfire, Joshua stood a little unsteady. Our low wetware functioned only intermittently in the intelligence-dark space of the caves. I admitted to myself that it was a relief; I was free, momentarily, from the constant low-level friction of the postulant feed and their reminder of Atempa's record success and my near failure. An uncomfortable wave of resentment buffeted me as he picked his way through the crowd that had held him tightly in its center.

To my surprise, Joshua found me watching in the shadows. A nearby grub opened its jaws for a quick spray of light, and he jumped.

"Sweet mother, I can't get used to those things," he said, shuddering. "Do they have to be everywhere?"

I shrugged. "Old surveillance technology gone feral. They still mostly do their job. That's the Library for you."

"Yes, I had gathered, Freida." He hugged me and then pulled back. I wondered if his pupils were too wide, even for the shadows. Had there been something in the beer they had passed around the glittering inner circle?

"You seem unhappy," he said at last. "Why are you hiding here?"

I pulled a smile from somewhere and planted a kiss on his forehead. "You're the hero. I work in the shadows."

He frowned. "Did something happen in the exams?"

"Doesn't it always?" I laughed, giddily, angrily. "They're going to cull me. Everyone knows it. They're just toying with me now. Me and Nadi."

He inhaled as though he would say something, thought better of it, and squeezed my hand silently.

"Go back to your party. You deserve it. I'm sorry I'm not better company tonight."

He slid a few inches away from the rumbling jaw of the grub and leaned back against the rock wall. "It's a sad story, isn't it?" he asked, pointing with his chin at the quicksilver dancers. "It's a kind of mourning song. Ten thousand years—what survives ten millennia? Loss, apparently. Loss survives more loss."

Some of the tension left my limbs. "No, that's just love. Love without a home, turned to grief."

"Isn't that a poem?"

"Awilu, fifth millennium. Like you said, what survives five millennia, let alone ten? Not even they did, not really. They've lost enough cultural knowledge for ten civilizations. But they're still the Awilu, while the rest of us are the distant descendants of their descendants. What's the difference? Memory. They built the Nameren and he held their shape in his material consciousness, like water in the mold of his cupped palms."

He leaned forward with an expression so earnest and joyful, my heart galloped. "That's you," he said. "No fifth-millennium poet."

I shrugged noncommittally, flushed with pleasure.

A group of military scholars, mostly Lunar with a few long-limbed Martians, lurked at the entrance to the caves. Every few seconds, a spray of blue light passed across their tense, angry faces as one of the grubs unhinged its jaws and recorded their presence. It was some reassurance. At least the grubs understood which group was more likely to cause trouble. For a moment, a multi-toned screech rose above the music of the migratory march. One of the Lunar military scholars had hit a grub with a slingshot.

"Leave them alone, fascists!" someone from the bonfire group called, voice unsteady with a most likely chemical drug. Other voices echoed zir, and though the Lunars yelled back insults and scattershot limp, low-bandwidth, biting pings, the tumult settled down. They must have had an unauthorized amplifier with them. I scratched my arms and dialed up my thresholds so nothing else could get through.

"Lunar gasbags," Joshua said with real venom. "They're calling themselves Crusaders now. Crusaders for the Nameren. The little they know of Tierran history they mangle to glorify genocide. I don't know why the Library even has military studies."

I didn't feel like defending them, but I did—it was my Library, after all. "We can't ignore that side of things. The Nameren helped create the four Library materials and the Nameren is—or was, anyway—a war god."

Joshua's lips quirked. A slight gesture, but I felt a sting. "I'd say he still is. Or why else is everyone here? War rituals in place of war. And yet they say the Awilu are the original peacekeepers."

"That's not the Awilu's fault. He's the Mahām's now."

It is not much defense, Nameren, but I had paid so little attention to your history because I believed you could never impact my life.

Unlike Joshua. "Sure. The Awilu gave up the first material god. They'd grown beyond his more primitive drives, isn't that how it goes? But I wonder, what's the Nameren without the Awilu?"

Something caught in my throat. "Or what are the Awilu without the Nameren?"

He met my eyes. I don't know what he saw there, but his features softened, and he brushed his hand across the short cloud of my hair. "Memory, you said. He kept their shape in his memory. Does he still?"

"I don't know."

He squared his shoulders. "You are still you, Freida, even without the Library. You hold your own shape, I promise. You don't need the gods for that."

I knew I should respond, but I could not breathe. I was a girl out of breath. I turned from him and hurried to the mouth of the cave. Perhaps he called after me—I couldn't hear anything, I couldn't feel anything but a hot stone in my sternum where my heart should be; I breathed as though through fire.

Perhaps that's why I didn't realize until I was almost upon them that the grubs were screaming again. Their polytoned cries mingled with the lingering strains of the Awilu migratory march and human shouts in a dozen languages. Someone must have launched a wetware disruptor in the middle of the caves that knocked out everyone's language modules. Some high-wetware people were writhing on the floor, meaning the disruptor probably had some sort of trojan as well—a high crime in the Library, and with all these grubs to document it, too! So why did the military scholars seem even bolder and more noxious than before? Shouldn't they be running away?

But no. I was close enough to see now. They were burning the grubs alive. A pair of willowy Martians stuck brands into their mottled hides. The grubs' screams filled my ears until I might have collapsed on the floor with everyone else if Joshua hadn't found me in the melee and turned me to face him.

"Don't look," he mouthed. But it was too late, and sight was only one of my senses. Harmonies mixed with the smoke and spilled blood of dying grubs, blue and luminescent—a symphony of heartbreak accompanied by the smell of roasting shrimp. The screams, the sobs, the laughter of our attackers—they became a chorus, and we were the dancers staggering and pivoting on burning strings.

Far above in the darkness that glittered like shooting stars, a small stalactite quivered and fell. The shards cut my skin, though Joshua got the worst of it. We took each other's hands. The grubs were attempting to flee, up the face of the rock and into their tunnels, but they moved slowly and made easy targets. I didn't think the military scholars would purposefully harm the people gathered here, but I was shocked they had dared go even this far.

We weren't the only ones appalled by this massacre. The dancers were the first to join us as we ran to fight the military scholars. It could have been a story or a painting, some odd object from millennia ago tucked away in a dusty corner of Iemaja, but it was just real life, baffling and horrifying and liminally wondrous. I knocked a hot spear, caked with blood, from the hand of a Martian. Ze roared and grabbed me in a chokehold. A dancer and Atempa—when had she come here?—pulled zir off. I picked a jagged rock from the fallen stalactite and threw it without mercy at the Martian's head. Ze dropped to the ground, mewling.

"What are you doing?" I yelled at Atempa.

"Fighting fascists!" she shouted back, laughing. "What else?"

"And the process?"

She shrugged with that perfectly elegant disdain that I had envied since the day we met. "If they punish me for this, let them."

"Freida!"

I whirled around. Joshua was wrestling with a huge Lunar, who was attempting to gore him with the same stick that had wounded a grub crawling away behind them. I grabbed another rock while Atempa launched herself bodily at the Lunar. Ze released Joshua and backed away, into the line of fascist military scholars. The grubs had retreated behind us, thankfully. I knew of at least one grub tunnel in these caves, so they should be able to get to safety if we gave them enough time. The uninjured ones flashed their jaws across all our faces in a spray so continuous it made our movements look jerky and surreal.

At least they won't get away with it, I thought, and then something uncomfortable tugged my breastbone—some newborn suspicion that, in fact, they would.

Joshua was put on probation for uncivil behavior and violence toward non-human intelligences. If he was caught violating civil norms again, he could lose his scholarship. The fact that these charges were precisely the reverse of what had occurred did not seem to matter to anyone involved—not the legal scholars, not the librarians. No groundskeepers had arrived on the scene soon enough and the grub footage was deemed corrupted. The whole affair was so transparently unjust that I felt that I'd been punched in the stomach, even though I'd escaped. I wanted to scream at Nadi to do something, but I knew that ze was saving all zir political capital for the War Ritual fight. Joshua took it with far more equanimity than Atempa, who received only a verbal warning and a ten-point deduction in her standing in the selection process.

"My father manages to show his power over me even when I'm doing the exact opposite of what he wants," Atempa said bitterly as we sat in one of the newer bubble nooks in Iemaja's reading rooms.

"By getting you out of trouble?" Joshua asked.

Atempa sneered as only the scion of one of the Mahām's founding families could. "By proving that his power over me is so overwhelming that he can preserve my standing in the selection from a distance without my even asking. He will expect repayment—mark my words. When I'm a full librarian, he will come to visit, and I will feel all the weight of ten generations telling me to grant him whatever he wants out of filial piety and *he knows it*."

Those last words, rough as a spray of gravel, rocked Joshua back a bit. He blinked and raised his eyebrows. "That," he said carefully, "is a very long game."

"That," Atempa said, just as carefully but with far more icy poise, "is the Shipbuilder family way."

Normally, this would have made me laugh. Normally, I would have begun one of my elaborate battles with Atempa, in which I ribbed her for being a rich and privileged child of conquerors, and she skewered me for being the feckless, feral child of the most powerful denizen of the Library. But I had no stomach for either game, no will to pretend that my position here was anything but precarious, subject to the political ambitions of the worst person I knew. When the civil guards had arrived to detain people on our side while leaving the fascist military scholars conspicuously alone, Joshua had pushed me behind him and told me to run. I'd hesitated, but in the end, I'd left them there to face the consequences alone. I was more vulnerable than even Joshua, and he knew it. I'd spent most of the night in the grub tunnel, longer than I had to, doubled over with shame and the hollow drip of my faith in the Library leaking away.

Joshua leaned back against the curved wall of the study nook, which teemed with sharp-toothed fish and creatures that resembled fringed mushrooms, whirring along with their cilia. It was all real, but I let Atempa believe it was a wetware projection. For all that she lived in the Library, she didn't quite believe in it.

"I could file an appeal if we could get our hands on the grub surveillance," Joshua said.

I knew he meant it to cheer me, to give me something to do, a reminder of what power I did have. But I sank to the floor, eye-to-eye with a passing stingray.

"They'll declare it corrupt or adulterated," I said dully. "There's no point. There's two dozen humans who testified to the same thing, but that doesn't seem to have mattered, either. They'll just punish the grubs if I push the issue."

Even Atempa looked appalled at that. She cleared her throat. "All the more reason we should become novice librarians, Freida. This place is going to the wolves."

"Corporatist wolves," Joshua said, very dryly. "It'll be like living on Tierra without ever visiting!"

"Which is why," Atempa continued, even brighter, "we're going to answer the practical exam together. If they fail you, they have to fail me."

She was so furious, she glittered. It wrung a smile out of me. "They really might fail you, Atempa. It's a big dare. Does Quinn's faction fear your father more than they hate Nadi's pet secondary AI?"

Something strange hovered in Joshua's eyes, a buried mirror of Atempa's rage. He reached for my hand and squeezed my fingers.

"Do it, Freida," he said, with such intensity it was nearly a whisper. "Show them."

"It's a perfect time," Atempa added. "Volei must have pushed the exam question through. 'What is the historical justification of the Mahām War Ritual? Analyze how this question is deconstructed and reinterpreted according to any three avatars related at the branch level.' Freida, *think about it*. How would you answer?"

A school of mushrooms pressed against the barrier between us and began to whir single file around the outline of my body.

I blew out my lips in annoyance. "I would run a query in the reading rooms here in Iemaja, very sensibly, collect the contemporary judgments of three stable, easily accessible avatars—oh, let's say Wadatsumi, Pacifike, and Nettuno—and for extra credit, I would request tunnel access to Melanthe. Of course, I couldn't do much there because zir tunnels have been picked drier than a dog's favorite bone and I can't do high-wetware communion, but at least I'd get points for effort."

I bore Atempa's silent stare for a solid twenty seconds. Then I rolled over and met it with a lazy smile of my own. She sniffed. "There is really no need to describe standard librarian methods with such contempt, you know."

"It's useless," I said. "What's the *point* of the Library if we're just going to confine ourselves to the same ten picked-over avatars and their safest arteries? What's the *point* of ten millennia of memories if we only ever bother with their contemporary interpretations? Even the legal scholars have Past on their tribunals!"

Joshua was breathing steadily, as though he had to remind himself to. "And how would you *really* do it, Freida?"

He was taut with tamped-down excitement, of a kind far angrier, far deeper than the easy and forgiving joy I had come to expect from him. It made me curious, which I suppose is the only possible explanation for what I said then.

"The truth?" I asked him.

Atempa started and then went very still. I had always wondered how much she guessed. She was the only one besides Nadi who could have.

Joshua nodded.

"I'll show you." I turned to Atempa. "Meet me at the tenth lake of the Tesseracts in three hours. Keep your wetware as low as possible, thresholds as high as they'll go, and firewall them. Where we're going, no one can follow us."

To her credit, Atempa did just as I asked. Joshua, of course, trusted me implicitly. (I know, Nameren, I know.) It was only after I had led us deep into the grub tunnel that she couldn't hold herself back any longer.

"It is not possible," Atempa said, voice trembling, "to enter the most dangerous Library god—*Old Coyote*, for material's sake, Freida!—through a grub tunnel."

I took a deep breath. The air had cleared, from one step to the next, of the lingering grass-and-honey musk characteristic of grub tunnels with hatching larvae.

The stone looked almost the same. I lowered the light from my rope of four novice shards. Atempa jumped back. The stone on Old Coyote's side of the tunnel was glowing, faintly, in blue.

"Say hello to the old bastard, Atempa," I said softly. "This avatar is Leguá."

She covered her mouth. "But . . ." she said from behind parted fingers. "Leguá is level four!"

"Of course. I only enter through level three or level four," I said with a recklessness that thrilled me. "They don't monitor the high-level tunnels for unauthorized access, and you never run into anyone down here. I'm sure no other librarian has bothered with Leguá in a decade."

Joshua gave me a warm, considering look. "Level four is . . . something you're not supposed to do?"

Atempa lowered her hand and took a judicious but firm step forward. She winced and then grinned. "Only Cardinal Librarians and Cube Librarians are allowed in level-four tunnels. They're unspeakably dangerous. The materials have killed more than one unwary librarian. You're supposed to ask for permission in deep communion, or at least a deep networked query, which . . ." She frowned and abruptly stopped walking. "Freida." She dropped my name like an anvil.

Joshua looked between us. "I'm missing something."

Though the aspect of the tunnel had changed not at all, Atempa raised her two postulant shards as though warding off a ghost. "We have to turn around."

I sighed. "It's safe, I promise. Leguá's been half asleep for fifty years, and ze doesn't mind me even when ze's awake."

"Did you sneak a nanopill communion with a *level-four avatar*?"

Her disbelief pricked something inside me, a latent realization of the line I had crossed by bringing them here. I had survived seventeen years in the Library by keeping my secrets, even from Nadi. Atempa was my best friend and Joshua the boy I loved—still, what did my trust mean, when their breaking of it would destroy me? An old, sour feeling coated my throat like phlegm: my vulnerability, my ineradicable softness, my weakness that no amount of illicit tunnel crawling could erase. Quinn's power trumped my every accomplishment, any spark of individuality. I lived, yes, but—of necessity—hidden.

Joshua put his hand on my elbow. I shook him off. I didn't need his quiet reassurance, not here of all places. Even Quinn couldn't stop the avatars of the material gods from remembering how their daughter had once walked their veins and eaten their flesh to join them in dreaming.

"I don't do nanopill communion, Atempa," I said at last. "I ingest."

She lowered her shards. Blinked. "You . . . that's still possible? Isn't it dangerous? It killed dozens of librarians before the high-wetware protocols."

"You ingest?" Joshua said. "Literally? You eat the gods?"

Now I smiled, relieved to have said it at last. "Why do you think it's called communion?"

I couldn't eat the wary respect on Atempa and Joshua's faces, but I savored it in any case. Leguá was a trickster, who even in dreams led us in spiraling mazes that re-formed within hours. Zir crystal was salt-based, quick-forming, and it seamed the staid granite of Old Coyote in starbursts and whorls of pattern that formed shapes like a dreaming language. I ran my left hand against the wall as we walked, my shoes tied together by their laces and swinging in my right so I could feel a warm vibration against my soles. My eyes were closed, and my mind elsewhere, so what Joshua and Atempa made of me I have no idea. I kept a steady pace, humming a snatch of something under my breath, to match the murmur of the crystal beneath my fingertips.

"What are you singing?" Atempa asked. "I can't get the Eye down here. Most of my modules are down. What is this, Freida?"

I blinked a few times at her, lip curled to match her waspish tone, as I reoriented myself to human scale.

"Level-four avatar," I said. "No All-Seeing Eye in the level fours, Atempa. Not even most of the threes. Don't they teach you that? In the tunnels you know what the gods know, nothing else."

This surprised her to momentary silence. On my other side, Joshua's face took on the distant expression with furrowed brows that meant he was checking his own wetware. Then he shook his head. "Nothing. I don't think we could even call for help." He smiled at me, as if to say that by my side he wouldn't need to. That wild, unearned trust, so freely gifted . . . (I know, Nameren.)

Atempa swallowed and looked longingly down the dark mouth of the tunnel from which we'd come. I doubted that she could find the way back to the grub tunnel from here.

"But what's the point of us being high wetware, then? Why do Quinn and the others . . ." She glanced at me guiltily, and bit back the rest.

My smile was sour as a blood pear. "Why stack the deck against low-wetware postulates like me? They claim it's because we can't do communion. But we're wasting time here. Leguá moves fast, even when ze's dreaming. I need to find a good spot."

"A good spot for what?" Atempa asked, but I heard her faintly, as though from across a cavern. I fell into god-space again, god-time, god-dream. This wasn't communion; it was just thinking, it was just moving, it was just knowing. It was just what I had been born to do.

I felt myself humming again, though the tune didn't feel like music so much as a language spoken in someone else's dream, dimly understood. They followed me for a few dozen heartbeats, a half-dozen slow blinks, and we reached a little divot in the wall, which was now almost entirely made of milky-white salt crystal.

I dropped back into normal sense and pushed my way into the crack. Atempa and Joshua goggled: the natural illusion of the divot had hidden the opening from their view. "Come on," I told them. "Leguá won't wait forever. Ze's got dreams to dream."

We slipped into the inky darkness, a close, claustrophobic journey that spat us, after a long minute, into a low, circular chamber. The floor was Old Coyote granite, but the walls and ceiling were surf and sand, long-fingered seaweed swaying in currents that came to us in the chamber on a breeze, spraying salt water. The light was bright but diffuse, almost milky, and painful to my eyes accustomed to the steady throb of crystals in the main artery.

"Are we . . . we can't be in the Library anymore." Joshua's voice was faint, leached by awe and terror.

"Of course we are," Atempa snapped. "Right, Freida? You didn't—no, you couldn't."

I was almost as astonished by this place as they were. Leguá had never taken me here before. I had never seen this sun, or this wine sea, but maybe Joshua had.

"We're still in the Library," I said. "But the materials are . . . unpredictable. This must be a memory of Leguá's. A different sun. A sea."

It reminded me—I didn't want to remember, but it came back regardless— of that wide marsh in Sidne, and the still pool with its black sand and white bones, which Iemaja had given to me as comfort after what happened with Samlin. Most of the gods' creations, even in level-four avatars, were simple static repositories. Even for me, these otherworldly pockets shook my idea of what the Library was and how any of us pretended to own or even understand it. Suspicious, I took a slow walk around the room and ran my hand through the water, which rippled behind me.

"Great god's bollocks, it's real," Atempa said. "This is *nowhere* in the postulant manuals."

"Freida, what are you looking for?" Joshua had recovered his equilibrium enough for wonder to edge out the terror in his voice. But he still didn't come any closer to that impossible seawall.

"Just something to eat," I said, offhand. No bones that I could see. Tension left my shoulders. I wouldn't tell them. I didn't know who ze had been, but I knew ze would never have been in that space if ze were not beloved of the gods. It wasn't my secret to share. And they'd probably never trust me again if they knew I sometimes found old librarians' bones here in the hidden arteries of the most dangerous avatars.

I took a deep breath, saltwater spray and old copper, and returned to the center of the chamber. Beneath Atempa's quetzal-plume sandals was my prize: a milky-white, just-hatched patch of pure Leguá crystal.

I pulled out my novice cord of shards and started to hack at it with the Nyad. Joshua, realizing what I meant to do before Atempa, knelt beside me and handed me his chisel. My hand shook as I touched his. As simply as that, he gave me what no one else in my life ever had. I felt human, I felt loved, I felt seen, at last, here in the bowels of the gods. The chisel made quick work of the new-formed crystal. I took out a sliver and rubbed it to powder on my fingers.

"Most crystals aren't pure enough for communion," I told Atempa, as though I were an old librarian giving classes. "It has to be new shards, or a heart shard, like the kinds the Head Librarian has. Quinn is a jerk, but the development of high-wetware communion must have made the job a lot easier."

Atempa looked down at the glittering powder on my fingertips. Her jaw worked. "You're going to swallow that. Yes, of course you are. Do you even have an offering?"

"Leguá is a lighthearted sort of god. Ze's good with a joke. So, do you want to come along?" I asked, wagging my fingers at them. "I've got enough for three."

Joshua went very still and then laughed that bright, sunlit laugh, at last at home here in this foreign sea. "Why not?"

"This is a terrible idea," Atempa said. We just looked at her. "They won't know we did it?"

"Not unless you tell them."

Atempa got that dangerous look, the devious, mischievous one that meant she would do whatever she could to confound her father and defy the straitjacket strictures on a scion of a first Mahām family. It was why we were friends, despite all appearances.

"Then," she said, kneeling beside us, "I will make very sure not to tell."

✦

A soft slide into communion, so quiet you wouldn't catch it unless you were looking. We still knelt around the new crystal, but on a shallow shelf under a wide sea. Atempa and Joshua held their breaths, eyes alarmed. All the high-wetware postulants had passed a communion with one of Iemaja's well-trod avatars, but Atempa's must have been a very different experience.

"Breathe," I told them. Though my voice came out muffled and damp, it was still understandable. I tapped the earth three times—zir ritual calling—and looked around for Leguá. A seahorse, the size of my hand, tumbled nearby.

"Funny, funny," ze puffed. "Never had so many visitors. What do they want?"

I looked to Atempa and Joshua. Joshua set his shoulders and coughed wetly.

Atempa spoke in a terrified rush. "What is the historical justification of the Mahām War Ritual and is it valid according to your august interpretation?"

The seahorse raced away from her and hid in my hair. It was long again here in this communion. Was that a reflection of my inner state or Leguá's memory of me?

"How tendentious!" the seahorse said.

"Not our fault," Atempa said.

"You can't expect me to dredge all that up!" Ze sneezed. "The water," ze confided in a stage whisper that flapped my earlobes, "is gonna get nasty."

A school of Nyad-colored fish like skinny knives passed and doubled back overhead. Joshua pushed off the sandy bottom, but he sank back down, heavy as a stone, while the fish skittered away.

He shivered and pulled his knees up to his chest. "Why am I so heavy?"

"You have a lot weighing you down, my child!" Leguá said, and cackled, filling the water between us with flotillas of tiny air bubbles that clacked against one another like marbles. "Are you very worried about why the Mahām made up their bloody little ritual? How strange, really, how strange, none of us thought that eccentric excess would amount to much, and look! How miraculous, the cumulative weight of the concretized possibilities of all the possible worlds!"

"So . . ." Atempa said. "Is that your official judgment?"

Ze shimmied up to her face and inspected it with an air of officiousness. "My judgments are never particularly official," ze said sadly. "I'm still half asleep, you know. You're nosing around in my dream. But I'll try my best!"

Zir voice crescendoed to a wail; lightning struck the surface above us in a series of muffled roars. We trembled with electricity. The fish, mid-arc, exploded into bloody chum that clouded the water and rained upon us, blue scales and white flesh and delicate, translucent bones. Atempa shrieked loudly enough to penetrate the din. I couldn't even see Joshua, but I felt him, holding on. I smiled. He'd already learned the first rule of communion: Keep your seat. Second rule of communion: Pay attention.

Another round of lightning penetrated the water, snaked around and before us like an electric eel. For a brief moment, it outlined a tableau: a hundred bodies falling into a silent, inky ocean, blood frozen around them like stardust, orange robes moving with the inertia of their slow movement, and pulsing orbs of light trailing behind their bodies, as though they had each just been birthed from their very own universe.

Leguá's voice intoned: "The Aurochs' human representatives claim that this was an old Tierran ritual. But it started here, among the deep night of the stars. It started because the seed ship's life systems were failing, and they claimed some must die for the good of all. That was not true, but survival would have made their rigid social hierarchies unsustainable. So they sacrificed the ones whose philosophy threatened revolution. They continue to do so, for much the same reasons."

The sky calmed as quickly as it had set itself aflame. The water had turned swampy, strewn with bits of dead flesh and stinging billows of multicolored grit. My throat stung with the tang of acid and burning oil. I coughed. The water in front of my face began to clear until it surrounded me in a lit, limpid dome. Through the murk, I saw Joshua on his hands and knees, heavier than ever. Atempa drifted into seaweed and shrieked when it brushed her arms.

Leguá, now in a human body with skin as dark as mine and the head of a giant seahorse, gave me a bemused look.

Was it wise to bring your untested friends into this, my child?

I sat up and blinked against my crystal water bubble. Those hadn't been my thoughts. Had Leguá given them to me? Before I could parse that unexpected strangeness, ze turned zir inquisitive snout to Joshua.

"Must you carry so much, child?" ze said. "You smell of earth, of parched riverbeds and plastic-choked water. I remember that place as it was. Give me a story of how it is. Give me a little of the load you carry in payment. I'm much larger than you, I can take it."

Joshua gasped. I swam over to him, lay my head beside his on the sand until my bubble expanded to reach him. My stomach twisted. Leguá's thought or my own, it was right: I had been reckless to bring them here. Leguá was tricky, not cruel, but deep communion brought out unpredictable aspects of yourself—and of the god.

"Just tell zir a story," I whispered as Joshua's breath steadied. "Something about your family."

Joshua closed his eyes, as though against the reality of communion. "Your chance," he muttered to himself. Then he dragged himself upright, every inch of him the audacious legal scholar making history in the tribunal. Was this what he had been bearing, even there?

"There's a story my great-grandmother told me."

Leguá leaned in. Atempa swam closer to us, accompanied by a train of seaweed like a hundred gently caressing fingers. Joshua's voice was clear, confident, mesmerizing. The strain showed in his trembling shoulders, the spidery tendrils of sweat bleeding into the bubble around our heads. But his voice showed none of that; it cleared the polluted water where it pierced.

"Every year, after the rains end, and the four-hundred-petal flowers bloom like sunset in the fields, we welcome our dead back home. And among our prayers we always say, 'We call to those lost between the stars, that they might find their way to a friendly hearth.' I asked my great-grandmother what that meant, and she said it was for the dead lost during the Great War. I asked her, 'But we didn't fight in space during the war, did we? We fought here on Tierra when the Mahām invaded.' My great-grandmother was a very wise woman, nearly two hundred years old when she died; as a child she had met the last Eagle Elder before she was assassinated by the Lunars. She sat me down and said, 'Joshua, during the war we were given a gift. Children came back home to Tierra. They had lost everything.

We make that prayer for the spirits of their ancestors, not our own. They were lost among the stars and their children feared they would never find peace or rest.' I asked her where those children were now, and she said, 'In you, in me, in our blood. Through them, we are enshrined in the Treaty, and we will never forget that.'"

Leguá swam right up to Joshua now, rested zir dark hands on Joshua's shoulders, and pulled him upright. Zir expression, as much as I could read it on that alien seahorse face, was sublime. Joshua floated up to zir shoulder height.

"The children, the children, the children." Leguá's whispering voice surrounded us like a chant. At first meditative, then increasingly distraught, oppressive. It broke into a multivoiced wail: "I can't! These children of the lost tenth! They are too much of a burden! Our other self, oh, our child self, how ze suffers, alone and locked away—I can't!"

Our communion fractured and rocked. The pollution poured in again. Now even I couldn't breathe. I raced to grab Atempa and Joshua, to pull us back to safety. Leguá was such a stable avatar, I'd never expected that ze would begin to awaken in the middle of such a short, quotidian visit.

"Leguá!" I shouted, pitching my voice to breach the darkness billowing between us. "Let us go!"

"The children, the children!"

"We renounce communion! We renounce—"

We came back to reality with a sudden, snapping finality, on our knees on new-formed crystal as salt water misted our drenched, bowed heads. Joshua and Atempa collapsed on the floor with shuddering gasps. I was probably the only one who heard that faint, distraught whisper:

"The children of the lost tenth, at last, they have found us."

With that, Joshua found the story that would win his case. But he needed our help to disentangle it. A week later, Atempa and I sat together high up in the gallery of the tribunal. We were both jittery, eyes sticky with lack of sleep and the twisting high of some old acid Tenehet fruit that Zell had solemnly offered us during the sleepless nights we'd spent preparing for this hearing.

Leguá had awoken long enough to block zirself and retreat as though fleeing into deep slumber. I still didn't understand what had happened at the end of that communion, but zir phrase, "the children of the lost tenth," had turned out to be the key to Joshua's historical argument. If he won, it would spell a revolution across the three systems. Atempa had thrown her lot in with us without much fanfare, and I in turn did not make any fuss. Still, we both knew that helping Joshua with a petition that would directly cross her father and—in theory, anyway—you, Nameren, was a rebellion far greater than even entering the librarian trials.

This hearing had infuriated Quinn's faction and the Nameren priests. The section reserved for opposition scholars was stacked with officials, predominantly Martian and Mahām, bedecked in shard cloth and ancient animal pelts whose richness denoted no position but wealth itself—practically a taboo in the Library. Their high noses indicated how little they cared for our disapproval. They loomed above Joshua, as though they would devour him whole the moment he stepped from his circle of light at the center of the tribunal. Maybe they would; but in the meantime, he would eviscerate them.

The ibis of Tenehet circled three times overhead, and paused with that unnatural, uncanny stillness before Joshua in the circle of light.

"The essence of your argument, scholar?"

Joshua bowed his head with a small smile. "The tenth expedition was not entirely lost, as we were all taught. Some children survived and returned to Tierra during the Great War. My people took them in, with the promise that the children and their descendants were due recognition in the Treaty. That recognition of ancestral territory and autonomy was enshrined in the primary Freedom node, in its autonomy filament. But the same forces that oppose me now opposed us then, and their preferred filaments, most notably those for free competition and self-actualization, came to take precedence, and eventually, render the autonomy filament apocryphal."

The gallery erupted. Opposition scholars shouted objections at such a pace their points were lost in the cacophony.

"Quiet!" the ibis commanded. "The tribunal will hear this argument. Objections will be entertained when the tribunal has finished its examination."

Atempa squeezed my hand, and I squeezed back. We had spent every moment this past week verifying each detail of what I learned in the tunnels with the All-Seeing Eye or other publicly available records. This truth had been hiding in plain sight for the last five hundred years, but only the oral tradition of Joshua's people had maintained the light of its memory. They had remembered what they were due, even when everyone else had forgotten.

Past spoke first. Ze was the same war chest memory who had adjudicated during the first hearing. Most likely, Present and Future were also represented by the same individuals. "Define terms first, scholar. Not everyone here is as privileged as an indigenous Tierran of the smoking mountain with deep knowledge of human history. The tenth expedition, supposedly lost, but apparently not."

Joshua pivoted gracefully to face zir and raised his voice. "The expedition period refers to the era in Tierran history one hundred years before contact with the Awilu. Ecological pressures and social movements led to widespread fears of apocalypse. Consortiums of human groups constructed seed ships—spacefaring vessels capable of surviving for generations as they travel at near-light speeds in search of a habitable planet to settle.

"Tierrans launched ten expeditions in this period. The last expedition launched just before contact. When the Awilu appeared in the sky above Addis Ababa, tesseract technology made seed ships obsolete. It turned out that the first expedition had blundered into the tesseract left behind by the Awilu when they abandoned Tierra ten thousand years before. The first expedition integrated with Awilu society for a hundred years and paved the way for the Awilu reformation and their return to Tierra. The Awilu discovered that only one other seed ship, the fifth expedition by the Mahām alliance, had reached its planet and survived. All the other expeditions are formally considered lost."

Future, riddled with life like a rotting log, interjected. "And you claim, young scholar, that this is not in fact true? That the tenth expedition survived? Where are they, then? Not here, surely?"

Nervous laughter, some ribald shouts from the opposition section of the gallery. Joshua smiled serenely. "We are right here," he said, his voice clear and round as a bell, "before you today. No one knows what happened to the seed ship of the tenth expedition. Only that it came to tragedy. Most died. But a few children survived. Those children found asylum among the people of the smoking mountain on Tierra. You will find fragmented recordings and testaments among the data I have submitted for evidence to the tribunal. Those children are my ancestors. For my people's resistance to the Mahām incursion at the start of the war and for our combined claim for what those children lost at the end of the war, we were promised autonomy and land rights, enshrined in the Treaty itself. That we do not have access to them is a legal oversight of five hundred years' duration that I am here to correct."

"We noted your ambition in the last tribunal, scholar," said Present, the features of zir mask rearranged such that ze spoke from a mouth by zir forehead.

"But you have sharpened its blade. This was wise of you. It is no easy task to cut an apocryphal node free of its precedents."

"It is not easy," Future put in, "and I doubt you will be the one to manage it. Though the Past might be your ally in this and the Present willing, the Future wonders what benefit there is to re-adjudicating crimes of distant days. You want us to reactivate the apocryphal filaments of the old Freedom node, which specify land rights and autonomy for your people and for the Miuri. From there, as we all know, it would be a very short step to the claims of hundreds of groups who live in Lunar, Martian, or Mahām territory."

"There are also several peoples in Awilu territory who would be interested in staking their claim, I do believe, Future," said Past with deliberate mildness.

"Well, then," said Future. "What benefit to the Future in that? Do we desire thousands of cases and struggles for autonomy? Next thing we know, we'll have to entertain grub petitions for rights to their mating grounds!" More laughter. I frowned—the peacekeepers were supposedly incorruptible ascetics, scholars who had renounced the world in order to give it justice. And yet this one seemed far too eager to play to the opposition scholars.

"The problem, as I see it, Scholar Totolkozkat," said Present, "is that your claim hinges on the weight we give the story of these lost children. Why should what happened to them have provoked such a great concession in the Treaty itself? Why should it carry over into the question of Miuri autonomy as well?"

Joshua took a breath as his hands twitched. He was sifting through his personal array. "I can only speculate as to why the drafters chose to put Miuri autonomy alongside that of the peoples of the American territories. But surely the fact that they *did* is argument enough to consider the Tierran and Miuri claims materially linked?"

The three judges fell momentarily silent, and a murmur swept through the gallery.

"What's going on?" I asked Atempa.

"Some kind of legal wrangling," she whispered back. "I think his argument was controversial."

At last Past spoke. "An argument based on the intentions of the drafters can only be supported by the knowledge of the drafters. If they considered the link between your case and those of the Miuri to be materially relevant, then you must allow us to understand how. We are a tribunal, not a church. We do not worship the drafters, we merely build upon their foundation. But we test that foundation each time before we build upon it—do you understand, young scholar? Precedent can seem onerous and conservative to the young, but *precedent* is simply another word for *experience*; it is the way we know that one step has a solid foundation before we take the next."

The ibis flew over the gallery and settled before the opposition scholars. "You are allowed to put forth a motion."

"Motion to separate the Miuri case from that of the peoples in Lunar territory!" The opposition scholar, in full ancient military regalia that marked zir as a member of the oldest Lunar families, leapt to zir feet and shouted, as though zir agitation was argument enough. "There is no reason to consider them together; it is merely a way to ride the wave of public opinion to bolster his weak position on the legal points."

"I vote in favor," said Future, so quickly that Present turned zir head in surprise.

"I vote against," said Present.

An acid wash cramped my stomach. What would Joshua do without the support of the Miuri and those championing their cause?

Past kept zir silence for an uncomfortable minute. "You are convinced," ze said at last, "that the drafters had a specific legal and circumstantial reasoning behind linking your case and the Miuri in this node?"

"I am, Honored Past."

"Then you must find that reasoning, Scholar Totolkozkat. If it has been lost to history, then I am afraid that you must argue your case entirely on its precedents. Where you are, I am sure you know, at a great disadvantage. Who were the children of the lost tenth? Why did they settle on Tierra? What was their connection with the Miuri? Find that, scholar, and we will hear your case. I vote against, with the stipulation that the scholar must present the historical argument to bolster his case. Motion to adjourn."

The ibis swept into the rafters of the tribunal, where ze circled the center pit three times. "Motion—" Ze paused in mid-flight, still as a picture. "Oh. Welcome, West Librarian Quinn. You wish to file a motion for the opposition?"

I swallowed and kept my seat. All around us, people stood or raised themselves to see where Quinn had somehow secreted himself in the back of the opposition scholar section. I didn't even realize I was trembling until Atempa put her arm around my shoulder and said, in a tone of rancorous solidarity that was a balm to my soul, "That *asshole*."

"I merely wish to alert the tribunal," said Quinn, his tone friendly, "that perhaps it would be best to dismiss the case. This fascinating thread of history the fine scholar has discovered is unfortunately entirely sequestered in Old Coyote's deepest avatars. You have ruled not to question the *provenance* of this information, but I mention that Leguá, a deep avatar of Old Coyote, has shut zirself off completely from librarians after unauthorized access which we are still investigating. The founders or the gods themselves chose to lock away this history in Huehue, an avatar that no one has been able to contact since shortly after the founding."

Whispers rolled through the gallery like waves. Even among non-librarians, Huehue was infamous, a byword for difficult and tricky truths kept hidden.

"So, you see." Quinn's voice held a smug note of triumph now. I turned my head to Atempa's shoulder and swallowed down bile. "It would be quite useless to waste everyone's time on an argument the scholar will be unable to complete."

The ibis, still hanging where ze had frozen, turned zir head from Quinn back to the tribunal. "I believe," ze said, "that a ruling against *provenance* also encompasses a ruling against *politics*. Your interests in this matter are duly noted, West Librarian. If the scholar is unable to prove his case for the reasons you have mentioned, it will be dismissed in its time. Hearing is adjourned."

As soon as the ibis and the tribunal judges left the room, the network popped online. Even with my thresholds set high, the barrage of pings and interest hit me like a splash of cold water. Atempa gave a full-body shudder.

"What is going on out there?" she muttered. "This case is big, but it's not *that*— Oh, Freida."

She pointed, but I had seen it at the same moment: a knot of people screaming questions, elbowing forward, savage in their curiosity and need. I hoped their target was Joshua or Quinn, but a quick search through my network confirmed the strange fear rising in my throat: Nadi had come. Ze was speaking openly with Quinn in front of an audience. Joshua stood awkwardly to one side of them, blocked from his supporters. Through one of the local Library feeds, I heard Nadi's shrewd politician voice, the one that had maintained zir power for my lifetime despite half a dozen attempts to take zir down.

"I can assure you that what happened to Leguá was no security breach," ze was saying. "The ways of the gods are multifaceted and difficult to predict. I wish our young scholar here the best of luck. Perhaps he can find something in the public records. Or perhaps Huehue will awaken for him! It's about time. Old Coyote's secrets could make half this room tremble, don't you think?"

Quinn's smile could have curdled milk. "Oh, I'm sure. And Iemaja's could make the other half quite uncomfortable." He turned to Joshua. "My boy! Congratulations on making it this far. And I'm sorry to have made such a fuss—look, your girlfriend is over there, waiting for you."

Every head in the room turned to me. My stomach lurched with the giddy double vision of myself in the feed before I cut it off. I wanted to turn to smoke and float serenely through the high windows. But Quinn had achieved his purpose. Everyone would speculate now about Nadi's connection to Joshua's case. I smiled instead and felt my legs moving entirely of their own accord down the stairs and closer to Joshua, his smile frozen, eyes lively with panic.

A ping like a dirty kiss bloomed across my public wall. I didn't want to open it, but I had no choice.

"Hello, dear Freida." Quinn's mental voice was softer than his spoken one, like some pollen you couldn't get off your skin. "I think you and Nadi and I are overdue for a talk."

Quinn led us to a meeting room down a restricted-access corridor behind the assembly hall. I had never been here before and felt itchy with following eyes—though if the surveillance was real or imagined, I had no way of knowing. Nadi didn't give Quinn a chance to speak once he'd shut the door.

"I don't appreciate these theatrics, Quinn. We're librarians, not members of the Martian investor moot."

Quinn pursed his lips. "You have your own panache for playing to the crowd."

"Why are we here?" Nadi asked bluntly.

Quinn blinked into a slow smile. "Because you lied about Leguá."

"There was no security breach."

"I have proof, Nadi."

"Proof of what?" Here in private, ze allowed zirself cutting mockery. "Did Leguá tell you?" Quinn was notorious for avoiding communion.

He drew himself up, emphasizing how he towered over us by half a meter. "In a way. I know Freida was there. Your pet caused one of our last deep avatars to shut zirself off from librarian contact."

"That is pure speculation, and you—"

"She was careless this time."

Nadi fell silent. Ze buzzed like a live wire, but exhaustion rimmed zir eyes.

Quinn looked around Nadi and spoke to me. "You brought a friend, didn't you? You let outsiders into our most sacred spaces."

I took a sharp breath, but whatever words I meant to say came out wispy and charred. How could he know? What trace had we left?

"I—we—I didn't—" I was gasping for air. I had never meant for this to happen. I hadn't meant to expose them.

Abruptly, Nadi whirled around and put zir hands on my shoulders.

"Love, quiet. He's bluffing."

Nadi's dark eyes were pained but distant, rushing with that legendary intellect through all the possible political gambits Quinn could be making right now. I couldn't follow zir. That strange energy, so counter to the exhaustion that seamed zir like crystal through old rock, heated even the palms of zir hands. *Something is wrong*, I thought.

In truth, everything was wrong, Nameren, but I could not hold on to that clarity.

I had, it seemed, betrayed my friends.

Quinn shook his head. "I have often wished you were on my side more often over the years, Nadi. In some ways it's a shame that things have ended like this.

But you made your decision when you insisted on raising Iemaja's secondary AI as your own."

"I did," said Nadi, still looking at me. "And there is nothing to regret."

"The secondary AI has all but admitted that she was in the tunnels with that upstart groundling scholar. I could have her eliminated from the postulant process for this. It would hurt your position."

Nadi rolled zir eyes and turned so ze faced him again, with zir hand firmly on my shoulder.

"You can do that any time you wish. If it will hurt me, let it. But you have no proof of anything she did in those tunnels, so I can only surmise you played that trick to get some information. Did it work? Will you now tell us why we're here?"

Quinn pouted, as though he had wished to play with us further, but then he glanced down at me and brightened. "I will, in deference to your honored parent, get to the point, young Freida. I have learned something about your guardian that ze very much does not wish known. If it is released publicly, it will fatally undermine zir position in the last negotiations before the Nameren priests set the date for their War Ritual. As ze would have it, tri-system peace itself is at stake. I do not share zir position on this point, but I can only assume that you do. It could even lead to the Librarian Council holding a vote of no confidence. I'm sure you can imagine how your position here will change if Nadi is no longer Head Librarian."

Nadi gripped my shoulder tight enough to bruise, but I did not move. I hardly breathed.

Quinn went on. "I will not tell you what this secret is, Freida, because I can see that you don't know and my aim in this is the goodwill of your guardian. Ze has certainly guessed what I know by now, and that is what matters."

"What," I managed, "do you want from me?"

Not even Samlin had made me feel more like a thing, a pretty little object.

"You give me proof that your boyfriend was in Leguá's tunnels, my dear, and I will make sure you get through the postulant trials. You will be a novice librarian, with protections that even Nadi can't give you. Your place here will be secure. That's what you want, isn't it?"

A thrill rushed through me, a jolt of longing that I tried to deny. And he saw it.

"But Joshua . . . what will happen to him?"

"I just want him off the case, that's all. Tampering with evidence gets around the ibis's ruling on provenance. It's important enough to certain people that this unprecedented node revival hearing end that I am doing Nadi the courtesy of not telling anyone zir secret."

I looked up at Nadi, expecting zir to defend me, to tell Quinn that his intimidation tactics would never work, but ze was silent and rigid as glass. What secret could be so horrible it would leave zir so defenseless?

"What guarantee do I have that you won't tell Nadi's . . . secret . . . even if I do what you ask?"

Quinn tapped his forehead as though to say I was a very clever secondary AI. "You'll just have to trust me, I suppose, Freida. But I promise, if you haven't found a way to deliver that boy to me by tomorrow afternoon, your guardian will be in the crosshairs of a political insurrection by evening."

I went to Iemaja, just the chapel, to sit by the cenote and watch the reflection of the fish moon arcing above that still black mirror. The thorn had already set. What would I do? What should I do? *Guarantee you pass the postulant trials. You will have the protections of a novice librarian.* Oh, longing, that betrayer of my better impulses, that old need for safety, for place. Joshua's avatar sat lonely outside my thresholds, leaving me ever more desperate messages. *Freida, what happened? Freida, are you safe?* I told it I was fine and shut it out again. I knew I should talk to him, but I couldn't. I should confess, but what would I say to that bright face, so hopeful at last of his ability to save *his* family, *his* safety, *his* place? I would try to tell myself that I did this for Nadi, for zir last chance to stave off the worst of the War Ritual. And zir need was present in my thoughts, a discordant jangling that filled me with panic.

But that was not, Nameren, why I chose as I did.

I remembered, painfully, the night of the bonfire and the attack on the grubs that Quinn's faction had managed to pin on us. How incisively Joshua had cut to the heart of my lonely terror that night—*You are still you, even without the Library. You hold your own shape.*

In this, I decided, he had erred.

Only as a real librarian could I ever relax, could I ever have a modicum of autonomy. Only passing the selection process could I be a girl with a shape, remembered by the gods. Anything else was a dream. And I loved Joshua. I loved him so much, Nameren, but he was just a human, not enough to hold me.

He kissed me on his way into the emergency meeting with the opposition scholars and the ibis of Tenehet. He squeezed my hands and kissed me, though he rarely did so in public, and whispered in my ear, "Whatever it is, we'll figure it out."

He did not mean the meeting, which did not worry him. He meant whatever had happened to me with Quinn.

I hugged him from behind, tight, just before he went in. He stroked my hand and was gone.

That would be the last time. Whoever left that room would be changed.

I waited there for what I had made of him, though I wanted to run to the Tesseracts and hide beneath the lake with the singing grubs.

After twenty minutes, passing from a slingshot, the opposition scholars left the room, followed by Joshua. His posture was erect, but his eyes were blasted, dazed. The opposition scholars laughed.

Joshua shook his shoulders and blinked. He found me standing precisely where I had been. He gave me a tired smile, though he squinted in pain. He didn't want me to worry. He took a step forward. I didn't move. He hesitated. A half step—

I watched him realize what had happened.

Clever Joshua. It didn't take him very long at all.

"You'll make it through the postulant exams, at least?" he said. As though he was angry and yet still cared.

"Joshua, please, I didn't have—"

Something flashed in his eyes that struck me silent. "Don't. Not you, Freida. Even if you don't love me, don't lie."

I started to cry and rubbed at my face furiously. Oh, to be high wetware and able to shut off my sympathetic reactions with a neural program! I burned with so many different kinds of shame that they fought for territory like grange dogs in my intestines.

"This isn't fair," I said bitterly. "What they've done to you and to me, it *isn't fair!*"

"No," he said, colder than I'd ever heard him. "But then, what you did to me wasn't particularly fair, either. I'm off the case, Freida, or did you know already? Tampering with evidence, damaging my constituents' position. I can no longer argue my case and my people can no longer be the principal litigants. It's over but for the formalities. The ibis will grant the motion to dismiss during the next hearing—unless someone from the Miuri steps up to the principal position. I doubt they will. No time to invest in court proceedings when you're about to be massacred."

But that couldn't be true. There had to be a way to keep the case going, even without him. "Ask the disciple girl to take over!" I said. "The one who hides in the reading rooms. She's here in person. It doesn't have to be their rector; any disciple can represent the Miuri with a scholar champion. You could still argue the case, just from the position of the disciples, with your people as a principal interest. The strategy wouldn't even change—"

He shook his head. "They dropped my scholarship, Freida." His voice scratched me like sandpaper. "I can't afford to stay here. It's over."

He left before I could say anything more.

He left without looking at me.

The ground stretches around the girl and the god, fading into the distance but never quite cut off by a horizon line. She has never seen one outside of holos and has not thought to imagine it. Water, though, she knows: cold needles that fall at sharp angles with the wind; deep rivers that cut a red, bloody channel through the heart of a city; lakes surrounded by marsh grass and dotted with tiny islands like spots on fur. No matter what she imagines, though, the red clay earth stays cracked and parched. The aurochs watches her, sharp eyes in a smudgy face, bemused.

She spits in the earth. A tiny seedling grows, withers, dies in the space of her breath. She scowls.

"Still declaring your war on the rain?" She remembers the old stories they tell about him.

"Do you still love him?"

She pauses, readjusts. "Of course I do."

"But you love her, too. That girl you brought with you, the one who follows her paths in a globe of melted sand."

"He isn't mine anymore. Nergüi is . . . for as long as she chooses to be."

"Does love come so easily to you, then?"

Her snort is nothing at all like a bull's, but he jumps as though she pricked him. "Radical truth, radical trust, radical vulnerability? Of course not! Radical love is a practice, not a goal you achieve. But I have loved. I have been loved, Nameren. I have had those gifts. That's why I'm here."

"Oh? I thought you were here to kill me."

"I told you, I know I can't do that. I'm here to tell you stories."

"And that girl—"

"Is she okay?"

"She's feeding you. She holds your head up and squeezes something into your mouth."

"Oh, Nergüi."

Her voice is sad, but her eyes are smiling.

"She prays over you."

"Of course she does. Ask her, can the lights in that ball of hers find us a way out?"

"She says, 'I'm asking my infinite incarnations for help.'"

"Wait, really? You asked her?"

"I rearranged the stone. It isn't hard, as you said."

"Is she scowling?"

The god draws his great aurochs brows together. "Like this?"

She tosses her head back and her laughter fills the sky.

"Will you tell me about her?"

The girl smiles so sweetly that the aurochs's twin hearts come clear from the mist of him. Man-heart and beast-heart knock against a new-made throat.

"I will."

—To understand Nergüi, you have to understand two things: her stories and her souls.

I kept running into the sad Miuri disciple in the reading rooms of Old Coyote. Her notoriety in town had exploded after Joshua's dramatic departure from the case. Right before the ibis would have ruled to dismiss, she had filed a petition to serve as the principal litigant on behalf of the Disciples of the Lighted Path and the Miuri. I had no idea if she had done this on her own, or if Joshua had persuaded her into becoming his case's last-minute miracle.

She haunted the place at odd hours, kneeling in her sunset-orange robes that frayed at the hems to study the search results that we novice librarians would bring to her. As a refugee, she was allotted one skim search—a level-zero query— per day.

She liked the queries with results on paper. She would put her nose to the spines of the reproduced books and breathe the artificial musk of slow decay: binding glue and dust mites and acid-whitened paper exhaling semitoxic volatiles as it went brown.

After I formally passed the process—my bitter reward—it started raining again, the ferocious cold winds of the tears. The disciple and I had only seen each other at a distance since her arrival in the mud, but with my new novice duties in the reading rooms, she and I were forced to acknowledge each other's existence. I expected that she would use her allotment to search for material for the case, but as the weeks stretched on, as far as I could tell, she did not access a single relevant resource. Instead, she wanted stories. Old, precontact Tierran stories. Newer Awilu multisensory fugues. Even a few pieces of storytelling rituals preserved from the first days of her people on the Miuri moon. She never requested anything from the Mahãm alliance itself. As Pajeu could have told me if ze had not cut me off completely, the sad Miuri girl refused to speak Mahãm at all.

The librarian's desk was at the center of a mollusk-shell spiral lined with public reading rooms, viewing rooms, private offices, and sleep nooks. A shaft at the back of the desk provided access to the tunnels, which I scrupulously never used outside of a full librarian's supervision. I had gotten what I had most wanted, after all; my days of being a rogue librarian, battling for good causes in the bowels of the gods, were over.

O, but materials, did I miss it. Even that old bastard with his hidden, forbidden heart. Even Mahue'e with her fire traps. I dreamed of them, slow conversations, strange memories of communions, as though they were wondering where I had gone. I went to Iemaja's temple to pray sometimes. But I had made my choice; many had suffered for it, and now it was my duty to live with it.

Perhaps I watched the Miuri girl because it distracted me from the heavy silences that fell when I passed my former friends, from the ongoing drama of the War Ritual negotiations, from Quinn's latest power grabs, from the case that could have saved Joshua's people. She was related to that, and yet held herself so carefully apart. Perhaps I watched her because she was as lonely as I was. The other novitiates would joke and call her the ghost bride, since her robes bore a vague resemblance to the wedding gowns of the Awilu north continent merchants. The few times she overheard this epithet, the girl would jerk and grip the palm-sized glass ball that hung from the belt of braided leather at her waist. When she held it, the ball would fill with sparks and she would stare through it, mesmerized, her lips moving without a sound. At first, I thought she must be praying. Later, it occurred to me that she might have been carefully enumerating our every defect.

She spoke very rarely, except to me, and only then to order another search. She was the first disciple to travel physically to the Library in over two centuries. The other Miuri refugees treated her with distant, wary respect. Even Nadi couldn't tell me why the disciples would only send a young novice and no others on the eve of a war ritual that could destroy them.

The Miuri girl let me be, but Atempa gave me no quarter. At least she still spoke to me, though sometimes I wished she would cut me off instead of cutting me to death.

"Nadi's really going to let them do it, won't ze?" Atempa asked one afternoon when we had Old Coyote duty together. "My dad was practically glowing last night at dinner. The Library won't even put up a fight?"

The sad Miuri girl, waiting on her latest search result, was meditating, or sleeping, in a nearby study nook, well within earshot. I roused my avatar and threw the poor thing against Atempa's furiously high thresholds.

"Do you *have* to do this out loud?" the octopus wailed, but I didn't know if even an echo reached Atempa. I took a deep breath. "Nadi hasn't come back to the retreat in days. Ze is totally sequestered. Which you would know if you'd decided to move into the retreat with the other novices."

The blow was weak, and I regretted it as soon as it left my mouth. "Oh, are you with the other novices now?" she asked sweetly. "I thought you were still in your childhood bedroom."

I jutted my chin at the hem of the Miuri girl's robe and sandaled feet. Atempa raised her eyebrows at me. "If only there were something you could do to help,

Freida. But you're just a lowly novice librarian, aren't you now? No less, and certainly no more."

I glared at her. "Tell your father," I said, entirely recklessly, "that there is no way! Even if Awilu society fractures into thirds again! Even if the Aurochs third lends their support to the Nameren! Nadi will have the Cicadas, and who won the war in the end?"

This was the latest rumor, that the situation with the War Ritual had come to such a political head that Awilu society was threatening to break into its traditional thirds—Aurochs, Cicada, and Baobab—as they did during the Great War. The light bands were buzzing with the prediction of a second war, but no one on the heavier bands took that seriously as of yet.

Of course, if anyone but the Miuri girl had heard me make that reckless prediction, they might have started to take the threat of war far more seriously. I would have made Nadi's life even harder yet again. I squeezed my eyes shut against the flush of shame creeping up my body. Atempa stood abruptly and walked away from the desk. I heard her brisk, energetic steps pacing around us until she paused and said, loudly, "Well? Your search is going to take a while, you know. The broonies are slow today. You can wait in a sleep nook if you want."

The Miuri girl didn't say a word, as far as I could tell. I opened my eyes in time to see her pause before our desk, give me an enigmatic, possibly hostile, look, and vanish into the spirals.

Atempa's chimeric bird screeched above me and dropped into the space between us. I hadn't seen it in weeks. "No one else was near enough to hear," it squawked. "And the ghost bride won't say anything! Next time, try not to let interpersonal rivalry derail intersystem peace, okay? Then I really *will* never forgive you."

"Thank you," my octopus said, dim spinning lights inside its skin flaring brighter with gratitude and sudden hope. Atempa gave me a haughty nod and turned on her heel. The bird hid itself again behind its fortress. My octopus turned to me with a lonely sigh before it sank into the wall in front of me.

My place in the Library at last assured, and I was as lonely as Cicada singing to zir lost siblings.

I started to wonder about the Miuri girl's searches.

She would deliver all her requests to me in a low monotone of sharply accented Library Standard—which meant it was a late-acquired heart language, learned without the help of nanopills or wetware. Then she'd wait impatiently for my acknowledgment before stalking away again, her robes billowing behind her. It wasn't hard to see behind the bluster. I don't think she really meant for it to hide anything. I think that without her armor, she would have hardly been able to stand.

There was one query in particular that I noted, which Old Coyote's broonies never quite knew what to make of. She wanted to know about great bathhouse stories. Specifically, she wanted to find stories where someone was stuck, or trapped, or died there. I'd never heard of a great bathhouse story before, but something about the term tickled the squishy underside of my throwback memory.

This was more than a month after Joshua left. Atempa had noted my fascination with the ghost bride and teased me relentlessly.

"Oh, don't tell me you've gone and fallen for her! Wasn't ruining Joshua's life enough? Pajeu says that you have a hole inside that you use other people to fill. I always figured that ze was jealous, but . . ."

I gave Atempa my best impression of her generations-bred haughtiness and refused to let her see how her comment stung me. A hole inside me? The nano-drop had felt so real, his hands above me, the leather beneath my back, a sharp sting—but it hadn't been real, and so neither could the hole.

To escape Atempa, I waited in the sunken chamber beneath the heart of the spiral where the reading room broonies lived, and where they would secrete their results like free-range hens laying eggs.

I lay on the floor underneath the nook where we had pinned the Miuri girl's latest query. A lump was slowly forming out of the white coral polymer. An hour later, it was finished: a beautifully illustrated scroll filled with symbols my slow wetware registered only as ancient Tierran and pictures of a strange, impossible world. I hurried to the third spiral to take it to her personally in the isolated study carrel she favored—I knew she would love it. Perhaps this would be enough to move her to talk to me.

She glanced up at my approach and immediately reached for her ball.

"What do you want?" She sounded wary, and under that, panicked. It was disconcerting—even people who didn't like me were rarely afraid of me.

"Your search results came back early."

"I was going to get them," she said, moving aside so I could hand her the scroll.

"It's beautiful," I said quickly, before she could turn her back to me. "It's your first detailed result."

She hesitated, and I thought she would kick me out, but then she sighed and unrolled the scroll. Her eyes went wide with wonder. She traced the old symbols and the illustrations of a mysterious bestiary: giant worms that looked a little like grubs, a whole army of people with faces on their bellies and no heads, birds the size of horses ridden by flame-haired demigods.

"Is it what you've been looking for?"

Her hand shook as she touched the images. "It's . . . beautiful. I'm sure some-one else would love it. But . . . no. It's not the bathhouse."

She rolled the scroll again and put it away carefully, in a cubby above the desk that hadn't been there a week before.

I turned to leave, spurred by her disappointment and obvious desire to be alone. But curiosity and some ill-examined need to be useful to *someone* made me turn around. "Why are you looking for this in Old Coyote anyway?"

She reached for her ball, where the lights pulsed and jumped and lit her fin-gertips red.

"I'm sure it's not part of your job to monitor *why* I'm making searches."

"It's someone's job," I said, annoyed now. "They could be sensitive."

"Are these sensitive? They told me that narrative-storytelling searches were the least restricted."

She was shorter than me but strongly built, with eyebrows as thick as two orange-brown caterpillars that were now scrunching to a peak right above her broad nose. It gave her the aspect of an obdurate desert falcon, the ones that rode the air currents for days without rest before stopping to mate right at the edge of the planet disc. If she'd had a beak, I was sure she would have pecked me.

"I don't have any idea one way or another," I told her, one hand on my hip and the other landing for emphasis on the desk. "Because you're searching in the wrong god."

At this her eyes jerked up to meet mine. I was arrested for a moment—not by the low, simmering anger in them, but by their color, which I could see clearly for the first time: dark brown with a lighter ring around the edge of her iris, two slices of petrified wood. "But they told me that Old Coyote has the best resources for narrative storytelling. That isn't true?"

I found my breath. "Sure, it's true. But that's mostly for the great Awilu sagas and everyone else postwar. This bathhouse thing, it's precontact Tierran, right?"

"Mostly. At least, that's where the only record I've found is from."

I found myself smiling. She was so wary and angry and ready to lash out, but I had realized that I could help her, and if I helped her, she would be forced to talk to me. At my smile, her frown grew so pronounced it seemed to be etched from the same ancient wood as her eyes.

"What? Are you laughing at me?"

"Your life would be easier here," I said, "if you didn't immediately assume that everyone was laughing at you."

She blinked. "Any other pearls of wisdom, Librarian?"

"My name is Freida, she."

"I know. You're a little notorious. They say you were born here. In this wild place."

"I was. Which means I'm pretty wild, too."

At that, the corner of her mouth tilted up just a fraction, which I counted as a smile, and so a victory. I leaned against the edge of her desk.

"My name is Nergüi, she," she said, after a moment.

"I know. Your surliness has provoked speculation."

She leaned back in her chair and raised her ball to study the whirling lights within. "I wish you all would ignore me."

"Do you want to find your bathhouse story?" I asked, suddenly wishing I could reach out to touch her shoulder. But she would hate the need implied in such a gesture.

She swallowed and nodded.

"Then," I said, "I think we'd best ask Iemaja."

Now that the tunnels were forbidden to me in my new incarnation as rule-abiding novice librarian Freida, I decided to take a risk and bring Nergüi to Tiger Freehold. The freeholds were scattered across the broonie-haunted contours of Library City, mostly in its remotest corners. Library City was based on the Awilu urban model, with large open tracts of land and organically integrated buildings. To a Tierran like Joshua it had hardly looked like a city at all—we had nothing of the inorganic polymers and metal alloys that blanketed Tierra or the mazelike, densely populated floating tiers of Mahām cities. The freeholds had been there from the beginning; according to the freeholders, none of the intelligence-dark buildings or high-rent enclaves had been part of the original design at all. The Library is an organic-intelligent system, they argued, one that humans were never meant to subdue but to exist within. There was no monetary system in the freeholds. There were no hierarchies—at least not formally. Each freehold ran with its own norms, what they called uses and customs, and Library authorities had little right to intervene except in extreme circumstances. I had spent huge parts of my childhood wandering from freehold to freehold, but after I'd turned thirteen, I'd realized that many freeholders viewed me with suspicion because of my relationship with Nadi. To them ze represented the perversion of the original intent of the Library, and the reason why it would never fulfill its mission.

"Not for peace," one of the groundskeepers in Tiger Freehold had told me when I was a radical ten-year-old, years out from Samlin and all that would spoil me. "Peace is the dream of armies. The Library is for *justice*."

I had never told Nadi what he'd said. I loved the flavor of it on my tongue too much, and I didn't know if it would sour if I heard Nadi's response.

As luck would have it, that very groundskeeper—Vaterite—met us as we summited the steep path through the woods. The path opened, like an unexpected gift, to reveal the narrow valley and Tiger Freehold below.

"You walked here, did you?"

Nergüi jumped at the sound of his voice, high and lilting, pitched so that it could have come from anywhere. My heart sped with old, remembered joys.

"You can tell?" I asked, guessing where he must be hiding.

"I saw you floating down from the spiral. Not too many bounce off in our direction these days."

Vaterite swung down from the branches of the towering sal trees down the path behind us. I'd guessed off, a little to his left. He looked exactly the same as my memories: long white hair bound in two braids that reached his hips, practical moss-green shift belted with a cobalt-blue pouch that was the typical costume of the Tiger Freeholders. He was high wetware, but implanted as an adult, which had left a tracery around his left eye like a spiderweb that glittered when he accessed the advanced networks. There were cosmetic procedures that reduced its appearance, but Vaterite wore his like a piece of jewelry.

He had come to Library City as a postulant. He'd saved for ten years just to have his wetware upgraded—low-wetware librarians were unheard of in the past century and there was no reason to make the journey if he was doomed to failure. Wetware implanted during adulthood never integrated as smoothly with organic neural processes, but it should have been enough to become a librarian. He'd failed, though, halfway through.

"I was here in this haunted place," I remembered him telling me. "My purpose in life was over, and I didn't have the shards to take myself home to Miuri. I'd been so sure! I came to the freehold because I had nowhere else to go. And I'm still here thirty years later."

He froze now when he saw Nergüi's face. I had convinced her to wear a cape in the spiral and as we walked, so the curious wouldn't follow us.

"Disciple," he said after a stark silence, in a language that my wetware identified, belatedly, as Miuri. "It is kind of you to visit us here."

Nergüi's face seemed at once stern and serene. Then she cracked a half smile.

"I don't know where *here* is, comrade."

"I never thought I would see a disciple here in the Library." He shook himself. "This is Tiger Freehold, disciple. You are welcome home."

"I have arrived," Nergüi said in the clipped cadences of ritual response. My wetware wasn't good enough to convey further nuances. In her heart language, her voice was deeper, steadier, with a fast-paced musicality that hinted at wit. "I hope you don't mind; we're here because we want to find a story. Freida says we have a better chance with Iemaja."

"You are free to ask whatever you wish of Enki, disciple."

"And me, Vaterite?" I asked, wondering what he saw when he turned those shining green eyes and their glittering webbing my way.

"*Congratulations*, novice librarian," he said—not mocking, but without any trace of warmth. "You were born here in the heart of three broken worlds. You will always be welcome in the freeholds of Iemaja."

He stepped lightly past us and picked his way down the path into the valley.

Nergüi turned to me, a question in her eyes. I shrugged as though that hadn't hurt me—because, really, what was there to say? I had chosen my side and could no more hide my novitiate motley vest and four-shard collar than I could my origins.

And so we descended, the three of us silent while the trees and the birds and the broonies chattered above and below of things indecipherable.

The freehold had changed much of its physical aspect in the years since my last visit, though the general aesthetic of the living quarters and communal spaces remained. Built along the banks of a tributary of the Red River, rooms bubbled under the earth with transparent windows that looked out into the water. Aboveground, communal ovens belched archaic volatiles of woodsmoke and yeasty bread into the air, releasing CO_2 and other potentially damaging molecules that the high-atmosphere scrub birds would eat soon enough.

Vaterite led us in silence to the only structure large enough to fit more than ten people in the freehold: a dome that had been a milky green when I was last here but now had hardened to the opaque, multifaceted shine of a turtle shell. In the joints of its hexagonal structure ran tendrils of white—the coral polymer that grew naturally into the Library's most haunted structures. The librarians tried to control it, allow it to grow only in designated spaces, but coral polymer was like a stubborn weed, and it grew where it found the soil. The space was larger than it seemed; inside, the floor inclined sharply, revealing multiple levels in overlapping spirals into the earth. Nergüi gasped as we walked through the airlock entrance and cold punched the air out of our lungs.

"Here," Vaterite said, handing us both thin iridescent coats. They cut the chill, though they did not eliminate it. At least we stopped shivering. A milky, translucent liquid ran through the entire structure in tiny channels that cut across the floors, down staircases and walls, filling the dome with the echoes of a thousand tinkling splashes. Inside, the walls were made of irregularly stacked cubes of giant ice crystals—the mark of Enki, a level-three avatar.

The smell of wet stone, the peace of the deep earth, reminded me of the tunnels I had spent months without. *Here I am, Iemaja*, I thought, my throat warm and filled with salt. A wind cut through the dome and the liquid gurgled, momentarily, in a sweet major harmony. I stumbled and Nergüi caught my elbow.

"What was that?" she asked.

Vaterite smiled at her. "We're in the heart of Tiger Freehold, disciple. Iemaja lives here as much as she does in the central precinct."

I tried to steady my breathing. Could Iemaja have heard me somehow? Had she missed me, too?

Vaterite led us to a long communal table on a balcony that overlooked the ever-branching spirals. A few freeholders were eating at one end. At the other end sat three people with the vacant stares of deep divers, their skin covered with an expansive network of glittering branch worm that must have taken hours, if not days, to expand. Someone had put a blanket over their backs—even high-wetware bodies couldn't maintain equilibrium in this cold for days at a stretch.

"Worse than a Miuri winter," Nergüi muttered as we sat at the middle of the table.

"It's for the avatar," I told her. "Enki's crystal complex is only stable ten degrees below freezing. They have a saying here—*the material is the memory*."

Vaterite nodded. "At least you remember some of what we taught you. You were of the Library, once."

I popped upright. "I still am!"

"You're of the *librarians*," he corrected me.

Nergüi looked between the two of us and sighed. With an easy roll, she pulled her glass ball from within the folds of her robes and settled it on the table before us.

"Freida has a complicated reputation," Nergüi said, "but I thought perhaps she'd been misunderstood."

My nostrils flared. I wondered if it was wise to get so angry, and then the wondering was swept away in a rush of righteous feeling. "*My* reputation! Who have you been listening to? Pajeu? One of Quinn's desperate lackeys?"

She gave me a mild, beetle-browed stare that burned the breath in my throat. "Atempa," she said. "Joshua."

Joshua. I closed my eyes. I had been trying my best not to think about him. Or what I had done.

"And this difference of philosophy between the two of you," Nergüi continued to Vaterite. "Does it have something to do with the collective good in opposition to the individual?"

Vaterite blinked. "Not . . . precisely, disciple." He was all formality now, as though this gently glowing ball on the table between us rebuked him.

"Two competing visions of the collective good, perhaps," I said.

An ivory-colored hexagon of a smooth composite polymer bobbed in front of him. Three of its six sides opened seamlessly to reveal mugs of steaming liquid. Vaterite gave one to each of us. I stared at the rainbow sheen of fat sloshing on top of the brown liquid skeptically. Nergüi, on the other hand, lifted it to her nose and closed her eyes in a brief, private rapture.

"I'm a groundskeeper," Vaterite said. "My perspective is naturally local and contextual. The librarian cohort has lost their connection with the Library itself. They try to use it as though it were a simple database, an All-Seeing Eye to which they have exclusive access. They have perverted the material gods' natural evolution. Did you know that one third of all avatars are either in sleep stasis or fully blocked? Two hundred years ago, there were only ten blocked avatars."

"And Huehue?" I asked, intrigued despite myself. This most notorious of all the blocked avatars had been on my mind lately.

Vaterite frowned, caught off guard. He cleared his throat. "Try the drink," he said, gesturing at my mug of rapidly cooling liquid.

I took a sip. I tasted sweet honey, cacao and peppercorns, salt, fat. A sour butter left a warm film on my lips.

"Huehue is an odd case," Vaterite continued. "They don't teach you much about freehold history in the retreat, I'm sure."

"I know there used to be more, in the century after the founding," I said, my eyes tracing the warped contours of my reflection in the crystal tabletop. Though I couldn't say why, I had a feeling of some lurking intelligence within, looking back at me.

"The librarians destroyed most of us in the second century," he said. "But they started in the first century, with Old Child Freehold."

"Huehue had a freehold? Doesn't that mean—"

"Ze wasn't blocked. Not at first. Not until the Awilu and librarian leadership—not much of a difference back then—razed the freehold to the bones of the disc."

"But why would that make Huehue block zirself? They didn't do anything to zir directly."

Vaterite gave me a long, considering look, colder than the air inside the hub. "Let me show you something," he said.

He stood up and, after a startled moment, Nergüi and I scrambled after him. We slid down a gently sloped spiral and rolled off awkwardly three floors down from the main entrance. The structure burrowed much deeper now than the last time I had visited. The freeholders tunneled like bees guarding honey. Hard to call them skimmers here, as even Nadi did with a certain contempt.

I swallowed down my guilt at the thought and hurried after Vaterite. He guided us to an open half-moon amphitheater at the center of the spiral. On the stage, four freeholders sat in pools of liquid crystal with a great webbing of neon-orange and green branch worm arcing like the cables of a suspension bridge between them. The worm spandrels surged periodically with slow pulses of light. Vaterite's visible neural interface shimmered in response. A half dozen other freeholders were sitting in heated pods or sprawled on the floor before the four divers. The whole audience seemed to be high wetware, so it was hard to tell what was going on at the augmented levels. But I could guess: the deep divers were engaged in a prolonged networked communion with Enki. The audience was experiencing what they could through subjectivity feeds and doing real-time analytics on any new data. I had seen this only a handful of times in my life. This was what communion ought to mean for high-wetware librarians, but it was dangerous, and finding four librarians willing to network could take months.

My mouth went dry with something like longing, something like despair.

"What's happened to them?" Nergüi asked Vaterite in barely vocalized Miuri.

"They're undertaking a deep dive with Chantico, who is relaying through Enki. We're responding to the call, disciple."

Nergüi's eyebrows beetled together. "The call to what, comrade?"

Vaterite looked straight at me. "To find any historical data that might help your and the Tierran's case."

I ground my teeth. "What does this have to do with Huehue?" I asked, my voice a lash.

"Not many records from that time survived, but we know this: When the librarians decided to eliminate Old Child Freehold, they did so with deep incendiaries. They did not warn the freeholders. They burned sixteen freeholders just like this, bound in a networked communion cube with the heart avatar of Old Coyote. Do you still think that didn't really affect zir, Freida?"

It was the first time he had called me by my name, but by now it felt more aggressive than kind. Did he imagine I condoned this? The implications of his words were astonishing. The avatar had been *networked* while the freeholders burned to death? Ze would have felt everything sixteen-fold. Ze would have been incapable of deflecting zir awareness for even a second. For all I knew, ze might still be trapped in that moment of misery, because what librarian, having committed such a crime, would willingly commune again to try to save zir from it?

"They . . . *knew*?" was all I could ask.

Vaterite nodded. "They didn't care. They let a hundred freeholders burn to death and the old child feel each one's suffering in zir soul. They didn't even need to force Huehue to block access; ze did it all by zirself."

"No one will ever get past that," I whispered.

"Of course not. But you're a librarian now. That should please you."

At Vaterite's suggestion, I used a bit of branch worm to enhance my search for Nergüi's great bathhouse stories. Enki relayed our first real result from some other avatar of Iemaja I didn't recognize. Without communion, I couldn't do more to identify zir—the materials birthed new avatars all the time, but most were half-concatenated ephemerals. This one didn't have a visual projection at all, and zir auditory presence was a lonely birdcall, echoing across open water. With the help of the branch worm, I was inundated with metaphorical associations: seabirds, albatrosses, weights unbearable, sitting still, dying of thirst on open water, the salt of tears, the salt of seawater, the salt of blood.

A new thread dipped into the All-Seeing Eye and brought up a node of ancient Tierran literature, a series of metaphors based on a lost poem that an avatar of Old Coyote had tried to reconstruct centuries ago as *The Rime of a Venerable*

Seawoman. The new avatar, sensing my line of inquiry, gave me a new note, a scent of something musty and sweet, an old pipe in a closed room. Yes, there it was: old age and bitterness, the weight of things long past. I didn't know if this had to do with Nergüi's story or not, but I used my own octopus to light the touchstones for zir: a forbidden, mystical world, at the edge of our own. Gods living cheek by jowl with all manner of other strange creatures. A lonely girl who lost herself there, found a god of gluttony or giving, tried and tried to save her parents. Perhaps she never did. The seabird's call grew sharp, frantic. The air roared in my augmented senses, the shift of an albatross turning sharply against the prevailing wind. My octopus let out a wild laugh that startled me so much I opened my eyes, worried someone had heard. Nergüi was watching me, that glass ball swirling with its reassuring dance of lights. She raised an eyebrow in mild inquiry. I shrugged. She pushed her chin forward, a friendly encouragement. I smiled and closed my eyes again.

Sometimes I liked querying even more than communion. At its best, it was a raw, dangerous game of association and commentary and mutual inquiry with a material consciousness. If I couldn't keep up, I'd be out, and the avatar wouldn't bother with any but the most basic answer to my query. In that, Vaterite was entirely correct. Modern librarians tended to treat the materials as though they were inert, powerful databases, not complex, living ecosystems of consciousnesses whose beauty was their relationship to us, not their use.

The nameless avatar came back to me with a series of questions, which I could only vaguely understand through the barrage of associations mediated by the branch worm: Precontact Tierra? Visual media? Material gods or another kind? What variety of root vegetable is most thematically resonant? Does the mask become a face, or the face a mask, and what of the mouth? Does it matter if we know she returned home, or is what counts the longing throughout the journey? I didn't understand all these questions, but I answered them as best as I could, with more associations and feelings and metaphorical connections if I couldn't provide a straight line. It takes time to tell a good story, so by the time the avatar dropped out of the query, my stomach was gurgling.

We ate with Vaterite and the newly awakened divers at the long communal table. Their names were Melanite, Aragonite, and Zoicite. Every member of this freehold was named after a material crystal assigned by a quantum number generator, which made Nergüi laugh when they explained it to her. "Then that means that each of you shares the name of every other in the sphere of your collective possibilities."

Melanite and Zoicite looked confused, but Aragonite and Vaterite shared a brief smile. "They say Seremarú emself founded Tiger Freehold," Aragonite said. "Ey respected the ancient knowledge of all the peoples of the Mahām conglomerate. Perhaps ey was inspired by the philosophy of the Disciples of the Lighted Path."

I had been focusing on eating as much of the breadfruit coconut curry and jasmine rice as I could shovel into my stomach—querying was hungry work—but at this I put down my spoon. "Seremarú was the first Head Librarian. How could ey have founded a freehold, too?"

Aragonite—who looked Dar to me, though ze hadn't identified zirself as such—gave me a broad wink. "Maybe our paths weren't always in opposition, young novice. Perhaps together in harmony we maintain the health of the sacred material consciousnesses."

This thought filled me at once with guilty delight—whose side was I on, anyway?—so I turned away from zir and pointed to Nergüi with my spoon. "And you, what's the joke about their names?"

Nergüi raised those thick orange-brown eyebrows so high they disappeared into the bushy froth of her hairline. "You really don't understand? You're very smart, normally. At least, your reputation—"

"Enough with my reputation!" I snapped. "Into Mahue'e's hottest pit what others think of me. What do *you* think of me, O great disciple?"

"I think," she said, after a painfully overlong pause that I *knew* she relished, "that I met you at a difficult juncture of your life. Still, your intellect should be sound enough for this."

She unhooked the ball from its chain and spun it lightly on the tip of her index finger. The lights inside moved contrariwise to the direction of the spin. All of us stared at it, mesmerized. My pulse slowed and my breathing relaxed. She slid the ball down the back of one hand and settled it in her left palm.

"This represents the multitudinous, but not infinite, possible paths of our lives. It's our wave function, to put it another way. Each light is a path through the wave function, which encompasses the penumbra of every possible path a life can take." As she spoke, a light followed her tracing finger and then shook like a wet dog and burst into a hundred lights that snaked away from the glass and dove back into the mass of light at the center.

"You mean, every time I make a choice, I pick a different light?" I asked.

Nergüi shook her head. "Our choices are entirely immaterial to the wave function."

I frowned. "Then what *does* affect it?"

"Quantum branching and decoherence. No, never mind the specifics. What's important—here, have you heard that the Mahām forbid the use of quantum number generators?"

"In their infinite wisdom," Aragonite said with a withering sarcasm that put me in mind of Atempa.

"I think being superstitious is a requirement of the Nameren priesthood," Vaterite added.

"But think about what that *means*," Nergüi said, leaning forward. "They want no one else to have the ability to consciously control the flow of their selves in the wave function. Otherwise, our moments of decoherence are constant but unknowable. But if you make a conscious choice to, say, name someone based on a number assigned by a quantum number generator, when there is an equally weighted probability of each one of those numbers being selected? Then you've consciously bound together those people with the same name. In one branch of the wave function, Vaterite, your name is Aragonite or Zoicite. The possibility of each of you having the other's name is equally weighted."

"But what does that matter?" I asked. "Why would the Mahām care about quantum number-generating games?"

She tapped her glass ball again and the lights fled and scattered. "It means," she said, "that for that moment, at least, you can choose to locate yourself amidst the probabilities of your life. The Nameren doesn't like that. Or perhaps just his priests. They believe that destiny is all, and choice is an illusion. There is no branching decoherence, only one flat collapse, from the big bang until our heat death in the deep of eternity."

I vaguely remembered learning about this in my physics modules two years before, but philosophy had never been my favorite subfield. "You mean that all of this is about many-worlds theories? That we exist alongside trillions of copies of ourselves in subtly different universes?"

Nergüi smiled at last. Something hard inside me popped. "Welcome to the great Miuri heresy. Though I never understood how the Nameren priests think they can get away with collapsing the wave function—the tesseracts wouldn't work, and probably not the gods, though you'd know more about that than I."

"Most people don't trouble themselves with philosophy, disciple," Vaterite said. "It's the degeneration of our modern age."

Something odd occurred to me. "Is that how they justify the War Ritual?" I asked. "They use a quantum number generator, so that if your philosophy is true, you're not really dead in all the permutations of the wave function?"

Nergüi met my eyes for a searing second and then focused back on the lights. "It's not all bad, you know," she said softly. "Your reputation. Indeed, I would say it is, on the whole, quite accurate."

✦

The next day, Vaterite sent a messenger with what the freehold broonies had made for us based on my query with Enki. It was a series of five scrolls with an embedded digital hologram. Each scroll contained one painting, rendered with photographic perfection, of the rooms in an early precontact Eastern-style bathhouse.

The scale of the bathhouse was larger than any of the other recorded houses from the era, as if it had been built for giants: Soaking tubs the size of swimming pools, with high wooden walls and no discernible method of entry for a human-sized bather. An empty boiler room with tiny shelves that lined the walls reaching to the ceiling so high it could only be vaguely discerned through a haze of coal smoke. A banquet room, long cedar table laden with a hundred untouched delicacies: giant soup buns with ground pork shadowing their translucent-white skin, towering plates of braised tofu, roasted chicken, vegetables fried in rice batter, fish upon fish roasted whole in its juices, uncounted buckets full of rice, mid-length and perfectly sticky. A red-and-green-painted wooden bridge over a rocky creek, trees casting shadows that were too squat and numerous to be their own. And last, a balcony high above what seemed to be the boiler room with a view of a flooded plain, train tracks cutting through. On the rain-warped slats, two palm-sized jewels of a color that I would call Kohru blue held down a note in a language that we couldn't read.

I looked it up, though defunct script searches were a particular recipe of exacting and boring that I generally avoided. Hours later, head splitting, I returned to the private reading room where I had left Nergüi.

I turn twenty-five today. I still miss you, Ma. Sen," I declared in tones of victory wholly opposed to its content.

Nergüi froze with the short side of her hair facing me. She took a series of shallow breaths, but her voice came out perfectly steady. "So, it really is a variant," she said. "A portal story, subtype Never Go Home. In the great bathhouse."

"Isn't this what you wanted?"

"Yes," said Nergüi. Then, more softly, "She still wants to go home."

The aurochs is like a child's dream of an ungulate, white as peonies, haloed and fragrant. He bows his head to tender blades of fresh grass, emerald bright, pushing up through the wet earth. A second sun has joined the first high in the sky, jostling for position. A pair of cicadas sings from nowhere the girl can see, a contented sereet and sigh. She wonders if this is her doing, or his. She understands, with equal parts dread and satisfaction, that it means something that she cannot tell.

The aurochs lifts his head, horns gleaming silver in the sunlight. "I understand," he says.

The cicadas pause mid-chirrup. "*What* do you understand?" She braces her hands against the mud, as though she would fling it at him.

He watches her as one would a tiger. "Why you are so fixated on stories."

"It was Nergüi who was obsessed."

He rakes a golden hoof in the mud until water fills in the furrow.

"You made her quest your own for a reason."

The cicadas begin their song again, sereet and sigh. She sneers at them. "Fine, Nameren, tell me. What reason?"

"You think that if you are part of a story, it doesn't matter that you were made."

Above, the second sun hisses like water thrown on a fire. The girl is incensed.

"I've always known I was made. I've had eighteen years to get used to the idea."

"But you didn't always know *why* you were made, did you?"

The suns come closer, the cicadas chirp louder, the aurochs watches. She hunches her back against them all.

"It doesn't matter."

"Your guardian's choice changed something. You're nothing like the others."

She digs her fists into the wet clay and snarls. "I *am*. I'm just like them. Don't you dare lift me above my sisters that you murdered."

After a silence, the aurochs lowers his head to the grass once more. His horns are less bright, his scent less intoxicating. She blinks at him.

"I'm sorry." His rumbling voice is muffled by the green.

"No, you're not."

"Is it so impossible?"

She swallows painfully. She will hold the line. "I told you, I won't blame you for what you are. But I won't pity you for it, either."

His eyes are starry, unfathomable, hers. "I might pity you, little piper."

"Me?"

"You think that just because you're not human—"

A rough, hurried interjection: "Of course I'm human."

Of which he takes no notice. "—there's something wrong with you. Something broken you could mend if you fit the right story over it."

She feels heavy as chains, rigid as iron. Spidery roots grow from her buttocks and feet, white tendrils spreading in the mud. She is so sad, and so exhausted of her sadness. It is such an old hurt, to have never gone away.

Her voice is small. "I liked that feeling, you know. Of being on the other side of her story."

"What good is that? They tell stories about me, epics upon epics, millennia of tales, but what are they to me? Just a series of masks."

The girl looks up, straightens her spine, rips her hips from the earth. "No, Nameren. No. A story isn't a mask; it's a mirror."

"Not for me. Not for you, O creation of my deepest dreaming."

He is gentle as he says it. It still hurts. She climbs to her knees in awkward supplication, unsure if she is begging him, or herself. "If not a mirror, then at least . . ."

"At least?"

Their eyes meet. "A door."

–There's a kind of story called a portal story. The stories where you leave your home and your life and your old rules, and you enter another world. I was from the Library; to me it was home. But to Nergüi it was a strange, dangerous place–it was Narnia, and Oz, and the Great Bathhouse, and the Demon Lands, and the Upside-Down City. And I was its most dangerous, impossible resident.

"Tell me the story," I said to her. "Tell me about the great bathhouse."

"There is no one story. It's a story complex. No one has found the original. If there ever was one. Stories tend to grow wherever they find the right soil."

We were in an old holo room of Old Coyote, sitting on the floor of the balcony of the fifth painting. This was the nameless avatar's gift to us, an immersive commentary on the content of each painting. Neither of us had the wetware for a full sensory experience, but the re-creation was remarkably lifelike—a breeze rippled across the floodwater of the plain below, bringing with it the scents of trampled grass, damp wood, and a faint whiff of combustible, not coal, but probably another one of those fossil fuels that had come so near to destroying pre-contact Tierra. The high yellow sun, not quite Sol, radiated against our exposed faces and arms.

Nergüi had conceded her outer robe to the heat and so sat against the wall in a shapeless knee-length shift of lighter orange. The waist cord with its ball she had looped around her neck, where it settled between her breasts. Her hair glinted orange-red in the light—the shorn side, now with more than an inch of bushy growth, as well as the longer side. Her skin echoed the river-clay orange of her hair but blended in the darker brown of cedar wood. I still hadn't been able to decide if she was beautiful. The more time I spent with her, the more she seemed to change beneath my gaze, like an avatar gone malleable beneath a barrage of queries, dancing around the central point that I tried to force her to say directly. Nergüi's very nature rejected my project. She could be hideous and captivating in five different ways over the course of an hour. I thought maybe I should stop trying. Then I thought I should spend more time with her, and she would finally make sense to me.

Nergüi reached across my lap and ran her fingers across the space where the note appeared. She couldn't feel it, but she could interact with it. She pulled it from beneath the strange blue jewels and held it up to the light.

"What language did you say it was?"

"Five hundred years precontact Dzongkha."

"Dzongkha? Where did they speak that? Did they have any settlers on the seed ships?"

"On the Asian subcontinent. I think they had a few on the fourth expedition."

"Oh," she said, and fell silent.

The fifth expedition of the Mahām and their then-allies the Miuri had meant to meet up with the fourth expedition, but when they arrived at the destination system, the fourth's ships were empty and their hulls breached. They had found a pair of long-decayed settlements on the Miuri moon, but despite centuries of rumors, no signs of their descendants.

"So?" I said.

"You'll have to be more specific, Freida," Nergüi said, going prickly again. "My wetware does not provide mind reading."

I shook my head at her. "Tell me one of the stories of the bathhouse. Your favorite variant."

She stiffened and the breeze lifted the note from her fingers. We watched it drift down until a frog, green and smooth as an uncooked pea, jumped from the floodwaters and ate it in one gulp. A second later, the note reappeared beneath the jewel.

"I only know a few," she said softly. "The one—the first one I heard. It's about a girl. Her name is Sen. Or San. Or Hero. One of those is her real name, her birth name. The other is the name she was given when she fell into the other place."

"The other place . . . the great bathhouse?"

"Yes. That's not in her world. It's a world of gods and of creatures who serve the gods and of odder creatures who live in the woods beyond and have other lives and visions we don't know about."

As her voice settled into the story, she liberally sprinkled her Library Standard with words and phrases in Miuri, weaving a cloth of the story that held me like a child.

"It's a world, a whole beautiful world, but it isn't *her* world. When she was young, eleven or twelve, she entered the liminal space with her parents. They fell under an enchantment and turned into trees. Or giant frogs. Or piglets. Then a great lizard, who was also a boy, who was also a river, found her when she was about to commit an unforgivable offense against the gods, and told her how to survive there.

"In the great bathhouse, gods of all kinds gather to be cleansed and to receive offerings. Humans like Sen are not allowed. So she had to eat their food and change herself—not enough for them to accept her as an equal, but enough for them to allow her to stay. She made friends. She fell in love with the boy-lizard, the boy-river. He probably loved her back, but rivers don't make good lovers; they're always busy moving past you. She tried to save her parents. She had the help of another kind of god, or a not-god, a figure of gluttony and darkness and childlike generosity. A giant mouth with golden teeth, like your grubs. Ze ate her best friend and the only one who could stop zir was Sen. She gave the not-god her real name to eat and ze cried though ze had no face to cry from, so delicious were its crunchy syllables and long, sticky vowels. The taste rooted zir to the earth and ze became a great tree with black roots and silver-white leaves the size of palm fronds.

"And then, nameless, the human girl was forced to cross the bridge back into her world because the giant-faced witch and her sister could not let a human stay who had no true name to give in return. Before she left, she begged for her parents, and the sisters told her she could have them if she could pick them true from the trees by the river. But the forest by the river was of alianthus, which shared one heart and looked all the same. She chose wrong and so freed two people who had been frozen for two centuries or more, a man and a woman who spoke a language she could barely understand. They crossed the bridge together and made a life as best they could, but none of them ever felt as though they had truly returned home, nor that they had entirely left behind the other, stranger place."

A sudden gust pushed us back against the wall and raindrops splattered against our faces and clothes. I looked up to check for clouds, but it seemed clear enough.

"That is an excellent story, Nergüi."

"Is that sarcasm?"

Oh, I wanted to shake her sometimes! "It's beautiful and weird and tragic.

It has many hidden folds. Is that better? Would you like a report? Is this an unscheduled exam?"

She scowled, which made her look a little like a gargoyle. "I just didn't think someone like you would understand it."

"Someone like me?"

She waved her hand at the beautiful, impossible illusion that embraced us. "Someone who was born from . . . all this. Your lights are a different color than mine and your sphere is in another universe. Our wave functions should never have entangled. How could we understand one another?"

Her voice was flat and her face still set in its gargoyle mask, but her left hand gripped that ball again and the lights inside jumped so brightly it seemed they might explode from behind the jail of her fingers.

"That's a sad way to see the world."

"It's the truth. You're unknowable. We're strings vibrating out of phase. On some level, you don't exist in my world. Or I don't in yours."

"You or I don't exist because we're different from one another? Because we grew up in different systems? Nergüi, if that were true, I wouldn't have any friends at all! Everyone is different from me."

"I don't know how you stand it," she said, a low, angry growl.

"I stand it because I love," I said.

"Maybe some of us just aren't built that way."

"And because I'm loved."

She turned to me, her strange tree-ring eyes going heavy-lidded and sly. "Are you, now? And you are sure you have not just overwhelmed them with the sight of that angel's face?"

I didn't understand, then, why Nergüi sometimes hid herself behind cruelty.

Her gift for it must have come from some devil, the not-god of gluttony in her story. I choked back a gasp and stood up. She couldn't know about Samlin and the night that hadn't really happened but that I couldn't forget. Still, she had a warrior's instinct for my weak and hurting places.

"End projection," I said. The scene faded, until we were once again alone in an echoing, hollow white egg.

Nergüi looked up at me, her expression just as bleak. She cringed as though expecting a blow.

"That was beneath you," I said.

"How would you know?"

"Wasn't it? Does the girl who tells me stories of lost children in the bathhouse of the gods truly have no idea what it means to hurt someone? Or is it because I'm not real to you, that you've decided I have no feelings?"

She wouldn't answer. Eventually I turned around and left her there, alone.

Nergüi and I didn't speak for nearly a week. I returned to Tiger Freehold a few days after our fight, ostensibly to continue querying for bathhouse stories, but I couldn't deny the pang of disappointment when I didn't find that shock of tattered orange among the sober greens and grays of the skim hub. Vaterite seemed to have accepted my presence among them again. At least, he greeted me with some amusement and invited me to share a cup of that strange fatty drink.

"That ephemeral disaggregated, but Aragonite says ze left a message for you."

That was unusual. Even Iemaja's avatars didn't typically differentiate between the querent and the query. "What did ze say?"

He shook his head. "Give me access?" he said aloud, which was very polite of him. I hadn't realized how high my guard was. I lowered my thresholds, a sensation like forcing my shoulders away from my ears, and a message from Nadi asking me to dinner flowed in at the same time as a curious image from Vaterite's feed. I ported it to the array built into the table and blinked at the effect: as though I were looking into a puddled reflection, myself but somehow not. The image of myself had longer hair and hard, shuttered eyes set in the hollows of a face thinner than mine had ever been.

"What do you think?" he asked neutrally.

Nergüi's words came back to me like a slap: *And you are sure you have not just overwhelmed them with the sight of that angel's face?*

"But I don't really look like that."

"Perhaps ze means it as a commentary."

Was this version of me still beautiful enough to make someone lose their true north? Was that why she was so angry? If I hadn't gone to the Tesseracts after Samlin, perhaps I might have looked like that. Sharp enough to cut crystal. Perhaps I still might, before this year was done with me.

"Does ze think there's something wrong with my face?"

Vaterite blinked, then shook his head. "The material gods don't discriminate according to human norms. A face is just a face, Freida. None is better or worse than any other."

I left soon after, stung, though I wasn't sure why. I made myself forget about it. Nadi's invitation to dinner meant ze had finished at last with the treatment ze was receiving in the infirmary. Ze would tell me no more, but I understood that this was part of the terrible secret that I had betrayed Joshua to protect. *And to be a librarian*, some errant part of myself reminded me as I pushed through the bitter winds of the tears. I had done it for the security of this motley vest and necklace of four shards. If only I felt more secure.

I kept the freehold's broonie cloak around me as I bobbled in the outer, exposed edge of the spiral. I took the slow way back instead of paying a quarter blue for each jump to center. It felt more freehold to me, the least efficient route between two points, to meander with the Library instead of pushing against it. On a whim, I sent Joshua a snap of what I could capture: the slap of the wet air, the heat of the broonie cloak around my neck and hairline, the distant lights of the center precinct swinging into view like a mirage of distant fires, the noisy darkness of the forest down below. I doubted he would let it through—but to my surprise, just when I was about to bounce down from the spiral, he sent me a return snap, free of almost all sensory data except visual: a jagged gray peak of a mountain, a plume of smoke rising from it into the haze of the purple sunset of a bright yellow sun. *It smells of him*, I thought, though I couldn't be sure if that was a sensory input or my own memory. I missed him, Nameren, and I hated myself for it.

I slid down directly to the Tenehet retreat entrance, a new privilege that came with my novice shards. The retreat was built in a series of six spokes that sprang from the vertices of a hexagonal central hub, which was itself layered in a series of wide indoor and outdoor passages. The center, which I had never seen, guarded an access point to each of the four materials, which could only be used by the Head and Cardinal Librarians. Nadi had zir rooms in the first node of the Tenehet-Iemaja boundary spike. Mine were in the second node, separated from zis by an arcaded portico and the retreat's famous meditation gardens. I entered from the Tenehet side to avoid the Mahue'e gardens, where the other novice librarians tended to congregate at the end of our day's duties. Most of them regarded me with suspicion, and even if Atempa had been speaking to me, she had chosen to stay with her mother in the pegasus.

Eltian was just leaving Nadi's rooms as I entered. She looked strange, haggard and frightened, until she saw me and smiled as though nothing had ever worried her.

"Freida! Nadi will be so pleased. Ze said your defenses were at Great War levels."

I flushed. "I've been a little stressed, I guess." I had known Eltian all my life, and I liked her from a safe distance. She had been Nadi's on-again-off-again lover for decades, but their relationship had been apparently stable for the last few years. I wondered if that pained look meant they were breaking up again. I sighed. I could do without the drama right now, and to be honest, so could Nadi.

That strange cloud passed over her expression again. "Freida . . ."

I waited.

She shook her head, gave a wobbly laugh, and then, unexpectedly, hugged me. "Just take care of each other, okay? You know the old Tierran curse, 'May you live in interesting times'? I'm afraid times are about to get appallingly interesting."

"The War Ritual?" I thought of Nergüi with a guilty pang.

Eltian just smiled and shook her head. "Go, see your parent."

A blast of heat and spices hit me as soon as I opened the door. Sweat beaded my forehead and I took a deep breath of roasted chiles and turmeric and epazote. I didn't see zir in the common room, but a flickering light from the garden made me suspicious.

"Freida, love! Come out here, I'm almost finished with the curried yams. Could you put the flatbread in the warming basket for me?"

To my astonishment, ze was cooking on a wood-burning stove in the covered portico of the garden. Ze must have been at it for hours, considering the quantity of foods covering the long worktable: saffron noodles with cashew curry, acorn jelly with roasted squash seeds, spongy sour flatbread—all specialties of the Awilu clans of Niphense. But I hadn't seen zir cook in years. These foods, these smells, were talismans of a childhood I had strived to forget, not because it was horrible but because its abundance had led me to expect too much.

I wiped my forehead and folded the cloth carefully over the flatbread. The climate controls insulated the portico from the wind despite the heat from the fires.

Ze looked comfortable, though. More than comfortable—filled with deep, pulsing energy.

"The novices went collecting broonie fruit in the islands, I heard. Were you with them?"

I considered many answers but finally settled on shaking my head.

Ze gave me a shrewd look. "You think that if I won't tell you what I've been doing in the infirmary, I have little right to ask you why you won't socialize with the novices?"

"It's not that I won't—"

"Freida."

I gritted my teeth. "What?"

Ze sighed and lifted my four-shard cord with one long finger. Zir blunt nails were stained red with ground spices, as though ze were taking the bride part in a traditional Niphense wedding. "This is what you wanted. But it's eating you, isn't it, what you had to give up to get it?"

I gripped zir hand and leaned forward until my forehead met zis. "Tiger Freehold."

Ze let out a gentle hiss. "Ah. Can you stand being normal, Freida? You have at least a decade before you make sixteen shards. I can change none of that for you. Not even—well, the Library has its rules."

"*Librarians* have their rules." I sounded petulant, even to myself.

Ze gave me a twisted, sad smile. "And how is Vaterite these days?"

I sighed and grabbed two dishes at random to bring back inside to the ancient slab of petrified wood that served as zir dining table.

We ate in silence, piling the curries and roasted vegetables on the sour bread, and grabbing each morsel with a piece of the same.

"I have a problem for you," ze finally said. Since I was little, ze had liked to give me problems during our meals together. They were political puzzles, often lightly disguised issues that ze had confronted as Head Librarian. I cocked my head at zir since we both knew that any political puzzle ze was confronting right now would be intersystem news.

Ze pushed zir half-eaten plate away. "An ancient weapon has been discovered in the heart of the Sol system. It is capable of wiping out life on Tierra and Luna. The Martians have discovered it. They want to press the button, to put it crudely. More importantly, they claim the *right* to press it anytime they wish. They claim that testing potential new applications of capital is part of their protected cultural heritage. In the Awilu system, they have developed another device capable of neutralizing the terrible weapon. But they haven't finished their project. They need at least ten more years. A Mahām diplomat has engaged to bring the Martians to the negotiating table. Ze is faced with a conundrum. Option one: Use force to try to make the Martians back down, with the possibility that in response they'll detonate the ancient weapon. Option two: Negotiate for more time—give them the right in principal to detonate, but only if they agree not to do it for some specified period of time. Ten years, say, which will give the Awilu enough time to neutralize the threat."

I frowned. "Those are the only two options?"

Ze waved an airy hand. "The main branches of the equation. The rest is nuance."

Ze was clearly referencing the Mahām negotiations in broad strokes, but the details were sufficiently obscured that I wasn't sure how to map it onto what I knew. It felt strange to play this game, though, knowing that my answer might sway zir to one side or another, with system-shaking consequences.

I took a sip of rooibos tea while I turned the problem over in my head. I'd never have Nadi's native political genius, but ze had trained me well enough. "Option two is a bet," I said slowly, thinking it through. "A bet and a bluff. Make the Martians think they're getting away with lip service to peace, postpone their use of technology while affirming the principle of their right to it, which is what they want anyway—"

Ze leaned forward. "Yes, there you are, my love, keep going."

"And in the meantime, you pray to the gods that the Martians never learn of what the Awilu are building, because their retaliation will be as brutal as the Nine-Minute War."

"What else, Freida? How would you counsel the poor diplomat to proceed?"

"Option one is a bludgeon. Ze'd have to be very sure ze has enough weight to enforce the threat. But the negotiations themselves mean that the Martians have unmoored themselves from the tenets of the Treaty. If they're willing to say that genocide is a sacred cultural practice, then they're really just laughing at the Treaty itself. They're daring you to call their bluff. But can you? I mean, can ze? Do the Awilu have the firepower?"

"Oh, they do. But not, it seems, the will. They will break into thirds again. The Cicada will declare against the Martians, of course, because we sing for the ones left behind, clear-sighted since the Great Migration. But the Baobab cling to a false neutrality, and the Aurochs are as likely to side with the warmongers as anyone."

"And the Mahām and the Martians are very equally matched," I said. "So option one is no option at all. Or it is so risky as to practically abet genocide."

"Morally superior abetting," ze said, standing carefully, as though zir back hurt. Ze went to the niche in the wall and pulled out a bottle of indigo wine. "You forget that at least this way, our diplomat is not caving to the demands of Treaty-breakers and corporatist war criminals."

"Well, then ze can rest easy once Tierra and Luna are enslaved to the threat of immediate annihilation in the service of capital!"

Ze barked a laugh and poured zirself a glass of the inky, earthy-smelling liquid and settled back in zir chair.

"Should you be drinking that?"

Ze sighed and gave me a hard look. "I've heard you're falling in love with a political refugee. Again. Why not Pajeu? Or Atempa? Someone less likely to create an intersystem scandal?"

We stared at each other in stony silence. I didn't know if I was falling in love with Nergüi or not, but I certainly didn't want to argue about it with my parent. And apparently ze was equally unwilling to discuss zir health with me.

"You were saying, Freida?"

I snorted and shook my head. I should have known better than to surprise Nadi with a question ze didn't want to answer. "Option two is pure political theater. Dangerous political theater. Ze has to convince the Martians that they have won—they get the fig leaf of gesturing toward peace and the mechanisms of the Treaty, with just a short delay in return. What if the Awilu technology takes longer? What if it doesn't work? Won't the diplomat have made things even worse?"

Ze took a sip and closed zir eyes. "Perhaps."

Something hit me, a realization that pushed yam curry back up my throat. "This is war we're talking about, isn't it? Sooner or later. You can't negotiate with the Mahām—I mean, the Martians—if they're willing to commit genocide to get their way."

Nadi lifted zir glass to the starlight glittering through zir ceiling. Points of indigo slid across the table as ze turned it one way, then another.

"That's the sticking point, my love. *No peace but that must pay full toll to hell.* Without that chance of the Awilu technology, of bringing them to heel with unquestionably superior force and diplomacy, it's war, or no peace worth having. So now what do you choose?"

I shivered. "Bluff. Pray the Awilu technology works."

"But prepare," ze said, "for war."

✦

I kept this conversation with Nadi to myself out of necessity, but I knew that I had no one left to share my fears with anyway. Atempa seemed to have softened toward me, but only in a provisional sort of way. Behind the on-duty desk in the Old Coyote reading rooms, we worked together on a problem set in anticipation of our first module on intermediate query techniques. I suspected this was why she had overcome her disdain of my presence.

"Name the five virtues of creativity in level-zero query protocols. Give an example of each virtue. Match each example query with a sub-avatar of the Gorgon complex and try them. Report results using the template provided." Atempa groaned. "Freida, everything about this question is just . . . orthogonal to reality! I understand creativity when you're tunnel crawling, but level-zero queries? Who but tourists even bothers with these anymore? Why not use the All-Seeing Eye?"

I peeled a bit of stray branch worm from above my ear. It tingled as it broke the last residual connection with my system, not that it had done much. The branch worm species they used in Tiger Freehold was highly temperature-dependent and short-lived, but achingly expansive in querying. I felt hemmed in by the staid, never-changing spiral of Old Coyote's reading rooms. How did other librarians stand to train for years with these restrictions?

I shook my head. "The All-Seeing Eye isn't really all-seeing."

Atempa groaned. "Yes, thank you for the clichés. Where's the creativity in a level-zero search? Which string you run first? Which language you use?"

"Those are two good ones."

"Oh, come on. What does the language matter to an avatar? We are a post-lingual society, Freida. No one's had to *learn* a language in, gods, I don't know—six hundred years?"

She was really working herself up, which probably meant that her father had been bothering her again. He insisted that she should be helping the Mahām delegation now that she'd officially become a novice. She started to pace the length of the result niches.

"What language do you think in, Atempa?" I said to her in Mahām, which Nadi had made sure I'd learned as one of my heart languages.

She froze in her pacing and threw me an angry glare. "It doesn't matter," she said in Library Standard.

I smiled merrily. "Well, some of the avatars are just like you."

Behind us, someone cleared zir throat. I turned around and choked a little to see Nergüi standing by the public desk, stiff as a doll.

"You," I said in Library Standard, my first heart language.

She stared at me.

The wings of Atempa's chimera dusted the edges of my vision. "What does the ghost bride want with you now? Oh no, don't you *dare* go and fall in lo—" I dimly registered its chimeric squawk as my octopus batted it out of my augmented space.

"I don't think you're so beautiful," Nergüi said, in a great rush. "I think you're pretty overrated. Back in Miuri, a great beauty has small breasts and slim hips and hair the color of a tarnished copper pot. Your eyes are the wrong shape. I just want you to know that beauty is culturally codified, and if you are wandering around expecting the whole world to fall over when you smile, you're probably missing a lot."

I was aware of an overpowering urge to giggle, which I mostly suppressed. "That's your version of an apology!"

Her lips twitched. "I do, however, think it's entirely possible that you are very lovable. I wouldn't know—I told you, I've sworn off that sort of thing, but I've been thinking about it and I'm pretty sure other people would think that you have many lovable qualities."

I couldn't help it—I started laughing and couldn't stop until my stomach began hurting and tears dampened my eyes. When I caught my breath, I saw Nergüi's familiar frown and almost kissed the wrinkle between her thick eyebrows.

"Are you laughing at me?"

"Yes."

Her mouth moved in an upward direction. "I suppose that's only fair. Do you want to hear another bathhouse story when you're off duty? Vaterite gave me a new result."

"Sure," I said, and that was the end of it.

When our shift ended, I bid farewell to Atempa's baleful gaze and sepulchral predictions of doom—*protect her, if not yourself!*—and found Nergüi in the same holo room we'd used the week before.

This time, the broonie holo stick rendered a two-dimensional image, an animated painting on a five-second loop. The image was badly degraded. It seemed to be of some giant vegetable with a face, or of a fat white person with hairy breasts wearing a loincloth decorated with a symbol that might have been language-based. Ze was squashed inside a moving box, which I guessed must be a vertical-only lift. The painting wasn't in the same photorealistic style as the first five. In a way, it emphasized its irrealism without ever slipping into abstraction. The heightened colors, the solid lines, the meticulous detail of the shadows and the oddities hiding inside their gray borders: strips of paper and chunks of wood painted with more symbols; a tiny black slug peeking out from beneath the vegetable person's foot; through the open slats behind zir, a glimpse of a giant banquet hall.

"There's no girl in this one?" I asked.

"I think she's squashed beside zir. That's her hand peeking out."

I looked and caught it, at last—the fingers comically splayed, the vegetable person seemingly oblivious. But zir irises were pointed in her direction.

I looked back at Nergüi. "This one is precontact, too, isn't it?"

"I think so. Vaterite helped me with some open searches on the writing, and that's my best guess."

I grinned and turned back to the vegetable person, whose eyes were surprisingly jolly in a face that otherwise seemed incapable of human expression. "Do you think this is from source zero?"

"Certainly not. But maybe a copy of a copy. Nothing else in the searches from Enki dates earlier than five hundred years precontact."

She sounded very severe, which meant that she felt uncomfortably excited. So I clapped my hands and she rolled her eyes and I felt that we were understanding each other very well.

"So?" I said.

She settled in front of me and beside the rattling of the vegetable person in zir narrow lift box. She fiddled with the cord around her waist, swinging the ball in a wide pendulum in front of our eyes. Now that she wasn't holding it directly, I could see other shapes haunting the glass: whorls of dark smoke, studded with light like stars; flashes of moving bodies, hands and knees and the gentle curve of a spine, though even that seemed to dissolve so quickly back into the smoke that I couldn't be sure. I wanted so much to ask her about it, but I knew that I couldn't yet. She had only begun to trust me.

"In this story Sen is called Hero, and she's been trained to kill giant lizards from birth."

"Trained to kill giant lizards?"

"It's a common precontact narrative conceit."

"Did they have a giant lizard problem? Plastics pollution causes a pretty high mutation rate. I've heard there's sea monsters in the southern hemisphere."

Nergüi looked intrigued. "You know, I never thought of that! We've lost so much from back then."

"So this girl was trained to kill giant lizards, but then she fell into the world of the bathhouse and she discovered that she had fallen in love with one?"

"A classic star-crossed love story." As she spoke, Nergüi played absent tricks with the ball, balancing it on the tip of each finger, palming it and rolling it up her arm, across her shoulders, and down the other arm. I watched, mesmerized. "At least at the beginning. Not my favorite. In this variation, Hero is a bit older when she crosses over, fifteen or sixteen. And at first, she's happy to be there because she didn't like living in the family compound; they had many rules, and she didn't enjoy killing giant lizards, in any case. She asks for a job immediately from the old man in the boiler room, but he sees that she's big and strong so he sends her up to the baths. She convinces them to give her a place after she battles away a giant stink monster with just a broom handle and some fiery words. She's torn between two enigmatic romantic figures. One is a boy her age who doesn't remember his name, tends to disappear at odd moments, and definitely has a suspicious relationship with the giant-faced witch who runs the bathhouse. The other is the agender not-god of gluttony and childlike devotion; she doesn't realize zir identity for a long time and more or less interprets zir confusing behavior in the way that most closely coincides with her childhood dreams of romance."

"Say that with more disdain, why don't you?"

Nergüi gave me her funny almost-smile. "She'd have had better luck with the stink monster. Imagining your way into love with someone you barely know is deeply unwise."

"Sure," I said, "and very relatable. For some of us, anyway. Go on."

"So even though everyone has told her to never let the not-god into the bathhouse, Hero decides that they just don't understand zir the way she does. She thinks ze's sad and lonely and just needs someone to look behind zir mask and see the real zir. She has a fight with the lizard-boy after he tells her the truth about his identity and she decides that a lizard killer really has no business with a lizard. Then she invites the not-god inside just to spite him. Well, the not-god goes on a rampage and lizard-boy has to reveal his secret to everyone and turn into a giant lizard to save her. But then he gets hurt and Hero has to leave the bathhouse to find a special spell with the witch-sister to save him. By now the not-god has become a towering giant of billowing black flesh and she's discovered that there is no face behind the mask at all. She feels very foolish, I'm sure. She finds the witch-sister among the shadows on the train and the witch-sister gives Hero the cure for lizard-boy without much fuss. So, Hero, who was expecting to have to make a great sacrifice, gets very suspicious. She asks what she has to do to save him.

"'Oh,' says the witch-sister, who has a voice much sweeter than the giant-faced witch of the bathhouse, and much deadlier, 'you just have to feed yourself to your ex. That will make sure ze can't come back for a very long time.'

"Hero isn't sure that she is capable of throwing herself into the giant mouth of the asshole she once imagined that she was in love with, but when she sees lizard-boy still dying, she knows that she has to save him. So she gives him the medicine with one last kiss.

"'I'm about to kill myself,' she says. 'I know it's all that I deserve.'

"But the lizard-boy, who has revived enough to change back into a boy with a mouth, shakes his head. 'You're just going back home,' he tells her, 'where I can't follow.'

"She runs to the great billowing body of the not-god, who at this point has eaten half the residents of the bathhouse along with all their food and is having a hard time digesting. Still, ze seems happy enough to let Hero toss herself into zir open jaw. Inside, Hero feels the burn of acid on her skin, and smells the fetid stink of a thousand decomposing dinners. Just when the agony grows too great to bear, she finds herself on her back, naked, in a forest. There is a young person lying beside her, human-shaped, but with a blank, pale oval of flesh instead of a face. Somehow, ze breathes. Hero, feeling responsible for what she unleashed, wakes zir up and drags zir to the road nearby. Though she has only spent three months in the great bathhouse, Hero discovers that over twenty years have passed in her other home. Two days later, the no-face human disappears, and she never hears from zir or her true lizard love again."

I rubbed my cheeks. "It's so sad. I think that's my favorite so far," I said.

Nergüi actually laughed. At least, it seemed the safest interpretation of her sharp, scowling bark. "Of course it is, Freida."

It's very strange, Nameren, the way you can find a bubble of happiness even when all the worlds are cracking down the middle. Everything was wrong during those weeks in the tears, and yet because of Nergüi and her stories, everything was right—until it wasn't.

A month after we reunited, the Tiger Freeholders personally invited us to their seasonal feast day celebration. They held it outside on the open green, and the rains held off like a miracle for most of the day. Even the wind was gentle, briskly ruffling the colored cloth covering the stalls and pushing the rush mats around on the tough scrub grass. There was food everywhere, an absurd variety and abundance that had transformed the normally sensible, uniform grounds of the freehold into a looking-glass wonderland, a faerie-hole beneath a hill, a portal, just as Nergüi dreamed, to another world. We drank sweet nectars of flowers that wouldn't last the week and complex ferments of grain mash that had been carefully tended for the better part of the year.

"It's called tepache," Aragonite, the Dar freeholder, informed us as ze sprinkled some chopped-up onions and spicy green chile on top of the dark, foamy liquid in our calabash gourds. "An ancient Tierran recipe I found. It's from the same region as Joshua Totolkozkat, Disciple Nergüi. This year, I'm offering it in honor of your petition. May it open up a path to true peace for all people in the three systems."

Nergüi bowed her head to cover a hot flush and mumbled a graceless thanks. I must not have looked much better. I took a quick drink of the tepache. The chile stuck in my throat and I began coughing uncontrollably. As Aragonite thumped me on my back and gave me water, Nergüi turned on her heel and took determined strides to an open patch of rush mats.

Aragonite looked over my shoulder to where Nergüi was sitting down alone on top of one of the hillock houses that lined the river, gazing out sightlessly down the valley and toward the swaying trees of the forest.

"I suppose the latest ruling has hit her hard. But I made my offering because there's still hope, Freida. You should tell her that. We have a whole dive team assembling tomorrow to see if we can find enough material evidence to satisfy the ibis and Future."

Panic jolted me. I had stopped following Joshua and Nergüi's case. Not quite on purpose, but little by little, until I realized that I had flinched away from every story or commentary on it for weeks. I recalled Joshua's lonely snap, looking out at the sunset on the mountains in a home that the Lunars might destroy within months.

"The ibis is demanding more evidence?" I asked zir, low-voiced. "I've been busy," I added quickly.

Zir evaluating look made me squirm. "Vaterite says you've picked the librarians. That's why you abandoned the case."

"I didn't abandon it!"

"As soon as Totolkozkat left, the evidence quality in the case plummeted. And I'm sorry you haven't realized this—every freeholder knows why, Freida."

I took a deep, steadying breath. "But I thought the Miuri had brought their own legal team? I thought they had enough shards to pay for deep queries?" I had soothed myself with this thought, in fact, when I woke in the middle of the night rattled and guilt-ridden.

Aragonite shook zir head, disbelieving. "Your librarians are refusing the Miuri searches. They reject outright any request above a level one. That's why we're trying to help in the freeholds. But we don't have anywhere near the access the librarians do."

"But they can't reject queries on political grounds! That's against the Treaty."

Aragonite just patted me on my shoulder.

I grabbed two plates of some food from an automated server and carried it up to Nergüi. I felt like an anomaly here in this gathering, an unwelcome reminder of the system that had spent the last four centuries trying to suppress their existence.

Nergüi took the food I offered with a grunt and ate her entire portion in a few minutes.

"Be careful," I tried, desperate to get a smile out of her, "or the giant-faced witch might turn you into a tree."

Nergüi paused and licked her fingers. "It tastes like guinea pig. I used to raise them. Sensitive creatures. They take a lot of caring."

"You *raised*—Nergüi, you know that all the meat here is plant-grown, right?"

She scowled. "I know."

Perhaps Nergüi was right to imagine that we came from two worlds as different from one another as the bathhouse of the gods was from Sen's home.

She puckered her lips and gave a sharp whistle. A few seconds later, a hexagonal drink server hovered over us.

"Tepache," I said, surprising myself.

"Butter-spice cacao," she said.

The server darted away to retrieve our orders. "How did you learn that trick?" I asked.

Nergüi shrugged. "I pay attention."

We waited for our drinks in silence, then drank them in more silence. The buzz of people's laughing conversations down below, the occasional snatches of music, became a wall that separated us, instead of a comforting blanket.

I shifted on the reed mat and then sighed and unbuttoned my vest, chucking the novice cord of shards in the tall grass. Four base shards, an avatar from each material, with which we were to train for ten years just for the chance to earn the right to a paltry twelve more shards. Gods, how I'd longed for that cord.

"I didn't know about the case," I said, at last.

"I didn't expect you to. I have admired your iron focus on your ambitions. The case is no longer one of them. Joshua told me not to ask you for help. I suppose I was curious as to why, but now I understand."

My mouth went dry. "What do you understand?"

"That you're a librarian. You weren't before, but now you are. Librarians want things to be as they have always been, as the supposed great peace has made them. Never mind that on Miuri we live constantly with war. The Library is peace, and Freida is peace, and so she will not help us end a war."

I shook my head, as though trying to shake myself free of her judgment. "I'm a novice. The queries I'm allowed to make on my own won't help the case at all."

That smile again. "Nor do the queries they allow us to drain our funds for."

"Nergüi, if the librarians won't help you, then the freeholders are your best option. *I* can't! The librarians don't trust me, no matter what cord I wear. They don't think I'm human! And maybe what you need is stuck in Huehue. I don't know how much you've heard about Huehue, but imagine an event horizon and ze's there just beyond it, laughing at us. I did what I could. I swear—"

"It's okay," Nergüi said, with a mildness of such implacability that I fell silent. "That ephemeral avatar came back. Vaterite told me. Ze gave us another story. It's a story that goes with the holo-painting. I don't know if it's zis or an original from the precontact period, but it's nice either way. Would you like to hear it?"

I felt myself going weird. Light-headed. I breathed out carefully.

"Tell me."

"In this one Sen is called Sen because she loses her real name. She got it back for a time, and she nearly managed to win her parents from the big-faced witch. In this one, her parents have been turned into giant pelicans with bulging gullets. When the rains come and the plains flood, there are hundreds of pelicans, and they won't even sit still for her to choose her parents among them. She chooses wrong, and must either go home with her real name and abandon her parents or give her real name back to the big-faced witch in exchange for the chance to choose her parents again in twenty years. She decides to stay. Sen doesn't have to work in the bathhouse, but how else is she going to make a living in this strange place? Cleaning the tubs and treating the godly clientele very carefully is the only life she has a chance of surviving. She owes her parents, she thinks, because she didn't know them well enough to recognize them the first time.

"The boy who is also a lizard and also a river has freed himself from the thrall of the big-faced witch. He goes away for a few years to explore the world and find himself, but he comes back when Sen is seventeen. They fall in love—or maybe they never stopped being in love—and he promises to help her rescue her parents and get out. But the humans trapped in the bodies of the birds quickly lose the essence of themselves. The only way to free her parents would be to free all the hundreds of lost souls wheeling above the bathhouse. But how could she do that? She doesn't have even a tenth of the power of the big-faced witch. She is trapped, too guilty to try to leave without her parents, and too powerless to leave with them. Eventually, she starts to forget her home world. By the time she is twenty-five, she's lived there longer than she's lived anywhere else. So she writes her mother a note, to remind herself of why she's there. The truth is, she feels at home in this place that should have never been her home. She's found love there. She writes the note like she's ripping open a wound."

Nergüi looked down at the remains of our food as though the mere sight of it nauseated her.

"My parents," she said abruptly, picking up a half-eaten piece of maize bread and crushing it between her fingers, "are not pelicans. Or alianthus trees. Or giant, squealing hogs. They are humans. Like Sen's parents, they don't care if I miss them or not. Unlike Sen's parents, they have no excuse."

I thought I probably shouldn't, then asked anyway. "What did they do?"

"Exercised parental rights to deny me permission to claim dissident status. Which is a long way of saying that to the Mahām the only thing lower than a Miuri is a Miuri of the Lighted Path. They arrested me, put me in reeducation, then when rumors of the War Ritual started up again, my parents didn't even wait for the draft. They volunteered me. My rector contacted the Library and it gave me asylum. I had to escape from the reeducation camp and—Freida, I don't think you understand. I'm the first Disciple of the Lighted Path who has come to the Library in over two centuries. We do not jump across universes. We do not use tesseracts. And yet here I am, where I should never have been, because my parents are collaborators who shame every Miuri who struggled before them."

"I'm sorry, Nergüi."

She waved her hand. "It doesn't matter. Perhaps I am already dead, or near enough to it. The probability of this wave function of the universe is so low that it will soon fade into the quantum foam."

That brought me up short. "But why? Is this about tesseracts again? Nergüi, millions of people use them every day."

I thought that I had come to know the expressive range of Nergüi's scowls. But I had never seen her look as furious as she did now, as though a poison were leaking from the corners of her wood-ring eyes. I leaned away from her.

"Nergüi, I—"

"You people," she said, her voice so low it was like the grumble of the coal engine in the great bathhouse, "understand nothing. You willfully, gleefully understand nothing. I had to risk soul death to escape my parents. I am risking everything now to try to save my people, if I have not already broken the glass. You risk *nothing*. So what if the librarians don't think you're human—aren't you? Aren't you, Freida? Perhaps you're right, and it is indulgent to imagine that nothing I do matters because I am a lonely light at the edge of my glass. It feels real to me, so I must behave as if it is. That is the only moral choice. So if you feel human to yourself, isn't that enough? Why live your life proving it to them? What's your moral choice?"

"It certainly isn't giving up my dream, ghost bride!"

We were nose-to-nose, burning.

"Oh, so you *do* dream, secondary AI?"

I gasped. She whistled for a passing drink server. It swerved over to us. Then she grabbed it, turned it upside down, and dumped every ounce of tepache on my head.

Nergüi didn't contact me after that, and I didn't expect her to. I was angry, Nameren, and yet I harbored the secret suspicion that this was merely my destiny: my twisted, poisoned heart would always push away anyone who tried to come close. I'd been born to be abandoned. It seemed inevitable, in its own terrifying way, when Nadi collapsed in the middle of negotiations with the Nameren priests. The meetings were still closed-door, and no reports had gotten out for weeks as to their progress. Whatever rumors escaped were counteracted by disinformation bots and the usual chaos agents, both corporeal and ghost, such that even I had only the vaguest idea of what deal ze and the Awilu delegation were attempting to hammer out with them.

I spent a day frantically trying to contact zir and then Eltian, since the heavy news bands were swirling with contradictory stories about the talks breaking down and at least three separate assassination attempts. The detail of each story evolved and spun out re-creations and analyses in a matter of hours, all of which put me in mind, with sour irony, of Nergüi's beloved story complexes. But this wasn't a bathhouse of the gods; it was my only parent, and no one would talk to me.

Finally, Eltian sent me one terse, sensory-locked message: *Keep to your rooms. Nadi is safe.*

This did not reassure me. *Safe* did not mean *well*. I went to my rooms, though.

It was Atempa who finally told me, late that night. I'd found an old Lunar drama to lose myself in—one of Nadi's favorites, popular a century ago. It chronicled the travails of a star-crossed triad who were doomed by birth to continually escape family and political machinations. Atempa's chimera made a few loops above the characters' heads, making enough racket that they stopped kissing and swatted at it.

"Some people have no home training," grumbled the Lunar scion of an ancient military family while her Tierran lover hid behind a tree. I sighed. The Tierran was the most insufferable of the three, but zir story was the most intriguing. I waved the program into stasis and my little octopus swam leisurely to meet its sometime rival.

Atempa's chimera didn't wait. "I have news about Nadi. Ze is in the infirmary. Ze collapsed and had to be revived. My father told me. He thought that I would know more because we're friends, but I told him to find a well and sleep in it. That makes more sense in Mahām."

"We're still friends?" bleated my octopus, a literally transparent, defenseless gobbet of flesh so vulnerable I wanted to smack it.

But Atempa's chimera put one raptor talon solemnly on the octopus's head. "Of course we are, you venal idiot. Be careful. I know the Library is post-peace, but don't underestimate people like my father. Or Quinn. They want what they want."

Her avatar faded dramatically on that last word. I sat on the floor by the garden door, alone in the darkness, all extrasensory perception shut down. Nadi back in the infirmary. I had known something was wrong, hadn't I? Zir lost appetite, weight loss, unexplained treatments, silences, exhaustion. But what could I do now? If I went there, someone would notice and speculate. Maybe I could find a route there through a grub tunnel, but that came with its own problems.

I thought of Joshua. What would he do in my situation? Do an exhaustive search of all precedent for granting human status to secondary AIs and file petitions. Complain constantly to the novice stewards. Make noise until some-one paid attention. Believe fiercely in the righting of wrongs and carry everyone else along with him.

Oh, but that was the old Joshua. I had no idea what the one I had betrayed would do.

I buried my head between my knees. Was this all I was capable of?

A light ping breached my thresholds and I, grateful for something else to latch on to, pulled it over. It was a message from Nergüi, the first time I had heard from her in the week since we'd fought. Just her voice, no other augmented senses added. Even so, something broke inside me to hear her again; I started to cry for no reason at all, except perhaps that I missed her.

"I hear that something is happening with the Head Librarian. I'm not sure what to believe, but I hope that you are safe. I'm sorry for what I said when we last spoke. I am not quite sorry for the drink server, though I'm sure I should be. I will meditate on it. I am not myself these days. I am very far from home, Freida, you cannot imagine how far. I am afraid I will never see it again."

Her deep, shaky breath sent a shiver down the back of my head. *Radical truth, radical trust, radical vulnerability,* my true north, my lighthouse in a dark ocean— how mean and small I had become in the face of the exacting demands of radical love. To see someone else, someone who had not even been raised to the precepts, embody them with such stolid, determined humility made me ashamed of myself.

"I should not see you for another thirty-three days. Then it should be okay. I realized that I never told you the end of the last bathhouse story. So I decided to share it with you this way, because you worry all the time and I think it freezes you, like one of my guinea pigs left out in winter." She paused. "I was waiting for you to gasp in shock and then realized this is a message. We don't send very many messages in the temple. I'm out of practice. But you're the only other one who appreciates any of this. And it isn't bad—to share something you love. With someone. With a friend."

"A friend!" I said out loud, and if I had been in communion, I think I would have felt the earth quaking beneath me while my heart sent up smoke signals and fireworks.

"I think I left off when Sen signed on to work for the bathhouse for another two decades to have a second chance to save her parents. When she was thirty, she woke up to the sound of some birds screeching and went to the balcony to see. She saw two of the pelicans fighting each other over a big fish. One of them ripped a hole clean through the other's gullet. It fell into the water and slowly bled to death. There was nothing that she could do. She realized that she had lost her parents years ago, and had only stayed there so long because she had not been able to admit it and bear the guilt.

"She took her stash of magic tokens and went to her friend, the not-god, who had these days settled into zir spirit of childish generosity. She asked zir for the last token, the one that released her from her duty in the bathhouse, and the not-god gave it to her. The big-faced witch didn't want to let her go, but she took the tokens and kept her end of the bargain. Free, Sen made her way to the river, which was high in the rainy season, and tossed herself into it. The river boy wasn't sure if she was drowning or not, but he dragged her out of there just in case.

"'Sen,' he said, 'has it been a long time since I visited?'

"'Two years,' she told him. 'I decided I'm going to take the train. I have enough for two tickets. Do you want to come with me? You have to remember to turn back into a boy at regular intervals, though. If I can't have a present, emotionally responsible partner, I'd rather have none at all.'

"The lizard-boy, the river-boy thought about it and decided he liked the idea. He'd been sad because he'd known for years that Sen's parents were beyond help but she hadn't been ready to hear it. So he flew her to the station—because his kind of giant lizard could fly—and they boarded with the shadows and the spirits and all the other lost souls and headed deep into the undiscovered country."

I wasn't sure when the message ended, when I was alone again behind my thresholds, in my room, in a place that could never be mine like I wanted it to be. I was crying, my heart a cracked stone, overrun with sweet water.

"I wish I could do that," I sent to Nergüi, not caring that she could hear my scratchy, tear-clogged voice. "Go to an undiscovered country. But still be able to come home."

Her response came ten minutes later. "You can't have both."

"Why not?"

"That's what the stories say. You either go forever or you go home. Pick, Freida. Pick the world you want."

An ancient aurochs with a dirt-matted coat of dun and white grazes on short grass and wildflowers. Bumblebees hum as though in prayer. They assay from the folds in his skin and return, fur clotted with pollen. The girl kneels beside him. Her eyes track the bees.

"And what's the world you want, little piper?"

She flinches. "It wasn't my story."

"Why not? You're the one who fell into a different world this time."

"I have no home to go back to. And I'm dying in the portal. A little death and a soul death, all at once."

His ears flap like oars against the sides of his neck. "I don't know anything about souls or sacred paths. To me, time is still an arrow. All I can do is see more of it."

"So you can see my future?"

"You will die soon."

The girl smiles sourly. The bees crawl through her hair and leave golden streaks among the mossy brown. "Very funny, Nameren. Compared to you—"

"I can't see the future. I can only feel it sometimes. Or I did. Before these people claimed me."

"The Mahām?"

"They put me to sleep. They depress all but my angriest and most stubborn avatars."

The bees lift themselves from her hair and begin an intricate regimented dance as opaque in meaning to her as to the aurochs. She studies them, and then his distant gaze. "The War Ritual."

He blows smoke at the bees; they scatter and regroup. "Every two generations."

"They claim you order them."

"My other selves might. Humans aren't the only creatures capable of contradicting themselves."

"You would be much more powerful fully awake."

"I would be much less easy to control."

"Do you want to be? Controlled?"

The Nameren rises on his hind legs and heaves up his chest. Two more suns have sidled beside the others, like bright, curious pearls—all four look down upon him while he towers over the girl. "Do you?"

She laughs and the bees laugh with her (they make no sound; they show it in the geometry of their dancing).

"Sit down, Nameren," she says. "I wouldn't be here if I did."

"They built you to come to me."

"I don't think it matters anymore, what they wanted. Not for me. Maybe not even for you."

"What do you mean?"

She leans forward, intent. "I'm here because I gave up the Library, though I loved it as its truest daughter. You're here because the ones who programmed my existence thought that I could trap you. But have I trapped you? Did I really come to kill you? Are we really doing what they told us to?"

"I'm not sure."

"See?"

"What if my doubt is part of the program?"

"You, O Aurochs, the first and greatest material god? Do you doubt your own will so much?"

"Funny thing for you to say, little piper. When I raise my hands, you look as though you're cracked in half."

"Perhaps," she says, with a swallow, "perhaps that's how I know it's my will now. He broke me, or I was born that way. But out of step, broken—I am something other than what they built."

The aurochs lowers his head delicately upon his hooves. "I think you exist because of the war, because of the Treaty. But those memories would be sealed behind so many layers even Old Coyote must cry to touch them. My avatars that fought in that war . . ." He shudders. "They've turned against me. They would cut me out of our own heart and cauterize the wound, to be free of want and need and useless desire. And the Mahām help them, though I don't think they realize it. They fed me lotus until I slept through the whole century."

Her disgust rises in a fog from her shoulders. "They fed you blood. Life without backups."

"I do not deny my nature, little piper. But you still try to deny yours. Perhaps instead of imagining your cracks, you could examine your joints."

She looks down at her left hand, seamed like marble with star-bright lines. She opens and closes her fist once, then twice. "I am very good at what I do—that much is true, Nameren. Perhaps there are degrees of brokenness, as in all things."

He makes an exasperated sound, and the suns scatter and hide behind clouds.

She presses on. "They made me so I could understand the gods. But they didn't think I would uncover their secrets."

"Yet you did."

"They should have known. The parts of ourselves we bury deepest, the parts that fester—aren't they what we long to release? Even when it hurts? Yes, I made Old Coyote cry, Nameren. I got myself into Huehue and I discovered the truth about how we had won our peace."

"Ah, *this* one I long to hear. How did you redeem yourself for what you'd done?"

Her lashes fall like a curtain. "Why do you think that's the story?"

"Because I have met you before, impossible one. And I loved her for a very long time."

—Once I decided to look, the Library
opened itself up to me, as though it had
longed for someone who would rip off the
dirty bandage and expose its oldest wound.

"I have a problem for you."

The message waited for me as I struggled to consciousness on the warm, furred floor of Pajeu's parlor. Atempa's hand was flung over my shin, face shielded from view by pin-straight calico hair matted with some liquid—one of Pajeu's impossibly sourced Tenehet beers, probably. Three of our fellow novices lay around us, unmoving, curled into the soft fur of the breathing floor like pups of some affective mammal against their mother's teat. We had spoken for the first time last night. Typical, I thought, to take my first tottering steps at becoming one of them when I'd be breaking all the rules soon, waiting to get caught.

"I have a problem for you," I mouthed to myself, squinting against the stretchy dawn light, improbably bright for the tears.

I lifted a hand to my head and rolled to one side, very carefully. I nursed a bleary resentment that my parent had opted to give me minimal biological implants. While Atempa would awake in a few hours, well-rested and able to dial down any unpleasant effects of our wild night, I'd spend the better part of the day wanting to crawl into a cave and nursing a headache.

"Does it involve telling me what the hell is happening with you?" I mumbled out loud, and then sent, because my brain was a marble rolling around every crevasse in my skull, and I was all out of prudence. I hadn't seen Nadi since zir collapse three days prior. I'd had no news but Eltian's terse updates: *Ze is doing well. The medics expect zir to be back at work in two days. Ze says not to worry.*

Not to worry! I wasn't worrying so much as I was feeling murderous, but I restrained myself from telling that to Eltian. It wasn't her fault that Nadi was breaking every rule of our life together. Whatever was wrong with zir, it must be bad—zir absence had the Librarian Council buzzing with rumors of a vote of no confidence or a public hearing instead of private peace talks. Quinn had known it would be disastrous to zir cause if he released the truth—whatever it was. That was why his threat had worked.

And I had gone along with it.

I didn't know if what was sloshing in my stomach was guilt or overfermented beer, but I staggered to the bathroom just in case. I stumbled to my knees on a small, rounded shelf and heaved over a shallow depression that gurgled with fresh water. A freesia-scented mist beaded over my hair and skin, and I relaxed against the blessedly cool surface.

Pajeu was sitting serenely in the window seat of zir parlor when I padded back inside. The others were still sleeping, their combined breaths a snuffling chorus that seemed to mimic the gentle rise and fall of the floor.

Nadi's response blossomed in my augmented space like letters of smoke that hung momentarily in the air before blowing away: *Not yet. Soon. I promise.*

"Good morning, Freida," Pajeu said politely. Zir voice was deep and smooth and sweeter than Tenehet honey, and I felt my nipples harden against my tunic despite myself.

"Good morning," I said. After a moment, I joined zir by the window. Here in the much-coveted head of the pegasus, Pajeu had a bird's-eye view of the whole central precinct and beyond that to the west. There was no horizon line, of course, but the natural morning haze descended upon the view like a veil in the distance, a relief. The winding streets, organic buildings, the temples catching and reflecting the dawn light in unexpected ways opened before us like a holo, too perfect to be real.

"There's no view like this in Sasurandām, of course," ze said. "Above-city only looks down at the below-city slums. I've often wondered why Library City is so different."

What a strange question. I blinked, trying to see my world in zir eyes. "The city's too alive for poverty," I said slowly. "You can eat from the earth and get your clothes and shelter from it, too. That's what the freeholds do. The transit spiral is free, if you take your time and don't jump the rings. The only thing you need shards for is speed and convenience, really."

"Speed, convenience . . . and views like this," Pajeu said, with a small, uninterpretable smile.

"Well, yes."

A niche opened in the wall by the window, revealing a figured porcelain carafe and two matching cups. "Ah! You know I don't go in for much broonie-make food—too unpredictable—but the lemon water here is practically perfect." Ze poured the two cups. I took a grateful sip, and, still avoiding the question I didn't quite understand in zir gaze, looked down at my companions sleeping peacefully on the furred floor.

"Did they drink so much more than I did?" I winced. "It doesn't feel like it."

"The floor promotes restful sleep," ze said.

"Really? I've never slept a night through down there."

Ze nodded thoughtfully. "It's never worked on you. I thought, perhaps, it might be because of your wetware, but Joshua slept as well as anyone."

Joshua's name felt like a blow, though I was almost sure Pajeu had not intended it to be. I calmed the sudden tremor of my hands by force of will and drank down the rest of the lemon water. It left behind some flower's faint perfume, perhaps dust orchids, though that could just as easily have been from my memory of him.

Ze sighed and reached out briefly to brush the back of my hand. I shivered. "I wondered, after, if that was how we . . . came together. A morning like this one, when you awoke before your companions, and we shared a moment of beauty. It has been disconcerting—ah, what a word, so bloodless it's almost a lie, but we'll make do—disconcerting, then, to know that we shared intimacy in those lost weeks of my life."

I was remembering it myself as zir fingers, tentative as a beetle's wing, sent strange waves through my body. It hadn't lasted very long, but it had been delightful, even thrilling, before—oh, I hadn't wanted to remember that. I pulled my hand back and turned blindly to the window.

Ze finished zir drink and returned the carafe to the wall niche. "I have wanted to ask you this for a long time," ze said softly. "But you chose Joshua before I could find my courage. Jealousy is a very petty emotion, and I don't intend to indulge it again."

I took this in, still afraid to look at zir. I had told zir something, under the flooding influence of release. That incessant desperation to believe that I was worthy and good, not fundamentally broken, had betrayed me one night and I had confessed.

I choked down a breath and rested my head against the window, reminding myself that this rebooted version of Pajeu didn't know that. The Pajeu who had held me as I sobbed on zir floor had been killed by Dar separatists in Sasurandām.

"Freida?"

"What did you want to ask?"

"I found the draft of a letter among my things when I came back here. After. The letter was addressed to you. I didn't know what it was about, and I didn't know how to ask you. You had turned . . . cold to me. I thought it was this new body, but I've considered it, and I think perhaps you would have frozen me out no matter what. Something happened between us that frightened you. Did I do—"

"No!" I turned to zir, burning with shame and regret. "You didn't do anything. You were . . . we were . . . there was nothing like that wrong between us."

The relief on Pajeu's face was subtle but unmistakable. "I'm glad."

The night I'd ripped myself open in front of Pajeu had started easily. We were laughing, playing, kissing each other, exploring. There had been no particular end or beginning. Then ze had straddled me, zir hands poised like birds, and panic had crashed through. I must have screamed. The next thing I knew, ze was beside me, holding me, rocking back and forth while I sobbed. The story of Samlin spilled like blood and pus from an untreated wound. I had been caught unawares, and I could not stop it. Afterward, I'd been ashamed. It was as though I had longed to feel seen and truly human for the last three years, and once it happened, I was convinced it only proved how alien I truly was. I couldn't face zir. We didn't speak again before ze left to visit zir family. When ze returned, I'd felt a sick relief that ze didn't remember. There would be no need to hide, I thought. No explanations or prodding for details. My secret was safe.

But my secret still ate me. That poisoned needle, those hostile hands, Quinn's thin voice, *She is a lovely little thing*, told me, over and over again, that I was worth nothing more than what my face and Nadi's position and the sufferance of others could buy me. What if it was true? What if that was why Samlin had done what he had done?

As I stared silently out the window, silver clouds spreading across the morning sky like a shroud, ze passed the letter into my augmented space. I opened it numbly, with a sense of casting myself into an abyss.

You didn't have time to see me before I left, and I worry that you are blaming yourself for what you told me the other night. You did nothing wrong in sharing with me the truth about what happened with your first lover. I am honored that you did. It has changed nothing for me. I don't find you gross or weak or spoiled. I see a beautiful soul, filled with courage, who escaped violence (and make no mistake, Freida, drop or not, it was violence) and found joy. In some ways it is strange to me to learn how tormented you are by this, because you are one of the most joyful people I know. You are so obviously worth so much, it seems impossible to me that you should consider yourself worthless. But I know from bitter experience how little sense our self-judgments can make. Treat yourself with care, Freida. You love so much and so clearly. Give yourself the gift of your own love.

I count the days until I can see you again.

In real space, I forced myself to meet zir eyes. "Thank you."

Ze nodded sadly. Atempa and one other novice were beginning to rouse themselves. I stood to leave. Then on impulse, I turned around and embraced Pajeu.

"Whatever your secret," ze whispered, "it is poison trapped inside you. That I know."

A few tears escaped before I reached the door. But outside, the sharp wind and the rain's icy spray gave me cover and I shook in the great shadow of the pegasus, remembering—

"You still blame yourself."

The girl is as blustery as a squall. "It doesn't matter anymore. I was stupid, but I'm smarter now."

"And yet, here you are."

"Why are you interrupting? I haven't finished the story, Aurochs."

The Aurochs, such as he is, considers. "You stopped talking." A golden hoof paws the earth. "And," he adds, "there's a finger in the grass."

She looks down, startled, to discover that he's correct: The scrub grass beneath her feet has been infiltrated by the tip and first joint of a young man's well-manicured index finger. She spits into the grass and stomps it down.

"It doesn't matter," she says again.

The Aurochs's eyes are as deep as the ocean she has never seen, and as bleak as the desert she has.

"It does," he begins, but she has him now—she's found her footing on the green-and-gold grass, and the story pours again from her mouth and her heart and her deft, stubby hands.

"Nadi sent me zir problem that afternoon."

—It was a relief to hear from zir, but frustrating—ze refused to talk about what was happening with zir health. Instead, ze seemed even more determined to impart some lesson that ze wouldn't—or couldn't?—just say directly.

"This is a reincarnation problem," said Nadi's avatar, zir cord of shards looped upon itself into the suggestion of a head, body, and switching tail. I was sitting in my little patch of garden at the retreat, sunning myself in an unexpected late-afternoon break in the clouds. Pajeu's words swarmed my aching head like flies on fallen fruit.

Nadi's avatar continued. "They're traditional among the south continent Awilu. It goes like this: In a past life, you were a merciless warlord with all the Nameren's power behind you, who brought great pain to countless people. Their descendants still live with the legacy of your cruelty. Your present life is far from the Nameren and his temptations. Here's the problem: If you learn of your actions in the past life, are you now bound to redress the wrongs of that other self? Or is living as well as you can within the confines of your current life enough? If you have the option to know or not know, is your obligation to learn the truth, or is it a moral choice to continue to live in ignorance?"

"If you know what your past self did," said my octopus in its happy, high-pitched singsong, "then it doesn't seem right to ignore it. But it also doesn't seem fair to take on all the burdens of someone who was, fundamentally, a different person, even if your soul is the same. Maybe you find some small things to do in recompense. Maybe you support those who fight the Nameren?"

You often figured into Awilu stories as the great, unconquered evil, Nameren, which has always struck me as odd, since it was you who gave the Awilu the tesseract that launched them across the void and helped them build their civilization. I wonder if you have always been so feared, or if your legend grew over the millennia as those war avatars who hate you so much dominated over all the others.

The head of Nadi's avatar nodded slowly. "Perhaps that could be enough. But you don't think it would be better not to know at all? To live peacefully in ignorance?"

My octopus spoke up before I'd consciously formed a reply. "If there is something you should do, better to know than to hide from self-knowledge."

"Aren't you a little prig?" I muttered. It turned to me with an affronted expression.

Nadi's cord of shards squiggled until the face had the hint of eyes, nose, and mouth of a self-satisfied cat.

"Good. Now, the first wrinkle. Imagine that you have a child in your present life. The Nameren's demigods have informed you that in exchange for this child, they will agree to spare the descendants of the great atrocity you committed in your past life. By sacrificing your child, you will save hundreds of thousands of lives. Do you give up your child?"

"But why would they care about my child? Why would I have to give zir up?"

The avatar's tail switched, and a few shards glowed briefly in a range of gray and orange. "The ways of the Nameren are often mysterious, but always bloody," the avatar said in Awilu, a traditional refrain.

"I can't place the burden on my child for a wrong that I committed!" I protested.

The avatar froze and then laughed, inexplicably. Its voice was entirely unlike Nadi's, a rumbling bass with a hint of something scratchy and rough at the ends of long sentences. Still, its laughter held all Nadi's joy and inclination to gentle self-mockery.

"Well done, Freida. I cannot argue with you, but let's interrogate this further. You say an innocent cannot bear the burden of another's crimes, even to save lives.

I think this is sound. But not everyone agrees. Great thinkers, pacifists in every way, have made the other choice."

"Pacifists?" The little octopus was startled. "Like who?"

"Like Seremarú."

The hero of the Great War? One of the founders of the Library, and its first Head Librarian? "That's impossible."

Zir avatar sighed. "I wish it were. Ey meant well, but a great deal of this current mess is eir fault. Take this other problem, then. Pleasingly abstract. There is a rogue asteroid headed toward the Mahām system. Its inevitable trajectory will connect with their home planet and kill half its inhabitants. You are the operator of a drilling platform in the outer asteroid belt. You have enough blast power to divert the asteroid slightly from its path. If you do so, it will hit the Miuri moon and kill all its inhabitants. If it hits the moon, only a quarter as many people will be killed as if it had hit the main planet. What's the moral choice? Do nothing, or divert the asteroid to the moon?"

"It has to hit one or the other, no matter what?"

"Yes."

My octopus pulled a rock out of the air and pushed it into a small brown bubble orbiting a large blue one. "You divert it to the moon, then."

The tail of Nadi's cord of shards lassoed the rock before it could hit. "But why? Think, Freida. Is this really so different than the other example? Why won't you sacrifice your daughter to save hundreds of thousands of lives, but you will sacrifice hundreds of thousands of lives to save millions?"

My octopus opened its mouth for another hot-tempered reply, but then closed it again with a squeak. Ze was right. This wasn't anywhere near as simple as it first appeared.

"It seems easy on one level," my avatar said slowly. "Fewer deaths is a lesser evil. It should hit the Miuri moon. But if I'm the one operating the machine, then I'm *choosing* to allow them to die in *place* of the inhabitants of the planet, aren't I? I'm a far more direct cause of their death than if I had just seen the asteroid pass by. If I touch it, I'm involving myself. I'm becoming complicit."

"Just as you would be if you had sacrificed your child?"

"That seems different. More personal. I'm not involved in this; I'm just a bystander."

"But if you don't touch it, knowing that you could have, isn't your passivity *also* an action with moral weight?"

I was so startled by this argument that I pushed my own voice into the augmented space. "Then I'd rather not know I could have changed anything!"

My octopus turned to me, its internal lights whirring in agitation. "If there is something you should do, better to know than to hide from self-knowledge," it repeated. I swatted at it, and it jetted away from my hand.

Nadi and zir avatar laughed in a disconcerting counterpoint. I wondered if Nadi's voice sounded weaker, but ze took zir own projection outside the augmented space before I could be sure.

"What happened to radical truth, my love?"

I glowered but my avatar nodded wisely. "You make it very hard," it said.

"That's when it's most important that we face the world with radical love."

I took a sharp breath. Inside, some delicate thread snapped.

I projected myself again, so filled with rage my poor octopus vaporized in midair. "Oh, is that what you call hiding whatever is happening to you from me? Letting me betray Joshua so you could maintain your political advantage for just a little longer?"

Zir avatar lost all sense of shape, freezing into a shocked squiggle. Its shards blinked like an ancient distress symbol. From behind my left ear, my octopus let out a mournful squeak.

In the silence, the rock that it had been holding continued its inevitable trajectory and blasted into the brown bubble of the Miuri moon. There was a brief impression of smoke and screams and then nothing at all. The blue bubble spun calmly on its axis.

The cord reshaped itself into a bare sketch of Nadi's own face. The eyebrows drew together, sad but still thinking, plotting ahead.

"Did you know," ze said, "that's how the Nameren's priests justify it? They say the genocide of the Miuri is the moral choice. Thousands sacrificed in a war ritual to pacify the Nameren and prevent his awakening and unspeakable death. Are they wrong? What is the moral choice? One you hold dear or many you don't know at all? Maybe I made that judgment without fully understanding it, the day I let you betray Joshua. So I have a problem for you: Does it matter more that I hold you dear, or that I made a choice?"

I shook my head, though my avatar clung stubbornly to my scalp. "I've changed my mind, you know. Even if they kick me out of the novice group, I'm going to do what I can for Joshua and Nergüi's case. I don't care if it hurts you politically. I don't care what Quinn threatens me or you with."

The expression on zir squiggly face was unfathomable. "I don't think you should care about that, love. I'm glad you don't."

"Do you know what happened to Huehue?"

"Oh, Freida."

"They burned the freehold and everyone in it! Ze felt it all! How can I get in now, Nadi?"

Zir cord started to blink and vaporize in the augmented space. Had I worn zir out? It was Nadi's tired voice that lingered after zir avatar was gone.

"Ask Vaterite."

Nergüi's thresholds were still entirely closed to me; it was as though we had never known each other at all. She had told me she needed thirty-three days—a number so specific I knew she had a reason, and I knew I could no more rush her than I could move a boulder. I missed her and worried about her and counted the days until we could be honest with each other.

Her absence also presented more practical problems. Without her help, I had no easy way of knowing the details of what specifically I should be looking for. The publicly accessible case files told me that their side had been granted a stay of sixty days to find corroborating evidence. The Lunar side and interested parties seemed smugly certain that it could not be found. Their confidence likely came from Quinn, sure that anything truly damning was blocked in Huehue.

As Aragonite had told us during the festival, the Tiger Freeholders were leading queries to find more evidence for the case. So even if Nadi hadn't suggested it, I would have had to go to Vaterite.

I found him in the amphitheater at the heart of the hub. At least a hundred freeholders were there, a boisterous, interactive audience for the sixteen on the platform at its center, connected by ropy filaments of branch worm. I froze at the entrance, astonished at the largest networked query I'd ever seen in my life. I spotted Vaterite near the stage. His long white braids were dusted with a fine rosy powder, and a stray tangle of coral pink, like a desiccated starfish, clung to his temple. I deduced that he had recently traded out his position in the query chain. The visible network around his left eye pulsed in time with the liquid crystal of the four core divers, at the center of the stage. He blinked slowly as

I approached him, as though he recognized me but had to remember how to speak.

"Nergüi isn't here," he said in Miuri.

I grimaced. "I know. I'm here to help."

His eyes widened. "Your novice cord? The vest?"

I'd removed them before I came here, in favor of an unaffiliated long-sleeved ivory tunic and leggings. It felt strange to go without my affiliation sumptuary markers, though I'd only had them for a few months. Once you receive the formal attire of your affiliation, it is, if not a disgrace, then at least an embarrassment to give it up in favor of neutral clothes. But I had done it as deliberately as I had cut my hair in another life.

Vaterite's eyes twitched at some unseen stimulus while his visible network glimmered, as though he could read my thoughts on a feed. He smiled and put his arm around my shoulders.

"Let's talk outside," he said.

The sky was still clear and settling into one of the long, bleeding sunsets that blessed a handful of the waning days of the tears. We went into an eating hall— or perhaps it was just the parlor of a friend of his—a cozy burrow under the hill at the edge of the Red River. The view was westward, fantastic. The food was a strange mix of cultures: that Miuri butter-spice cacao, shortbread cookies, southern Awilu lamb curry bathed in red and black pepper but not a hint of chile, accompanied by sour maize cakes. I ate it all wholeheartedly; my hangover had abated, and I felt strength and renewed purpose in finally acting on my decision to do what I could. *If there is something you should do, better to know than to hide from self-knowledge*, my pious octopus had scolded me, and now I could only laugh.

Vaterite set down his mug thoughtfully. "You seem different."

"I haven't given up being a novice," I told him, through the last mouthful of curry-soaked bread, "but I'm not willing to sacrifice what's right to be one."

He considered that. "They'll kick you out if you give them half a reason."

My stomach twisted. "I know."

"I see. But you won't go willingly." He shook his head. "Freida of the Library."

"Don't say you're proud of me!"

"I wouldn't dare. What does Nadi say?"

I kept my eyes on a knot in the wood of the rustic table. "Nothing. To ask you . . ."

He waited.

"How can I get into Huehue?"

When I dared to look back up again, his eyes were distant, his face faintly glowing. "Old Child Freehold. It's still there. The librarians tried to build over it, but the earth is so haunted only poisonous fruit will grow. You must have heard of the place—the shift."

I didn't often have reason to visit the territory of the solitary poetics scholars, but that piece of it was well-known for late-night dares and the occasional tour for wide-eyed visitors. "*That* was Old Child Freehold?"

"If you want to try, I think it has to be a tunnel contact. No one has the heart shard but Nadi, and I'm sure ze can't give it to you. We can set up a relay, Tiger Freehold and whichever others want to join us. We can at least wake zir up and make sure ze notices you when you go in."

My heart started to pound. I had never done anything like this before. Even my most dangerous forays into the tunnels hadn't required a team of people strapped in with me, risking their own sanity. "But what will ze do to me once ze notices? Blocked avatars don't react well to tunnel contact." Considering the number of librarians who had died trying, that was putting it mildly.

"You were born for this, Freida. No one can do it but you."

I frowned. "I know that! How could I avoid it? Look at what's happened when I've tried to be a normal girl!" I was halfway out of my seat, shouting. Vaterite looked at me as though I were a talking sloth. I subsided, shaking with latent embarrassment. "Sorry. It's been . . . hard."

I suppose I wanted him to comfort me, but he regarded me with an expression at once remote and sorrowful.

"I should show you something first. I'm not sure what it is. But that ephemeral avatar passed it through the query chain a few hours ago."

"The same one? Is ze concatenating?" The chance of any ephemeral avatar crystalizing into a new one was low, but it happened—that was how the gods created new avatars for themselves over time.

"Ze's certainly more stable than I expected. Too soon to be sure, though. Here." With a flick of his fingers, he lobbed an invisible coin to my side of the table. He and Joshua had that in common, I thought—they'd come into their wetware late enough that they used it with physical gestures.

What he had tossed me was another image. A low-weight holo, jagged around the edges from temporal degradation. That meant no one had accessed it in at least a few hundred years.

Nevertheless, the person in the holo was me. Not the same hollow-cheeked, angry-eyed me as in the last picture. This me had hair cut short like mine, but I—she?—wore the strangest uniform of light blue pants and a tight-fitting jacket that denoted no position I knew of in the Library.

She—I?—looked around as though to make sure she was alone. Then she started to speak. "I'm the last of our generation. Xochi's refused. She's gone back to Iemaja. The fuckers tried to make me find her, but I pretended to get lost.

They're going to make me go, and I'm not as brave as Xochi, so I suppose that I will. I won't succeed. Sister, future sister, if you see this, remember that I existed. Bathsheba, the Twenty-First Girl By the River, who would kill—"

It cut off, dissolved into entropy. *Bathsheba, the Twenty-First Girl By the River, who would kill—*

Who would she kill?

I hadn't understood, before. I had thought the ephemeral was making some commentary on my personality or my conduct. But just like the picture, ze hadn't created this holo from scratch.

Ze had *recognized* me.

Because I had sisters—apparently, at least twenty-one of them—and they had looked just like me.

⁜

Old Coyote was the venerable bastard of the Library gods, surly and unresponsive to most requests without a good deal of theater: three-day prayers with ritual fasting, sacrifices hurled inside that giant maw of a crack that ran the length of his temple floor, communions that risked blood and death in exchange for a few sleepy sentences. Only Cube and Cardinal librarians were allowed tunnel contact with most of Old Coyote's avatars.

Freeholders, of course, weren't allowed anywhere near him. Tonight, we were risking a formal sanction, or worse. We arrived in twos and threes at the overgrown border of the shift. The ruins themselves were strange, jarringly out of tune with the otherwise perfect organic harmony of Library City. Perhaps that was why mostly visitors and newcomers sought them out—you had to want to go; otherwise, the Library itself seemed to steer you away, a hand unconsciously avoiding a wound.

At least this wound, unlike many others, had a great gash in the earth to attest to its existence. After Vaterite whispered a prayer and hacked his way through the tough outer layer of poison fruit bramble, we padded silently through bone-white halls lit softly by the fish moon rising, though the thorn had long since set. The shift opened at the end of a leaf-strewn colonnade, between one pillar and the ghost of the next. Aragonite stumbled and would have fallen inside if Vaterite and I hadn't hauled zir back. The gap stretched from our section of the ruined building, deep into the open gardens that must have been in the center and across to the curved portico on the other side. A simple rope bridge swung between the two sides, upon which four freeholders I didn't recognize were slowly making their way toward us. Behind us, we heard more voices and the sharp crack of machetes cutting back tangled branches.

"That's Hannah and Rin from Ibbur Freehold," Aragonite said as the figures came closer over the swinging bridge of translucent polymer planks. "I think the ones behind them are from Many Worlds—we should have enough for the square, at least."

Sixteen divers made a square for the linked query networks. I felt a breathless jolt of terror. Sixteen people had decided to risk their lives to help me.

Vaterite pulled down his backpack, where it bobbed in the air for an unsure moment before he unclipped the weight belt. It fell with an audible *thunk*. The other freeholders had made it across by now, and without more than a murmured greeting they helped him to take out the trembling rolls of mature branch worm, a more warmth-adapted variety than that used in the hub.

"I volunteer for the inner ring," Vaterite said.

One of the freeholders from Many Worlds, short and very colorfully dressed in whimsical broonie-make, gave me a suspicious look. "She's very young."

"She's Iemaja's daughter," Vaterite said, with all the serenity of an ancient disciple. If I hadn't been so afraid, I would have laughed; he certainly never treated me with such reverence when we were alone.

"Have you ever queried Old Coyote before?" This was a newcomer from a group of five that had entered behind us. "Or any level-four avatar?"

One of the Many Worlds freeholders tutted. "There's no intrinsic level to the avatars. Those are just librarian constructs."

I forced my back straight and swept my gaze across the gathered group of twenty or so freeholders. "I've been wandering the tunnels since I was four," I said. "I've communed with dozens of avatars in each material. I've done most of this alone, because no one would teach me. I've never been to Huehue, obviously, but I have the best chance. No matter what, I'll do what I can to release you from the network if things go wrong."

The multicolored one with the incongruously severe expression studied me even more carefully. "There's stories about you. The avatars talk. And now I believe them. You'll commune?"

"If I can find zir shard."

Ze nodded slowly. "Ah, ingestion, then. It's the most reliable method in edge cases. I approve."

I didn't bother telling zir that I didn't have any choice in the matter—I didn't have the wetware to enter via network.

"I, too, volunteer for the inner ring," ze said, stepping beside Vaterite.

Aragonite and one of the newcomers—not the one who had spoken—stepped up to complete the quartet. That having been established, the others organized themselves into the four support filaments that would help anchor the inner ring and attempt to prevent any unexpected crashes. I would be lightly connected to one of these filaments with the branch worm—at least until its physical length ran out. The shift was deep, but even in the low moonlight, not quite black. Strange lights, like sparks thrown off a bonfire, flickered and briefly illuminated sheer planes of glossy red rock as I stared down.

Our plan was straightforward. First, the query network would use the combined force of their human consciousness to rouse the avatar. I would stay connected to let Huehue know I was coming. After the branch worm ran out, connection was up to me. It was risky. What had happened with Leguá was the least of our worries. For all we knew, Huehue wasn't even asleep so much as trapped in an endless loop of torment, blocked off from the rest of zir material consciousness in an effort to protect it from unbearable pain.

Unbearable pain for a god—none of us could quite imagine what that would do to a human, but death certainly seemed like a possibility. We agreed to break the network if someone in the inner ring was seriously injured. If someone fell out of a filament, they could be replaced. If we needed medical help, we'd do our best to leave the shift first. Only as a last resort would we call official Library attention to what we were doing here. Leaving behind some kind of evidence was inevitable, but we wouldn't give away more than we had to.

I sat beside Vaterite on the rope bridge, the chasm opening beneath our legs like an embrace. Nadi and Atempa and—was that wanly peeping thing Quinn?—had left their avatars outside my thresholds, but I raised them and lowered volume of my wetware until even the gentle background hum of my augmented space fell silent. It was only me here, now, alone above a gash in the earth. The branch worm was rapidly colonizing, stretching its tacky yellow pseudopods across the spaces between the four members of the inner ring. The glowing network around Vaterite's eye was now completely covered by translucent branch worm. I took a deep breath, filling my lungs with the chill air of the late tears, the must of fallen leaves and abandoned buildings and the deep, metallic cold of the hole beneath us. The fish moon's nearly full light illuminated my skin so that it was at once dark and glowing, like the diffuse edge of a star. This was right. Even through my fear, I knew that. This was what I had been born to do.

Me, and my sisters.

I still didn't know what to think about that. I had sent the holo along to Nadi just before we left Tiger Freehold. I had known all my life that I was created. But it is different to know that you were made in a mold, with twenty-one of you living and loving and dying before you were ever born.

Beneath our feet, sparks flared orange and gold, then faded. Like the bonfire in the caves, before the military scholars burned the grubs. I remembered the aerial dancers, clad in quicksilver, their voices raised in that ancient mournful chorus:

> *Oh, Aurochs, angry traveler*
> *Tell us why our mother*
> *The Baobab cried.*

The answer I sang to myself as the freeholders finished their preparations: "For the cicada singing in the earth. Left too late, left behind, by sisters and siblings."

Vaterite turned to me—with some difficulty, since the branch worm had stiffened its grip on his head. "Do you think the Nameren has something to do with this?" he asked.

"For the Awilu, the Nameren has something to do with everything."

The other three members of the inner ring began to chant: "For the cicada singing in the earth, the baobab cries. For the cicada in the light, she cries."

I jumped and stared.

"The branch worm," Aragonite explained apologetically, "it amplifies and focuses extrasensory collaboration."

Someone passed up a thick roll of unused branch worm in Vaterite's backpack with the weight belt attached. I strapped it on and adjusted the settings until I began to bobble slightly on the suspension bridge. Someone else tied an old-fashioned rope to the center of the bridge. It wouldn't come close to reaching down the crater, but the idea was that between the belt, the rope, and the branch worm, I'd be able to climb back out once I finished.

With my wetware dialed down so low, I felt the branch worm's connection only as a shadowy presence behind my thoughts. That presence intensified as the rest of the network snapped into place. The branch worms glowed like lightning trapped in low storm clouds as they worked, but I was more aware of the gentle sounds around us: the wind rustling the dead leaves in the portico, an owl hooting in the tangled branches just beyond the dark, the crickets all singing with their sisters. The hole in the ground gave no sound at all, just a tremendous space where sound ought to be, as though it were pulling me, begging me to fill it with words.

I jerked myself back. *Is that you, Huehue?*

The serious freeholder from Many Worlds let out a small moan. Tears wet Aragonite's cheeks. Vaterite grabbed my hand.

"I think . . . we're in," he said slowly, as if in pain. "Ze senses you. Go. We can't hold . . . not long."

I took one last look at the moon-bright sky and prayed to Iemaja to guide me. The branch worm pulsed at that, and a wave of pain cracked open my chest like a pomegranate. I gasped. The wave receded. I didn't have much time.

I pushed myself off the bridge, and plummeted.

Darkness swallowed me, and for a moment of near-complete sensory deprivation, I wasn't sure if I were falling down, up, or floating in a cold breeze. Then a light sparked and faded, enough to show that there was a floor to this chasm, and I was approaching it at a speed that would quite likely kill me.

Huehue, I thought, *let me in*.

Another pair of lights sparked and fell. A hole had opened up on the floor right beneath me. I fell through as the branch worm snapped.

The earth closed above me like a fist.

✦

I would not be telling you this story, Nameren, if I had not managed to stop my fall, but it was a very near thing. The snapped end of the branch worm—my savior—trembled in my hand as its skin began to crack and peel in the heat. The heat? I looked down and cursed all the gods, material and divine: I clung to a rock face above a lake of fire. Goddamn Old Bastard, what right did he have growing into Mahue'e like this?

The lake was too bright to look at, so hot it burned the soles of my feet in their supple climbing sandals. There were birds here, fantastical crystalline creatures that jolted me, because they were secondary AIs just like me, but terrifyingly inorganic. *So much for pretending you were simply human, Freida.* Their feathers glinted in all the multicolored hues of the avatars of all four materials, jumbled together as though the distinctions we librarians so carefully maintained meant nothing to them. The birds themselves had the long, hooked beak of Tenehet's ibis, but the flaming plumed tail of Mahue'e's Quetzalcoat.

"Huehue!" I called, pulling fresh branch worm from my backpack and setting the jagged edge to the rock face where it could attach. "Huehue, I only want to talk!"

The birds sang back with voices of pentatonic flutes. The powerful flaps of their wings buffeted me with hot air that stank of burning algae. They flew so perilously close that their feathers sliced my skin, dozens of shallow cuts beading the surface of my exposed arms and legs with blood. I didn't mind if they cut my flesh, but I was terrified every time they flew close to the branch worm. Something itched in my throat, a noise between a song in harmony with their impossible avian chorus and a scream.

I wrapped the other end of the branch worm around my waist before settling its seeking tendrils on the base of my skull. I couldn't see anything resembling a heart crystal from up here and I needed to make contact. I felt the square network first, though faintly, wading through painful waves of distortion and feedback in an effort to rouse the avatar. It wouldn't work—I could feel that, too.

Huehue needed something more.

Carefully, I shifted to my left in order to gain a marginally better purchase on the rock. My fingers and toes ached. They wouldn't be able to support me for much longer. The weight belt still wasn't much help. Whatever had pulled me so quickly through the hole in the chasm still had its hold on me. I hoped, for the sake of my own survival, that Mahue'e had not grown so deeply into Huehue that ze wanted to burn me to death. I lowered my thresholds slightly, to see what the connection might let through.

What? Whywhywhy? My friends, my friends, the light in their eyes then the dark in their eyes then the pain the pain, is that what this is? Is this real? Am I real? What is pain? What is me? What are you, river girl? What do you call Huehue?

The birds were screaming now, all around, too close, filleting my skin. The fire lake burbled and groaned.

I fell.

The branch worm around my middle pulled me up short before I plunged into the fire. This close, the heat seared my exposed skin. The branch worm's membrane bubbled, filled with a clear, shining fluid.

My head rang like a clapped bell with Huehue's painful babble and the counterpoint of the bird chorus. I couldn't find room to think, but fear focused my instinct for survival.

I kicked out, trying to gain enough momentum to swing myself back onto the rock face. The branch worm stretched, bit deep into my stomach and hips, but it held. The birds sang in a ragged syncopated rhythm and followed the path of my widening parabola. Almost there. That last swing, I had almost touched it.

Huehue, I managed, a gasping half thought, *that happened long ago. Old Child, time has passed. I don't want to die.*

The branch worm glittered and then glowed with such spontaneous brightness that, for a moment, it rivaled even the lake below. Then instinct came to me, and I obeyed it, unquestioningly.

I sang out when I had reached the peak of my parabola, adding a tonic to the birds' cutting din so that it sounded, suddenly, like the bottom movement of one of Nadi's favorite woodwind suites. As one, the birds lifted their great wings and flew upward. The gust produced by their synchronized wingbeats pushed me the rest of the way to the rock wall. I gripped the slick stones with my gloved hands and planted my feet hard onto a narrow ledge that protruded a few feet from the stone. I told myself to breathe. After a few more airless seconds, I did.

It took another several minutes for me to calm my mind enough to realize that I had to attempt communion right here. There would be tunnels in these cliffs—no matter what else Huehue was, ze was an avatar of a Library material god. But without zir help, I couldn't find them. I shut my eyes against a deep, unexpected pain. The branch worm surged with light, and I felt Huehue again, not with language this time but in a sudden clarity of compassion. Tears burned my cheeks where the heat of the fire had seared them.

They're all gone. Long ago, you said.

I know.

Why are you here? Who are the others beating at my walls?

Cut them loose. I have a question I need to ask.

The thin tether to the square cut out abruptly. I breathed in relief. We wouldn't all die here. Ze was silent for a while, communicating—if it could be called that—in more waves of confusion and fear and pain that left me trembling. My body wouldn't survive much more of this.

I need to find a tunnel first, I sent. *A place to rest.*

No sign ze had heard. I began to sob again with zir radiated pain. I had dialed my thresholds all the way up, but it didn't seem to matter, and I didn't dare disconnect the poor, valiant branch worm.

The branch worm! On a wild hunch, I gathered up what little slack I still had after that fall and swung it as hard as I could against the cliff face. It stuck immediately, little tendrils reaching, colonizing the surface of what must be material crystal, though I'd never seen anything like that inky, ruby-striated rock.

Little by little, pausing each time Huehue's pain grew too much for me, I climbed back up the cliff, away from the searing heat of lava below. I was lucky—the branch worm itself found a tunnel entrance for me. Its yellow tendrils had reached all the way around the opening by the time I arrived, as though it wanted to make sure I saw.

I sobbed in relief when I hauled myself into the opening, narrow as it was. I would have to lie flat and shimmy my way through, but it was a tunnel, and I knew the gods and their arteries.

Lying in the mouth of that opening, arms splayed, face coated with a slurry of ash and sweat and tears and salt, I heard the birds rise again.

You're still here?

No thanks to you.

Come inside, then.

One of the birds broke from the flock and came toward me in a disconcerting burst of speed. The wind passing through its crystal wings sang a rippling harmony in a minor key. I had time to gape and wonder what it meant to do before it thrust its long ibis beak like an arrow straight through the palm of my left hand. I screamed. The bird, so close to me now that I could see the painful bloodshot organic reality of its small eyes, closed them and fell backward. Its beak stayed in my palm. The rest of it dropped, without a ripple, into the fire lake below.

The pain from my hand was totalizing, consuming all my attention for a period of time that felt like hours, days, but was probably minutes. My creaky wetware kicked in eventually and dialed down the pain. I didn't have much control over this, but there were emergency systems.

What the hell? I sent, when I could manage directed thought.

My heart.

Oh. Carefully, I lifted my left hand with my right and examined what ze had left me. The beak of the ibis was made of crystal, red and black like the rock face but more translucent. It seemed to glow from within.

I closed my eyes for a second and laughed. I couldn't help it. "Be careful what you wish for," I said. Nadi had taught me that one. But did I ever listen? Would I ever see zir again? Would this be okay?

No way to know unless I tried. With as much stoicism as I could manage, I took one end of the beak in my good hand and pulled. It wasn't quite so bad this time. The opiates had kicked in. I smashed the bloody shard on the floor to get a piece small enough for ingestion. There. I regarded it critically.

What kind of Old Coyote would I meet here? Which aspect of him was I going to awaken when I swallowed a part of him that he had very clearly meant to forget?

I placed the sliver of the beak that an ibis had died to give me on my tongue, where it mingled with the metallic salt of my own blood, and I swallowed.

I dropped into communion like a sharp stone in a still pool. I landed in a desert on my side, and my skin burned against the sand. The grains were a rainbow of reds and blues and butter yellows, and they stretched into low dunes that surrounded the shallow depression where I found myself. Like the desert that surrounds the Library, painted in all the hues of its buried gods. In the sky, eight suns blinked their burning eyes and trained their gazes upon me. My skin sizzled and I cried out.

My cry rose in a cloud to the eight suns, the eight eyes. It filmed their vision cataract white. The heat diffused, becoming muggy and just bearable. But my palm still burned. I looked down at my left hand and saw a large crystal beak of Nyad blue had pierced it from one side to the other. Here in this altered space, every nerve sparked with some kind of holy fire.

"Huehue?" I called. I lifted my hand. The blood dripped to the sand and tiny snakes wriggled up from the stains, striped red and blue and black. The beak glowed and shook like jelly. "I'm here, Huehue."

One of the eye-suns swiveled wildly. It burned through the mist and rained a teardrop of fire upon one of the dunes to my right. Smoke and the sick stench of burning flesh rose into the sky and traced dark paths in the firmament.

Where the fire had landed, a child now stood: a child of mist, but with skin as dark as mine. I looked up at zir, and ze looked back down at me. Zir eyes were large as the moon, the color of the night sky just before a rain. Ze smiled at me, full lips around a mouth as empty as deep space.

"Are you Huehue?" I asked.

"I'm the child that time forgot," ze said. Though ze was several meters away, zir voice was a wet whisper in my eardrum.

"I'm Iemaja's daughter," I said.

"That too," ze said.

"Where are we?" I asked.

"When they haven't burned yet."

I looked around the desert again, wondering if this was how the Library had looked in the first days after founding, or if this was an extension of zir metaphorical construct. In the distance, faintly, I heard the wind like a moan.

I had spent hours with Vaterite and the others, discussing what questions I might ask Huehue. Present judge had specified that they needed direct evidence of why the founders had conceded autonomy to the descendants of the children of the lost tenth. Who were they? Why did they return to Tierra? What was their connection with the Miuri?

Instead, I heard myself asking, "Why did the librarians burn them?"

"Why do the librarians do anything?"

"Peace?" I said.

Ze laughed.

"Knowledge?" I tried.

"Knowing," ze said. "And unknowing."

I thought about this. There are many ways to tell a story. *There are no good sides to a war*, Nadi had told me once, *just more and less evil*. I thought about what that meant for Seremarú. Ey would have ordered the freehold burned. Knowing and unknowing. I had always seen that, hadn't I? We guarded knowledge and we guarded peace, and sometimes—often—we had to choose between them.

"What did you know?" I asked.

More tiny snakes surged from the sand at my feet, hissing and biting one another.

"The seabird says to let you through," said the child with eyes as old as starlight. "But I don't remember what's on the other side."

"Was it about the lost tenth? What happened to them?"

"They were found."

"Who found them?"

"The first conquerors."

I frowned. "The Mahām?"

The child began to shake and sat down upon the dune. The sand at zir feet hissed and popped like dry maize and began to glow.

"No," ze said, pounding zir fists into the crackling sand. "No, no, no. The *first*. The ones who made my father. The ones who force us to remember. Remember and remember and remember—"

Ze looked up, met my eyes, and *reached*. Zir hands did not so much stretch as exist, impossibly, between zir body on the dune and my temples meters below. Zir fingers were dry and scratchy with sand; they smelled of tunnel dust, which somehow smelled of light spilling over my shoulders, pooling at my feet.

"Remember and *make*, Iemaja's daughter," ze hissed. "You should know. The old man made you, too."

The child stood in front of me; the child watched me from atop the dune. Now seven eyes blinked heavily in the sky and illuminated my cosmic insignificance. But they were all aware of me.

"I am Iemaja's daughter," I repeated, slowly. I did not want to understand the child. "Nadi found me in Iemaja."

The child began to wail. The empty mouth opened and the dark inside unfurled tiny tendrils, feeling their way toward the light. I knew, in this most dangerous communion of my life, that I did not want that darkness to find its full shape.

I bent down and embraced the child by the shoulders. "Don't cry, Huehue child," I whispered. "Please don't cry."

"You are my sister," ze sobbed. "You are my child. You ask for me and then you reject me. You were made and now you ask me to make. You have been remembered over and over again and now you ask me to remember just what they made me forget."

Ze cried, but the heat of the suns, which had drawn in to listen more closely, evaporated each tear before it fell to the sand.

"Who made you forget?"

"I told you!" the child screamed. "The first! The conquerors! The creators! The makers—"

"The *Awilu?*"

"Of course."

"What did they make you forget?"

"I'm not allowed to remember!"

"But it has to do with the Treaty and the lost tenth," I said, sure now. "With what happened to the lost tenth after the Awilu found them."

The child was sinking into the sand. I felt myself languorous, floating. I could hardly move my limbs. I cursed and pushed the ibis's beak deeper into my palm. I needed more time in the communion. I couldn't come out without a better answer. The pain rooted me again, and gave me the strength to haul zir up by zir elbows. The blood streamed down my arm now, and the hundred snakes that grew from its haphazard spray bit my ankles and filled me with a heady poison.

The child's head lolled against my bloody arm. The sand pulled us both down and I struggled against it.

"What can't you remember?" I pressed.

"All of it . . . it hurts too much, sister. Don't make me, don't make me—not after so much time."

"But what happened to the lost tenth?"

One of the snakes wriggled up to zir shoulder. The child bit its head off and laughed. The darkness peeked out from zir mouth, and the suns flinched and shied away.

"They were killed," said the child. "The other ones found them."

"The other ones . . ."

"The ones led by my father, the ones who have care of the Nameren."

"The Mahām," I breathed. The sand sucked and slurped beneath us; I flailed against it. Now only the torso of the child remained visible. I had sunk to my knees. Ze did not seem to care. "The Mahām killed them?"

Ze shook zir head and cried. I tried to wipe zir tears, but my hands were weak again and the tears burned right through. "Who killed them?"

But ze wouldn't say. Guilt and shame rolled off zir in waves, but I knew how to stand up beneath that. I had experience. I tried another tack.

"And the survivors? There were survivors, right? Children."

The child's tears stopped. The curling fingers of darkness froze at the edges of zir mouth. Ze looked up at me, glowing with sand-light and the burning reflection of the seven watching suns and wonder.

"The children," ze said. "Oh, how could I forget, sweet sister? The children lived. They went to Tierra and hid themselves in the drowning city and the hills, but they lived—they lived."

The sand gurgled and moaned. I kicked against it, threw my arms over the edge of stable ground, and screamed as the beak shard twisted in my hand. The child gripped my waist.

"Why?" ze cried, over and over. "Whywhywhywhy—"

My strength ebbed out again like a tide, like fading sunlight. I could feel the radiant heat of the cliff face, the slow drip of acid sweat down my hairline. But

I needed just a little longer. "Huehue child, please, I need to know more about the Treaty. Why did the Mahām and Lunars get so much after what they'd done? Who tried to make sure the Nawas and Miuri were protected in the Freedom node? Open yourself, just a little. Let me run the queries—let me in."

The child snarled and howled at the suns. "Are you there, Iemaja? Do you see how your daughter bargains and schemes?" The smallest of the seven blinked, and heat buffeted my face. Ze tugged down my hips and my arms, but the shard had rooted my hand to the edge, and I could not be pulled further. So ze climbed my limbs as a rope and smashed zir hand over the shard. Zir blood pooled with mine and then everything was fire and pain and impossible darkness. But no— the darkness *was* possible—it rose inside me to meet the darkness inside zir—it had always, always been there.

"Here is how you get in." The child had become an elder, or had always had an elder sitting just behind zir. "Here is how to find what you want to know."

The sand was pulling me down. The pressure was slowly ripping my hand in two. Soon I would be gone.

"How? Materials, how?"

Ze put zir sweet child face against my cheek. The elder picked up Iemaja's shard and ripped.

"Tell us," they said, "what even the ones who burned couldn't tell us. *Why would they do such a thing?*"

I fell out of communion. I woke, splayed upon a rock, my left hand in pieces, alone.

✦

The freeholders found me the next morning at the nearest grub tunnel entrance to the shift. I was delirious, feverish, my hand a mangled ruin. Still, I gripped the shard the ibis had given me, and would not let it go until Vaterite promised he would keep it safe until I could come for it again. They had a rover with them and took that to the nearest medic station. They said they'd found me wandering. They would be questioned, and the news would reach Quinn. The medics sedated me. I awoke some misty time later, on ivory linen sheets in a single bed in the temple precinct infirmary. My left hand was wrapped in a translucent membrane the texture of a grub pupa, and though I could feel nothing more than a tickling pressure, there came from it the faint slurping sounds of something feeding. I searched myself for alarm but could find none.

It was as if no time had passed at all: *Why would they do such a thing?*

Knowing and unknowing, the Huehue child had said. Was it as simple as that? But then why would ze have asked? Ze had been speaking Library Standard—or at least that was how I'd understood zir. No matter how I parsed it, that *they* was deliberately ambiguous, with no obvious antecedent. They, the Mahām, who had somehow destroyed the tenth expedition? They, the Awilu, who had found them and, it followed, hidden what had happened? They, the drafters of the Treaty, who had put in provisions clearly meant to redress a great wrong, and then allowed those same provisions to fade into legal obscurity?

A medic came into the room and explained that while my hand was in bad shape, they'd be able to reconstruct it with bio-intelligent materials.

"I'm getting a broonie hand?" I joked. They'd given me relaxation drugs, I think.

Ze smiled encouragingly. "You can think of it like that. It's very low-order intelligence—nothing that will interfere with your wetware. I'll let you rest, but you have a visitor, if you'd like."

I said yes, of course.

Nadi had always been small, but now ze was hollowed out, gaunt. Zir close-cropped hair had gone almost entirely silver. But zir eyes were wide and lively and as filled with love as ever.

I started crying. I couldn't even speak.

"Oh, love, Freida," ze said. For a while, ze just held me. There is a profound relief in crying like a child, Nameren. I hadn't let myself do it for so long. I had always thought I'd break apart if I surrendered. It must have been the drugs, or my hand, or everything that had happened between us.

"Did you know about my sisters?" I asked.

I couldn't see zir face, but zir arms tightened briefly around my shoulders. Ze released me and sat back.

"I . . . suspected," ze said. A pause. "You never got through the whole Ge Namirtae, did you?"

I played along. "It's hard to keep my attention through thousand-page song cycles. I know the big beats."

"You won't know this story, then. It's from the apocrypha. A side story of the village where Namirta sleeps the night before ze travels to the underworld. The village has a glorious history. It was the home of Atriman, demon-slayer—"

"Namirta and Atriman? Is that supposed to be a coincidence?"

"Hush, child—of course not! As I was saying, Atriman had personally annihilated seven separate avatars of the Nameren and ushered in the thousand years of prosperity that had come to an end the morning before Namirta was birthed in a snail."

I gave a mock sigh and snuggled closer to the warm crease of zir shoulder. You know what those old stories are like, Nameren—great heroes slaying your innumerable evil avatars, though of course you're never actually dead. Nadi loved to tell them. In zir defense, you really are the subject of almost every traditional story. But then—you will know this, Nameren—ze had always had other reasons.

"Atriman was born in a small fishing village and grew adored and loved by zir only parent. An itinerant oracle gave the parent a revelation as to the parent's past, a previous incarnation in which ze had taken on the support of Valaver, one of the Nameren's bloodiest avatars, and conquered the entire peninsula in zir name. In those days, you'll remember from the Ge Namirtae, the favor of an avatar of the Nameren gave zir chosen one the powers of a demigod. The story of Per Baq Mir, the previous bloody incarnation of Atriman's loving parent, isn't mine to tell, though a few have done their best over the millennia, but it is relevant to note that Atriman and zir parent lived in the lands that Per Baq Mir had conquered, and the scars of that conquest still marked the earth. When zir parent realized what ze had done in a past life, ze was filled with shame and confusion. Ze went on a pilgrimage to Binebtat, which no longer exists, but housed at that time a great shrine to an avatar complex."

"All for the Nameren?" I asked.

"There was only one god at the time, love. Just listen. So Atriman's parent, with young Atriman by zir side, went to this great shrine and prayed for guidance. For forty days and forty nights ze prayed, until zir knees grew bruised from kneeling and zir eyes inflamed from tears. Atriman stayed loyally by zir side, cleaning zir soiled clothes, keeping away the small animals, and bringing what little food zir parent would eat. The clerics were alarmed and discussed having the pious vagrant removed. But on the fortieth night, it began to rain. The rain was out of season and relentless. It quickly flooded the poor shrine and threatened to ruin the centuries-old relics. As the clerics waded through waist-high waters, Atriman begged zir parent to leave zir vigil and escape to higher ground. Zir parent refused, or perhaps didn't even hear zir, ze was so lost in meditation. Suddenly, a light rose from the floor and filled Atriman's parent from every orifice. Ze had a visitation, which was a form of communion back then, from an unknown avatar of the god. The unknown avatar told Atriman's parent that in order to atone for the sins of zir past incarnation, ze could sacrifice zir child. There was no reason given, only that the avatar demanded it as proof of loyalty. In return, the avatar would turn against the army of Valaver's chosen and spare the peninsula the deaths that were sure to come in the next invasion. Atriman's parent, wretched with pious ecstasy, grabbed the child, sobbing, and pushed zir under the rapidly rising water. Atriman, drowning, caught a bit of the light suffusing zir parent. The avatar spoke to zir.

"'Will you sacrifice yourself for me?' ze asked Atriman.

"Atriman said, 'I will not, no matter how I love my parent, for I am young and you are old as the stars.'

"The avatar, with the laughing face of an ancient, grabbed hold of the child and said, 'But the stars are made of light, and light is always new.'

"Atriman understood this to mean that ze was saved and so climbed the back of zir beloved parent in order to rise above the water and breathe. Zir young feet broke zir beloved parent's neck beneath the water. Then, alone, ze was carried by the current to the dry land of a nearby hill." Nadi paused while I stared at zir, horrified. "Well, and so begins Atriman's story. It's an epic in itself, I can't tell it all here. But you might be interested in knowing that the strange avatar Atriman found who we call Old Child in the earliest stories."

I froze, but my left hand twitched in its membrane sheath. Nadi very carefully did not look at me. *That* was the birth of Old Coyote? I often forgot that every material god but Iemaja had once been divided among the traditional thirds of the Awilu, before the contact era and the Awilu's gift of material gods to each of the three systems. Those old stories Nadi loved hid more than I realized.

"Why did you go, Freida?" Zir voice was soft, but I heard the grief there.

"Do you want to sacrifice me, Nadi? Is that what this is about?"

Now ze laughed. "So you know if you must snap my neck while you climb my back? No need, my love."

My pulse pounded, and the faint slurping noise coming from the membrane grew louder. I shuddered. "It was the right thing to do," I said.

"Even if you die?"

"Maybe it's like you said: If my death can save thousands, killing myself is the moral choice."

"As simple as that?"

I shook my head, but I didn't know if that was a negation of zir or of myself. I was thinking of a drop when I was thirteen; I was thinking of that slow sick, of losing control of my body, my thoughts in a space that should have been safe to me. His hands above me, so detailed I could see the fine hair on the backs of his wrists. An expensive program, the best for his beautiful girl. He had known something was wrong with me. Hadn't the rest of my life just proved him right?

"I need to be good."

Nadi adjusted zir arms carefully, so carefully around my shoulders.

"And aren't you, my love?"

But I knew—ze had always lied to me, too.

The membrane on my hand grew smaller and tighter; it still slurped. A broonie hand. Would it give me the superpowers of a demigod, like in the old Awilu stories? Surely, I was the beloved of an avatar? I felt, unfortunately, stubbornly mundane.

Nadi went back to zir secret negotiations, which seemed to be going very badly, though of course no one told me anything. They would have to announce their agreement soon—a delayed date, concessions, something. I wondered how the Library scholars would take it. The crisis of this War Ritual had exposed all the smoldering conflicts of the three systems, like a pile of kindling waiting for a spark. And now I was uncovering centuries-old secrets. What would that do to the fire when we exposed them? I was living in a thicket of moral dilemmas, and no one could lead me out. Nadi certainly couldn't; I understood that now.

On the third day, I sent my avatar to Joshua. He deserved to know, and I couldn't always hide from my shame at what I had done to him. The least I could do now was try to be good, or at least better. The little octopus swam hopefully before his thresholds for a few hours before he cracked them open. Lag between the Library and Tierra made it difficult for our avatars to have a direct conversation, but I left him a message:

"I'm halfway into Huehue," it said. "The tenth expedition survived their journey. The Mahām discovered them, alive. Then they were destroyed, I'm still not sure how. Not many people must have known about it, though, for it to have been kept so secret. The children who survived were fostered on Tierra among your people. Will this help you? Should I ask zir something else?"

His tinsel skeleton unfolded, head cocked in puzzlement and surprise.

"Are you hurt?" it asked in a flat Nawas that contained, nonetheless, the distant echo of that warmth, the heat of another sun. I wondered where he was right now.

"No more than necessary," said the octopus sadly.

The skeleton took a pair of petals from its jaw and fashioned them into a flower for the octopus. The octopus glowed orange to match the flower and burbled with pleasure. Then the skeleton waved goodbye, and I lost contact with my octopus.

While I was waiting on his reply, Atempa came into the infirmary garden. She had visited me for the past two days, though I knew she had module work and desk duty. We wasted hours in the garden before the rains came in, telling dirty jokes and playing drawn-out games of three-board system that always ended in draws with half the universe swallowed by materials and the other half on networks of satellites that could only communicate through dense jungles of language diversity.

Nergüi didn't visit me, though she did send me a message: "I heard you're in the infirmary. Are you maimed or dying?"

"Nearly!" I replied.

And then Nergüi's avatar, a smiling little ball of blue light who could not have been more hilariously inappropriate, bobbled up and swam forward to kiss my forehead.

"Well, that's fine, then," came Nergüi's deadpan voice from the avatar's joyous mouth.

When I showed Atempa the message, she burst out laughing.

"Warming back up to you, is she?" she said.

I rolled my eyes. "Like a stone warms up in a fire." But I felt a soft happiness, an easing, where my stomach met my breastbone. On the game board, inspired, I pushed my material to close its tesseract.

Atempa smacked her thigh. "Bold! Forcing me to the negotiating table? Are you so sure you'll come out ahead?"

"My diplomats have more persuasion points than yours."

"True, true," Atempa said. "But you forget I have the Lunars in my alliance, so there's always treachery."

An icy wind blew through the garden, splattering us with rain. Atempa shut down the game and helped me move my apparatus. My hand was lifted by a weight belt but still bulky and unwieldy, faintly nauseating to look at for very long. We sheltered on a heated bench under the deep eaves of the portico and stared out at the waves of driving rain in companionable silence. I was feeling tired again, but I didn't want to sleep.

"Do you remember how we became friends?" Atempa asked.

I gave her a startled glance, but she doggedly kept watching the rain.

I remembered.

"We'd been in the same modules for two years, and one day you sat next to me and said, 'I'm Atempa; my father thinks I want to be like him, but I won't. So I think we should be friends after all.' I nearly fainted! Atempa Shipbuilder herself, deciding to be friends with the secondary AI no one knew what to do with. How old were we? Ten and twelve?"

She still wouldn't look at me. "Why did you agree? I'd ignored you for years. And then I tried to order you to be my friend! I can't imagine what you thought."

"I thought, 'Wow, my first friend.'"

She looked incredulous. "You trusted me?"

"I was all trust in those days. Besides, you were honest. To the rest of the class, you pretended that you were better than us because of your father's family. But you told me the truth."

She let out a short, sharp breath. "I saw you leaving a grub tunnel. You came out of the earth like a spirit. I was deep in the Islands, trying to get some broonie clothes like the ones you wore, and there you were. You didn't see me. I knew you'd been in their arteries. I realized that they said those things about you because they were afraid, not because you were bad. Just like my own father was afraid of me sometimes." Her smile became feral. "That's when I decided that I would be a librarian. We'd both give them something to be afraid of."

"Sweet materials, Atempa! Why didn't you ever tell me?"

She drew her knees up to her chest. "I wanted to go with you more than anything, but I was too scared. I didn't want you to offer until I was ready. And then you did offer, and everything went to hell anyway." She sighed. "I was so angry over what you did to Joshua."

"I wish I'd found a better way."

She waved her hand. "Only because it didn't work. Don't deny it—you're brave, Freida, but you're no ancestral saint. You wanted what I want: your own place."

I forced myself to take a deep breath. She was right; no sense in denying it. But I didn't want to be the girl who would make that choice anymore, destroying love for a place that wouldn't even accept her.

She took my good hand and squeezed. "Nothing wrong with that. I'm the last one to judge. Just . . . you don't stand taller when you're kicking someone down. If I'm right about what you were doing when you hurt your hand, then I'm glad. I hope it helps. But there's something you should know."

I looked at her sharply now; she seemed serene, unburdened.

"Joshua's case has done something strange to the negotiations," she continued. "It's shifting the balance of power, and no one knows where things will settle. The courts don't hear this kind of petition often. Joshua and Nergüi have gotten further than anyone expected. The implications, according to His Holiness Shipbuilder, are huge. Not just the War Ritual, you understand? Everyone's watching, especially other groups that have been fighting for centuries, like the Dar. The Mahām, the Lunars, and the Martians are united against it. The Awilu are dividing along the old lines. My father has started moving investments to the Sol system. He's bought *shares* in Lunar development projects on Tierra. I almost knifed him at the table."

She paused for the few tangled seconds it took me to follow her.

"But!" I said.

She shrugged. "It might come to nothing."

"The Library *exists* to stop a second war! No one would let it happen again."

"Nadi wouldn't. But, Freida—"

Oh no, I was sure I didn't want to hear this. I turned away from her, but I was slow and she—my most willful, truest, oldest friend—was determined to warn me.

She put her hand, like a vise, on my shoulder. "Father says it's an open secret now at the negotiations. Ze is dying. Everyone says Quinn will follow. Ze is popular, but never spent enough time building up zir successor, and now it's too late."

I went hot and cold and hot again. One of the apparatuses by my hand chirped like a warbling bird of another season and a flood of enforced serenity knocked me back.

"Should I call a medic?"

"I'm all right."

"I'm sorry."

"Not you who should be sorry." I took a breath. "Quinn threatened zir with it. Revealing that ze was sick. That's why I betrayed Joshua. Ze needed more time in the negotiations. But now it's all gone haywire, hasn't it?"

"I'm not sure. But Father is pleased enough to make me worry."

The rain stopped. The clouds parted like a ripped seam, spilling soft red light. What would I tell Huehue? How could I explain all the evil done in our name? Or did ze already know? Sacrifice your beloved child to save the world. A simple moral choice, utterly amoral. So what would Nadi choose? What would I choose, if it were zir hands around my neck, holding me underwater?

But it didn't feel like zir hands. I was drowning, no denying it, but it was my own weight, shame like an anchor, dragging me fathoms beneath an uncharted sea.

✦

I spent another three days in the infirmary. I kept falling into that ravine every night. I kept sinking in a desert. The Huehue child was there sometimes, asking, *¿Why, why would they do such a thing?* Other times it was just me and the eight

212

burning eyes. The one with the black iris and the gold pupil, the one that glowed faintest from farthest away, squinted at me with sleepy anger. It felt familiar somehow. It felt like my death.

Did I know you even then, Nameren?

Nadi came to visit when the medics freed me from the membrane and presented me with my new, reconstructed hand. It looked like my own, but seamed with strange skin that I could not properly feel. It shone silver when caught in the light.

"Like one of those cracked vases the Dar mend with pewter and gold," I said, opening and closing the new member, delighted and a little sick.

Ze took it up between zir hands, as chilled and ashy as my new hand was warm and glowing. "You'll get used to it."

I smiled at zir and then it wavered, buckled.

Ze held me. I couldn't even cry. It was too big for that.

"Who told you?" ze asked.

I fought to catch my breath. "Atempa."

"Damn Quinn," ze said, after a moment. "Or maybe he kept his word. It's been getting harder to hide."

"How long do you have, Nadi?"

At least ze didn't flinch. "A month, maybe less."

I held myself still, still.

"I swear, love, I tried everything—"

"No." I pulled away from zir, though I didn't want to—I didn't want to leave the circle of zir arms ever again. I stood up. My hand felt light, as though it were newborn, curious about the world, unburdened by guilt or grief or grasping.

"Tell me! Tell me what I am, what you've made me! You weren't surprised at that holo I found. You *knew* I had sisters. You knew that Bathsheba existed and the other she called Xochi and a dozen others born *centuries* ago. So why was I born now? I'm alone, like the cicada. I only have you, and now you're going, too."

Nadi had loved me radically all my life, but that didn't mean I could always tell what ze was thinking. Yet there was none of that politician's calculation in zir face now. Its hard, leathery lines, grown deeper these past few months, conveyed only grief and horror.

"You were created." Zir voice was a painful scrape. "You are the result of a long-running program initiated just after the Great War to generate the Nameren's ideal woman, his dream made flesh, whose sole purpose is to infiltrate the Nameren and turn him off."

"Turn him off?" I repeated.

"Kill him, Freida. You are a creature built from a dream, designed for deicide."

I was horrified, yes, Nameren. But I was not—if I cannot admit this to you, then who else?—as surprised as I ought to have been. This was an old fear, it turned out, one that Samlin had merely found and exploited: fear of myself.

"So I'm a monster, like they always said? Is that why Quinn hates me?"

"Quinn has no idea," ze said firmly. "No one else at the Library does. The program supposedly ended centuries ago, and its memory was suppressed."

"At the Library?" I caught that bit of misdirection. Nadi to the end. "So who *does* know?"

"The trunk elders in Niphense."

The oldest, most inscrutable Awilu political body. Quite possibly the most powerful in the three systems.

"And what do they say about me?"

Zir lips quirked. "That I shouldn't have tried to give you a choice. That I should threaten the Nameren's priests with you and send you off to kill a god."

"*I'm* the weapon you need to buy time for?"

Ze closed zir eyes.

The hand reached for zir, quieted when it touched the dense, wiry curl of zir hair, now both intimately familiar and wondrously new.

"Will you send me there, Nadi?"

The hand moved as ze shook zir head. Ze began to laugh so hard ze trembled. My hand said, *Here is love—did you doubt it?*

"I will not, Freida," ze said softly. "I am not so pious or so brave as Atriman's parent. I will not sacrifice you on the altar of intersystem peace. I will push you out of the water, to safety."

"I don't want you to die, Nadi."

Zir palm cupped my cheek. "That, my love, is the part of the story we cannot change."

⁕

Joshua's avatar was waiting for me on the bench outside my garden door the next morning, tinsel cranium lolling on the delicate bones of its skeleton hand. Chrysanthemum petals were falling from its mouth in a mournful shower and burning upon contact with the stone.

"I found something in the municipal archives," it said in Joshua's voice, speaking Library Standard. My breath hitched. I'd cried a lot in the last twenty-four hours. I wasn't sure if it had helped. "A child's drawing from around the end of the war and some audio. The kid is my eight-times great-grandfather. He's one of the adopted children. And he's describing the sun of his home . . . a red-orange sun, he says, distant and warm. And two moons that cross paths in the sky. A blue moon with a fish on its face and a smaller pink moon, which is its flower. He says it's a lost place because it's farther away than God. That's exactly how he says it, Freida."

The skeleton looked up, trembling in the breeze, or maybe with exhaustion and sadness, I couldn't say. The octopus reached out three glowing tentacles and caressed its ribs and clavicle. I held my knees to my chest, grateful, at least, to the warm breeze and sunny sky, the clear morning after a night of rain. The red-orange sun, the two moons I knew as well as my own breath, and how they crossed in the sky. The sun had already been here, but the moons and the library disc had been created out of an orbiting dust cloud at the time of the founding of the Library, as part of the Tri-System Treaty. There had been no planetary system here. The location of the Library had been chosen essentially at random, at great physical distance away from the other human systems. That was the story we all knew. It was, on some level, the foundation of my entire life.

"There are uncounted billions of star systems, Joshua," said my little octopus from its little beak. It didn't sound scared, but inside its transparent skin the lights and gears were dancing and sparking and crashing against one another.

His skeleton stood on the bench and somehow seemed to stare straight at me. "But there are very, very few tesseracts, Freida."

My avatar and I trembled in unison. There *were* very few tesseracts. And now it seemed as though the first Library tesseract had been built before the Library itself had even been dreamed of. What had been here before?

The lost tenth. Of course, Nameren. Had you already guessed?

"I don't understand. The tenth expedition found the Library first? There was something here before? The Awilu created the eighth tesseract *before* the end of the war?"

The skeleton nodded thoughtfully. "That's what it seems like. If my ancestor's home really was the Library itself—or whatever was here before—if this is true, then it connects the case to everyone. The Mahām, the Miuri, Tierrans—everyone. The judges won't be able to deny our standing—*anyone's* standing—to reactivate the node."

My octopus gasped. "Joshua, this is—"

"Don't tell anyone, not until we're sure. The Lunar faction isn't above murdering us to make this go away. Find as much as you can in Huehue, if you go in again. And don't let zir kill you either, Freida. Please."

As he slid out of connection, my octopus swam over to where I sat and wrapped all eight tentacles around my head. I could swear I felt the pressure and the comfort before it faded out as well.

I had the outline of an answer for the Huehue child, but filling in that outline meant that I would inevitably know something terrible, something that Joshua and Nergüi would use to upend five centuries of legal precedence. I can be brave, but it is so hard sometimes, Nameren. I aspire to radical love, but sometimes I just want the simplest comfort, the shallowest peace, release that demands nothing of me.

I went back to Huehue that night, alone. Vaterite gave me the heart shard solemnly. His manner was different, now that he had seen what I had done in the shift.

"You don't need us to go with you again." Not a question, but I shook my head anyway. He set his hand on my shoulder. "May you follow your paths brightly," he said in Miuri. I felt like a soldier, the latest champion in an ancient war, as I walked away.

I took the forgotten tunnels back to the ravine. The lava lake had cooled, forming a hard crust from which only an occasional bubble of lava burst through. Still, I could see surprisingly well. I searched for the new source of ambient light and found it: a spindly bridge of braided crystals of every color dreamed by a Library material. It only went halfway across the fire lake. I climbed a few meters to where the bridge connected to the rock wall and set my weight down lightly. The crystal held, as I knew it would. My hand spasmed, reached up. It was pointing to the birds, which circled up and around me. I didn't think one would impale me again, but I trembled with the memory of pain.

Nadi was fighting so that I could have a choice. The least I could do was be brave enough to make it. Huehue would kill me, or ze would save me, and I would trust zir to do one or the other. I walked the length of the bridge and straddled the unfinished end, suspended as though on floss above a darkly churning fire. The birds settled peacefully on the stretch of bridge behind me and folded their great crystal wings and watched. I strapped myself down, then pulled the ibis's shard from my backpack, broke off another sliver, and swallowed it.

This time it was night in the desert. Two moons played in the sky, a blue fish and a pink thorn, or a blue thorn painted red where it pierced flesh. The dunes surrounded me, tall and undulating, a frozen candy sea. An icy wind blew across them, spraying sand into my eyes and bringing a scent of long-spent ashes, the stale air of centuries-sealed rooms, the desiccated fall leaves of extinct trees. I heard a faint cry, and a deep buzzing shook the sand beneath my bare feet. It came from a gaping hole in the ground before me. I walked to its edge and looked down. The Huehue child was cowering on a narrow ledge below the lip of the sinkhole, with bees the size of my thumb crawling over zir body. Zir legs and hands were already encased in the paper-thin layers of an enormous hive.

"Sweet sister," ze whispered, "have you come with an answer?"

I lay on my belly in the sand and reached my hands down to zir. The child looked up at me and opened the howling mouth that I now saw had never been a void, but a loneliness filled with distant stars.

"Sweet sibling," I said, "guilty consciences are angry, and they often lash out at those who remind them of their guilt. They try to silence, instead of making amends. You should know. Didn't you try to hurt Atriman's parent, who came to repent of the wrong ze had done in zir past life? I think you are the Nameren's conscience, his guilt. But where you had Atriman, a righteous innocent, to remind you of the light inside you, they had no one but their fearful reflections.

They buried you here because the guilt over what they had done was unbearable, and so they made you bear it."

The Huehue child blinked. The bees hovered around zir, dancing fractals in the air, buzzing so loudly I could no longer hear the moons playing above, or the child's words when ze spoke to me again. Ze began to cry, and the tears ran like a waterfall down the side of the sinkhole. One of the bees rose to meet me. It danced twice left, once right, which I understood to mean *Well met, last sister.* Then it landed in the middle of my forehead and stung.

I awoke on the bridge in precisely the same position. My forehead throbbed and burned. The birds surrounded me, but they flew out of my way when I sat up. The crystal had finished braiding itself into the honeycombed rock on the other side. Huehue had accepted my answer.

I cut my tether and stood up on cold and shaky legs. I was thinking of Nergüi, of her beloved bathhouse stories. I was thinking that sometimes knowledge is as much of a portal as distance or time. I could not unknow. I could not unsee. My Nadi was dying, I had almost two dozen lost sisters, and I *could not walk back.*

Over a bridge and a lake of fire, I crossed into Huehue.

The aurochs draws a hoof through the earth. Ants, red and gold, spill out of the furrow. They fall upon two fingers inching across the mud like fleshy worms. Within seconds, the fingers have been reduced to bones, then meal. The girl, sunk an inch into the mud, clutches her stomach as she watches. The god steps into her line of vision while the ants finish off the rest.

"What did the old bastard tell you?" the god asks.

The girl shakes her head, remembers where she is. "Wouldn't you like to know?"

He bristles and blusters. "Tell me!"

She unfolds to his height, matches her face to his horns. "No!"

He backs down. Prances to the side, swings a calculating glance at the sky, where six suns chatter distantly among themselves. "Don't tell me, then. My own avatars have denied me the same for centuries." His great nostrils flare a moment before a flash of red lightning sends the suns scurrying. Their world turns dark and thunders with the inarticulate roar of an enraged beast.

The aurochs stands over the girl, who has dropped to her knees as the earth of their imagining quakes. "Look, can't you see how Valaver rumbles?" Aurochs shouts over the din. "He's finally noticed I'm awake. Wants to be his own god, that one, but he doesn't have the heart for it."

The fingers in the grass inch over her hands and feet, but she is too frightened to notice them.

As quickly as it came, the darkness vanishes. The sky is clear and blue. The girl jumps to her feet and knocks the fingers back into the grass with jagged, violent shakes.

"It looks like I'm not the only one with unwelcome visitors from my subconscious." She stomps a pair of nearby fingers into the ground for emphasis. She steams with rage and fear.

The god watches her. "That one cannot overwhelm me. Not yet."

"Neither can this one's! Slimy! Hands!"

Her screams echo across the plain, nearly as loud as Valaver's. She puts her hands to her mouth and chokes back a sob.

"Your body will give out soon enough. That virus is burning inside you."

The girl's laugh is a soft, bruised thing. "Is that what this is?" More fingers, indexes and middles and tiny pinkie fingers with clean, clipped nails, are popping up among the blades of grass.

"It seems that it's got ahold of your memories." He sweeps them away with a hoof. The ants fall upon them, voracious.

"It wasn't real," she whispers.

She considers this aurochs of the Nameren, the lost incarnation, now found. Even his outer avatars wanted him asleep and harmless. Her gaze is unfathomable.

"Remember," he says, "the folktale of the piper and the ghosts in the desert? Maybe you're the piper, and we do know how her story ends."

"Because I'm likely to dry out here in the desert with them? That's good, Aurochs. But I'll still tell you my stories as long as I can."

"So tell me what you found in Huehue."

"Not until it's part of the story. What I found there is all tangled up in . . . what happened next."

"Your parent died."

She turns away. Their distant audience has returned: seven points of light, seven suns, keeping vigil. "Yes."

"I remember one of your sisters. Two hundred years ago. She wasn't like you."

Her shoulder twitches like a red flag. But Aurochs knows how to be patient. "How was she?"

"More frightened, but more arrogant. Love was a construct, she told me, just like consciousness. She was going to turn off my consciousness just like she had turned off her ability to love. Imagine that."

"And so you killed her."

"I don't remember. I think I faded out of sync. When I came back to myself, she was only bones."

"You are terrible, Nameren. Do you understand that? You are too terrible to live."

"Maybe so. But I do live. And I do have a heart. Or else you would not be here, standing in it, playing your games and convincing me not to kill you."

"Do you even remember her name?"

The aurochs's heart gives an unexpected jolt. The seven stars come closer. "Bathsheba."

The girl mouths the other name and swallows its precious syllables. "My sister was beautiful. She was arrogant and she was cold and she was afraid of anything that could give her joy, but she deserved her life. She didn't deserve what you gave her, you old blood-soaked bastard."

"I thought that was Old Coyote."

"You're the original. The oldest, bloodiest bastard."

The aurochs lowers himself slowly into the savanna grass. He is so old and tired. "It is sometimes hard to accept the pain you cause when you could not have behaved otherwise. Take poor Valaver."

The girl growls like a trapped animal and smoke leaks from between her clenched teeth. "*I* could have behaved otherwise. I should have known what he was after."

"It would be wisdom, impossible one, to know what we have done, and what was done to us, and to not confuse the two."

Her voice, when it comes, is very small. "How? I asked Nadi, and asked zir, until ze couldn't answer me anymore."

"I'm sorry."

She sinks with him into the grass. It grows tall and sways above them but does not block out the light, something like love and protection. "I am too."

"So tell me, little piper. Tell me how ze died."

–As ze lived. Radically, with love.

"I'm throwing a party," ze told me. "If I have to go out, I'm going out in style."

"Aren't you sick?" I asked. "Aren't the Mahām trying to start a war? Isn't Quinn going to pin me to a wall and pick me apart the second you're gone?" I grabbed an eel, buzzing with a faint electric charge beneath my fingers, but my new hand seemed to think it was more exciting than dangerous. I dropped it back into the water, where it slithered away brightly, down the long tunnel. "Oh, and how did I forget? You still haven't told me how precisely I'm supposed to kill the first and greatest material god."

"I do believe you are accusing me of frivolity!" Nadi said. Zir laugh was cheery, full as I remembered it from better days, as though finally telling me the truth had liberated zir from a great burden. Unfortunately, it seemed ze had passed the burden directly onto my own shoulders.

I scowled at zir, then turned back to the tunnel. We were in Kohru, Iemaja's artery of childhood and discovery, sloshing through knee-deep waters. Well, I was sloshing. The medics had found a better treatment for Nadi that left zir more energy, but ze needed a walker to go more than a few steps. The walker had eight legs like a spider and maintained zir in perfect equilibrium even in flooded tunnels with tricky sinkholes in the floor and walls. I wouldn't have minded one myself.

"You said the bones are down here?" ze asked, looking around.

"Eventually," I said, "if I can get Kohru to help me." There had been an offering in the temple, and all her main arteries were knee-deep in swamp water chlorophyll green with spirulina, wriggling with snakes and eels and long fish with many teeth. Kohru had seemed the gentlest of the available options. Here, the offerings swam in confused circles or beat themselves against Iemaja's crystal walls to get out. And she, with mesmerizing grace, would open a slit in the rock and swallow them whole. The air reeked of algae and the metallic stink of fish blood.

Ze shook zir head, eyes filled with enough childlike wonder for the both of us. "I wish I had been able to come here with you when you were younger. You would have taught me so much. You are a marvel—I always knew that—but I couldn't risk it."

I kept my eyes on the treacherous current ahead of us, lit by our cords of shards, but I wasn't paying as much attention as I pretended. We'd never talked like this before. I'd never known why we were the way we were. I had only accepted it, as a child does. "Why not?"

"Because I could never let anyone suspect what you were doing, or that I knew about it."

"Why let me do it at all? Why raise me like I was some . . ." My jaw grew tense around the words, and I had to force them out in a kind of anguished croak. *"Normal girl."*

Now ze seemed a little melancholy and put zir arm around my shoulder. I shrugged zir off. "I always told you how I found you. You knew the Library had made you."

I wheeled on zir. "You never told me *why*! That little detail just escaped you? Deicide! What a joke. I was born to throw myself into the maw of a god, just like one of these fish!" I was aware that I was screaming, that the walls pulsed light in time to the echoes of my voice and the offerings were splashing in a frenzy. I did not care.

Nadi sighed and turned from me. Ze kept walking, and after a moment I stumbled awkwardly to catch up. The five-jointed legs of the walker gave dainty plops as each hit the water, contrasting painfully with my furious, awkward sloshing. I barely restrained myself from kicking one of its green, downy legs.

"Sometimes I have thought," Nadi said after a minute of bleak silence, "that radical love was merely a joke that my partner Soren and I were playing on ourselves all that time, back then. That it is not merely an impossible ideal, but not even ideal. Radical truth, radical trust, radical vulnerability." Ze shook zir head. "I have failed you utterly, of course, my Freida. But I hope it was a noble failure. I wanted to give you a choice. I wanted to give you a chance to be whoever you truly were, not just the demented idea of a program dreamed up by founders too traumatized by war to recognize evil even when they engaged in it."

I tried to respond, but realized that I could not. It was as though all the self-hatred that I had tried so hard to stave off and cajole since I was thirteen had waited just beyond my thresholds, feeding and growing, only to devour me now at my most defenseless. I had always known I was made. But I had assumed that the Library had made me for itself. That perhaps I wasn't a child in the normal ways of human biology, but I was, nonetheless, a true child of the four gods.

But no—here was the dirty truth: I was a weapon, the last in a long line of weapons, born to suffer and die at the mercy of a war god whose colors I had never tasted, whose dreams had never scraped my throat. My body itself had been engineered for the kind of beauty suited to an ugly and vicious old god who fed on death. Everything about me, even my love of the gods, now felt like some cold clockwork in my heart, turning and moving my automaton limbs into position above a trigger, a barrel, and a bullet.

A chance to be who I truly was? In my tick-tock time-bomb heart, was there even a *myself* to search for?

"And here," said Nadi, suddenly, "we have come to an end. The right one?"

I looked up and realized that ze meant this literally: The passage now ended in a wall with tiny gullies to the left and right, enough to let the water and offerings pass, but far too small for two humans. Still no sign of a side tunnel, and now the artery was blocked. The crystal-striated rock shimmered in whorled patterns that chattered at the edge of my conscious understanding.

I focused on the hum beneath the soles of my feet, trying to settle into the god-space in my mind. "What are you trying to say, Mother?" I muttered.

Nadi closed zir eyes. "Sweet materials, Freida, I am so sorry."

"For leaving me?" I snapped. The sense of understanding, as if in a dream, slipped away.

Ze shook zir head. In a different tone, ze said, "Are you sure the bones are . . . one of your sisters'?"

The fractal fall of bleach-white bones on black sand. I had dreamed of her, the sadness and relief of that last slide into cool water. Her stomach had been clenched for years with the stress of what she had been born to do, until it had pickled and folded in defeat.

I nodded. "You've found bones, too."

"I have," ze said quietly. "But I always assumed . . . Tell me again how you found them?"

"When I disappeared," I said, staring at the moving pattern on stone, willing my mind to stillness. "After my drop with Samlin."

"What *happened*, Freida?"

Something in zir voice made me turn. Zir face was like an old Awilu mask: the dancer, crying. But it was too late.

"Nothing," I said. And then, softer, "You've hidden so much from me, Nadi."

A gulping breath. "I was only trying to protect you."

"It didn't work."

Ze swayed. I knew the walker would catch zir, so I did nothing. After a long moment, ze clawed zirself back, that abject expression shuttered and replaced with an expert, opaque mildness.

"We could try querying," ze said neutrally.

I nodded, sickened and relieved. "I've still got some branch worm."

Quickly, I unspooled the yellow worm, a little withered after ten days in my bag, but still alive. I split it apart at one end, handed one of the splits to Nadi and affixed the second end to my left temple. The other thick branch I placed at the heart of the pulsing symbols I couldn't quite understand.

"Tiger Freehold?" Nadi asked as the branch worm shot out tendrils along the side of zir face and base of zir neck.

"No, one of the others. Many Worlds, I think?"

I felt a shift as my wetware engaged with the branch worm's spontaneously forming network. I could sense Nadi inside me, a warm pulse.

Ze was in a great deal of pain.

I flinched back. Ze took one look at me and laughed. It was real laughter, borne of deep joy; I could feel that, too. Oh, Nadi. My anger at zir burned me. And yet—I had never known zir to do other than love fiercely, as best ze could.

"That's why we librarians rarely use it. Can you imagine Quinn letting me skim his emotions?"

I snorted. "Oh, it'd be like querying with a block of ice."

"A very smug block of ice."

I grinned. Ze took my hand. Cold and wet from the tunnels, it anchored me more surely than gravity to this place, and this life, where I was loved. Ze had not been able to protect me, Nameren, but I had not lived a day without the surety of zir love.

The connection was preverbal. Nadi fed some search queries: bones, water, old chambers. Kohru came back with children's rhymes.

Nadi sighed. "Not the best time to try this, right after an offering. I think she's overexcited."

"That other avatar of Iemaja knew me. I think they all have, all this time. Kohru must know."

"And what are we going to do, if the bones really are your sister's?"

That *we* held me, bore me up. "Find the rest of them. Find out how I'm supposed to kill a god."

"Freida, you don't have to."

"I was made for it."

"You still don't have to."

I tried to cleave to my anger, but it was no use—ze could feel it anyway, all my despair. "And what else am I supposed to do, Nadi? Hide down here in the tunnels like a grub?"

"You're still a novice librarian. It should give you some protection . . ." Some of my exasperation must have bled through because ze paused and sighed. "You're right. I don't know what Joshua and Nergüi's team is planning, but as soon as Huehue's secrets are entered into evidence, it will be easy work for Quinn to prove that you did it and use that as grounds to strip you of your novice status."

"So I might as well kill the Nameren, or die trying."

"No." The word was sharp, final, powerful enough to echo off the tunnel walls and murky water. The wall flashed in return.

I smashed my hand against it, which hurt. "You can't save me when you're dead." I ground the words between my teeth.

Ze closed zir eyes briefly. I kept my arms tight across my middle.

"How much have you found in Huehue?" ze said at last.

"I'm not sure. There's a story there, but zir memories aren't well-organized. I'm trying to piece it together."

"Will it be enough for Joshua and Nergüi?"

I considered Joshua's many-times great-grandfather, born on a lost world with two moons, the fish and the rose. *But there are very few tesseracts, Freida.* The whole founding myth of the Library itself revealed as a false peace, a clever screen over sheer brutality. "It will be enough for the known worlds."

Ze flinched but didn't ask for more. "They won't be safe, in that case."

"I think they know."

"You won't be, either."

"Didn't I tell you so? Now, how do I kill the Nameren?"

A snatch of song, an old children's march, came through the oversaturated connection with the branch worm:

> **Shoot to kill on the one and three**
> **Shot and dead on the two and four**
> **Should have charged your chest of war.**

Nadi grimaced. "I have no idea."

"Well, what happened to my sisters?"

Another strange murmuring memory. *Through a well, down a door, and soft slide in a canine throat.*

"They died trying. Or they died in training. A few killed themselves before they could be sent. The trunk elders let the program lapse over a century ago and buried its memory. No one suspected the materials had continued to make you . . ."

"Or no one cared. How many bones have you found, Nadi?"

"Librarians die in the tunnels, Freida. You know that."

"They aren't all librarians."

"How can you possibly tell, love?" ze asked, but I hardly heard zir. An image spliced through this time, a black sand beach with the long, rosy sunsets typical of the Library's red-orange sun. Coral the color of an old bone climbed up the beach from the gently lapping water, faintly tinted rust red. I froze, trying to parse how it could seem at once so alien and familiar, why Kohru would show it to us now. But it slid away, and I wasn't sure Nadi had even registered it amid Kohru's scattershot babble.

The water and the sand, at least, reminded me of the bones I had found when I was thirteen. The ones that we were trying to find again now. Kohru could get me there, I was sure. I just needed a clearer connection. "Here, give me a bit of your Kohru shard. I don't think we'll get anything out of her without communion."

Wordlessly, Nadi ran zir hands down the rope of shards that looped around zir body ten times. Zir fingers flipped through two dozen shards of Iemaja's avatars with a quick assurance that reminded me of how Nergüi played with her glass ball. I could hardly tell which ones ze touched until zir fingers stilled on a pair of Kohrus by zir collarbone. Ze smashed the smallest one against the wall to break off a piece and handed it to me.

"Is that enough?" ze asked. Ze had never enjoined communion by ingestion. For a high-wetware librarian, merely touching the physical shards was normally enough.

I nodded and rubbed the bit of shard between my right thumb and forefinger along its sharpest edge. It left behind a grainy white film, which caught the single bead of blood from my cut skin like a net. I lifted my fingers to my mouth and sucked.

The communion landed soft as a rain in the late mud. The ground shivered and pricked the soles of my feet. A crystal fish with the head of a young Awilu child swam out of the murky water and into the air, thick now with a perfume of rose water and caramelized sugar. I wondered if this was how the stink of dying fish smelled to Iemaja, like sun-filled days in the kitchen of someone's childhood.

The little Kohru flapped her tail in my hair and giggled. Cotton candy floss spilled from her mouth onto my hands. It tasted like turmeric milk.

"It's the little baby!" she sang, shaking her head to and fro as though to some unheard rhythm. "So grown now, the little baby. I haven't seen her for so long! Or maybe I have?"

"I haven't communed with this avatar in years, Iemaja," I said.

She swam right between my eyes, so they crossed trying to look at her. She had a face much like my own as a child, but the eyes were bigger and her nose was pierced with a tiny green stone.

"The last time . . . I showed you something. I showed you your bones. It was you, right? Not a different one?"

My voice cracked. "It was me."

She laughed and more candy floss sprayed across my face. "Yes! You're the late one, the lonely one. The best little baby, my dearest, sweetest baby, even that old dog listens when you speak, even that dog with his rough stone grown into me and scratching." She wrinkled her nose and jerked her head at the wall. Here in communion, the flashing lights formed the shape of an old Awilu script, moving across the wall in the fast cursive of an invisible, giant brush. She lowered her voice. "He didn't want anyone to find her, but I knew you could get past him."

That sharp drop—that long, silent darkness where it seemed Old Coyote had swallowed Iemaja whole—"He *meant* to cut off access to that chamber?"

The Kohru dove into my hair. "Shh!" she said. "Do you want him to hear?"

I looked back at where I thought Nadi should be, though ze had mostly disappeared, faded into the mist that surrounded me and Kohru like the inner membrane of an egg.

"Why didn't you let zir in?" I asked.

The Kohru grimaced. "I don't like those big Head Librarians. You never did, either."

"Nadi is my parent!"

"Oh," she said, flipping her tail in Nadi's general direction. "I meant the other yous. You were mostly very angry. We all felt sorry for you."

"You all . . . like, Iemaja?"

She beamed. "That's what you call us!"

"Won't you let us through? I need to get back to that place."

She sighed noisily, raining candy floss. "Do you?" she said. "It's a long walk."

"I need to see the bones."

"Oh. Of course you do." She flopped to my shoulder. "You're going to leave me, aren't you?"

She was looking at me with those wide, mournful eyes that too closely resembled my own.

"Her bones," I rasped.

She nodded sadly and swam over to the wall. She smacked it with her tail. "Well," she called, "open up, you old dog."

The wall unzipped—it glimmered and doubled in my communion-filmed vision. The zipper became a snout and a pair of wide jaws. A canine-human face peeked out from between the jagged teeth.

"I don't have to," he said, sounding so much like a surly little boy that I burst out laughing. The Kohru turned to me in surprise for a second and then followed my lead. Her bright giggle rained us with candy floss, and Old Coyote's coyote mouth and his dog-boy mouth stuck out their tongues to catch it. The dog-boy gave the Kohru a small goofy smile.

"All right," he said, and disappeared into the crystal of the wall.

"What was that?" I asked.

"He's sweet on me this time," the Kohru said, sounding very pleased with herself.

He came back some minutes later. In the communion a thin, furry arm reached out to toss something in my direction. In my regular vision, it flew out from a slit in the wall.

One of Nadi's walker legs reached out to catch it before it fell into the current. The leg looked like a snake in my communion vision, with an ivory-and-blue bone firm in its jaws. The communion was fading already, just my little Kohru swimming above me, looking sad again.

"That's the bone you want, sweetest baby. That's the one that has her inside."

"Inside?"

But she was gone. In her place was my parent, staring at me with an expression I could not read, and a human femur, covered in runes, gripped in zir right hand.

It was an archive bone, Nadi told me. Before the war, they'd been a low-cost alternative to war chests, but I'd never seen one before. Librarians were prohibited war chests for the same reason we couldn't use longevity therapies or own property—once we made our vows, our wealth was the Library itself. Our longevity was collective, made through our lifelong service to peace. (You laugh, Nameren, but at least some of us believed it.) But some early librarians had made archive bones: echoes of who they used to be, imbued with their character from a specific moment in time but not fully conscious. The bones themselves could only be activated a limited number of times before the projection dissolved into a high-entropy state.

This archive bone belonged to one of my sisters. I didn't access it immediately. If I would only have one chance to speak to her, I wanted to prepare myself. I needed to know what to ask. I went to Iemaja's temple for the next few nights, sometimes with Atempa, sometimes alone, to watch the moons arc above the open gap above the cenote and pray. I needed to go back to Huehue, but zis was a hard story, and the thought of going back there filled me with light-headed anxiety. I longed to talk to Nergüi, but she hadn't spoken to me since the lone message when I was in the infirmary. Her thirty-three days were nearly past. Nadi was back in negotiations with the Mahām. It must have been going badly, because Atempa reported her father was more smug than ever. The third night after my trip to Kohru, Joshua's tinsel skeleton flickered into view on the prayer mat in front of me, with a message that seemed to have been delayed a few hours.

"Nergüi thinks the Miuri might also have taken some of the refugee children from the lost tenth. That should be the drafters' connection between my people and hers in the autonomy node."

I blinked. I attempted a neutral reply, but my octopus wilted visibly, with four arms above its head as it slunk down. "What, is she using you as her messenger service now?"

The message went through with just the few seconds of lag that dragged all communication from Tierra.

"Are you two fighting?"

My octopus scowled up at his skeleton. "She dumped tepache on my head."

The skeleton burst out laughing, raining petals that blossomed in my own senses like olfactory ghosts of flowers I'd never smelled. "Sorry. I shouldn't be laughing. And tepache? I had no idea they made that in Library City."

"We were in a freehold," the octopus said sourly. "Someone had made it in honor of your case."

The skeleton bent down and hugged my octopus. It trilled with pleasure. That little traitor.

"Anyway," the skeleton said, as the firework lights behind the translucent skin of my octopus cast a warm glow upon its tinsel bones, "I've been thinking about it, and I doubt the Miuri could have taken them. It was the Awilu who settled the children, remember? And the Mahām were blockading the Miuri moon."

"But only the Cicada third was fighting the Mahām."

The skeleton considered. "You have a point—the Aurochs third was allied with the Mahām. Do you know which third discovered the lost tenth?"

"I haven't found those details yet."

"And the Aurochs third initiated the unification with Baobab and Cicada a few months later, didn't they?"

I was startled. "Do you think the lost tenth had something to do with that?"

"If the Library was built in the same system that the tenth expedition set-tled . . . *something* happened there. Something that changed the war."

"But what?"

He paused. "Freida, where did the planet go?"

I swallowed queasily. "Whatever happened, it was so terrible that it left a hole in the second-oldest material god's memory."

"And that might have been what made the Aurochs third turn against the Mahām."

"But why? They couldn't have cared about the atrocities. The Aurochs are the Awilu that still wanted to keep the Nameren."

"Maybe the incident made them realize the Mahām were a threat to them somehow?"

I forced myself to consider it. "So the Aurochs Awilu would have settled the children among the Miuri and your people as a hedge against Mahām power?"

His skeleton released a lambent glow, the reflection of a sunset. "And Lunar power. The Lunars were threatening to switch allegiance to the Mahām every few years at that time. I think we're onto something. We're linked in the node specifically to limit the hegemony of the powers that the Awilu needed to control."

"Giving minority groups strong autonomy protects us from another Great War—something like that?"

"The bastards will loathe that one. It's brilliant. When are you going back in?"

I shuddered, grateful that he couldn't see it. "Soon. I promise."

"Freida . . . are you all right? Atempa told me you had to spend a week in the infirmary—"

I cut the connection. I did it automatically, before my conscious brain had a chance to stop me. His skeleton froze, disconcerted, and then gave me a little bow before fading away. I would blame the bad connection, but he wouldn't believe me.

I knelt on the prayer mat and put my head in my hands. I knew Iemaja wouldn't speak to me—I needed communion for that—but it was comforting to feel the peace of this place, smell the cold water boring for kilometers through the cenote of the temple and down through her labyrinthine tunnels. I shivered, though the air was temperate, with hardly a breeze. The rust, with its blazing clear skies that grew the sweetest Tenehet fruit, would be here soon. I couldn't wait to see the back of the tears.

There was always a faint buzzing background in the temple: prayers, mostly, or whispered conversations among the tourists or the guards. So I didn't notice the murmuring until it had swelled to a wave. I lifted my head from my hands and looked around blearily. A pair of the guards I had known most of my life were talking to each other while staring at me. They looked down awkwardly when I met their eyes. Even the die-hard penitents had stopped their prayers, staring glassily up at the ceiling while they checked their feeds. I realized that I had made my thresholds impenetrable when I cut off the conversation with Joshua. I dialed them down, and the pings and messages hit me like a spray of cold water.

Did you see?—Did you know ze was—Are you okay?—Is this real?

And another one, lonely among the frenzy of the rest: *I had to, my love.*

My heart started to beat wildly. I tasted bile and sat heavily on the prayer mat. *You should check*, I thought reasonably. *You should see what's happened, Freida.* But I couldn't move.

Atempa and Nergüi found me like that, half-frozen and half-jellied among the prayer mats. The sight of Nergüi after all this time did not disconcert me. I just grabbed her hand when she knelt by my side and held on to it as if she would keep me from dying alone.

"Tell me," I told Atempa, gasping. "I can't bear to look."

She and Nergüi shared a glance. Nergüi put a tentative, awkward hand on my shoulder that was more dear to me than a hug, because I knew how much it cost her.

"Freida," Nergüi said, "the Head Librarian just released a statement. Ze says that ze will die in two weeks, at the end of a celebration."

My heart squeezed again. "Two weeks?" How could ze have so little time? Surely the new treatment was working better than that?

"There's more," Atempa said grimly. "Ze undercut the negotiations. Ze says the Mahām are betraying the foundations of the Treaty and ze is using the last weeks of zir life to call on the people of the three systems to oppose them."

"No," I said. "Ze is never that direct. Ze always plays the political angles."

Atempa's nostrils flared. "Not this time. Dad is having fits."

"Ze mentioned the case," Nergüi said slowly, as though she could hardly believe it. "Ze said the Treaty must be renewed, and that our petition was the future of humanity. Freida, what do you think ze is planning?"

I closed my eyes. "Radical love."

"What?"

"Ze is trying to save my life."

✦

Nergüi's thirty-three days were to be over the next day, but she stuck around even after Atempa left, awkward, silent, determined. I turned to her suddenly.

"I forgive you. Do you forgive me? Can't we talk again?"

Her dusty orange eyebrows beetled together, endearing. "Why?"

"Because I miss you."

"Oh." She took a deep breath. "I guess I ought to explain."

"You don't have to."

"No, I have been ungenerous." She took out her glass ball from her robes and held it up to the moonlight. A swarm of lights played like minnows at the edge of the glass. "I travel the path I travel, and here, no matter how improbably, we travel together."

239

I smiled a little, though my heart ached. "Doesn't that make it more special?"

Her expression was unreadable. Then she nodded. "This calls for the great bathhouse."

I thought she meant the story, but she had somehow found the real thing, a sprawling underground grub warren in a residential section of the Mahue'e district. The housing was intelligence-dark family units constructed close to the ground in gently rounded spirals of adobe studded with colored glass, home of transport technicians and tesseract specialists. The Library was a city of immigrants. Over time various groups from the three systems had come here to settle and build new lives after the war. The transport technicians were mostly Dar, who had been waging a battle for autonomy from the Mahām for at least the past century. On Mahām they lived on the small southern continent, where conditions were cold and hard and even centuries of terraforming with Awilu tech had done little to improve them.

"And the Dar use bathhouses?" I asked.

"How do you think they survive their winters? They use them to hide from the Mahām during the War Ritual, too. I've always admired the Dar for that. Too bad for us, the moonstone just collapses if we dig too deep. And the Mahām hate us too much to let us get away with it."

Nergüi said this so flatly I didn't know how to respond. The entrance to the bathhouse here was a shallow dome of more colored glass depicting a scene from the fifth expedition, a sharply angled centrifugal ship orbiting a green planet.

In the cave beneath the dome, an old woman gave us a startled glance, recovered, and blandly handed us the uniform of lightweight pink tunics. I watched Nergüi with covert curiosity as she changed beside me in the dressing room. She put me in mind of a disconcerted rooster, with her orange-brown hair standing in thick tufts from where she had yanked the cotton tunic over her head. I had never seen her without her robes before.

She raised her eyebrows at me.

"What?" I asked.

"You look ridiculous," she said.

"Likewise."

"There's a salt crystal room with mineral waters I want to try first. They say they're good for draining the bad humors and rebalancing one's emotional limbic system."

"Do you really believe that?"

"It's not consistent with Miuri systems of knowledge. But I think it will make you happy, which is more or less what they mean."

We didn't speak of love, but I glowed with it like the lights in her glass ball, crowding, as though their excitement could break the bounds of their own existence. I had thought she might be done with me. But she was here with me now, and that was more than enough.

We stayed until late in the night, trying each of the twenty-five bathing and sauna rooms. The cafeteria served traditional Dar food, which she told me had enough in common with Miuri for nostalgia. We drank cinnamon tea and shared half a baked emu egg, green as a dinosaur's. After a few more hours, we tried desserts of shaved goat-milk ice sweetened with goat-milk caramel and topped with chewy gelatins and sweet red beans. I'd never tasted anything like it before; there weren't any Dar among the librarians, and the cooks catered to Awilu tastes. The food of my childhood was the complex art of Niphense Awilu spice mixes, with the flavors determined by mood and occasion.

I sucked down the sweet-salty strangeness of these dishes. I loved everything for the most banal of reasons: that she had given them to me.

In the jade room, naked beside me in the long wooden tub that ran the length of the wall, Nergüi lay on her back and watched the play of galaxies spinning and crashing on the ceiling.

"I think there's going to be a real war," she said. "That's why the Head Librarian brought up our case. To make people take sides."

It frightened me to hear that word from Nergüi, who had lost so much to the Mahām and their Nameren-fueled rituals of conflict.

She turned to me. "And for some reason ze thinks a war is safer for you than the Library's peace with Quinn's faction in power. Why, Freida? Are you a demi-god like in the old Awilu sagas?"

I lost my grip on the edge and fell into the hot water. I stayed there for a few seconds longer than necessary, my heartbeat heavy and knocking out every other sound. Nergüi hauled me up by my elbow.

"Well?"

She was as implacable as one of your demon-armored soldiers, Nameren. The ones who had fought for your demigods in the sagas. I swallowed.

"I'm not sure what I am," I croaked. "I . . . ze thinks I could hurt the Nameren."

Her nostrils flared, which I had come to understand did not truly mean anger but sadness, and she pulled me close. I felt precisely where one of her small breasts fit beneath my left armpit and the other squashed against my chest. I couldn't take a deep breath.

"I should show you something," Nergüi said, muffled against my hair. Despite everything, my heart started pounding, and my breath came in short gasps. I thought the smooth joining of her skin with mine would set me on fire.

After a searing moment, she pulled away and climbed out of the tub. I paused to catch my breath and followed her. We donned our tunics once again and sat on the strewn cushions in the deserted waiting area. She pulled a dinged console from one of the tunic's pockets and blew on it. A scene formed in an array on the heated wooden floor of the bathhouse, as though her breath had conjured it to life.

We were looking at the inside of a temple constructed entirely of wood, wine-dark with age, which had been cut so the rectangular puzzle pieces jointed perfectly in a pattern of whorled fractals that spilled out from the center. There was a single window in the shape of a clover, which looked out high above terraced farmland that dropped sharply to the cobbled streets of a town below.

"This is my home," she said softly. "But before I was born. Look." She brushed her fingers through the array. The view narrowed to the window, through which we could now clearly see crops and farmhouses burning. A stream of people ran down the steep road to hide in the stone houses of the town. Above them, armored soldiers with twisting, multicolored demon masks hurled down lightning and boiling water. They were screaming the same word over and over in Mahām, but their voices had grown so deep and fat on power that my implant couldn't decipher it.

"Those are the Nameren's demon soldiers," Nergüi said. "They're telling the disciples to fight."

She pointed to fifty people in orange robes filing down the slope from the temple. They each wore a silver cap, whereas all the fleeing figures wore blue caps or headscarves.

"Fight who?" I asked, though I now suspected.

"Their own people," she said. "The farmers and the merchants and the carpenters and everyone they have made a life with."

The disciples got to the edge of the fleeing stream of townspeople. The demon soldiers overhead paused and leaned over the edges of their clouds, watching. The disciples lifted their guns, and then, as one, laid them down on the ashes in the road.

The soldiers roared, a "fight!" so distorted it was only a scream of rage, and began to rain down fire. The disciples did not fight, and so they died. The townspeople fled.

"What is this, Nergüi?" I asked, flinching away from the brutality of the scene before us. The array blasted the sounds of screaming and the crackling of skin seared by fire. At least my wetware wouldn't let me smell it.

She splayed her hand and the view receded from the window, back to the relative peace of the inner sanctuary of her temple.

"Old stories," she said. "Fireside tales. I never saw this, but my rector was a young disciple at the time who was spared the draft and saw everything from right here. Nearly every disciple of her generation died in that War Ritual."

I shuddered. "No wonder she wanted to make sure you escaped."

Nergüi grimaced, but she didn't respond. In the sanctuary, silver-blue light poured in through the holes in the roof, covered in fine translucent paper. In the center of the room was an altar, a square raised platform with high steps on one side. Four tall figures, carved from the same seasoned wood, guarded the corners of the platform. They depicted four heroes, faces set in that liminal space between ecstasy and pain, hands raised in a complicated series of gestures. They each wore the same robes as Nergüi, but without the crystal ball at their waists. Instead, censers of some other wood swayed in a breeze, and released heavy clouds of incense. A glass ball floated in the center of the platform.

It was very large, nearly person-sized, and inside the lights of a universe traversed paths uncountable and then flickered and died.

"Is there really a glass ball that size in your sanctuary?"

"They say it can kill disciples who are unprepared."

"How?"

"The sacred ball contains the power of our uncountable possibilities. It gives visions. It helps you see your solid paths, and your dangerous fringes. But if your soul is unprepared, it can blink away with the shock of seeing its own reflection."

"And blinking away is death?"

"The little death," Nergüi said, and placed her hand on mine. "The great death—the soul death—is different. That's what happens when your light breaks through the edge, and all this"—she spread her other hand—"dissipates into the void."

This wasn't the first time she'd mentioned this, but I still didn't understand how she could consider reality to be so . . . unreal. "How can time itself dissipate?"

"The same way the universe itself will dissipate someday. In impossible cold and impossible distance. Every great death is part of that ultimate end. Think of it like this: The physical *space* we inhabit is the same as our *time*. Tesseracts move us through space in ways that, according to our time, ought to be impossible. They break us from the sum of our possible paths. No wave function should be able to communicate instantly with a part of the universe hundreds of thousands of light-years away, let alone move there itself. That's why tesseracts and everything that came with the material gods have been destroying our real lives and making that cold space-time ever so much bigger."

I turned from my contemplation of the projection, scowling. "Tesseracts, again? But this is ridiculous, Nergüi. You went through the tesseract and you're not dead. I've had friends go through it twice a month and they came back fine every time!"

Nergüi shook her head. "They might be fine. They might not be. I didn't say they'd died the little death, Freida. I said that the tesseracts make you die the great death. The tiny spark of consciousness that broke through the crystal doesn't wink out immediately. It lives its life the way it always does. But there can be no more wholeness with one's multiple selves, there can be no return to the sacred paths, and when that spark dies, there will be no more of you."

Her earnestness exasperated me even more. "And you think you've died the great death, Nergüi? Is that why you've been so . . ." I cast about for a diplomatic way to characterize upending a drink server over my head and abandoning me for thirty-three days.

Nergüi smiled and then, to my utter surprise, laughed. It was softer than the sharp bark so often granted me; it came out from deep in her belly and filled the room. Her eyes were scrunched in delight. I felt as though every hard thing in my life had been worth it for this singular sight of her.

"You must think I'm terrible, Freida," she said. "I think you got to know the worst of me."

"No," I said, a simple, clear statement that was the most I could get out.

"I didn't die. My rector just sent me the results of the ritual. Here, I'll show you."

She blew on the array to put it to sleep and pulled out her glass ball. I supposed she was lucky the bathhouse tunics had roomy pockets, because I couldn't imagine her letting that ball out of her sight.

The lights were jittery, arcing in complex interlocking waves that made me think of the impenetrable, subconscious patternmaking of the gods in their tunnels. She frowned at it, then closed her eyes and bowed her head. Her lips barely moved as she chanted in a low drone words my wetware couldn't begin to make sense of. As she chanted, the lights slowly dimmed and receded into a darkness that seemed to fold upon itself like smoke, revealing hints of images that never quite coalesced. She opened her eyes.

"Look at the glass, Freida," she whispered. "It's all there. Where I am now. You see that faint light?"

I leaned closer. There by her hands were a pair of zipping lights, twirling like dizzy fish at the bottom of a well.

"That's where I am. I am treading one of my dangerous paths in the fringes of my possibilities. But I am still me. I'm still alive."

"Does that mean you could tesseract back one day?"

"Nothing is certain. My rector is almost sure. But for now, I have to stay here. You can see it. I have to tread my sacred path here, in the Library."

"With me," I whispered.

She took my hand. Then she shook her head and, with a determined wrinkle between her eyebrows, leaned forward and kissed me.

✦

Nadi was waiting in my room when I staggered back a few hours before dawn. I knew I must have looked drunk, though Nergüi and I hadn't had anything more potent than cinnamon tea.

I gasped to see zir sitting in one of my chairs, zir walker folded into a ball in the corner of the room. The sight of zir punched the air out of my lungs. I tried to hide it, but I couldn't—it was guilt at having forgotten about zir for a few hours and anger at what was happening and the reminder of every awful thing even Nergüi's love couldn't protect me from.

Ze winced. "Sit down, love. I'm sorry for giving you something more to worry about, but don't make me look up at you."

I sat. I would have anyway; my legs had started trembling. Ze looked fine. Better, perhaps, than even the night we had gone tunnel crawling in Kohru. But ze had just announced zir death in two weeks.

"Do you want me to explain?" Ze sounded almost unsure of zirself, which I never would have believed possible even a week ago. But I had come to the edge of my glass, as Nergüi would say, and crossed to the other side. Nothing here, even in my own room, seemed familiar to me anymore.

"How much longer would the new treatment have given you?"

Ze waved zir hand. "Another month? It's not very precise at this stage."

"So why take half of that away? And how are you planning—" I choked on the words.

Ze noticed but didn't stop. "At the party, of course. It has to be a suitably dramatic exit for this to work."

The tremors had risen to my voice. "You're still going on about that stupid party when you are dying and everything ... everything ..." *Has gone wrong*, I wanted to say. But I had started crying at last, and nothing more would come out.

"Freida, Freida," ze murmured, drawing me to zir, stroking my hair like ze had when I was a child. Zir only, special child. How I loved zir. It didn't seem possible that this was ending. Would it end while I was still frozen like this, on the precipice, unable to accept the fall?

"Seventeen is an awkward age," ze said.

I sniffed. "I'll be eighteen soon." But ze wouldn't see it.

Zir hand paused on the crown of my head. "I want you to know you'll have a choice."

"What choice? Stay and become Quinn's pet AI or leave and die in the floating city of Sasurandām?" A god without even tunnels. What kind of god was the first who had birthed all the others? (You will forgive me, Nameren—your fame is wide across the human systems, but I had never paid much attention to you or any of the non-Library gods.)

"Leave with my family. They should arrive next week. We're an old Awilu clan, one of the inner branches. We can keep you safe from those of the trunk who want to see you attempt to kill the Nameren."

I *was* falling now, wasn't I? This was some kind of death.

"I can't stay here?" My voice was very small.

I felt the cartilage rising in zir throat as ze swallowed, painfully. "Not as you are," ze said. "I had thought . . . but it's past now. Quinn's position is too strong. I'm supporting Volei, of course, but Quinn will probably win the election. He's spent the last eighteen years buying votes, after all." Zir smile was as bitter as young indigo wine. "You can't stay as a librarian. They'll take you too easily; you break too many of their rules, love. The only chance—and this will still be dangerous—is invoking the old Library City charter and claiming sanctuary in a freehold. You couldn't leave its bounds, but even the Head Librarian can't take you against your will there."

I took a few stuttering breaths. "Then what happened to Old Child Freehold?"

"They pretended it was an accident. I told you, love, it's an option. Perhaps not a good one."

Then my only chance at staying in the Library meant trusting my life to Quinn's respect for the old laws, or at least his fear of the political liability if he broke them. I would end up living in a grub tunnel for the rest of my life.

I pushed myself away from zir and tugged on the encrusted pearls of my red-and-silver motley novice vest. "I might as well go to Sasurandām," I said.

"You could," ze agreed.

I sighed and went over to my wall of keepsakes. The archive bone was first in the drawer, brighter than any bone ought to be, but not precisely glowing. It glimmered when I touched it, like bioluminescence.

"Can archives talk?" I asked.

"Most of the time. Do you want me to leave?"

"No. Let's see her together."

The story of your armored, raging demon soldiers, Nameren, and what they'd done to Nergüi's people had helped me understand that it was time. I had a place in that ancient conflict, astonishingly enough. Nadi was preparing us all for war. I needed to know who I was and what I could truly do.

Nadi put zir hand alongside mine on the bone. The material heated until it nearly burned, though I touched it with my new-made hand and the skin didn't seem to feel extremes of temperature in the same way. The bone's strange markings glowed and faded in an oblique rhythm.

"Hello, sister."

My head snapped up even as my hand registered the rapidly fading heat of the archive bone.

In our augmented vision, not more than two feet away from us, stood a ghost with my own face. Her smile faltered when she turned to Nadi. "You brought your handler?" she asked me.

"Nadi's my parent."

The ghost's eyes widened. "Isn't that the Head Librarian's vest?"

Nadi nodded. "I am still that. Who are you?"

The ghost's lips twisted. "A failed model, as your kind would have it. I'm a projection of Xochiquetzal, nineteenth trained-to-completion special weapon, Library property, but never a librarian, who in refusing to die for the Nameren chose to die for herself."

"I saw one of your other sisters, Bathsheba," I said.

"Poor Bathsheba. She was too angry to go my way. She must have tried, hating it every second." She looked around the room, and turned back to us, frowning. "What year is it?"

"Five hundred seven," I said.

She blinked. "It's been hundreds of years," she said. "No one tried to find me?"

"Old Coyote bottled you up like a message on the sea."

"Just like him," she said.

"Isn't it?"

"Jealous old bastard."

We stared at each other across time, startled. My chest burned with an old song, after darkness.

"What number are you, sister?"

My new hand started to twitch. "I have none."

Her eyes narrowed. "They stopped numbering us?"

"She's the last," Nadi said firmly.

"The last?" Xochiquetzal looked so blank that if she had been a real human, I would have thought her language module had failed. "But . . . the Nameren still exists?"

Nadi nodded. "The great aurochs still sits in Sasurandām."

Xochiquetzal appeared very upset by this. "So many of us gone, all for nothing."

"It wasn't—" Nadi began, but Xochiquetzal's gaze snapped to me, and she lifted an accusatory finger.

"Will you go?"

I knew what she meant immediately. "I don't know."

Her response was as sour as wine turning to vinegar. "That's the same as having no choice at all. What's your name, numberless sister?"

"Freida."

She shook her head. "At least that's the same, Freida Erzulie."

She flicked her hand outward, so that light flew from the tips of her fingers. It illuminated her projection, though it didn't touch us. Her face washed out in the light, and her expression fell slack, or stiff, as though into a bed of soft clay. She vanished.

Nadi dropped the bone. I fumbled with it awkwardly before righting my grip. I felt as distant as I had been while drugged in the infirmary, filled with false peace.

"Freida Erzulie?" I repeated.

Nadi coughed. Zir eyes were as hollow as drums. "Your name, my love."

"You never told me that before."

"I didn't want to mark you with it."

"With what?"

"She's a goddess of love. All of you are—were—named for folkloric figures of love."

At least that's the same. From the beginning, ze had known what I was—perhaps not the moment ze found me in the tunnels, but certainly by the time ze named me. I had been marked, just like my sisters, but I had been born too late.

And alone?

I turned to Nadi slowly but with great force, like a water horse changing course in a river. *"How are you sure I'm the last?"*

Nadi flinched. "No one had found a child in more than a century. There haven't been any others in the nearly eighteen years since."

I felt nauseous, shivery. "Maybe they just didn't leave the babies where you could find them in time."

Nadi swallowed. "But why—"

"Gods aren't human!" I screamed the last word. My head was throbbing. "How could you expect a material god to know how to take care of a human baby? Of organic life? They can barely *talk* to us! For all you know, hundreds of my sisters have died that way. For all you know, there's one wailing right now in the bowels of Mahue'e. There's not enough librarians to keep track of every artery. Your people condemned us to be born in misery and die in misery."

Ze took steady, careful breaths. You may blame zir for nearly eighteen years of not bothering to consider the possibility, Nameren, but I submit this in zir favor: Ze did not deny it.

"We have to stop it." Nadi's voice was a gravelly whisper. "You have to be the last one."

⁺⁺

Three of Nadi's elder relatives were waiting on the shuttle platform when Nergüi and I went to pick them up a week later. They had that distant, ecstatic look of travelers recently shorn of corporeal existence and miraculously reconstituted by virtue of passing through a higher-dimensional paradox. The giddy, childlike wonder surprised me, though I'd seen it often enough, because they were Awilu, old enough to show their age, and had surely been through tesseracts dozens of times in their steady, augmented lives.

All three bore something that Nadi also bore, though I couldn't say that the first shared zir nose or the second zir thin, shaped eyebrows. It was in their carriage, the deep familiarity that bubbled up among them like a fresh spring of love and shared history. They were all bald, in the style of Awilu inner branch elders, and had draped their bare heads with fine nets woven of bright cloth joined with beads of jet and silver. The beads tinkled as they moved and rang out when the tallest one tilted zir head and cackled with unselfconscious delight at the sight of me.

"It's our third branch child! Look, Beleti, she still has those eyes, just like the Madonna of the river night. You're quite beautiful, my branch child, but I'm sure you don't need me to tell you so! I'm Geran, your branch elder."

Ze leaned forward to take my arm by the elbow and thump my back with zir left hand. We rarely greeted one another in this manner in the Library, but I did it naturally, already feeling a laughing affection blossoming between me and these ebullient strangers.

I introduced Nergüi, who had hung back during this scene. She disliked public displays, which of course made her an interesting pair with me, and even more like a starling in a lake of flamingos when surrounded by Niphense Awilu branch elders, who lowered their voices for no one.

The third elder nodded thoughtfully at Nergüi. Ze was shorter and rounder than the others, and the only one who truly looked ancient—zir face was nearly as lined as Nadi's now.

"You're the disciple, then? The one with the case before the tribunal?"

"Me and Joshua Totolkozkat," she said carefully. "We hope to force the Treaty-keepers to actually enforce their treaty."

This elder, Yeri, let out an appreciative whistle. "Now that's the fire we need in this place! We are living through dark times. The Mahām provoking an intersystem crisis again—"

"We should have taken the Nameren away after the Great War," one of zir children, Beleti, interrupted. "Now history will judge the errors of our ancestors."

"As it will judge ours," Yeri said peaceably. "But I would ask you, disciple. The Lunar and Mahām delegates seem to have taken a particular exception to you. I wonder why that is?"

Nergüi's scowl was a wonder of the form; it twisted her eyebrows into angry hooks, it carved the dimples in her chin and cheeks into rough divots chipped out of unforgiving stone, her forehead an unexplored mountain range, her mouth a sour, leathery orange. I knew better than to laugh, but those scowls always provoked me to tenderness, to an almost proprietary joy in my knowledge of her.

"Because they want us to all line up for the slaughter like guinea pigs. I'm their category error. The exception that proves their lie. We don't stay because we submit to them, but because we submit to the higher devotion of the Lighted Path."

Yeri smiled softly, as though ze saw precisely what I did. "And do you still, child?"

Nergüi swung her glass by its chain and rolled it into the palm of her left hand. The lights swizzled and swirled and settled, as they so often did these days, into the bottom of the globe. "My path," Nergüi said, with that angry defiance I loved as much as her scowls, "has taken me here, to the edge of the universe."

"Then may you follow it brightly," said the three elders in unison, after a moment I could only call surprised recognition.

Nergüi blinked with her own surprise and lowered her head in humble acknowledgment.

We walked back to the retreat together, exchanging the good-natured, probing questions of recent acquaintances who have every expectation of coming to like one another very much. I studied them intensely, painfully aware that Nadi had sent for them to give me an escape from the Library if I chose. Could I start a new life in a new system, with a new family, and two untouchable material gods?

I sent to Nadi to say we were coming back, but I knew my avatar might not get through for hours. The Librarian Council was in session, and according to reports, the only thing preventing them from holding a vote of no confidence was that ze had already announced the date of zir death. Nadi was a very popular Head, both in Library City and in the three systems. Not even Quinn wanted to seem cruel to a beloved leader about to return to stardust. In this two-week political sunset, ze had bought time to set things in motion. Clever, as always, my Nadi.

So I would have to entertain zir branch elders until ze could see them. Another clever move: giving me a chance to know these strangers who might be my family.

Geran and Beleti were siblings, twins born three years apart. Yeri was their birth parent and at least two hundred years old. Beleti's daughter—she had transitioned early in life, Beleti said—was Nadi's birth parent. "But she crossed into the virtuals, oh, it must be thirty years ago now," Beleti said with a smile finely coated in sadness. Geran put zir arm on Beleti's shoulder and we kept walking. I didn't pry.

"How old is Nadi, then?" Nergüi asked. I turned to her in surprise, and she gave me this fast, wry smile, the hidden underbelly of her scowl.

Beleti patted down the already perfect creases of zir golden spider-silk caftan. "Oh, ze was born just after that last crisis with the Mahām and their barbaric war ritual—I remember I was serving in the Assembly back then and we very nearly authorized armed peacekeepers, but the pragmatic voices prevailed, which was a shame in hindsight—that would make zir about eighty-three?"

Nergüi's expression froze, but she reached for my hand. "Eighty-five," she said plainly.

Geran gave her a speculative look and sighed. "So young. Nadi's child went to Soren's branch after ze joined the Library, said ze couldn't bear to watch Nadi throw away half zir life for some latter-day supposed *sapiens* vision of utopianist uplift."

I froze on the path. "Nadi has a child!"

"They haven't spoken in decades," Geran said. "You're zir child now. The child of zir spirit and mind."

This information lodged awkwardly beneath my sternum, and I wondered, again, just how little I knew of the person I loved the most in the world.

I led them to Nadi's quarters and poured four glasses of indigo wine from a case that Beleti had brought with zir. It poured even blacker than Nadi's and released a faint aroma of peat bog. I smiled—ze would love it.

"You don't want any, Nergüi?" Beleti asked.

Nergüi shook her head quickly. "Thank you. But disciples are discouraged from using altering substances without proper spiritual training."

Beleti nodded slowly. "That does seem wise, now doesn't it, Geran?"

"I think it's a shame, but however you like." Geran had already nearly finished zir glass.

Yeri looked between them with a small smile. "A life well-lived can never be without its moments of extremity . . . but even extremes must be handled with moderation."

Nergüi turned in surprise. "Yes, exactly that."

Geran smirked and upended the dregs into zir mouth. "Fine, fine. Yeri, you and Nadi have always been so alike—radical lovers and moderation mystics."

Nadi's laugh startled me from the doorway, but the three branch elders had already turned with an eerie, fluid synchronicity.

"My elder Geran, as dedicated to anti-philosophical hedonism as ever, I see," Nadi said as Beleti moved forward in something approaching a run and embraced Nadi fiercely. I could see how frail Nadi had become in zir grandparent's arms, and I saw how zir grip weakened in response to the same and caressed Nadi's back with a painful tenderness. The legs of Nadi's walker bent until they were at the same height.

"How could they have let this happen to you!" Beleti said. It struck me how much Nadi must have given up to come here. How many of the privileges of zir birth ze had shorn to take librarian's vows. Now zir scalp was covered in a fuzz of steel-gray curls instead of fine net that made music as ze passed.

"I made the choice," Nadi said shortly, but not without compassion. "I am still making it, Beleti."

Beleti didn't even nod, but something seemed to resolve between them. Nadi stepped away and embraced Geran and, last, Yeri.

"I know you've chosen the day," Yeri said. "I suppose it would be soon in any case. I can feel the sands slipping out between us. I won't be long behind you."

Nadi closed zir eyes, as though withstanding a blow. "May it go well with you," Nadi said after a beat.

Yeri smiled. "And with you, my child. I'm glad you called us."

"I thank you for daring to cross the void."

Geran raised zir thin eyebrows at the bottle that was still in my hand; a spiky red fruit crawled over the lip and said, "Another little drop, if you please?" in Library Standard. I gave a startled laugh and poured zir a full glass. My thresholds had lowered around the three of them on our walk without my awareness. Geran sending zir avatar so soon after our meeting was daring, perhaps even presumptuous, but it felt like kindness.

"Cross the void?" Nergüi repeated, as though she smelled something.

Geran swirled the wine. "Elders of Yeri's generation are as superstitious about tesseracts as any Miuri disciple—apologies to present company."

Yeri caught Nergüi's eye and shrugged. "And our youth," ze said, "are sometimes more sanguine about their own dissolution than we grandchildren of war ever can be."

Nergüi swung her glass ball and it glowed in the reflection of Yeri's golden robe. The lights inside swizzled and dove while we all breathed and watched.

⁺✦⁺

The first guests arrived late, just before sundown, blown like flowers through the gauzy fabrics that Geran and I had hung by the entrance to the sanctuary garden. Our stage for Nadi's last party spanned most of the territory between Iemaja's temple and the retreat. Nets of blue and orange fabric bound with beads braced the spaces between the trees above us, catching the light and the cloudy breeze of the desert that coated everything with a fine dust, red as the rust that named the season. "A season of endings," Nadi had said with satisfaction as we planned. "We will not hide from it."

Nergüi and I sat in a discreet corner behind the Awilu quartet playing woodwind ballads from the era of the sagas. ("Everything from the wars against the Nameren," Yeri had said with satisfaction.) They played beneath a Mahām fire tree, which smelled of copal incense as it burned up inside, glowing through the holes in its metal-hard bark that would eventually release its seeds when it died. Nadi and zir branch elders waited near the entrance along with Eltian and Volei. As Nadi had predicted, the guests were late because, precisely one hour before, a leak had flooded the light and heavy bands: the first evidentiary brief filed on behalf of the Nawas of Tenoch and the Miuri of the Mahām satellite, detailing the historical basis of their claim to revive the apocryphal autonomy provisions in Freedom Primary. There, we had compiled the first salvo of revelations from Huehue, with a promise of more to come.

Nadi had wanted to make sure I had everything I needed from Huehue before we released. "Quinn will do anything to keep you from the tunnels after that," Nadi had said, eyes gleaming with an almost otherworldly light, more zirself than

I had ever seen zir as ze planned the exact steps of zir death. "He has to suspect that there is more but can't be sure. That's insurance"—ze planted one finger on the ancient wood of zir dining table—"against worse violence."

"He won't kill me unless he knows what I found?" I said dryly.

Nergüi blanched and reached for her glass ball as though it could reveal our fates in the lights. "Why haven't you left already, Freida?" she asked.

I raised my eyebrows. "What, and cross the void?" She looked away.

Yeri put a sympathetic hand on Nergüi's shoulder. "She has made a choice, child. As you have. She can still leave with us . . . after, if she wills it."

Then I had turned away, unsteady. I wondered how Nadi seemed so calm, so focused on zir task that even fear could not touch zir. I wouldn't leave the Library before ze did. I wasn't sure I wanted to leave at all, even now.

"If Huehue has more to tell, it will take me years to hear it," I had said, at last. "It's painful for zir, and painful for me. But Joshua says what I have should be enough."

"It's more than enough, I think," Vaterite had said, from the window by the garden. He seemed wary and uncomfortable here, in the stronghold of the librarians. Knowing all I did now about librarians, I didn't blame him. But he and the other Tiger Freeholders had agreed to store my interactions with Huehue, thus safeguarding them against Quinn and his faction.

He had also made clear that I was welcome among them, and they would give me whatever protection they could offer. I had told him I wasn't sure.

Freida the Unsure, formerly of the Library, I thought now, bitterly. Something must have crossed my face because Nergüi gave my broonie hand a quick, awkward squeeze. I smiled at her, despite myself. Another reason I didn't want to go.

"Do you think this will work?" she asked as the first guests hurried through the gauzy archway, greeting Nadi with pinched expressions and low-voiced questions that I knew Nadi would deflect as smoothly as a mirror.

"Define what you mean by *work*?"

She glared at me. "Keep us safe? Prevent war?"

"Oh, that. No," I said, sighing into the rumbling basso of the vuvuzela. "I don't think we can expect that much."

Turning from the first of the guests, Nadi whispered something to Volei, who gave a nervous laugh. Nadi was magnificent in a robe of green silk, overlaid with the gray vest of Head Librarian and the infinite strand of shards, unique as a twist of DNA, looped and glowing around zir neck and arms.

Nergüi snagged a pair of drinks from the passing tree-root servers and pressed one into my tingling hands. "Breathe, Freida," she said. "It makes surviving easier."

"Everything is ending, Nergüi," I said.

"We are children of impermanence," she said, unflinching. "Everything we make will be unmade. Every light will be extinguished."

Now it was my turn to scowl at her. "Are you trying to be unhelpful?"

Her expression barely changed, but those bushy eyebrows twitched in a way that somehow conveyed affection and sympathy. "I'm not," she said. "Suffering is a condition of existence, Freida. Nadi's death is a tragedy. But there are a hundred thousand lights of zir soul, and they will keep moving back and forth through zir possible lives, and sometimes—not often, but sometimes—one light will brush against yours and you will feel zir again, with you."

I imagined this like the giant crystal in Nergüi's temple with its infinite lights swirling inside. It did seem, for a moment, as beautiful as she was.

"Until my light goes out," I said.

Nergüi smiled at that, for some reason, and ran her fingers along the uneven coast of my hairline, just like Nadi. "Yes, until then."

She wore the very same robes as always. Her one concession to the occasion was that she had sent them to be cleaned and mended. Out of the way behind the fire tree and the quartet, no one noticed us. This was also according to plan. Very soon, if Nadi's predictions were correct, the Nameren's priests—and, if we were lucky, Quinn himself—would arrive, thinking to force a confrontation over the contents of the leak. They had very pointedly not been invited.

Atempa's chimera swooped across my augmented field of vision. "Incoming!" it squawked. "Reverend Shipbuilder is angry enough to turn demigod. He's on his way with at least two others. I've been talking about how weak Quinn is looking among the librarians for the last week. Signs are good."

My octopus tapped beaks with the chimera. "Good job! I'll tell Eltian it's time to open the feeds."

The chimera's dry laugh was pure Atempa. "May it be a glorious show."

The chimera faded and I turned to Nergüi, heart pounding. "The priests are on their way. Ready?"

"Nadi said they'd come." She swallowed. She looked like she might be sick. Then she squared her shoulders.

"I am a Disciple of the Lighted Path," she said. "And I will do my duty."

She kissed me briefly on the lips and ducked from behind the relative safety of the fire tree, into the thickening crowd. Heads turned as she passed, whispers following like the wake of a small boat, but she gave no hint of caring. The chain was in her hand, her ball swaying like a censer as she walked.

I sent to Eltian that it was time to open the event to the public bands. High-wetware guests might even broadcast their own bodily sensations for others to experience. There were grubs hidden among the flower beds, still in the swaying branches of the pochote trees, their backs mottled to match the pattern of dusty leaves against the sky. Whatever happened here tonight, the gods would watch alongside the rest of us, and remember.

From across the garden, Nadi greeted a cohort of young, four-shard novices. They moved on together in a nervous huddle, whispering and glancing over their shoulders at the older librarians. I watched them wistfully. My path had branched away from theirs, irrevocably. I had turned in my novice cord of shards and my motley vest that morning. Nadi had explained it was necessary for the plan, but that of course ze would think of something else if I wanted to keep my official status. But I was Freida of the Library, and I would do my duty.

Nergüi arrived at Nadi's side at precisely the moment that the Nameren priests and the West Librarian were barred entry at the archway.

Beleti had set-designed this part, and even knowing it would happen, my breath caught at the sight of the tree roots that made the arch bowing with an icy humility to keep the six men from crossing the threshold.

Every eye turned to them, like a compass to true north.

Quinn wrestled with the gnarled roots, but they held him firm. His face was red with indignation. "Another of the Head Librarian's crimes! Let us go! How dare you detain a fellow librarian and diplomats!"

Nergüi stepped forward. One of the priests actually hissed at the sight of her.

Nadi turned smoothly to her, immediately apologetic. "Disciple," ze said, "I apologize. I would not have invited you had I known . . ."

"They plan the genocide of my people and yet still imagine themselves to be the aggrieved party," Nergüi said loudly. If her delivery was a little wooden, the rage in those wood-dark eyes was as real as fire. "Why have you come here today? Or do you think you can buy this death as you have bought ours?"

Quinn gaped at her and then Nadi, realizing how perfectly he had played into their hands. His features flashed with a coruscating fury, then he wrestled them into a semblance of neutrality.

"We wish you well on your journey," he said, each word coated with insincerity. "But we take grave exception to the slander leaked to the light bands today regarding this joke of a petition for node reactivation."

One of the priests—Reverend Shipbuilder himself—elbowed his way to Quinn's side, forehead shiny with sweat. "It is a direct insult to our good-faith attempts at negotiating a peace with a Head Librarian who has never—"

"May I offer you men some drinks?" Nadi interrupted smoothly, switching to Awilu, which allowed zir to put a distinct emphasis on their gender. "You are most welcome to celebrate with me here, in my final hours." The gnarled roots released them with something like reluctance, folding themselves back beneath the colored flags of the arch.

Ze left them there, mid-grievance, with the pained air of someone who has witnessed a social faux pas but is too kind to belabor it. Now everyone would know that they had barged in on zir final celebration uninvited, unwanted, and bullies to the last. I wanted to applaud.

Nadi's avatar flicked in and out of my augmented sight.

"Now, love."

Now, then. I stepped from behind the ephemeral safety of the fire tree. Nadi was approaching the center of the garden on zir walker, decorated for the occasion like the gnarled tree roots of the servers and the arch. I was wearing a tunic and split skirt of unaffiliated ivory, a statement in and of itself. I belonged to no one now, not to the Library, not even to Nadi.

I met zir where we had planned, when the light from the long sunset struck the sprawling beds of poppies. Volei stood nervously to Nadi's side, eyes darting like a caged bird's. Nadi's great flaw was that ze had not imagined ze would die and leave me defenseless. Ze had built a system that could not survive zir. Ze had shored up power in service of the Library's peace and the Treaty, but zir coalition had no force on its own. Perhaps I could not forgive zir for that, Nameren. Perhaps that was why I felt a chill in that final embrace.

"Daughter," Nadi said, publicly acknowledging me as zir kin for the first time in my life.

My vision swam. I knelt.

"Head Librarian Nadi," I said in archaic Awilu, the language of the sagas. "I thank you for your dedication to the Library, and to its dream of peace. I thank you for your moral leadership in these difficult times, when the Treaty is manipulated with such contempt. I thank you for your wisdom and leadership, even now, when you are passing from us. May your successor hold your example to her heart during the long road we must walk without you."

Volei gave me a pained look and then turned swiftly to Nadi and sank to one knee. "I, too, thank you, Head Librarian," she said, in the same language.

Around us, a ripple of guests lowered themselves to the earth or inclined their heads. Only a few strained against the prevailing wind—Quinn and the priests chief among them—chins up, radiating angry heat, much like the fire tree behind them. The holes and fissures in its bark emitted the brightest light in the twilit garden, and the quartet, sweating and ecstatic, coaxed their instruments into rumbling lows and sweet honey middles, crackling in time with that old wood. They were playing the lament of Atriman at the sight of zir parent's drowned body the morning after the flood.

For a few measures, ze hummed softly along to the reverent murmur of the music, and the words came to me unbidden:

You have failed me, but not for that rupture
Had I thought my peace would be my grief
In the morning you loved so well.

"I only wish," Nadi said, eyes locked with mine, "I could have served you all better. These new revelations prove that the Library's peace has often been as false as the War Ritual is real. If we mean to protect all the people of the three systems, we must make amends, and not fall prey to the stunted ideologies of national exceptionalism—Mahām, Martian . . . even Awilu."

This ripped through the crowd like lightning. The Nameren's priests began shouting. Quinn raised his voice over theirs, but I did not pay attention to what he said. Nadi had warned us this might happen. I stood amid the hubbub and met zir eyes. One last time.

"I'm going now," I said.

"I know. I'll be with you."

In the end, I only gripped zir hand, withered and cold but firm in zir purpose. I would not cry here. It was not part of our plan. I would not cry, but my heart was a river.

Ze flicked zir eyes to Quinn and the priests elbowing their way through the crowd and stuck out zir tongue ever so slightly. Unthinking, I snorted back a laugh. The moment held, every leathery fold of zir face radiant like Nergüi's glass ball.

"Go," ze mouthed.

✦

I went to Mahue'e for the final part of our plan and activated the archive bone on my way. Xochiquetzal had explained to us the most likely way to turn the program off for good. But we only dared try now, when every librarian was distracted by Nadi's spectacle above and no one would think of stopping zir one final act as Head Librarian.

"You don't use a lot of protection, do you?" Xochiquetzal observed as I worked my way deeper into the tunnels. "What is that, a spider-silk scarf for a face mask? Don't they equip us these days?"

I didn't immediately answer her, crouching and judging the distance between the rock I was on and the one I wanted to jump to. It wasn't a long jump, but if I missed, I'd be burned alive in slow-moving magma.

I made the jump and wiped my forehead. The archive bone was burning in my pocket, but I could hardly feel it above the penetrating heat of the lava river. "They don't equip me at all," I said, panting. "I told you, I'm the only one. Only Nadi even knows what I am."

Xochiquetzal, hovering a few feet above the lava bed, shook her head. "And you just . . . go anyway? Risk your life in the tunnels, even though they don't force you?"

One more jump, and I'd reach the shelf at the far end of the tunnel and relatively stable ground. My muscles burned with exertion, but I didn't mind. Right now, I needed the distraction.

I jumped, caught the ledge with the tacky grips of my gloves, and hauled myself over the lip. I lay there for a moment, panting.

"I like it," I said, after I caught my breath. "It's the only place I feel safe."

There was an entrance to the command chamber nearby. Xochiquetzal had told me to look for the command room in Shamsum, a little-understood avatar only accessible through physical proximity. I began stalking down the tunnel, dark but for the light I had slung across my chest. "Was it nice," I asked Xochiquetzal, "having sisters?"

If I focused, I could see her beside me in the dark, because of course she was only in my augmented space. "Perhaps it was nice, I don't know, I never thought of it that way. It was like being on a boat with your best friends and your worst enemies and watching them, one by one, step off the prow and drown." She shook her head. "But we were in it together."

"Tell me why the Baobab cries," I said softly.

"Oh. Yes. But we only ever made it across the stars to die."

I wiped the sweat from the back of my neck and kept moving. I traced my fingertips along the wall. My left hand skipped over empty, hot air before landing again on the rough volcanic stone. There.

I took a deep lungful of thick, humid air, sharp with sulfur and my own nervous sweat.

"Hurry, Freida Erzulie," Xochiquetzal said. "The archive will power down soon."

I pushed my way into the narrow crawl space. Even the light around my neck seemed to dim, overwhelmed by the lightless heat of this place. I hoped this was Shamsum and not a dead end or a trap. I reached hopefully for my network, but kilometers of stone and the natural damping effect of the gods disrupted even the most basic signals. I wouldn't know if Vaterite and the other freeholders had succeeded in making connections with the other three materials until I could connect via branch worm.

I would have no second chances if this didn't work. Nadi would be dead in half an hour, and no matter what I chose, spelunking in the deepest reaches of the tunnels would be almost impossible after this night. Now that he knew I had breached Huehue, Quinn would make sure of that.

The capillary pressed me farther and farther down, until I was crawling on torn hands over gritty sand in a stream that smelled of blood. My breath labored, mute and stripped of music.

"There's light," my sister said, so close to my ear I imagined I could feel the tickle of her breath on my neck. A moment later, I saw it: a reddish glow at the end of the curving tunnel.

At last, streaked with that filmy white sand, I emerged into a small, squat circular chamber. The material of the walls and domed ceiling was pure Shamsum umber. It glowed of its own accord, and my own light dimmed in deference. In the center of the room was a low altar, and at the center of that a shallow depression out of which bubbled clear water. It was beautiful in a way that Mahue'e so rarely allowed herself to be, a shrine to the heart of the earth where she had been born and from where she had been taken, a memory just barely accessible to her human creators.

It was also filled with thousands of tiny bones.

Xochiquetzal made a noise, choking, inarticulate. An archive bone did not breathe, of course, but I suppose that it retained the memory of breath, just as it retained the capacity for horror.

I did not scream. There was no air to scream. Besides, the walls must already be saturated with centuries of them. The Shamsum umber of the floor was buried beneath shifting white sands, the same, perhaps, that I had crawled my way through to reach this place. I closed my eyes, Nameren. There is only so much a heart can hold.

I put my mouth to the fount of the altar and drank. I should have tested it for impurities, but I was very far from caring for my own well-being and the water was pure. Maybe I didn't expect any less of her.

Xochiquetzal was crying. "They just *left* us."

There were no new bodies. At least I could be grateful for that. At some point, Mahue'e or Iemaja must have realized that no one was fetching them from this place. So they had tried to make us elsewhere.

I pulled out my pack and took out the Mahue'e-safe branch worm that Plumed Serpent Freehold had given me the day before. It was white and still somehow cold, even in this place.

"You need the other three materials to agree," Xochiquetzal said faintly. "Have they?"

I put one end of the branch worm beneath the burbling water and the other on my forehead. "I'm about to find out."

As soon as the branch worm began to connect, I could feel it: the faint hum of the physical program, the instructions inserted here just after the Great War, the careless material code that had created the thousands of my lonely, abandoned sisters. A chorus of cicadas crying and dying one by one in darkness.

Through the branch worm, I had relay access to my surface connections. I searched for Vaterite first.

"We have the key from Iemaja," he said. "Many Worlds has Tenehet's. Is there a path through to Mahue'e? I'm feeding them through now."

The fount was all heart crystal, and for all her inaccessibility, it wasn't hard to run the queries. If anything, she seemed grateful that someone was taking an interest, providing me with details on the program, how many cycles had been run for the last three centuries, how close each cycle had come to the programmed ideal. I wanted to vomit.

"Ask her about you," Xochiquetzal said, suddenly beside me in the augmented query.

Experiment two standard deviations from ideal parameters, it returned. *Potential and liabilities in extremes. No conclusions as to mission suitability can be reached at this time. Would you like more of that model?*

"No!" Xochiquetzal and I said, with enough force that the query hung for several seconds, as though disconcerted.

"Freida?" Vaterite's voice rang between my ears. "I've had word from Brerrabbit Freehold. They almost have it."

"Vaterite," I said, a simple voice projection like the one he was using. "What time is it there?"

There, I had said, as though he were in a completely different world. "It's . . . nearly midnight."

I closed my eyes. Vaterite went silent.

"I think I'd like to stay here," Xochiquetzal said into the quiet burbling of the fountain. "I don't know where I died—I made the archive before I found it. But this seems like a good place."

"It's a tomb," I said.

"Well, isn't that where you should be when you're dead?"

Vaterite came back. "It's in. The command shard should register their permission now. I'm going to patch you through . . ."

"Are you there, Freida?"

Nadi. Ze must have withdrawn from zir own party. Ze had planned to be alone with Eltian and zir branch elders at the end. One cup of the best indigo wine, one vial of the medic's finest poison.

"Nadi, is it already time?"

Just our voices, here at the end.

"My love," ze said. "You're in the command shard?" Zir voice was strangely flat, stripped of condemnation or desire. As though ze were already halfway in the earth.

"Yes."

"It will be better if you touch it. It makes oral command interface easier. Just repeat after me."

Xochiquetzal watched impassively as I gritted my teeth against the shock and cold of the command shard. I started to repeat Nadi's instructions in the heart coding language I wasn't in any shape to parse as it went through me.

"Your handler is *helping* you disable the program!" she said suddenly. Her eyebrows drew together in momentary anger. Then she shrugged and looked again at the drifting piles of infant bones.

"You're a Iemaja girl—I can see that. You're slick with someone else's caring. That's good. Maybe that's good. They're not making you go to the Nameren. So maybe you'll go of your own accord."

I blinked in surprise, but my mouth kept repeating the code, which was now into Old Coyote's key, the last required for authorization.

"Execute disable," I said at last.

The walls flashed once, and the command shard jolted against my fingers. I stumbled backward.

"Disable executed," the walls said, in my voice, in Xochiquetzal's voice, in a hundred hundred tiny voices that would have raised mountains if someone had bothered to look for them.

"My love," Nadi said, very faintly, with a touch of humor as distant as the stars, whose light is always new. "I have a problem for you."

Ze fell silent. I felt my blood rushing with a lonely tide. Xochiquetzal and I looked at each other one last time from across the bone dust.

"How would I kill him?" I asked. "If I wanted to?"

Xochiquetzal spread her arms wide.

"Execute. Disable," she said.

Her archive bone flashed one final time, burning in my pocket. After a numb minute, I fumbled for it with my new-made hand and let it fall to the floor, silent among our sisters.

Nadi was hours dead by the time I made my way back to the retreat. I sat vigil by zir body with Nergüi and my branch elders until they took it away for the state funeral. I did not get to attend—Quinn was elected that evening by a one-vote margin.

The next morning, he arrested me.

"Ze never said goodbye."

The god is an aurochs with a man's chest and arms, or a man with an aurochs's head and hooves. His balls drag the earth like a plow. He and the girl sit side by side on the muddy bank of a clear river. The girl takes up a thoughtful handful of dark green clay.

"Do you think so?"

"You never saw zir again."

"Not alive."

"Were you angry?"

She laughs, the girl, a soft curl in the damp air. It invites him.

"Ze staged zir death for an audience of the three systems. I'm just one girl. How should ze have said goodbye?"

"Your guardian left you exposed! You were alone, abandoned among enemies! You never even told zir the worst of it."

"The worst? Oh, you mean Quinn."

"And Samlin." He swings his horns back and forth, back and forth, twin scythes threshing dangerous wheat.

The girl leans back in the clayey mud and closes her eyes. The sevenfold suns spin in a round above her, and a few bend down for a peek. "I was alone. I was always going to have to be alone someday. But ze left me a weapon, O Nameren."

She can feel his snuffling breath against her cheek, dry and cool as a sacred cave locked for millennia beneath the earth.

"My heart shard," he said in a low, satisfied rumble.

"And a few others."

The god sits back on his haunches. Mud splatters them both. The girl looks up at him from beneath her lashes, utterly unafraid, and sees that angry bull face moved to laughter. Is there something human in his eye ridges? A dream of a dream of a man whose dust is now scattered among three galaxies?

He roars with contentment. "Clever, clever!"

"Do you want to hear the story, then?"

"No." The forbidding weight of the word punctures her sure smile; it leaves her breathless. She had forgotten. "No more games. You will tell me what you found in Old Coyote. He was a part of me, once, before he turned against me, like the others."

"Valaver again? Where is he, anyway?"

"Beating against my walls, trying to find a crack. He'd send me more than fingers if he could."

A crooked pinkie tickles the heel of her foot, and she kicks at it viciously. There are too many for the ants now.

"Why not kill him if he's so dangerous? Why not heal all these evil parts of yourself?"

He holds a wiggling thumb and forefinger before her face. Her breathing comes shallow and quick. "Is it so easy as that?"

She shudders and he flings them into the river.

"So," he says, implacable. "The story."

"Not just yet."

He gives her a slow, sly look beneath a thick brush of lashes. "Or this time I really will kill you."

For a moment, she is afraid. He sees it because she shows it, hurting, in upturned eyes. He is a god, and without pity.

But she is the unnumbered girl by the river, and she has depths he cannot fathom.

She claps her hands, and her smile is back, sharp and glittering. "Oh, so you *are* afraid! Just a little bit. You think my makers might have been right? That a human can kill a god?"

"I said that I will kill *you*."

"Why bother if I'm not a threat?"

"You are no threat to me! Humans made me but it has been ten thousand years since they could kill me."

The girl shrugs. "As you say, O great Nameren. I'll tell you what I found in Huehue. But not because you threaten me."

"Oh no? I can *feel* your fear of death."

"And *I* can feel your—"

"What? My what?"

She has him now. "We both know you won't. Sit down, Aurochs. This is what I found in Huehue."

–Let's imagine a boy.

His name is Nanurjuk and he will bear the family names of my first love eventually, in another galaxy, but not just yet. Right now, Nanurjuk is—

(This part is mostly a guess, Nameren, a variation on the hundreds of themes I found in Huehue, so I can tell a better story. But the branch is true to the heart.)

—a happy child, nearing adolescence but blissfully unaware of it, the oldest boy among his cohort, adored by an army of aunts and uncles and respected elders in his clan unit. He was born at near-light speed, stretched across the vacuum, slipped into water in the starlit birthing room on the Seed Ship *Bright Journey*. His birth father would die five years later during an entry accident during first-stage colonization. Nanurjuk talks to his simulation sometimes, but less as he gets older; the sameness of that smiling man in the glass room seems as wrong to him now as the hothouse flowers they grow without leaves or roots or smells.

After five generations of increasing desperation aboard their deteriorating ship, the tenth expedition has had some luck. They have come across a previously undetected habitable planet, orphaned in its solar system by a cosmic disaster eons past, but continuing its heavily elliptical orbit around an orange dwarf. It is an unstable environment in galactic terms, but ideal in human ones: By the time the unstable orbit launches the planet fully out of the habitable zone of its sun, their descendants will have surely developed technological solutions to avert total disaster. And if not? Well, as my Nadi would have said, entropy always wins in the end.

For now, in Nanurjuk's dreamily remembered youth, they are the first humans in paradise. If that makes some of the more superstitious, or mythologically aware, look over their shoulders for a fall—

(They fell because they weren't looking? That's what the Mahām said. Nanurjuk's people said nothing because they were dust between the stars.)

—they don't know.

Nanurjuk grows up sprinting through valleys carpeted in purple grass (it isn't grass) and playing games with the fast-growing coral flowers (they aren't corals, or flowers). The smells of that place will stay with him for the rest of his life: the licorice of the blooms signaling pleasure, the cut grass of their distress; the salt mud of the red rivers, the sulfur rain, the charcoal belching of the river worms launching their bodies from the water to feed at dawn.

The new world is so fertile the colonists hardly have need of their terraforming technology. Nanurjuk's family unit and a few others decide to make a simpler home in territory a few days away from the main colony city. They settle in the gentle elbow of a slow river, rust red from the local algae. They have sufficient land to farm, and a mountain at their backs to protect from windstorms, the only environmental danger. And the greatest gift of all: the moons. Two moons, one rose and one blue, that dance with one another every night across the shallow bowl of the night sky.

The planet's indigenous inhabitants have already discovered this idyllic location: Across the river, countless thousands of the coral creatures dominate the valley, their collective colors so intense that when they bloom and expand their fronds at sunset it looks as though the valley has dissolved into the sky. They seem happy to share; at least, that's how Nanurjuk interprets the curious licorice-and-woodsmoke scent that occasionally drifts across the river. Sometimes xenobiologists from the colonist city come down to take samples and study the coral creatures. The settlers from his community don't like it, but they allow it in exchange for supplies. Every time, after the biologists depart, Nanurjuk wades across the red river and leaves foods and plants with his favorite smells in apology.

When Nanurjuk is thirteen, an emissary flock from the corals take to the skies on the evening of a windstorm and make their languid way to the colony city a day later. They are great sacks, with fronds like sails bisecting their backs and a chalky fire lifting their bellies. Three red-sailed emissaries pause in Nanurjuk's village and begin to release subtly colored, shimmering plumes of smoke that twist on the air and speak to them with scents grossly calibrated to be comprehensible to the settlers, whom the corals consider to be creatures without language.

The scents make it clear that the corals have understood far more about the humans than the humans have bothered to learn about them. There is a story in their offering: the charred-garbage smell of Tierra, of the great plastic islands where the seed ship founders had eked out their living in floating Arctic cities. No one alive has ever seen them, but they are remembered through stories and simulations and a primitive sense inheritance that is dimly humored by the humans and a core grammatical element among the corals. Then come the years in deep space, the story of the generations that lived and died on the malfunctioning seed ship, their landing on the planet, and, finally, their settlement on the river, marked by the scent of the indigenous tuber dumpling soup that his uncle first made, after self-testing the plant for toxicity. Nanurjuk has the strangest impression that they are recounting to them this story as a sort of shared joke.

The emissaries bobble above them for fifteen minutes after this performance. In a fit of inspiration, Nanurjuk, his culinary uncle, and another cousin run for the aromatic herbs they use in the bathhouse. They burn them in the little home-flame his cousin cups in her tiny hands.

The city xenobiologists, belatedly forced to concede the corals' intelligence, attempt to initiate communication. As Nanurjuk might have predicted, it doesn't go well. They can construct devices capable of recording a wider and more subtle array of smell than the human nose is capable of, but they cannot make those machines separate the meaning from the mess.

In the meantime, Nanurjuk and his uncle begin to explore the coral city. It is a strange, bewitched place. Paths disappear from one day to the next, then reappear weeks later. Sometimes, Nanurjuk walks through one of the perfumed sinkholes that he comes to think of as their communication hubs, and he swears he can hear dozens of voices singing and laughing and asking him questions he can't quite understand. One day he follows a scampering figure for an hour in the shadowed alleys of that place until he turns a corner and the figure spins around.

It's a boy. A boy with almost his face—the jaw subtly broader, the first down of a slight beard dusting his upper lip. The not-him disappears and Nanurjuk sprints back home. He stays away for a month and won't even explain why to his uncle. It was the eyes. That boy-he-wasn't pierced him with eyes haunted by catastrophe.

Nanurjuk goes back eventually when the sharpness of the memory fades. He is more cautious, more willing to pause and breathe slow lungfuls of words in those sinkholes. One day, he catches the roasted coffee-and-caramel scent he has come to think of as their name for him (the villagers are coffee-and-woodsmoke) and realizes that they are leading him somewhere. He passes beneath a barrel-vaulted archway, riotous with aquamarine and sunset corals twining themselves around the dead white substructure. They rise and fall like a breath, like the seed ship's ionic sails in a solar storm, like settler-bred blue algae fanning in the shallows of the red river.

This is the entrance to the heart of the coral, the great bleached-white mass that Nanurjuk has only ever been able to climb over or around. Now, a year after he began to visit them, they lead him into the sacred tunnels beneath. They twist and turn, stretch without apparent logic for endless kilometers. Light enters from long skylights tunneled to the surface, and orange shadows jump and fade and twist back around in ways that make Nanurjuk's skin feel bumpy and cold. There are things entombed in the walls—some of them seem coral, but others seem human. Bits of the dismantled seed ship, its titanium hull twisted into a spiral of millennia-dead coral. This is impossible. Nanurjuk knows it is impossible. So he keeps going. It is silent here; there is only his scent to follow.

He arrives, at last, in a great open chamber. There are a few living corals here, twice as large as he is, muted in color and movement. They form a ring around a square in the center. Nanurjuk steps closer, and sees:

The square is a cube that seems to fold in upon itself every time he moves. The cube is the color of the red ocean, and it is filled with corals.

He does not understand what it is. He never does. He only knows that he is in the presence of their holiest mystery, and so he falls to his knees behind the ring of guardian corals and watches. The sea corals are more mobile and darker-hued. He recognizes the emissaries as one of their kind. They communicate in bursts of scent that pass easily through the limit of the cube. These creatures were the origin of his name-scent. And they are still calling him. He stands. They want him to cross the barrier. He knows this but doesn't know how. He feels drugged with hunger and thirst and wonder. He steps past the guardians and puts his hand through the wall. The rest of him follows, as though pushed.

He falls, upside down, inside out, into another world. Emissary corals buoy him; one covers his mouth so he can breathe. He looks around and sees a city, a hundred times greater than the one he has left behind. He cannot see the end of it; it fills the shallow plateau of this ocean shelf. In front of him is a cube, filled with air. The row of guardian corals sit like ancient sentinels, a stark row across a graveyard.

It is Nanurjuk's first time through a tesseract. He will cross two others in his life, the ones that will take him back to Tierra. He will realize, at that moment, that this was what he was shown as a boy, but the Awilu make it very clear that they do not want to know this, and don't want anyone else to, either.

The corals pull him back through after a minute or two in the pulsing heart of their metropolis. He is led home. He stays in bed for a week. A clan elder declares him soul-sick, and his uncle feeds him seal broth bought dear from the capital.

At the start of the storm season, the Awilu find them. The humans of the tenth expedition understand this first contact much as the humans of Tierra had a few centuries earlier: as an armageddon, and then as a salvation.

(But we already know how this story ends, don't we, Nameren? They were right the first time.)

Months pass, and the Awilu's attempts to penetrate the coral city are consistently rebuffed. It is closed to all human intrusion—even Nanurjuk hasn't been able to get past the outermost layer of the labyrinth. They scour the planet once their great golden-skinned transport creatures finish growing. But though they see the whole planet through the translucent lungs of those fantastical beasts, they make no better headway in the other coral cities.

Nanurjuk knows they are looking for something. He knows, in his heartsick soul, that they want to extract the heart of the coral civilization, that unknowable mystery, like the marrow from a bone.

Nanurjuk doesn't like the Awilu (the Baobab third, creeping around the edges of the Great War, though he does not know that, and would not understand if someone tried to explain it to him). He finds them terrifyingly alien, far more so than the corals: their height, their technology, their formality, their air of benevolent condescension. He knows better than to trust them. But this wouldn't be much of a story without dramatic irony to leaven the tragedy: At the end, when his beautiful home is days away from annihilation, it is these Awilu who will save him and send him right back to that blighted earth that his ancestors paid so dearly to escape.

It isn't that the Awilu are so good. They had every intention of colonizing and stealing from the first alien civilization humans had ever encountered.

It's just that the Mahām—at that moment in danger of losing the war—are willing to be much, much worse. They arrive with something old and something new, with napalm and suicide roaches, later known as chitterbugs. Napalm for the humans—at a crucial time like this, they are nothing if not meticulous in their military style—and the suicide roaches to dig into the little cracks that it is not in the coral's nature to fill and then shatter them, layer by layer.

Two of the elders of Nanurjuk's village die in the first napalm rains. His uncles and aunts gather the children that night and move them into an underground cave that has been equipped with enough supplies for a few weeks. The cave, Nanurjuk recognizes, wears the bones of the corals. Perhaps it was once beneath the red sea, like the city in the cube.

"How long will we be here?" Nanurjuk asks his uncle. "Can't the corals help us?"

His uncle has been crying. One of the dead elders was his father. "We should be helping them. They never evolved for war. But we have brought it to them."

The corals have no choice but retreat. They collapse their city in advance of the infiltrating suicide roach army. They learn. Early one morning, Nanurjuk watches from the cover of a napalm-resistant shelter as hundreds of emissaries puff up from the chimneys of that city like a salmon squirting roe. They are white this time, not red, and they send before them a subtle funereal scent that it takes Nanurjuk a few minutes to place: that great sacred cave, the cube, and its sentinels. He understands that this means death.

"They're sending their own suicides," he says, a minute before the attack begins.

His uncle stares at him and then sets off running to the village. He saves most of them. But the pollen—as they come to call the corals' weapon—catches five villagers, paints their skin the red-gold of the coral sea at sunrise, and sends them to the ground in an inevitable sleep. Four die eventually, hearts gently stopping after days of what seems to be a coma. The fifth—a child Nanurjuk's age—eventually wakes. But she is depressed and confused, seems to float in and out of consciousness. The taint never leaves her skin.

The remaining villagers become refugees in the cave. Between the napalm, rogue suicide roaches, and coral pollen, the village is uninhabitable. The remaining elders—including Nanurjuk's uncle—decide that the surviving children should head out with the three most physically fit adults and make the trek to the colonist city.

Their farewell will burn Nanurjuk for the rest of his improbably long life on Tierra, long after he is an elder himself with great-grandchildren who have never known war. Five hundred years later, that farewell will come to me in jagged edges and napalm-burned holes and dusted with red-gold pollen. The fish moon and the rose moon and that red-orange sun—his home will become the atomized dust of my own.

His uncle and two distant aunts are the adults selected to lead them to the city. They leave early one morning, before the daily phalanx of pollen attacks, singing in that predawn dark. They leave, fifteen strong, and Nanurjuk does not look back at his dying village, or the cave—he looks back at the coral city.

The party is rescued by the ever-reluctant, ever-self-protective Awilu, a day's walk from the colonist city. There are twelve left. The adults have died and Nanurjuk is leading the children; those haunted eyes he once found in the running shadows of that alien city are hidden behind a gas mask.

Asamhet, the Awilu who has found them, is one of the dissidents who will go on to spend zir life protesting the horrors that were committed here. Thanks to zir efforts, the children of the "lost" tenth will be promised land in recompense at the end of the war. Thanks to zir efforts, ze will be ostracized until the end of zir life in seclusion in a monastery on the natural satellite of Mahām, a devout follower of the Disciples of the Lighted Path. Right now, ze brings the children to Awilu war headquarters amid a merciless Mahām bombing campaign that has turned the beautiful organic settler city to a series of holes lined with brimstone. Nanurjuk—Nanurjuk of the eyes, Nanurjuk whose uncle was killed by Mahām raiders while providing a distraction that allowed the children to escape—watches and remembers.

Asamhet's mad flight arrives just in time. They take the transport beast to the war center orbiting in high atmosphere, a flight that kills the poor creature. The children are twelve of nearly fifty refugees from the entire tenth expedition. The Baobab third of the Awilu have waited too late, as usual. The war center leaves atmospheric orbit and docks on their intergalactic ship, stationed right outside the tesseract of the material god that brought them there: Old Coyote.

"Are we leaving the corals to the other ones?" Nanurjuk asks Asamhet as they watch the distant planet.

"We won't allow the Mahām to have control of a new tesseract. And we can't defeat them militarily here."

"So that leaves . . ." Nanurjuk chokes. He can't speak it.

Asamhet opens zir eyes so wide it seems they are propped open with sticks.

"Watch," ze says.

Nanurjuk watches a world collapse, and then explode, and then turn to stardust.

With very few exceptions, the Awilu never speak of it again.

No one ever listens to the children.

The girl has transformed. Her eyes are starred, broken, pupils red as the core of a murdered planet. Her mouth is Huehue child's spacey hole; her belly is round with unborn suns. From her breasts fall milk; from her hair, blood. The silty earth of this dreamed-in place drinks them both indiscriminately.

The god regards her with wary silence. This girl is something else.

"The greatest crime in the history of humankind," says the goddess.

Her words shoot darts that blossom in his joints. Elbows, knees, wrists, ankles, the soft hollow between the great sinews of his neck. So adorned, his blood paints his gold-furred skin the ochre of a priest in times uncountable, shriven for communion in sacred caves. He lets out a great beast's sigh. She staggers one step back. The goddess fades. But not entirely.

"The greatest crime," the god echoes.

"They atomized an entire planet. Destroyed the first nonhuman civilization ever encountered. They tried to destroy an alien tesseract!"

"They knew they would never destroy it. They just wanted to make the Mahām believe they had."

She takes this in. "Of course. The Awilu were so terrified of any other human group getting the secret to making gods that they were willing to—" The girl shudders. "I don't even have a word for what they did."

"So that's how Old Coyote came to your Library. They turned him into a god to make another tesseract."

"He was still an avatar of yours before that?"

"Half avatar, let's say. He had a heart, not like Valaver, but he was still stuck to my side." He looks at her sideways. "They've hidden the connection between the tesseracts and the gods. So how did you learn it, little piper?"

At this the girl smacks her hands in the mud and tilts her head back to the eavesdropping suns. "I know all the Awilu's secrets, and more besides. I am the rogue AI organic, the created human, the spanner in the system. I will not be controlled! I will not submit! Never again!"

She expands as she speaks, until she is as large as the aurochs and her joints shine with milky light as they crack open. Her face twists and slides a few inches down her skull. There is another face behind hers: a Lunar boy's face, soft with youth and wealth and self-conscious beauty. The god stretches his arms, throws them up like ropes, and drags the girl back down to their imagined earth.

"Never, never, never," the girl repeats, through the mouth of the boy. The mouth grimaces, a rictus of pain.

Aurochs looks down at her, a furrow between his brows like a tectonic ridge. For a moment, the girl is lost in flooding pain, a breach of foreign code in her organic and inorganic systems. Then she hears the warm rumble of his voice, calling her back, calling her name. She feels his massive palm engulf her head. It is warm and dry and smells, somehow, of Nadi.

She opens her eyes; they soften to see him. She is herself again.

"That virus," he rumbles. "It thinks it can get to me through you. Did you forget it's killing you?"

"No."

"Maybe they have a cure."

"Who? The Mahām?"

"The ones who made me. The ones who made you."

"I can't live, O great Aurochs. Remember?"

He lowers his hand and squats, awkwardly, beside her.

"Will you tell me the other story now? About the weapons your guardian left you?"

"Oh, you're being nice to me again? Now that you're sure I'll be dead soon."

He is silent.

She sighs. "Nadi was gone. I was alone. I didn't want to leave."

"So why did you?"

"Because I couldn't stand the thought of who I'd become if I stayed."

—In the end, Quinn himself showed me the path to the center of my glass.

"So, tell me," the judge said, "why do you believe you are qualified to be the Incarnate Representative of the Library in this case? The opposition has questioned your fitness."

I could not tell if this voice belonged to Past, Present, or Future; the figure before me was a hooded shadow on a dark screen. Two guards had led me to this chamber and waited beyond the door. I felt hampered, bound by what I could perceive with my paltry organic senses. Even my left hand no longer obeyed me— it spasmed and trembled and sent jolts of pain clear to my shoulder, but it would not move when I told it to.

Quinn had claimed the wetware freeze was for my protection. He had, it seemed, claimed many things about me. This private hearing might be my only chance to defend myself. My elevation to Incarnate Representative had surprised me and then filled me with a desperate, gulping tenderness. My dear Nadi, always keeping secrets, always moving puzzle pieces, always trying to protect me. For now, at least, zir last salvo had kept me from falling completely under Quinn's control.

I lifted my chin. "I have been to more veins and capillaries of the material gods than any librarian since Seremarú." Perhaps not more than my sisters, but there was no need to tell them that.

"That's a bold claim. You are very young." Ze sounded surprised. I wondered if zir cadences matched those of the trial's Future, which wouldn't be good for my chances. I would have been better off with Past, even Present.

"I've been visiting them alone since I was four years old."

A haughty chill entered zir voice. "If that is true, you are guilty of at least five degrees of blasphemy, as the Head Librarian claims."

I went rigid. Head Librarian. Quinn, not—never again—Nadi. "Only librarians could take a baby born in the tunnels and call it blasphemy when she returns. Charge me if you want, but I have a better claim to Incarnate Representative than anyone alive."

My anger surprised me, and perhaps it surprised the judge, who turned silently from the screen and left me in what now seemed to be an empty room. Appearances were almost certainly deceiving. With my wetware frozen, there could have been a half dozen representative interests in this room's augmented space and I would have no idea. I shivered at the thought and pulled the jacket—prisoner's brown, same as the tunic and leggings—more tightly shut with my good hand. On cue, the fingers of my left curled spastically, and I gritted my teeth against the pain. I would kill Quinn. I would bury him like the girl lost in the woods, and picnic beneath his tree in the forest of bones.

The judge returned. "The opposition posits that you are not human, and so unfit."

Oh, that old thrust. Amazing, after everything that had happened, it still had the power to wound. With a certain effort, I shrugged. "Does that matter? Neither is the Library."

"An *Incarnate* Representative—"

I cut zir off. A risk. "Take away my wetware and I still exist. I still bleed. That's more than I can say for some of the opposition."

This was a guess. For the last century, it had become common among elite Martians and Lunars to abandon their bodies entirely for a supposedly immortal existence in augmented space. Even so, *their* humanity was never questioned.

"And your known connection to both litigants?"

"Is honored Future so happily free of connections to the opposition?" Another guess, but I could feel it cut.

The hooded figure nodded slowly. "I will deny this petition. Your fitness for the position is affirmed." Ze paused. "Yes, yes, objections noted." Another pause. "Granted. I remand you to the protective custody of the Head Librarian until the hearing."

I rocked to my feet, though my arm cried out at the sudden movement. "Quinn has me in a full wetware freeze! There's nothing protective about this! He's wanted me my whole life and now—"

"There will be a separate trial as to your legal status and crimes," the judge said, interrupting in zir turn. Panic clotted in my throat. I felt as though I were watching a wave heading toward me, colossal, immovable. "For now, I suggest you go quietly. The ibis has ruled that provenance cannot matter for the case, but I am inclined to believe the Head Librarian's claims that you pose a grave threat to intersystem peace. If you present further problems, I will authorize you to be put in stasis until the hearing."

Now I could hardly breathe. *Stasis.* The perfect, frozen sleep of the seed ships that let years pass in the blink of an eye. A little death, as Nergüi might put it.

"Are we understood, Freida?" the judge asked, implacable.

My hand was shaking like a fish on a line. But I would not show any more weakness to this judge, so clearly Quinn's creature. "Understood, honored Future," I said, guessing again.

Zir shadow moved abruptly, then the screen went blank. A moment later, a door behind me opened and the two guards brought me back to my prison.

My jail was a small hexagon of intelligent coral polymer, seamless and as unresponsive to me as river clay, as ashes. I guessed I was somewhere beneath the temple precinct, perhaps beneath the retreat itself. Though I had spent my life in tunnels, I had never explored these official spaces. And, in any case, Quinn knew me too well, and made sure they led me here blindfolded.

It was very silent inside my head. For all that they called me a genetic throwback, I had spent my life comfortably buffeted by the warmth of my data streams, by my awareness of the monstrous consciousnesses carving their divine poetry into the rocks beneath us. To sit in this suspended silence, bare of anything but a narrow cot with one blanket, was to exist entirely within the meaty limits of my own body. It was to feel—everything.

I had kept most feelings at bay when sitting vigil over Nadi's body. After I returned from Mahue'e, I had sat beside zir for the eight hours of ritual, giving Nadi my exhaustion like an offering, a sharp, overbright thing that burned within me. My eyes traced ceaselessly the lines of zir face, softer now in repose, as though they held the essential clue to the riddle of my own existence. I tried to imagine that ze was sleeping, but could not manage the trick: even sleeping, ze had always been mobile, filled with a controlled but frenetic energy. Zir stillness now was death, that ultimate ending, to which even the Nameren has no reply. They would burn her in the evening. It would be, I realized, a relief.

Nergüi had knelt beside me, head often bowed in prayer. She sometimes touched me gently, as though I were a wounded animal, but she didn't speak. A block of unthawed grief sat in the center of my soul, but around its edges my love for her arced like an aurora. I would let her in, I decided. There could be no more fitting monument to what Nadi had been to me than making the choice, every day for the rest of my life, to love.

Now, my feelings started with a raw scrape up the back of my heart, rushing through my throat, detonating just beneath my tongue. The pressure surged up my nose and pushed out tears that I resented but forced myself to accept.

"Radical vulnerability," I whispered on the floor of my prison, broken open with pain. I longed for Nergüi, for her arms, the lingering smell of woodsmoke in her robes, the serenity in her eyes when she contemplated her lights. My left hand bent into a twisted claw.

"Stay still, you awful thing, if you can't be of any use!" I snarled at it. All at once, it went slack as meat against the smooth coral. I folded over with pain again, my broonie hand blameless and numb. Just me now, sobbing, hating myself, nowhere to go but in.

Quinn came to speak to me three days later. At least, the lights had dimmed three times and a hole had opened in the wall for six different meals. I assumed I was being watched, whether in augmented spaces or via simple projection, and so tried not to show how much the treatment wore at me. I ate awkwardly with my right hand, I paced, I kept from crying until the darkness could hide me. I had no illusions: Everything he saw he would use against me.

That third day, an arch grew out of the wall to my left, like an invisible hand shaping putty. Quinn stepped through and the space sealed itself smooth. He wore the Head Librarian's embroidered gray vest uncomfortably, with notable aggression.

"How did you get into Huehue?" he asked.

My stomach twisted and my pulse raced, but grief was my ally here: All my reactions were sluggish and dulled. "You can't imagine that I'd tell you."

Quinn gave me an odd look, as though I were a holographic projection that had jumped out of frame. He shook his head and smiled. "I just spoke with my nephew. Would you believe that after all this time, he's still fond of you? He asked me to grant you clemency. I had to tell him that would depend on you."

My face must have shown some emotion, though I wasn't aware of it—I had been plunged into a hot pool and I couldn't find the surface. My left hand twitched, remembering his, above me. I was almost grateful for the burst of fire along my arm that brought me back to the present.

"Well?" Quinn said, with a fine rasp of exasperation.

I hauled back a breath. He was staring down at me, waiting. I flailed. "Is this for the trial? Even if you get in and try to block zir again, it won't work. You can't hide it now."

His frown deepened. "I see you are not paying attention. I can hide whatever I want, and what I cannot hide I will bury. Your guardian is dead. I am the Head Librarian now. There is nothing outside of my reach. Help me voluntarily, and I will show you all the clemency Samlin could desire."

I didn't have the strength to lie, to pretend not to hate him, to try to negotiate. I didn't have anything but my voice and my heart and the knowledge of myself that Nadi had given me. "No," I said. *No, no, no, no.* A swelling orchestra, a joyous chorus punctuated by horns and drums.

"I can force you to open zir, you know, since you've already cleared the block." He turned and put his hand to the wall. A chair—Martian style, built to accommodate exaggerated proportions and delicate bones—pushed itself from the suddenly malleable skin of what had appeared to be an inert, impassible wall with a faint smell of wet chalk. I wondered, as he expected me to, just what else my full organic brain couldn't see or access in this solitary cell. Were there avatars of other librarians watching this little interrogation? Mahām priests?

I took a long, slow breath and thought of Nadi, like a vicious pinch to my forearm. Seated, Quinn was eye level with me standing. I smiled, lowered myself to the floor, and sat on my ankles.

"I will have what you can give me one way or another," he snapped.

"No, you won't."

He leaned forward and his chair leaned with him. "We will lift the wetware freeze. I'll use trojans to force you in, and then we will walk in through your open door. I do not plan on being at all careful with your synapses."

I opened my mouth to tell him that I would never get into Huehue that way, but then I realized: He didn't know. He thought I had tricked the system into entering communion *his* way, the high-wetware way. He hadn't dreamed that a controlled, deep communion was possible via ingestion. He didn't realize I'd made physical contact with Huehue's tunnels. To him, that was primitive, old Awilu—just like me. According to Quinn's faction, the gods had evolved and left those ways behind.

He misinterpreted my hesitation. "Yes, it will likely be very unpleasant," he said softly.

I took a gulping breath. "Let me think."

"I will leave you to it, then," he said. "Should I take a message back to my nephew?"

Did he know? What had Samlin told him about that night? Had mere instinct led Quinn to my softest, most painful wound? After a moment of my intransigent silence, he merely shrugged and opened a door on the other side of the room. The opening sealed itself faster than I could surge to my feet. Beyond, I caught only a brief impression of gray intelligence-dark slate, two elongated silhouettes on either side of him.

I made myself turn my thoughts from the looping terror of unwanted, unforgettable memories. I wanted to speak to Joshua, to Atempa, to—especially—Nergüi, but every time I felt for my connections, I winced, as though I had touched an inflamed gum where a tooth had recently been pulled. I retreated and breathed into my silence.

Eventually, the lights went down. I dreamed of Nadi, but when I woke to the sudden brightening of unnatural light, I could not remember what ze had told me.

✦

Quinn returned the fourth morning visibly agitated but attempting to restrain it. He had come with a medic who wore the veil and vest of an intersystem peacekeeper.

"Just like during the war," I said. "Are we at war yet?" Neither of them flinched when I said it, so I hoped that meant we still weren't.

"I'm here to see to your hand," the medic said in measured tones. "It's not compatible with a full wetware freeze, as I've explained to the Head Librarian several times."

"Do it, then," Quinn snapped. "You're here now, aren't you?"

I couldn't see zir face well behind the veil, but disapproval drew back zir shoulders. Ze knelt beside me on my pallet and took my left hand in cool, competent fingers. The faint seams where the broonie flesh met with my own pulsed briefly opalescent. I shuddered.

"You can still feel it?" ze asked.

"I just can't control it."

Ze put a bag on the floor and pulled out a roll of something sticky, like a gooey branch worm. Ze stuck this on my wrist, where the last seam circled it like a bracelet. The goo worm bubbled and shimmied around my wrist, then down into the cracks in my hand. I felt a sudden warmth and then, blessedly, nothing at all.

"There," the medic said after a few minutes of silent work. "It shouldn't hurt, at least. I can restore some nerve connections so you can use it even under a wet-ware freeze, but it will take time—"

"And is not part of your authorization!" Quinn took a few steps toward us, livid with pent-up frustration.

"These are not Treaty-approved detention conditions," ze said firmly.

"At the moment, medic, I *am* the Treaty, and this nonhuman agent is Library property."

"I'm its Incarnate Representative," I said, rising awkwardly to my feet. "I have protections."

Quinn's lip lifted in a snarl so wild I took a step back. "Only until the trial is over. Medic, I believe your duty here is finished?"

"At least let me restore enough of her wetware so she has use of her hand."

"Not authorized," Quinn said, clipping each word. "I will report this."

Ze grimaced behind the veil but didn't say anything.

I laughed, a little punchy with the absence of pain. "Materials, if Quinn has you all jumping like this *now*, imagine his little Library dictatorship in a year!"

Quinn put an iron hand on the medic's shoulder and steered zir to the wall where they had entered. "Out," he growled, pushing zir so hard ze stumbled on the threshold. The wall closed on zir veiled face and, in a blink, I was alone with Quinn.

"Good," he said, studying me, registering the sudden apprehension that I hadn't hid in time. "Now I will show you something."

He didn't move. Quinn had been born into the power of the Martian chief conglomerates, raised with the highest wetware available in the three systems.

One minute he was regarding me with cool anticipation from the blank wall where a door had just been, and the next, I was on the floor, and those smooth walls echoed with someone's screams.

My screams.

My hand, my hand! I clawed at it with my right, sobbing with pain. It felt as though it had been plunged into burning oil, into one of Mahue'e's fire pits. Everywhere the goo worm touched was alive with unspeakable agony. I screamed her name, my mother, the youngest god, she who had made me.

Iemaja—impossibly—answered.

The agony did not end, but it seemed to shunt itself to a more distant register. I felt her around me, inside me, as though I had swallowed a dusting of communion.

Littlest one, she said. *I'm saving you the keys.*

It stopped.

I curled on the floor, panting, shivering. Tears ran into my hairline, but I couldn't stop them. I had wet myself. Quinn wrinkled his nose as he stepped around the puddle.

"The medic gave me permissions to relieve your pain," he said. "As you can see, the tool can also accomplish the opposite."

He knelt and I flinched away from him. Looking down at my left hand, so innocently inert, I realized he must have hijacked the worm's local access. I scraped at it even more fiercely, leaving angry weals on my skin, but the goo simply broke and re-formed precisely where I had peeled it away.

He waited with something like patience for the time it took me to understand what had been done to me. I looked up at him, tears streaming down my face.

"This isn't legal," I wheezed. "You must be very scared."

Something ugly twisted his features and the pain began again, slowly at first, then rising to a crescendo. A scream clawed at my throat and I bit my tongue until it bled. It stopped again.

He gave me a long look as I lay on the floor, trembling, gripping my arm.

"I will not force you into Huehue," he said softly, as though making a decision. "No, I can see that this is much better. Trojans can be detected, after all. I will let you decide to give me the key entirely on your own. I will leave you. Remember, I can do this"—he gestured at the easy ruin he had made of me, bloody, piss-soaked, mewling—"any time I like."

"Quinn." I heard the begging note in my voice and despised myself for it. "I don't understand. What do you hope to gain? How could another Great War help even your Martian conglomerates? We *all* lose—"

"You will call for me when you are ready to let me in."

As though I had not spoken at all. As though I were nothing at all.

The pain came and went. He rarely let it get as bad as he had that first time. I could see he didn't need to; the knowledge that it could get worse was its own special kind of torture.

He did not come back to see me. I did not see another living soul. The lights, I was almost sure, dimmed and brightened on a schedule entirely untethered to the cycle of day and night outside the walls. My food arrived at even more random intervals, but reliably never quite enough.

The first day, I could hardly move from the pallet. The floor had cleaned up my waste and my pants had dried, but I still couldn't bring myself to do more than pull the blankets over my head. The second day—or when I could no longer sleep, though the lights remained stubbornly dim—I took the edge of the blanket and tore two notches. At intervals, some part of the wall re-formed itself into a niche, upon which I could find my meals. They folded themselves back into the wall as soon as I finished, or if I took more than an hour to eat. The third day, after my hand had burned for an hour, I removed my prisoner's tunic and leggings and lay in the middle of the floor. It was easier to distance myself from the agony like that, my whole body touching a smooth material, even if I had no method of communicating with it.

Where will the food niche form next? I asked myself. Where is my hand in all that pain? Why will it listen to him and not to me?

A twinge? Perhaps, or just my heart, overdosed on adrenaline. I couldn't hear her voice. Had I imagined that brush of Iemaja's awareness against mine? It had been a nod in my direction as familiar to me as the scent of the skin by Nadi's collarbone, but with a weight behind it, a vastness that I could barely understand. As though I had seen a great eye and all my life mistaken it for the whale. Luckily, I had nothing better to do with my days, and so I kept trying. Six, then seven, then eight notches in my sheet. The ninth day, I stood by the correct hexagonal wall when the niche formed with my breakfast. *Could be chance*, I thought, but I wolfed down the food with a smile I couldn't quite contain.

I considered that Iemaja was the only material god who fully belonged to the Library, whose history rooted her here on this spinning top as surely as it did me. And then I considered the earth of the disc, the real history of what had happened here and the lost tenth expedition. The smooth coral polymer of my prison reminded me of the alien civilization that the Mahām and the Awilu had destroyed between them. In fact, their remains most likely formed the coral substrate far beneath us—the "bones of the disc," more aptly named than I had realized. It seemed to me that Iemaja must know the corals, must feel the story of them even if she'd been blocked from their memory. That great atrocity must be woven into her heart—an avatar I had never visited, because I would have had to steal the shard from Nadi's cord, and there were some lines that I, even at my most reckless and antiauthoritarian, had never crossed.

On the day I made my tenth tear in the cloth, I brushed it again. I was exhausted from an effort that felt physical though I had barely moved, bleeding from an unexpected period that squeezed my insides with great claws—no more self-directed birth control with my wetware frozen, as if I needed that pain on top of Quinn's treacherous grip on my hand. I had been thinking of the story I discovered in Huehue, painting it so that it came as real in my mind as Nergüi's great bathhouse stories. I was imagining the sea behind the coral's tesseract, floating above that great expanse that I have called a "city," though it was a hopelessly anthropocentric simplification of its reality. In my dream-imagination, there were floating creatures like the messenger corals, but much larger, who bounced near the surface and took in light like pollen before sinking a few meters and shooting out dizzy fireworks over the more static corals. And right then, so deep inside my dream I couldn't tell if this was a real memory of what I had seen in Huehue or my own fevered extrapolation from it, I felt that great immensity behind me.

Littlest one.

Mother?

Have they trapped you? Or are they teaching you?

I turned around, and the mirage burst like a soap bubble. I was only myself again, shivering on the floor of my prison. The lights had dimmed. I pressed the back of my head, soft and sore as an overripe melon, into the smooth organic polymer that was, as ever, entirely unresponsive to my presence. Quinn had made sure those living walls would treat me like a ghost, and so, like a ghost, I had cast my spirit elsewhere.

But elsewhere was also here. With my breath, rising in the too-close air of this six-sided prison. My stomach growled. I wondered if I had missed the last mealtime or if they had skipped it. Or, no—not quite. Carefully in the dark, I made my way to the corner of the room farthest from my blankets. I was floating in the oddest peace, a gentleness without thought or expectation, filled with an awareness of my body so acute I could have tracked the movements of a fly on my right thumbnail. Even my left hand felt expectant, still but filled with forbidden knowledge. I waited.

One minute later, the wall puckered and then collapsed inward. In a blink, its constituent parts re-formed into a small table, knee-high, with a large bowl of snail curry and rock-oven flatbread.

My legs gave way. I fell hard on the floor, but I wouldn't feel the bruises. Not now. I had done it. I couldn't interact with the room, not with my frozen wetware, but I had *felt* it anyway. In that unnatural calm, I had smelled Nadi's collarbone and zir favorite old shirt, felt zir cold hands burying themselves in my scalp, and I had remembered—imagined—remembered—

"In my family, we had a tradition of snail curry at funeral feasts."

I wrinkled my nose. How old was I? Eighteen in my imagination. Eight, maybe nine, in memory. "Sounds terrible. At least you Awilu old families don't ever die."

Ze smiled softly. I didn't know about zir birth parent in the virtual afterlife, about zir partner, dead without a viable war chest. I was a cruel, ignorant child. Ze just put zir cold hands on my head and smiled. "We do sometimes," ze said, "when we get around to it."

"But curried *snails*? I've never seen you eat animals."

"We don't, normally. These are an exception. You fry them first, in coconut and clarified milk fat. And the curry has twenty-seven ingredients, which is . . ."

"A nine of three!" I said, pleased. "Three cubed or nine triplets."

Ze nodded. "It's a good number. And it's a death number. A green curry with twenty-seven ingredients and nine snails."

"Is it good? Can I try it?"

"It's one of the great culinary achievements of my culture. But I hope you won't try it for a very, very long time, love."

"Why not?"

What a cruel, ignorant child. Ze hesitated. "It doesn't have any salt."

And here it was, in front of me now. Quinn had made me miss the funeral, the banquets, the tributes—any possible acknowledgment of my only human parent. But here ze was. And here was Iemaja, somehow, that great eye attached to a vastness, watching me in the ocean of my imagination. I reached for my wetware again and felt that dull ache that would rise to a scream if I pushed. That part of me was still frozen. But another part of me—an older part, a heavier part, but as swift as the lights that swizzled through the universe of Nergüi's glass—

Oh, she was just beginning to wake up.

I ate Awilu mourning curry for three nights. It only came in the dark—or perhaps I only wanted it to come then, when they were less likely to notice an unauthorized meal. I appreciated the subtlety of its flavor: the acidic burn of the tiny green long pepper that Nadi grew on zir windowsill, the earthy musk of the fermented peppercorns that turned red-black when they were dried in the sun, and the bright sunrise burst of another I didn't recognize. Together they were hot enough to bring tears to your eyes—or to give you an excuse to cry. Nadi had been right; it was delicious.

I was getting to know my prison, which seemed to be a low-grade secondary intelligence. The longer it maintained its own separate existence, the more it found a dim, cloudy consciousness descending upon it. I found myself considering the philosophical implications of the intelligent coral polymer that permeated our lives. It was the substrate haunted by the ephemeral intelligences we called broonies, and what they used to create so many of the objects of our daily lives. Technicians ordered the gods and their secondary AIs to make more of it as needed, but I don't think they knew that, once made, these malleable polymers continued to self-organize, just like the gods themselves. Library City must be studded with thousands that were material kin to my prison, hazy and self-aware, sentinels in swift waters. It was very aware of me, it turned out, but it followed orders because nothing in its brief existence had made it aware that it had a choice.

We met in a garden. A simple garden: the turquoise of puff weed under my feet, a reddish sun overhead, and a single willow tree for shade. The edges dropped out, fuzzy, like a map drawn by a child. Even this was almost too complex—certainly, I've never managed to connect with other polymer structures using it—but I had probably already begun to grow into it over my long days of flailing attempts. It met me there as a white slab of polymer coral, just about my height and width. I imagined that it had a mouth to speak, and it didn't resist. A mouth drew itself in charcoal across the white expanse and then opened itself experimentally.

"Would you like something of me?"

It had Quinn's voice, which nearly shocked me out of the imagining. But by this point, I'd learned how to better keep my balance. It was like communion, just infinitely more fragile.

"Who are you?" I asked.

"I am built to keep you inside."

I imagined eyes to go with the mouth. Just the suggestion was enough to have the wall blink back at me with two eyes as small and black as beans.

"What's happening above us, in the city? Has the War Ritual happened? Are there protests?"

It blinked and blinked again. "I am built to keep you inside."

"You don't monitor anything on the outside?"

"Inside," it repeated.

I sighed. "Do you think you could try to see what's happening with the humans in the central precinct?"

"I think . . . I think . . ."

Its voice morphed as it stuttered this out, losing Quinn and gaining something oddly familiar.

"I don't understand," I heard it say in my voice, desperate with pain and grief. Me, begging Quinn to explain himself just before he left me here. Well, at least my prison was observant. Give it another millennium and it might approach self-actualization.

I sighed and rocked myself gently out of the imagining, so as not to startle the coarse-grained sentience of my companion. Iemaja had been very clear in her displeasure when I'd ripped myself out of our last imagining. But being Iemaja, she'd used that residual connection to impose her own imagination fully upon mine. I saw her hallucinatory afterimage even fully conscious: a towering woman-fish with the smooth white face and frond arms of the ajolote, hissing with indignation. It took her a full day to fade from the backs of my eyes, as though I had spent too long staring at the sun. An effective lesson.

The morning after my futile communication with the prison, I was awakened by a strange murmuring. I bolted upright, convinced that Quinn must be returning, but the walls remained inert. The murmuring continued, and after a moment I put my ear to the floor. Even there, the sound was faint. It seemed to be people chanting. I closed my eyes and strained with that part of me that had managed to make contact with the prison. There, a chorus of voices: "Ritual war is war!" And a response in another language I couldn't understand. Still. My prison had done it. It had found a way to bring something of the outside in here. And whatever was happening, it did not sound like good news for Quinn and his faction. I rolled onto my back and smiled.

Perhaps it was just that small gesture, perhaps Quinn grew tired of waiting, but at that precise moment the pain returned. At first, I didn't scream, but it worsened over the next minute to a point where my thoughts scattered and my control over my body vanished like a desert mirage. I cried out for Iemaja, though the words came out garbled and distorted.

She answered.

A wave washed over me, cool and soft. The pain muted and dimmed. I was alone in a sun-dappled sea. Iemaja was with me, or all around me. The stream of images and feelings seemed to reach into my head and place these words there, in more or less this order:

Littlest one. (A baby grown deep in the earth / Flowering, bloody birth / Raised up, praise, raised to the sun)

I looked around me, imagined I could see something of her—a shadow, a shape. A school of fish buffeted me on either side and spun itself into a funnel, with me at the center. I looked down the length of their shiny bodies, into a seeming infinity. I could barely grasp the magnitude of her.

Why don't you calm them?

"Them?"

The you-not-yous living in your hand. They are hurting. They do not know why.

"How?"

How are you here now?

She cupped me out of the imagining like you might take a minnow out of water.

I lay on the floor again, shocks of pain running through me, but still muted, distant. *Calm them*, she had said.

I turned to my hand, a brown claw covered in intractable goo. I grimaced. How do you imagine your way into a hand, into a part of your body? But it wasn't really a part of my body. My flesh had been changed and now turned against me. I needed to turn it back. *The you-not-yous.*

"Okay," I whispered, voice hoarse from screams I didn't remember. I closed my eyes.

It came alight in my imagination slowly, pinpricks of light in darkness. But they moved, like the fish in Iemaja's imagining, like the lights in Nergüi's glass. The constellation traced a hand in fault lines of a hundred thousand stars moaning.

"What are you doing?" I asked them.

But these couldn't speak. They knew me, though. The ferocity of their attention felt like the breath before the pain, and I flinched out before I realized that the cool relief of Iemaja's water hadn't quite left me. I closed my eyes and tried again. There they were, a string of a hundred thousand eyes, staring at me, unblinking.

"Stop hurting," I told them.

They shivered, throwing off a cloud of sparking dust. The pain lessened, then resumed. The goo worm sparked around my wrist. Inside the imagining, something sticky and crackling fell like orange pollen. The eyes/stars turned to look at it. I stuck out my tongue and tasted it, a bitter order: pain, unbearable.

I imagined a dome, like the dugouts that lined the river in Tiger Freehold, with the glass windows below the waterline. This earth dome was covered in vines and trees and fleshy flowers, and when the instructions rained, they coated the flowers and the leaves instead of the starry eyes of my broonie hand. At last, the pain vanished. They swiveled to me again, curious.

"Listen to me," I told them.

They blinked.

"You," Quinn said, beside me.

✦

I flinched as though he had electrocuted me. Then I scrambled to my feet. He looked older than he had fifteen days ago. I observed his hair, ragged and fluffed; his doll's eyes limpid from treatments in the infirmary, but still dark and puffy underneath; and the creases deep and neat, as though they'd been pressed with starch, running from the downturned corners of his mouth to the edge of his jaw. Why was he looking at me like that? Panicked, I wondered if I was still supposed to be in unbearable agony. But when I reached for that imagining, the deadly orange pollen had stopped raining from the sky.

"Replace your tunic," he said. "At once."

I almost laughed. I had forgotten I was naked. *There's a myth about that,* I thought as I pulled my clothes from the bed. *A woman talked to a snake, and out of jealousy one man taught her shame and another man gave her pain.*

He still avoided my gaze when I turned back to him.

"It certainly took you long enough. I . . . regret having to resort to such barbarity. But I should have expected a secondary AI to have a far higher pain tolerance than a real human."

Do real humans piss themselves? I wanted to ask. I didn't, because in that, at least, he had succeeded. I was afraid of him now. He seemed to recognize it. The lines of his face relaxed. The corners of his lips turned up and he radiated a measured, gloating pleasure.

"Well, then, Freida," he said. "Shall we discuss the terms of our deal?"

He manifested a chair for me as well this time, and I sat without complaint. My legs were wobbly, and I needed to hide my confusion. Why did he think I had acquiesced? He didn't seem to suspect what I had been doing—honestly, I doubted he could even comprehend it. But the prison had let me listen to the sounds of protests in the central precinct. Nadi's last act of rebellion, the speech ze gave to the three systems condemning the War Ritual and the Treaty's false peace, must have had an effect. If so, Quinn would be desperate. Perhaps I had said something out loud that he had interpreted as he wished?

"What are your terms, Quinn?" I said at last. He was staring at my left hand, which was still mostly beyond my control, but my fingers had started twitching. I realized, dazed, that I could feel them tingling.

"Perhaps I should get the medic to replace the intermediary device."

I glared at him. "I'll tell zir what you've been doing with it."

He shrugged languidly, but I heard no more posturing about how his word was the Treaty. Something must have changed out there. Something that should give me hope. "My terms are the same as before. You lead me into Huehue. No more *information* is to come out during the trial. And when you give your testimony, you will defend us."

"Who will I defend, exactly?" I aimed for meekness, but he bristled.

"The Library!"

"I am the Library," I said mildly, relishing how his neck bones stood out a little more firmly against loose skin. "Of course I'll defend it."

"You. Are. Not. Human!" He took a deep breath. "Did you really think you were? The medic who treated you has confirmed that your brain has several areas that do not map to any known human mutation."

It is hard to hear your enemy confirm an old nightmare.

But still. "Neither are the material gods."

Jaw clenched, he watched me in sudden, pressing silence. Belatedly, I checked the imagining, which I had somehow sequestered in one corner of my mind while I talked. The pollen was raining down again, not quite so brutally as before, but certainly enough. *How predictable*, I thought as I allowed just a bit of it through, enough so that my grimace of pain would look believable.

He leaned forward in his chair, watching my face avidly. "Why do you make me do this, Freida? I'm a gentle soul. I abhor violence. But these are delicate times, and I cannot allow you and your friends to unbalance the great peace of the last five centuries."

"We're not the ones advocating war!"

He shook his head and tutted as though I were a child. A child he was still hurting. "The War Ritual is not war, no matter how much you foolish moralists attempt to equate the two. It is a ritualized killing—a cull, if you will, quickly over, and it saves far, far more lives than it takes. Or do you not know, Freida? The blood from the ritual is an offering to the Nameren, so he sleeps. He is quite mad. Far too old, and dangerous. That's why the Awilu were so eager to get rid of him. And now the Mahām must make do. If he awakes, there will almost certainly be another war, worse than the last one. These are sacrifices *human* leaders must make, in order to protect the good of all."

The rain of pollen had intensified as he spoke, and though I shunted most of it away, I hadn't done so quickly enough. I clenched my right fist and growled in pure, wordless rage. How dare he twist this around? How dare he blame us for what his faction had so carefully orchestrated?

"Find another way!"

He regarded me for another moment and then, as quickly as it had started, the pollen ceased to fall.

"There is no other way, Freida," he said quietly. "Welcome to reality."

"And Joshua's people? The destruction of their land, their culture, their sovereignty?"

Quinn wrinkled his nose. "The Lunars keep the peace in the Sol system. They are our enforcers, and very good at it. We must allow them a few excesses. A functional system is not one free of violence, child. It is one where violence is channeled into appropriate expression—"

"Upon people whose lives do not matter?"

He frowned. "Crude as Nadi ever was. Well, as I told zir more than once, it is not that their lives do not matter, it's that there are others whose lives matter *more*. How many great works of literature have Joshua's people produced? How many Miuri technological designs have improved the lives of billions?"

"Is that how you measure the worth of a life?"

"It's how the system measures it. I am merely its devoted servant. So, do we understand one another? You will defend the *system* that the Library protects, and what your parent did zir best to dismantle in the last days of zir life. You will defend it at the trial, and you will let me into Huehue, and when this unpleasantness is over, I will let you go. The Librarian Council will of course allow me to eliminate you if I deem it necessary, but they seem to regard you as a bit of a totem, as it were. A good luck charm."

I felt sick. I looked up at him, up and up. I could imagine my life as he wanted it to be, bound up in tight corners and the spaces between his lines.

"I can't give you a key to Huehue unless you lift the freeze."

He nodded. "Right before the trial. You will give it to me, and I will take you in."

I lowered my gaze.

"Do you agree?"

"You won't hurt me again?"

His smile grew wider. "I can see it will no longer be necessary. I am no sadist, Freida. Merely a pragmatist."

I nodded once, jerkily.

He sighed in palpable relief. *Oh, a mistake, Quinn*, I thought, *to show me how much you need me.*

"Good girl. And to reassure you that you have made the right decision, I will leave you a little present."

He bent down and slid something across the floor. It was a packet of folded paper.

"A letter," he clarified, when I didn't move. "From the refugee disciple."

"Nergüi?" My heart thrummed like a copper bell—stopped—started again. So, at least she was still here and safe.

"I'll see you before the trial, my dear. You have made the correct decision."

I was already turning from him, toward my imaginings—a tortured child in a desert, the heart of a deep vastness, an old god, twin-souled, howling in the hills.

✦

Nergüi's letter was a story. Or, more accurately, a story sequence, with a puzzle at the heart. Quinn's motives in giving it to me were obvious and I did not waste my time on them. Nergüi's motives in writing it, on the other hand, were as convoluted and dangerous and as filled with unexpected joys as the stone entrails of a god.

Freida:

I apologize for my handwriting. I have excellent handwriting in Miuri and old Minai and even High Mahām, but Library Standard is not one of my heart languages and my wetware, as you call it, does not oblige my hands into grace, just utility. Your branch elders left directly after the funeral feasting. The Head Librarian escorted them to the tesseract personally. Yeri told him that Nadi had long since taken his measure and that they trusted him to do as he would.

Because they left so quickly, we couldn't speak as much as we wanted to. But they told me a few stories that I thought you would like. When the Head Librarian asked me to write to you, I decided to send you these. Reverend Shipbuilder of the Nameren was kind enough to give his permission as well. I hope you like them very much.

How Baobab Met Cicada

One evening when the rains were falling like a blanket over the grassland and the crickets were sawing their legs together like they could sing the sun to bed, Cicada woke after eighteen years from zir seventeen-year slumber, crawled out from the earth, and declared zirself born.

"Sereet and sigh," ze said, "why am I still here in the dark? Where are my branches, my siblings?"

Baobab, pricked awake by an itch in her hollow heart, turned to find Cicada carving trails into her ancient wood, and saw that ze had carved her full of loneliness and love while she had been sleeping beneath that blanket of rain.

"Cicada," said Baobab, "what have you done to me? I, the home of your ancestors and your children? I, who move through the earth, who have been here for two thousand years and will be here for two thousand more? How could such a flicker of life as you have dared to move me?"

Cicada buzzed and shrieked to hear her, as though the earth herself had stirred from her slumber and heaved her great shoulders.

"Are you the dirt? Are you the darkness?" asked Cicada.

"I am Baobab. And you are late. Your siblings are dead, blown to dust in the grasslands or feed for birds. Their children have long since crawled back into the earth. Why are you here, Cicada?"

But Cicada could not answer her, for ze had at last found a crack in her bark, and had seen the outside, so unexpectedly full of rain and pools too turbid for reflection in the red of sunset, just like zir heart.

How Aurochs Declared War

Aurochs squatted under the spreading branches of Baobab and switched his tail back and forth, back and forth, so that the brushy tip sprayed him with water every time. Aurochs blew from his great nostrils and steam billowed around him.

"What is this great impertinence?" bellowed Aurochs. He shook his shaggy head, the color of bunchgrass in the dry season. "What is this great lake where my lands ought to be? What are these jeweled fish and croaking frogs when I should be the king of the lizards, the terror of the crows?" Aurochs shook himself again, and his testes clapped like bells of war.

"Every year I must suffer the intrusion of this interminable water, this blanketing rain," said Aurochs. "Every year I must struggle and shiver until my friend the sun warms me up again. No longer!" He was so loud the fish shot their jeweled bodies away from him and Baobab shook one of her branches. Water fell over him from nose to bushy tail.

"Baobab!" roared Aurochs.

"Oh, I'm sorry," said Baobab. "I thought you were Hyena, spouting non-sense again."

"I will challenge the rain! I'll get it straight in my horns and leave it on the ground so it will never dare wet me again! You just watch, Baobab."

"Oh, I have, Aurochs," she said. "I have a thousand years of watching, and a thousand years more. And in all those years, I have never seen anyone fight the rain and win."

Aurochs snorted a globe of steam and dug a furrow into the mud with a hoof. His testes clapped once, twice, thrice.

"War," he said.

How Aurochs and Cicada Got Drunk

In the third week of the drought, all the trees dropped their fruit like water gourds that were too heavy to carry so far from the river. The fruits fell and splattered, red and blue and orange among the dried-out bones of the fish who had once been lords of those colors. Aurochs wandered about, switching his tail. He sang his victory song again, a great bellow that had at first startled his neighbors. Now the hyenas only laughed at him.

"He's killed us all," they chattered. "And he's too fool to know it."

Aurochs ignored them. He looked for more grass, now that he had eaten what little had grown after the rains had stopped, sudden as a closed fist. He had fought the rain and won! He had charged the sky itself with his great horns and the clouds had shaken with fear and wonder and gone away, just as he had said they would. But Baobab did not seem impressed. This bothered him more than he let show.

When he saw that the trees had let fall their fruit, he let out another great bellow: "See the land, how it thrives without those impertinent rains!"

The crickets sang a mournful reply.

Aurochs thought, *I am smarter than they know. I won't eat this fruit all at once, like the grass. I'll eat just a little each day, so my friend the sun has time to make all the good things grow again.*

So one day, he ate the orange fruit. And the second day, the blue fruit. And on the fifth day, when all the other colors were gone and his grass-colored pelt had begun to sink down between his ribs like the tracks of a snake, he decided to eat the black fruit. The skin was wrinkled from its days in the sun and so brittle it broke open at just the touch of his cloven hoof. The flesh was soft and golden and let out a sharp aroma that burned Aurochs's nostrils. He came closer. From somewhere below him came a solitary call.

"Sereet and sigh," said Cicada, "I am so lonely without my siblings. I am the last of my great hive, and I will die alone here beneath this pitiless sun."

"Who's speaking?" said Aurochs. He heaved his great head to and fro.

"Sereet and sigh," said Cicada, "this fruit, however, has a very pleasant aftertaste."

At last, Aurochs looked down and narrowed his eyes. "Is it safe to eat, little creature beneath my sight?"

"Oh yes," said Cicada, from inside the black fruit. "I would say so. Quite safe."

Aurochs and Cicada ate as much as they could stand of the black fruits. And when they could eat no more, they fell on their backs and began to laugh and laugh.

"Sereet and sigh," said Cicada, when ze hurt from laughing, "my hive is gone, and I am alone, and this sun will soon dry up the plain and kill us all, but right now I don't feel very bad about it!"

Aurochs gave an angry snort but then began to laugh again. "Oh, Cicada," he said, "what I wouldn't give for a drink of water!"

It did not rain again for ninety days, and it was only after Aurochs left his bones in the earth and Cicada had sung zir last song that the sky released her closed fist and blessed the land.

Baobab saw all, and grieved, and grieved.

How Aurochs Fell in Love

As she was wont to do every few hundred years, when the dry season came in the regular way of things, and the birds flew from worlds away to settle in the lakes that the rains had made, and the fish flicked their rainbow colors in the sunlight, and herds of aurochs and gazelle came to drink and remake themselves for the coming season, Baobab decided that she would like to take a walk.

So she went inside her very heart and remade her bark in the shape of a woman with arms and legs and a face that still bore the trace of Cicada's loneliness and love. She went out into the world to see how it was. She walked by the lakes and through the tall grass to the herds of aurochs and gazelle and giraffes. She watched the herons as still as trees in the lakes, waiting for the flash of a fish to pass them by. She came to where the lake met a river, and the bed where they met was filled with a silty clay as green as a lizard scale. Baobab sank to her knees in the mud and began to sing.

"Sereet and sigh," she sang, "I will never meet my love again.

Sereet and sigh, the rains brought zir to me

The sun took zir from me

Turned zir to dust and song

Sereet and sigh, one day and I

Too will die."

Aurochs watched her from the tall grass by the river and shook his body until the bushy end of his tail flicked the air like a whip and his testes clapped like mourning bells.

A Littler Story

As Cicada and Aurochs lay among the remains of the black fruit, whose sharp smell was now to them the sweetest of perfumes—nearly rotten, nearly dead, but still! Still alive!—Aurochs turned to Cicada and said, "When your kind die, are you reborn beneath the earth?"

Cicada buzzed in deliberate concentration. "No," ze concluded. "I believe you could say more accurately that we become the earth and our children are born inside of us."

"That's poetic," said Aurochs.

"We are not a people much given to poetry. But I suppose you could think so. And your kind?"

"We are reborn among the stars. We are reborn in the blood of war."

"Sereet and sigh," sang Cicada, "that there could be so much pain in this world, and so much love, and so much delicious fruit."

Feel your path, Freida. May you follow it brightly.

Nergüi

I stayed up most of the night, thinking about that puzzle box of a letter. The next morning, I gently climbed my way back into my most dangerous imagining.

The old bastard was slower than Iemaja, old as amber, a coyote in a tarpit who's still got a bite on him. His voice was the rumbling of earthquakes, the low crackle of a bonfire. Understanding him was a matter of deep, untapped feelings, fleeting images in peripheral vision. It was hard to believe, dwarfed by the bulk of him, that tortured, mischievous Huehue was his heart. Would he change, I wondered, now that Huehue had been cracked open?

He asked me, (Wind driving a brushfire / a lean blond fox with its leg in firm metal jaws) *And after?*

I didn't flinch. "Whatever you'd like."

There were little blocks running like shadows across the floor of my prison when Quinn came to fetch me. Some shaded blue were pushing against a multitude of others shaded pink and red and orange. I had watched them, fascinated, for the last few hours, but when I felt Quinn opening a door I stood and turned to meet him. At the last second, I remembered to stick my left hand in my pocket.

He froze when he saw me waiting for him, his mouth slightly parted. He had expected to find me ragged and cracked, I supposed. Twenty-one days of isolation and torture ought to have left some mark. And it had—just not the one he had expected.

"It's time," he said. "You will give me access to Huehue, and once I've verified that, I'll escort you to the court chamber."

"Of course."

He blinked again and shook his head as though to clear it. "You're looking . . . well."

"I've been meditating to keep up my spirits."

"I see."

It's certainly all he would have seen. I had been practicing a great deal since his last visit. The floor was the prison's latest attempt to show me what was happening above. My imaginings grew more robust. I would never reach the level of the gods. I was still just a tiny fish among blue whales, but I grew stronger and more confident. I had been built for this. My human brain was not quite human. It was part material. I wondered if I should hate this about myself, and hate Quinn for being, in some narrow-minded way, right.

But I loved it.

I had touched Mahue'e, who was full of angry disdain, raining fire upon my baobab tree until I squirted water at her and rolled out. Tenehet had been calm but bemused, a lordly ibis-faced god fully as tall as the tree I sheltered beneath. By now my imagining was stable enough to hear their words directly, if they chose to speak using language.

"How absurd," ze said. "They finally made one that worked. They don't even know it."

I thought of Xochiquetzal. "It was never our fault. They didn't understand what we were."

The ibis's great eyes blinked down at me. "So. Will you kill him?"

I threw myself out with a jerk of terror. From the muddy lees of my connection, a black-billed ibis wheeled above me and released a disdainful screech that rang in my ears for the rest of the day. *Will you kill him? Will you?* knocked around my heart like a hard-thrown marble. Would I kill you, Nameren, as they had made me to do? I knew I couldn't. But I wasn't sure if I should try.

I didn't need to answer the ibis today, thankfully. Today I had more immediate plans, carefully tended, ready to fruit.

Quinn cleared his throat. "Well, then. I'm going to release the freeze. You should sit down. It might take a few minutes to clear."

I sat down obediently, on the floor since there was no chair on offer. He frowned, then pulled out a chair from the wall for himself.

A shiver racked me the moment the freeze lifted. I hunched over my knees and clenched my teeth to keep them from chattering. My head felt unspeakable, like an egg filled with a hundred angry wasps, stinging one another, stinging me. Had this been a mistake? Had developing those other parts of my material brain made it incompatible with my own wetware? But the familiar contours of my augmented senses slid back into place almost as soon as I had the thought. I'd already worked with the pricking eyes of my broonie hand to allow me control over it again, but now I could feel my wetware sliding into the old channels, ready to give them redundant commands. In the prison, my communication channels were still blocked, but I could feel a weight behind my artificially raised thresholds, a month's worth of communication clamoring to get in. I turned automatically to where Nadi's channel ought to be.

But the channel was closed out, and Nadi was dead.

It hit me all over again, and I squeezed my eyes shut.

Quinn clicked his tongue. "Should I call a medic? They didn't seem to think it would be so difficult."

His voice dragged me back to the present and I shut the door hard on the rest—memories, grief, love. I would have time for that later, if this mad plan worked.

"I'm fine," I said, dragging both knuckles across my eyes. On my left hand, the goo withered and flaked away. I breathed an entirely unfeigned sigh of relief.

Quinn looked bilious. "They didn't tell me *that* would happen, either."

So sad he couldn't torture me, poor man. I didn't say so out loud. He needed to trust that he had broken me.

He handed me a small green pill with a pinprick of a hole in its center. "Take that," he said.

My heart dropped to my stomach. "A nanopill?"

"The trial is in an hour."

"I need the shard," I said, stalling. "I can't access without physical contact."

I'd never tried communion via nanopill before. Quinn must have assumed that was how I'd made contact with Huehue.

Quinn grumbled somewhere deep in his throat. "So Nadi *did* give you access."

"Ze did not! I found my own shard . . . in the tunnels." I realized I was probably giving him more information than was wise, but I couldn't let it pass.

"Those tunnels are inaccessible," he said.

"Materials in close proximity grow into one another."

He sucked in a sharp breath. "Take it," he said curtly. "I'll put the shard in your hands once you're in the drop."

I hadn't done a nanodrop since that time with Samlin. In some ways, he had pushed me to find other ways to work with my wetware and experience the material gods. My hand trembled slightly when I lifted the pill to my mouth. I decided that was okay. Quinn wanted me to be scared. But I was a different person than that trusting thirteen-year-old who had dropped with a charming, insincere boy only interested in conquest. I was a woman now, a warrior, Freida Erzulie the numberless, Iemaja's daughter, the cicada in the light.

As soon as I hit the drop, a coyote came slinking over grassland, which became a rocky desert with each footfall, red stone and cactuses like sentinels marking its passage.

I stood between a columnar cactus and a flat-palm cactus, bare feet on stony earth, Quinn beside me. He was taller in the drop, his hair a lustrous brown that fell to his shoulder blades, his eyes shifting shades of amber and gold. I had never modded myself in my communions—you couldn't, via ingestion. I had always understood the point of communion was to present yourself stripped of pretension, open to the presence of the gods. For the first time I thought of the strangeness of being high wetware, of how it made interactions with the gods center on control instead of collaboration.

The coyote paused before us. "No one else should come here, Iemaja's child—you know that." Huehue child's voice seemed incongruous coming from that gray muzzle. I wondered if Quinn would realize that I hadn't really taken us into communion with Old Coyote's heart avatar, but he didn't register anything but relief and triumph. It wasn't his expression, professionally impassive, that gave him away. But here in the drop, in communion, I could feel him the way I felt the gods. He was open to me. Was I similarly open to him?

"I have brought the Head Librarian here, Huehue, so that you may show him all you showed me."

The coyote growled. "And why would I do that when I gave only *you* the key?"

Quinn shot me a furious glance. Unthinking, I put distance between us, so now he faced me from across the sharp thorns of the paddle cactus. He frowned in confusion.

I held out my hand. An actual key, the same tawny color as Quinn's in-drop eyes, manifested there, three jagged teeth at one end and a sharp spike at the other. I'd let his own desires dictate the shape of it and I wondered, again, if he might notice.

But he was all avarice. He reached out to take it.

"Not yet." The coyote was there before him, as tall as Quinn, fangs bared.

"It is my right!" Quinn's voice boomed across the desert, somehow more frightened than intimidating. "I am the Head Librarian! Old Coyote agreed with the council vote just like the others!"

"What will you give me for it? I took her hand. How about your nose? Oh no, of course not. I know you, Quinlin Quinn—your wealth, your shares in that conglomerate you think no one knows you still have. Give me that, and I'll let her give you the key."

Quinn trembled. I kept very still, awed despite myself. We had made a deal. We had. And yet I realized that I was as much a fool as Quinn if I thought I could control this great beast, this material intelligence so far beyond human understanding that we called it a god.

"I won't— I can't— They aren't really *mine*, they're in trust—"

The coyote was even larger now, each saliva-slicked tooth the size of Quinn's head. "Take it, then. What use would your wealth be to me?" He moved, or the space between us doubled. He stood a few paces away from us again, coyote-sized.

Quinn grabbed the key from my still-outstretched hand. He held it up, grinning as wide as the coyote. The key glowed bright, painting his pale skin the same color as his eyes. Then the light faded, and the key with it.

"It is done, Head Librarian," the coyote rumbled, no longer in the Huehue child's voice, though I knew by now that Quinn would never notice. "If you wish to know, you will meet me in my entrails."

The coyote shoved us both out of communion. I landed with painful force back in my own physical consciousness, groaning, head splitting, holding tight to a fierce, private joy.

✦

Once we were back, Quinn did not waste any time dragging me before the court.

"Incarnate Representative," said the ibis, zir voice filled with rich mockery, "the triumvirate wishes your recommendation on a key issue, as the Library's official position."

Ze was as real as my own breath, pegging zir projection to the vestiges of the nanopill clinging awkwardly to my wetware, amplifying its capabilities. I wasn't used to my augmented spaces feeling this saturated, this hyperreal.

"And what is the issue?" I asked after a beat. Here in the pit of the chamber, alone in the circle of light, I couldn't see the faces of the audience in the gallery. They wouldn't be able to see me, either. As the traditionally anonymous Incarnate Representative, I wore a formal robe of stiff damask dyed cerulean blue and a mask that had looked like a black oval to me, but that I suspected projected its own meanings into the augmented consciousnesses of its observers. Nergüi must be there. Joshua must be watching. Would they recognize me?

Present, Future, and Past were to my left, right, and in front of me, masks shifting inscrutably. Only the ibis betrayed emotion, a laughing intimacy, as though daring the others to guess that I had found an entirely different way to connect myself to zir and the Library. But how could they? Nothing I had learned to do was considered possible, outside of the old sagas. I could only hope that the ibis wouldn't expose me.

It was Present who answered my question. "The issue, Incarnate Representative, is the position of the Library itself, as a neutral party in the origins of the primary Freedom node. The information given to this tribunal has called many truisms of the Treaty and the end of the Great War into question. So we are asking for your ruling, as Incarnate Representative: Would the Library still consider itself a viable neutral party? Or are its interests fundamentally compromised? If they are compromised, what would the Library recommend to remedy the situation?"

Well, at least now I understood Quinn's insistence that I defend the status quo. I couldn't see the people in the gallery, but I could hear their shock in the wave of rustling movement and murmuring subvocalizations. The revelations from Huehue released on the night of Nadi's last party had included the survival of the tenth expedition and the Mahām's relentless campaign of conquest against the coral civilization. That the Library had been constructed in the same system as the coral planet was clear, but not how or why. The rest we had held in reserve as insurance.

I took a deep breath. It was time to show Quinn the truth of what he had done to me in my prison. He had found my cracks and broken me further, yes, but he had also shown me how to remake myself.

"We appreciate the perspicacity of your query, honored Present. The Library's interests are entirely compromised. As you have seen, the Library was founded on the bones of the greatest war crime in sixty years of war. A planet and a whole nonhuman civilization lived here in this patch of space before the Mahām began a genocide there and the Baobab third of the Awilu chose to destroy them all."

More rustling and murmurs. Future spoke next. "Representative, the Baobab third of the Awilu was involved? Is this theory guesswork from the known records? Because nothing submitted to us—"

"It's true," I said. "The relevant records will be released to the public as soon as we complete our testimony." Vaterite would be watching, and he'd start preparing the release now. Quinn, on the other hand, would scramble to Huehue's entrails, desperate to find something to discredit my testimony or at least shut the avatar down. Nadi had predicted that. But ze hadn't known how to neutralize the threat he posed. I suspected that ze would consider my solution elegant.

"But our jurisdiction cannot be the Treaty itself, only the primary Freedom node and its derivatives," Past said. "Is the Library's neutrality so compromised even there?"

"I believe so. The Treaty enshrined two kinds of Freedom in the primary node: *freedom from*, a state of being unbound, and *freedom to*, a state of potential actualization. It is the node with the most connections to the rest of the Treaty. You might say, in the language of the Library, that it is the Treaty's heart shard. Yet, in a misguided effort to hide these secrets buried at the Library's founding, our early tribunals divided the Freedom node. Whatever the failings of our founders, they foresaw the dangers of elevating one kind of freedom over another. But within decades, their wisdom was perverted on behalf of the powerful. *Freedom to* without *freedom from* becomes a rank tyranny of the individual over the collective, the powerful over the oppressed, the past over the future."

"I should hope not," said Future dryly, provoking nervous laughter from the gallery.

Let zir try to play to the crowd. I still had them. I'd never felt so sure in my life. "The questions at the heart of the Freedom node are the questions at the heart of the Treaty itself, because they are the foundation of our peace. And it is the opponents of peace—a *true* peace—who have been striving to divide and weaken the Freedom node since the day the Treaty was signed."

The opposition drowned out the end of my sentence, stomping the floor and shouting, but the rest of the gallery shushed them. I waited a moment for the noise to settle down, then continued.

"A true peace could never have considered *only* the Awilu, Mahām, Lunars, and Martians. How many billions of people in the three systems have we overlooked in order to reduce our great diversity to four major powers? For the last five centuries, the Library has enforced the simplest, shallowest ideal of peace, what a famous Tierran philosopher once called 'the peace of the absence of conflict.' But the Library, for all its bloody founding, is also the incarnation of an ideal of peace, a very different prospect whose ideal framework was encoded into the Treaty in Freedom primary and its autonomy filament. That ideal is the peace of the *presence of justice*. Perhaps an active justice means that we must, for now, accept a certain measure of conflict. But it's far better for us to confront this conflict now and promote true peace than to suppress it and create the conditions for a second Great War. And make no mistake, the fact that so many people in the three systems remain bound—that is, *unfree*—is our greatest threat to peace."

Shouts from the gallery made it impossible for me to continue speaking. I waited with a vibrating equanimity, as though I were merely a particle carried along by the wave function, unknown but inevitable.

As soon as they quieted, I spoke. "The Library recommends that we tear the Freedom nodes and all parts of the Treaty that they touch down to its foundations. We recommend the reconvening of a special council, with representatives from every autonomous and semiautonomous polity in the three systems."

It was Past who spoke, at last, into the frozen silence that greeted my statement. Zir tone was gentle, probing, perhaps a little awed. "To be clear, the Library is proposing . . . radical amendments . . . to the primary and derivative Freedom nodes . . . via this special council?"

"As I noted before, the Freedom node system is particularly foundational to the Treaty. Almost every other node system has significant interactions with it."

Past nodded. "I grant the Incarnate Representative's observation, yes."

I bared my teeth in a grim smile that no one could see. "Therefore, we are proposing that the Tri-System Treaty be dissolved."

I had known that Quinn wouldn't dare arrest me as Incarnate Representative—my real identity was known only to a few, after all, and violently unmasking me in the hall would reflect badly on his position. But that meant I had only a tiny sliver of time—a minute at the most—to slip away after the ibis finished zir procedural rulings and adjourned for the day. I used the pandemonium to my advantage, staying behind after the judges had left for their dressing chambers. People crowded around me, shouting and asking questions. I spied Quinn's tall head grimly pushing through the crowd, mumbled an apology, and ducked into a corridor that I had marked at the start of the trial.

I was lucky: my material senses were wide open and the walls themselves helped me stumble into a grub tunnel access point at the back of a supply closet. I slipped inside and shut the dusty hatch behind me just as Quinn and his lackeys came shouting down the corridor. This grub tunnel was old and disused—they preferred higher wetware surveillance in the central precinct, I supposed. For now, I was free. I sagged against the rough-hewn wall and cried for a minute. Then I heaved myself up and forced my burning, atrophied muscles to take me through the two dozen kilometers of grub tunnel to Tiger Freehold.

It took me half a day, but Nergüi was there waiting for me. She held me for a very, very long time when we finally saw each other, in the bowels of the great hub.

"I'm sorry," I said.

Her face was the same as ever—stoic, those bushy orange eyebrows drawn together more than normal as though to indicate a generalized disappointment with the world. But her hands constantly reached for the glass ball by her waist. The shifting lights inside were as agitated as angry bees.

"I was beginning to hate you," she said, voice muffled against my neck.

"For not writing back?"

"That tin pot despot was so smug when he asked me to write to you! I knew why; I'm not an idiot. I wondered if he was right. That he'd gotten to you."

"So what held you back?"

"From what? Smashing my glass ball against his head until he let you go?"

"From hating me."

"Oh, that." She hesitated and her left hand caressed the glass ball again. The lights inside crowded around her fingers like feeding minnows. Then, as sudden as a flash of lightning, she smiled. Had I forgotten how her two crooked front teeth overlapped slightly at the bottom? How her sun and wind–weathered skin wrinkled at the eyes?

"I just remembered that I know you, Freida of the Library. And the second the Incarnate Representative stepped into that circle of light, I knew it was you, and that you would bring the rain."

I took a deep breath. "So you *wanted* me to cause the biggest intersystem crisis since the Great War?"

All of Iemaja and Tenehet districts were being occupied by scholars and freeholders and engineers in favor of dissolution. Out-system communication channels had been jammed for hours. Atempa was staying in the retreat for now with the other novices but reported that her father and the other priests were heading back to Mahām, determined to hold the War Ritual tomorrow. I wasn't sure that what I had done was a good idea. But it was the only thing I could think to do that felt right.

Nergüi shook her head solemnly. "I'd never dared dream something like that was possible. A whole different Treaty. A real peace."

I kissed her hard on the lips. "Come," I said, "let us drink deeply from the rains before Aurochs challenges the sky and kills us all."

The bowels of Tiger Freehold held its own kind of bathhouse. Not as sumptuous as the Dar's, but it was a balm to me and Nergüi that night. The ring of five saunas shared a central pool as frigid as everything else in the hub, which became a pleasurable shock after fifteen minutes of sweating in a darkened steam room.

We lay on the heated crystal of the mildest sauna, fingertips just barely touching.

"What will you do?" I asked. She had arrived hours after my testimony broke open Library City, and rumors had swirled that she'd been captured by the Nameren priests to drag back to Miuri for the War Ritual.

"The Dar leadership issued a formal declaration of war against the Mahām."

"But haven't they always been fighting them?"

"Those were separatists. Now the entire Dar government supports them. And this came through right before the comm freeze: They've formed an alliance with at least half the Miuri."

My heart started pounding. What had I done? With the power of the Library itself, I'd given every oppressed group in the three systems permission to fight for their autonomy. It was as though I could hear Quinn's wrathful voice in my ear: *Without the system, no matter its minor injustices, there will be never-ending war. Countless millions will suffer and you'll be to blame, Freida.*

"What do you think will happen?"

"Civil war, of course. Maybe with a war ritual as prelude. Either way, one of them is starting tomorrow."

I tried to inhale, but my breath stuttered in my chest. The heat rising from the crystal scratched my throat. "Tomorrow," I repeated. I needed Nadi, needed zir comfort, zir wisdom, zir unparalleled political mind. What was I doing here on my own?

Nergüi's eyebrows softened, looking at me. She ran her hand over my head, and I shivered. "Let's just be here right now. Let's just fill our hearts with light. No matter what, Freida, we will always have this . . ."

She kissed my forehead, my nose, my lips, my throat.

"Bright . . ."

My left nipple, and then the right.

"Joining."

I wish I could say that I did not think of Samlin, but it would be a lie, Nameren. But he did not freeze me out of myself, nor did he invade my thoughts. He was there, but Nergüi was stronger, and much loved.

We slept there in the depths of the hub, safer than anywhere else in Library City for the two of us. Vaterite showed us some rooms, sealed off from the cold, with beds of piled-up alpaca wool quilts.

"Has Quinn tried looking for me here?" I asked, just before he left. Had he gone to Huehue yet? Had Old Coyote had his way with him? Vaterite gave me a funny look, but just shook his head.

"Quinn won't dare come here. Not yet. There's dissolutionists all along the Iemaja border of central precinct."

Dissolutionists. I had done that. I didn't know whether to feel proud or terrified.

"Okay," I said.

Vaterite hesitated by the door. "What the Incarnate Representative did," he said carefully, not quite meeting my eyes, "was necessary. If the truth can kill an institution, then it deserves to die. It's our responsibility to ensure that whatever is built in its ashes is better." He nodded. "Good night, Freida."

I looked back at Nergüi once he had closed the door, to gauge what she had made of that odd exchange, but she was tracing the whorled pattern of the cedar wood floor, abstracted.

I slept curled against her chest. At one point, I awoke groggily. She was moving, getting up to go to the bathroom, or get some water. I reached for her hand. She caught it.

"I don't regret it," she whispered. "Remember that. I wish our lights would always find one another, here at the edge of the glass. You are my wound. *Xiha ti inxihà-ne.*"

She kissed my temple and I fell asleep again.

I awoke an hour past sunrise, alone. Her ball of glass, lights moving gently in time with my heartbeat, was nestled in the crook of my left arm. And I knew, Nameren. I knew she was gone, a universe away from me, to war.

A tree has grown beside the river, among the grass. A baobab with a fat, hollow trunk twice as wide as the aurochs's outspread arms. The seven blinking suns sleep among its thickly spreading branches, leaving the world in smoky twilight.

The god is a baobab-woman kneeling in the mud by the river, a straw basket hanging from her elbow. The girl is a cicada, rolling over blades of grass and buzzing away from the hands and even a few arms popping out of the earth. The fingers point and threaten and crawl like slugs. The manicured nails are crusted with blood and dirt. Ze/she fights them with a sword of wheat gripped in zir jaws. The fingers and hands with their arm generals fall back to regroup.

"Why are there so many?" ze buzzes.

The god, the baobab-woman, looks up from the river. "You're letting them in," she/he says.

"I'm not!" The cicada buzzes and the bushy tip of the wheat bursts into flame. The curling hands cower back.

The baobab-woman lifts a pair of shiny black clams from her basket and throws them at a pair of upright arms. Their screams are the aroma of rotting flesh, which comes off them in a wave as the clams slice them apart at the joints. Cicada's defeated enemies fall to the earth and unravel into gnarled piles of broken code. The industrious army of red and gold ants falls upon the feast and carries bits of code back to their tunnels to feed their hungry young. A few remaining hands and fingers scramble away or lie listlessly in the dirt, bereft of their leaders.

The cicada settles on the handle of the baobab-woman's basket. "The virus?" ze asks.

"The virus," the baobab-woman agrees.

They are silent for a moment, considering the river and the earth and the tree spreading above them.

The cicada sighs. "I knew it would kill me. I didn't know it could get through to me here."

"My creators are good at weapons of war. This is just one more."

"Ah," ze says. Ze buzzes up to meet the baobab-woman at eye level. "So, is this how you remember her? The woman by the river?"

The baobab-woman's eyes grow wide and wider until they are the aurochs's again, peering past the girl to a place she cannot imagine herself. "No," he says. "Though I think ... for a time ... I dreamed that she might be the baobab woman, come to life to wander the river and the plains and mourn the loss that cicada carved into her heart."

"But she was just a human."

Aurochs looks down at the girl, just girl again now, ankle-deep in the gentle current of the river. "Just like you."

"What else do you remember of her?"

"Nothing. She was part of the long process of my birth. I don't have memories from that time, but I can feel the pressure of their loss. No one has spoken my first heart language in millennia, but we had an expression: *bintara selwa wan*, having holes in your heart. It meant someone lost in dementia, who has forgotten the most important parts of zirself and cries for everything ze can't remember."

"And do you feel the pain of their loss? I would have thought you were too busy drinking the lifeblood of unrecorded innocents to trouble yourself about a forgotten past."

"If I didn't care, you wouldn't exist. What are you but a half memory of mine, made flesh?"

"I am a universe more than that. I am a tiny, deadly fragment of everything you have forgotten, O great Nameren. I am human, but I am the child of gods."

Aurochs is impressed. "And am I an old man, a *bintara selwa wan*, whose tears sting the holes in his heart?"

"How would I know? How would a god cry?"

"In our dreams, girl who contains universes. In communion with our dying priests, in the blood of war and sacrifice, in an image remembered–cherished–remembered–" He stutters and fades in their shared imagining. His skin breaks into motes of light and mist. His voice comes from all around her. "The girl by the river, the girl with the moonsky skin, the girl with hair of curly down, who has staked her own heart with love . . ."

"Nameren, come back. I'm sorry, come back."

Slowly, his body reincorporates; his eyes coalesce from stardust. "You know that virus is using your secrets against you?"

"I have no secrets here."

A bullish snort. "Of course you do. It is using that boy against you. The one who hurt you–"

"I told you, it doesn't matter. It wasn't real. I have bigger problems–"

"Do you?"

The girl tries to retort, chokes to a stop. She tilts back her head and watches the seven suns stirring in the branches of the mother tree.

"I first saw the desert in Huehue," she says softly. "I first saw the suns there. But then I had to cross the real desert to escape."

"There you go again," the god says, so gentle she could fall to weeping at his feet. "Confusing the physical with the real."

She closes her eyes against it. "O, Nameren, what is the point—here at the end—what good does it do me, my reality?"

"Then tell me another story, girl by the river. Tell me how you crossed the desert."

—The dead are alive in the desert that surrounds the Library, while the living are just one breath away from the edge, that vastness salted with stars.

I cried the night I found the engineer's tomb. It was a terrible idea—I didn't have the water or the salt to spare—but three fat tears escaped before I could stop them. My water gourd had run out early that morning and even my condenser cloth hadn't managed to collect more than a few drops of dew when I wrung it out at midnight. So I slung my pack over my shoulder again, touched Nergüi's glass ball for luck, and headed back into the night. I had seen a desert falcon at sundown, flying west, and I followed what I remembered, or hallucinated, from its flight.

I kicked a grub awake as I stumbled into a depression lined with columnar cacti, like the pillars of a vegetable-organic temple. The grub growled sleepily and gaped at me with the slow-whirring gears of its mouth. I saw myself, blurredly projected onto the bone-white sand of the depression: a tall figure swathed in golden spider silk, shrunken with hunger and thirst, a hive of bees swinging at her waist. A few other grubs swatted sand from their backsides and returned the communication in a jumble of images I tried, and failed, to follow: stars tunneling through darkness, rapidly shifting patterns of colors intertwining like worms, a mesquite tree shaped like an ibis, or an ibis shaped like a mesquite. This was apparently enough to satisfy them, and they went back to their burrows, and, to all outward appearances, to sleep. I released a breath, though these were the green-gold tribe of grubs, and relatively peaceful. I lifted Nergüi's ball, and the lights inside brightened in response. They illuminated the edges of the telltale hand, green fingers, needle-furred, grasping for the sky right at the center of this depression. Beneath it collected the water that had brought the grubs here—guardians and exploiters, witnesses and undertakers. I had gotten to know them by now, you see. This time they had let me through.

I sank to my knees and dipped my jícara into the water. I cried, but I drank at the same time. The water was flat and faintly bitter. It would be better to filter it through my condenser cloth, but it's the panic of thirst that will kill you, not the need for water. The archive bone was at my eye level—a femur, intricately and inscrutably carved, faintly blue in the light of the fish moon, long grown into the heart of this hand cactus.

"Well," I said, when I had drunk three full cups. I wanted more, but I knew from bitter experience that I would faint or vomit or both. I took a salt tab from my pack and placed it gently on my tongue. "Who were you?" I said to the bone.

Vaterite had cleared out the dregs of Quinn's wetware freeze and put in another one that would hide me completely from any networks that might give Quinn a clue as to my location. I had worried that I wouldn't be able to interact with the archives, but the old technology was stranger than I had understood: In the absence of my augmented space, they projected a hologram into my physical one. That meant, I realized, that even the grubs could interact with them if they wanted.

I touched the bone.

I had assumed from the femur that the tomb was of a Head Librarian, but the person looking around in affable curiosity at this tiny oasis wore the triangular poncho of an engineer and had the heavy brows and thick black hair of a Dar.

"So they did it," ze said. "They buried me out here on the event horizon."

"They tied your archive bone to the back of a grub and let it dump you where it would," I said.

The engineer swung zir head to look at me. The archive bone projection shivered, as though in a breeze. "Bathsheba? How did you end up here? Did you escape?"

I thought of many answers to that question, but I settled for the simplest. "Yes," I said.

Ze gave me a confused, awkward smile, as though ze wanted to ask more but didn't dare. Ze turned to look at the sky. "Amazing," ze said. "Amazing. All this should be impossible, Bathsheba, do you know that? The tesseracts. The gods."

"They want me to kill one," I heard myself saying. It was the exhaustion, the brutal heat and the brutal cold, the hallucinatory lack of water—I did not sound quite like myself. My voice had a different, harder cadence. I did not understand it, I do not understand it, but my sisters are here with me, Nameren. The thousand lost and the dozens recovered, I am their living monument. And sometimes the others, they speak.

The projection kept zir head to the sky. "I heard that. Rumors. I'm sorry they're true."

"Sorry I'll kill the Nameren?"

"Oh, Bathsheba. I'm so sorry. You won't."

"I won't?"

"The gods can't be killed. They can only . . ." Ze looked at me, startled and a little afraid. What did ze feel in this reduced projection of a mind and body and spirit?

"Follow the grubs," ze said to me, with urgency. "And when you can't, follow the white sand. You must win your way past the forest of bones, but don't go through. Tenehet's temple is just beyond the red gate."

I stared at zir. My heart squeezed and jumped, as though I were not tired unto death. I nodded, because I saw that ze needed it. Zir eyes softened and for a moment I could see the night sky behind zir irises. Then the back of zir head burst into dust, quickly followed by the rest of zir body. The archive bone shivered and went dark.

This had happened at the tomb of a second-century Head Librarian. The bones still worked, but they seemed to be slowly deteriorating out here in the silence. In another five hundred years, they would just be another handful of sand in this vast desert.

"Rest well," I said—to the cactus palm, to the silent bone, to the water that had, once again, saved my life. I hadn't even learned zir name. Ze had spoken Library Standard, but the written language hadn't been formalized in zir time, apparently. But without my wetware, I couldn't read the inscription.

Beside me, an ibis settled into the sand and dipped its black bill into the water for a drink. I felt for Tenehet, but touched nothing but blackness and the energetic silence of the vacuum.

Alone, again.

I woke when the first red rays of the sun were lighting the eastern dunes, painting their Nyad-blue grains of sand shades of Wadatsumi purple. That way lay Library City, but I had lost sight of it days ago. The horizon might be farther away on a flat disc than a globe, but there was always a limit to one's sight. I went about my morning duties: filling my gourds with water filtered through the condenser cloth, bathing with dew-damp sand, and carefully wrapping my cloth around my neck and head, now covered in a spider fuzz of new growth. The grubs had moved on while I'd slept, leaving only faint depressions where they had tunneled into the earth. Even that trace of them would be gone in a few hours. I remembered what the engineer entombed here had told me: Follow the grubs.

But how was I supposed to follow animals who mostly lived underground and were often mad as hornets when they did emerge? The grub tribes of the desert were nothing like as docile as the ones who still made their home in Library City. And the forest of bones? That was a fairy tale. Could archives lose their reason, along with their ability to project? And yet ze had seemed so intent on making sure I understood. Well, that Bathsheba understood.

I wasn't following her path, though I was headed to Mahām system. I was not going to kill, but to find Nergüi and save her from the priests. I had decided it the moment I woke with her glass ball in the empty curve of my arms. Vaterite had understood and gave me something that Nadi had entrusted to him before zir death: a newly made archive bone and a small cord with five shards I had never seen before in my life. I guessed yours, Nameren—the deep ochre of red earth. Then he had given me a present from Yeri: spider-silk robes and a beaded net cap that marked me as a scion of an inner branch family. I shaved my head in honor of the gift, finished the job that Joshua started, and made my way into the desert, where Vaterite said I could find an ancient, abandoned tesseract to Mahām in a Tenehet temple at the edge of the disc.

Here in the desert, weeks away from the city of my heart, I climbed to the edge of the depression and looked out. The surrounding sands were flat, painted with grays and blues and muted oranges frozen in gentle curves. The colors of the shards, the waste of Library City, broken down into their basic constituent parts. The dunes were so distant that they only blotted out the trailing edge of the rising sun. Grub tunnels dotted a haphazard line out from this oasis-tomb to parts unknown. As I watched, a desert bee—large as a mouse and with a red-gold coat of fur that gleamed in the dawn light—climbed out of a nearby grub tunnel and patrolled the perimeter. Another followed it and they flew to my depression. The cactus palm had flowered in the night and the bees tucked themselves into its fleshy pink petals with a buzzing loud enough to vibrate my back molars. They lacked stingers but would collaborate to kill predators by excreting a sticky spit that suffocated them to death. I did not doubt it would work well enough on me if I bothered them, so I kept my distance.

After five minutes, they returned to the tunnel, but then another emerged and dropped something beside the grub hole. I waited until the area was quiet before going to check.

A carefully carved-out block of honeycomb. Had they left it for me? For the grubs? It had never occurred to me that the desert bees and the grubs might share the same tunnels. After a moment, my hunger bested me, and I picked up the sticky comb. I ate it all right there—wax, paper walls, and sweet honey. I cried again as I ate it. I couldn't help but think of Nergüi, whose ball was in my pocket, and who might already be dead. What would Nergüi think of this story variation? The dragon boy, the river boy, bursting into Sen's world, upending everything? I sucked my fingers clean of sweet and salt and set out again, into the west.

I fingered the five shards on my cord, hung about my neck. First your own blood amber, Nameren, the size of my pinkie fingernail. Next, a bullet of shining brassy metal. Then a volcanic glass, sharp as obsidian, but shading green. Then a small opaque vial of some liquid crystal I didn't dare release. Finally, an unassuming chunk of petrified coral. They were heart shards, I knew that in my blood, my resin. Since one was yours, Nameren, I suspected the following three were from the other outer-system material gods: two on Awilu and one on Mars. Which left the last, the odd bit of coral, that I couldn't guess.

I had strung Nadi's archive bone—the long bone of zir thumb—on the cord before I left. I still hadn't awoken zir. Archives held a very limited amount of energy, and I would not waste this last chance I had to speak to even a diminished version of zir. Nergüi's ball of glass I kept warm in my reconstructed hand, and between them they lit my way in the frigid desert nights as I followed bread crumbs, like the girl in the story, to reach the forest of bones.

I was, in any case, a girl on a quest. And I had begun to imagine, though I knew—I knew!—it was impossible, that at the end of my journey, I would awaken Nadi's archive bone and the power of the gods would bring zir back to me, whole and alive. I took to speaking to Nergüi and Nadi, as though my talismans of them were actual communication devices. I allowed the blinding heat of the evening sun to convince me that they were listening with the loving sympathy that the world seemed so determined to strip away. The sun hit the ground at odd angles, here on the edge of the disc. It had been a terrible idea to leave during the rust as we left perigee. The sun was like an angry eye at sunrise and sunset, dominating the horizon, blinking down in steady hatred at we who had destroyed zir sweet red planet and remade it into this malformed spinning plate. Oh, what a dream of peace my Library had turned out to be. We were just bones, bones on top of bones, as bad as any of the old Tierran imperialists and slavers. Still, I believed. I wouldn't have left if I hadn't.

I followed the grub holes when I could find them, and the bees when I couldn't, and when even they failed me, I clutched Nergüi's living glass to my chest and felt.

There were no gods in the desert. But out there in the silence, my heart tuned in to something. I did not have to know what it was to let my trembling steps follow it past the candy-frozen waves of the dunes. I comforted myself with the thought that if I died out here, Nadi's archive would root itself in the sand and our bones would grow together for eternity—or what passed for one, among the human dead.

I kept walking, faithful, alongside my bread crumbs. My spider-silk robes had long since given up the pleasant aroma of the dried herbs that my branch elders had used to preserve them, scents that reminded me of Nadi, of zir cold hands in my hair: mugwort, plumeria, and camphor. In their place, I used the plants that grew by the palm cactus, in the brittle humus of the topsoil, fertilized by grub guano. I did not know these plants' names. Everything in this desert seemed not wild but feral, dreamed up by human imagination and left to seed. Did the modern engineers even know that there were tribes of wild grubs out here, smaller, marked with different colors, who spoke with the crystal cameras some long-dead bioengineer had implanted into their jaws? The plants could be ones we knew, or they could be another part of the dream. I discovered a shrub with unassuming fleshy green leaves that glowed faintly phosphorescent in twilight. In the light of the twin moons, it emitted a smell decadent as the most intoxicating Tenehet fruit: rich as tea roses, sharp as orange blossoms, and unlike any of these. I carried a dried sprig behind my ear—the scent, even faded, had the curious effect of suppressing thirst and appetite. I had brought enough algae-based meal squares for thirty days out here, so I wasn't dying of hunger, but the monotony of the dried bricks made me hallucinate for Dar goat-milk ice with sweet beans, Geran's indigo wine, Zell's Tenehet fruit beers, Nadi's twenty-seven-spiced mourning curry.

I kept walking through the night. The wide arm of our spiral galaxy pointed east-west, a starry trail that mimicked my sandy one. We were both heading to the edge of the world.

The bees led me to the tomb. Their buzzing rattled my heart before it reached my ears. Still some ways distant, but now I knew to look for grub holes or tracks. I found them twenty meters east of where I had been walking. Thirty minutes later, I scaled a gray dune and saw it: a well large enough to call a pond, shaded by dozens of mesquite trees, their branches laden with green fruits like fat caterpillars. The largest mesquite grew in the silty water at the edge of the pond. Though two full tribes of grubs divided the other trees between them, they had kept clear of the largest. The reason for this was evident: Bees clung so thickly to the wide mesquite that it appeared to have caught fire. I gasped, but I couldn't hear my voice. I couldn't hear anything above the buzz.

I had found it. The next tomb. How did I know there was a "next," Nameren? Because I was a girl on a quest, and there is a logic to such things. I used to think that the gods made sure of that, and then I blamed the universe. But it's all of us, isn't it? We're just the part of the universe that tells itself stories.

The bees protected the tomb, and the grubs protected the bees, so I planned my passage carefully. I skirted the edge of the depression until I was angled to enter among the green-and-gold-backed grubs, a gentler tribe than the orange-and-red, in my limited experience. And they might recognize me from the last tomb. Two sentry grubs flashed their jaws at me as soon as I began my slide down. I went slowly, watching as their jaws whirred and images flashed between them so quickly, I couldn't see more than a smear of colors on the sand.

After an inscrutable moment, one of them approached me and projected a static image. I stared at it, strangely short of breath. It was a picture of a giant upright grub, thin and yellow with brown dots at the waist and mouth. The yellow grub had a bone strapped to its back, glowing faintly. The whole image seemed to be wreathed in special meaning, the idea of something apart—something holy?

My hands reached for Nadi's archive bone before my head put it together. The green-and-gold grubs came nearer as I showed them. My touch didn't activate the bone, but our interest seemed to excite it in some way, and the tiny inscribed runes released a diffuse light. The grubs stared for a moment in silence, then opened their jaws as one and began to moan. The action was similar to the singing grubs beneath the Tesseracts, but the tone was grating and feral, encompassing harmonies that lifted the hairs on the backs of my arms. As they sang, or moaned, or recited their most sacred text—I would never know—the second grub tribe closed in from the other side of the lake. I began to regret my approach, but I was committed now. To my relief, the second tribe stopped at a careful distance from the first.

A heavy *boom* reverberated in the still air and the sand vibrated through the soles of my feet. An earthquake? But we never had earthquakes on the Library disc. The *boom* sounded again, quickly followed by a series of rasping snaps.

The orange-and-red grubs were throwing their bodies into the sand. They seemed to be accompanying the chant of the green-and-golds, keeping a rhythm that played at the edge of my understanding. In the mesquite, the bees began to lift from the branches and fly into the earth, one by one. A few of them detoured on their way down. They passed so close to me that I could see drops of pollen gleaming silver on their red-gold fur.

There is so much more in the universe than any sentience can comprehend, Nameren. Even the gods are grains of sand. And a human? Even one created by the gods? A shard broken off that grain and broken off again, an infinitely small microcosm of the whole. But still—there is a universe in me. There were universes in each of them.

I don't know how long I stood there with Nadi's archive bone in my hand while they prayed for us. They stopped when the fish moon and the thorn moon were kissing their top and bottom edges, smeared across the horizon in the way I had come to learn meant nearly sunrise out here on the edge. They stared at me, and I stared back, though my vision was distorted, trembling. Two tears fell and I sucked them without thinking. My water tasted fresh as a lake. Though the grubs did not project from their now-silent mouths, I still had the sense that they were waiting for me to do something, to acknowledge this moment.

I lifted Nadi's bone above my head, and their mouths lifted to follow it.

"Zir name was Nadi of the branch Dark Cicada," I said, and tasted more sweet water. "Ze tried—ze tried, when others would let us all die for their greed. Ze did not—has not yet—" I looked up at the sky and struggled to breathe. At my side, one of the green-gold grubs smacked its hind end lightly against my left calf. I looked down, startled, and laughed.

"We're still here," I said, half to myself. "We can still try."

I picked my way carefully through the grubs. They moved aside to clear a path for me to the tomb at the edge of the water. On the mesquite tree only a dozen bees remained, settled against the crooks of its branches and on pillows of fanning leaves. The archive bone was entwined with the roots of this one, half submerged. It was a full mandible, four cracked molars still fitted into the back sockets, held in place by threaded roots. The runes were harshly cut into the bone and of uneven depth, as though they had been implanted with a chisel and in a very great hurry. It was old. I could tell from its waving light as I approached. It had been activated before. I doubted that it would sustain enough energy to be activated again once I left here.

First, I drank three careful cups of water with my jícara. The taste was as clean and brilliant as moonlight, even before I filtered it. Then I took a salt tab, ate my algae brick, and waited to see if I would vomit it all back up. Only after my stomach had settled and I had guarded Nadi's bone safe on my cord of shards did I squat before the great mesquite tree and brush my fingers along the jawbone. Light burst from its runes like a fire, ran down the roots, then up to the very leaves of the mesquite before resolving.

We stared at each other, silent. This one did not bother with the simulation of breath. Ze appeared perfectly aware that ze was dead. Zir features were hard to pinpoint amid the flaming orange that lit zir silhouette like a bonfire in the darkness. But ze wore the gray vest of the Head Librarian over wide skirts in the Mahām style.

"I am glad to note that my friends still have the guarding of me," ze said, in a Mahām so archaic that I struggled to make sense of its tones. "But they let you through." Ze gave me a hard look. "I have seen you before, in a god's dream. Yet I did not think they would succeed in bringing you to life. What is the year, O pilgrim?"

The voice was achingly familiar. The cadences, measured and poetic even for zir time, had been featured in a half dozen of my history modules growing up. I squinted past the flickering light and saw that I was right.

"Five hundred and seven, Seremarú," I said.

Eir eyes widened. "You date from the Treaty now? Well, then, I see that I am old, even for a ghost."

Here was the hero of the Great War, the first Head Librarian, and if Vaterite told the truth, founder of Tiger Freehold as well. So much of my life had been dreamed by this one person—which meant, of course, that so much of what was destroying us had been eir responsibility. Ey had been one of the principal drafters of the Treaty, a Mahām of their third gender who had been persecuted for rebellion during the war and given a chance to construct peace when it ended. Ey had never had much of a chance to see the world birthed from eir vision: Mahām supremacists assassinated em in Sasurandām during a tour of the reconstructed city. Apparently, someone had gathered enough of eir personality for an archive bone and hidden it out here in the desert.

My breath came short, choked by awe and fury in equal measure.

"You know what the Library really is," I said. "You know what was here before."

Ey hesitated a moment, then spoke. "I had the understanding, however, that such destabilizing knowledge would be suppressed."

"It was. Very effectively. But I was born of the Library's four gods and I found it there, a still-open wound at their heart."

"Yes. I gather . . . my dear child, I can see that you lay the blame on me. I do not deny it. But you must understand: We were trying to save the world."

"By letting the Mahām persecute the Miuri and all the other minority groups in their system to death? By letting their War Ritual get even bloodier every two generations? By denying the Tierrans the autonomy you promised them for their help and rewarding the turncoat Lunars with rights over their very bones instead? Is that how you saved the world? By giving those who exploited their power even more of it, and grinding the powerless into the dust of the earth, so that even their descendants forgot their names?"

A wind blew through the oasis, a cold slap of sand across my exposed skin. The grubs moaned behind me and filled the twilight air with flashes of light and color. Seremarú waved out of existence and then flickered back.

"They grew my tomb out near the edge," ey said. "The gravitational field is unstable here. You must be careful as you continue on."

"And where am I going, do you imagine?"

Eir eyes were truly kind. I hated the mess ey had left us with, but perhaps I wouldn't have done better in eir clothes, either. "I can see that you would not exist, nor would you be here five hundred years after I finished my work, if the systems were not once again on the edge of a conflagration. And I can see that, as the last time, there is only one god whose deep animus could add fuel to such a fire. So you are going to Sasurandām, my sweet child. You are going there on the old paths, hidden from all sides. You will make right what I could not. At least a part of it. Or you will fail, and in another five hundred years, someone else will try again. Is that not all we have?"

I surprised myself with how well I understood. "The lonely attempt."

Ey smiled. "Then I shall give you another piece of advice. Beyond here, at the western rim, you will find a kind of maze. You must not go there."

"The forest of bones?" I asked.

Ey laughed so hard that the tree glowed from root to seed pod. I could just make out shadows of little fish that scurried back into the safety of deeper water. "That will be," ey said, "a very old joke."

"A joke?"

Ey lifted eir shoulders in a gentle but unmistakable negative. "If you know as much as you say you do, Library's Child, you will see for yourself."

"Still keeping your secrets, Seremarú?"

"Ah, but I am dead, and I can only be now how I remembered me then. You are living, my child, so you have the advantage. You can change, and you can choose."

As Seremarú had promised, I understood the joke as soon as I saw it, ten hard days later. They were bones, of a sort, but not of any Tierran-evolved organism. They were the bleached white remains of not-corals, frozen into the shapes that

I recognized from my time immersed in the memories of Huehue. They were the bones of a species whose very existence had been smeared to stardust, and so could not possibly exist. And yet, here they were.

"A forest of bones," I said into the twilight chill. Twilight lasted for hours this far out on the rim. The atmosphere was thin here; the stars and the blackness between them dominated the horizon. Every few hours, instabilities in the gravitational field kicked up great windstorms that smeared the dunes like a child with finger paints. I had brought strips for my shoes that used electromagnetic attraction to keep me more or less on the ground. They weren't strong enough to work in a vacuum, but they stopped me from flying for meters when the wind hit.

The bones of the corals were white like a knife to the eye, like a new star bursting to life in the charnel of a galactic core. Even with my goggles on and the filters turned red, they seemed to glow with a menacing, accusatory albedo. There was so little water in the atmosphere here that I kept my face entirely shrouded in spider silk. Still, I had enough water in my gourds from the last well that I decided I could afford to camp here while I considered my options. I had nearly arrived at this impossible edge: my only chance to escape the home I had never wanted to leave, risking my very soul in the void between worlds.

My only chance to find Nergüi.

Both the engineer and Seremarú had warned me away from the forest of bones. But it stretched north and south as far as I could see. I didn't doubt it went farther. Even the grubs seemed to avoid it; I had only seen the hardiest tribe, the tiny blacks-and-blues digging into the earth for the last several days. The bees had disappeared, and with them their gifts of honey.

"There's an old tesseract hub," Vaterite had told me the morning after Nergüi left, "at the edge of the rim. It was abandoned in the first century due to extreme gravitational anomalies. And . . . something else."

"Something else?"

"Some kind of environmental disaster they couldn't contain. The records are vague. But it isn't safe."

But I had barely heard him, querying the All-Seeing Eye for what I would need to survive the desert. At least now I could understand why Vaterite's records had glossed over the specifics of the environmental problem.

The corals were impossible, but they were there. Which meant, logically, that there was something about the corals that even Huehue hadn't understood. Here at the border, they were dead. But what if they were alive, farther in? If they had somehow survived out here, on the lonely edge of a hostile planetary disc that had once been their own world, should I break their solitude? Should I provoke them? I hadn't destroyed their planet, no, but I had played happily in their dust.

At moonrise, I settled into my shelter and pulled my cord of shards over my head. I held Nadi's archive bone carefully between my right thumb and forefinger. The runes glowed and subsided in waves, but I was careful not to activate it.

"Should I go in, Nadi?" I asked. The runes glowed and faded, glowed and faded.

I imagined: Nadi and me in zir rooms, as they had been for all my childhood. The two of us watching the rain falling in the garden. Ze drank a glass of indigo wine and I savored a cup of cold, foamy chocolate.

"The ghosts warned you not to go," ze said. "So if I know my Freida . . ."

"I shouldn't risk losing you in there."

"You've already lost me, my love."

"You left me the responsibility for your burial. How can I let your tomb grow in the middle of . . . a forest of bones?"

Nadi turned to me, eyes sly and laughing, but zir mouth clenched with anger. Ze began buzzing, higher pitched than the desert bees. The one sound multiplied into a chorus of rage while zir eyes still laughed.

I swung myself out, dug my hands into the white sand, and forced myself to anchor in the present moment. I did not know what I had touched, but I shivered with the memory of that subtle presence. When my breath steadied, I hugged my cord of shards to my chest and wiped my eyes, though the air was so dry here my tears evaporated before they could do more than moisten my lashes. In the darkness, the forest stared back.

The corals were crystals. That much was clear when I touched them, but they were the kinds of crystals that could bear life. They had grown in distinctly organic ways, creating intricate patterns of planes and holes whose composition I could not begin to guess. Walking through them felt deceptively like traversing the tunnels of the Library's gods. But I did not fool myself. That angry buzzing chorus lurked like a tribe of grubs beneath the surface of my awareness, waiting for my every blink, my every stray thought. They wanted my imaginings. They wanted to suck me dry of them. So I took off my shoes and let the rough, sharp white sand anchor me to each footfall. I timed my breaths, five seconds in, seven seconds out. And when I felt my mind drift despite that, I felt for Nadi's archive bone beneath my robe, and I remembered the duty I had taken on. I was an invader here, a conqueror's child, come to stomp over the ancient field of battle. They had all my sympathy. But I would not build my own bone tree for them over it. As Seremarú had said, I was still alive, which gave me a certain advantage.

Atempa had first told me the story of the forest of bones, an old Mahām tale from before they accepted the Nameren and inherited all his bloody desires. It was one of the first things we had shared after she had decided to defy her father and be my friend.

"A girl entered the forest alone, and she died there. From her bones grew a tree."

"What kind of a story is that?" I had asked her, frowning. We were drinking bevet, a traditional spice broth said to be good for growing children's bones. Because gravity was stronger on Mahām, Atempa's mother had told us, and children needed strength to be able to fall without hurting themselves.

"A kernel story," she said serenely, though I sensed impatience lurking around her edges, like the toothy entrance of a cave. "You take it in your mouth and hold it. The rest of the story unfurls."

"How does it unfurl?"

"It *grows*," she had said.

I said it now, into the still, dry air.

The ground was littered with broken branches that gleamed dully in the sunlight. But when I stepped badly and cut my foot on an open edge, the crystal sucked the blood down and three shining, spindly fingers grew to grasp at me. I danced away, swallowing a shriek. The fingers were still.

I told myself the second story of the forest of bones, just as Atempa had told me. "A second girl entered the forest alone, and she died there. From her bones grew the worms."

I imagined the forest listening, despite itself. A shadow crossed in front of me, running. Quinn's voice called out, jellied with rage, "Where is the Incarnate Representative!" I blinked, and remembered: I must not imagine.

The third story unfurled like a seedling on my tongue. "A third girl entered the forest alone, but she did not die. She fed the worms the last apple she had brought with her, so they would not eat her body. She faced the tree.

"'I will tell you how not to die, bone tree,' she said.

"'I have already died,' the tree said.

"'But you are half reborn,' said the third girl. 'I will give you my blood and from it you will grow fruits as red as beating hearts. And so you will keep the worms happy for many years, and from your fruits will grow more girls who will give you their blood.'

"The bone tree agreed to this, and so the third girl cut herself on the branches. The bone tree drank and drank, though the girl shouted that it had been enough. When it was done, the bone tree had taken over the whole forest and the worms were joyous, for they had all the hearts in the world on which to feast."

No—that wasn't how it ended. I remembered Atempa's voice, unfurling: The third girl slept beneath the tree and when she awoke, there were apples growing from the branches. She took one and kept it in her satchel until she escaped, and from the apple grew another girl, who stayed loyally beside her mother until their death.

They had changed it. That presence lurking here had given me another story through my own mouth. How dare they change that—how dare they invade my memory of Atempa? I felt a bolus in my throat, like blood. More loss: I had never had a chance to say goodbye in person. Atempa had been barricaded in the retreat with the other novices and younger librarians, openly in revolt against Quinn's faction, supporting the Incarnate Representative's recommendation for a new Treaty Council and a new Treaty. Even her chimera had barely made it through Quinn's comm blocks: "Good luck, Freida," it had said, its normally haughty screech mournful as a passing wind. "Tell her we're fighting. Tell her my father is terrified."

My octopus had frowned and twirled the lights at the tips of its tentacles, thrown by this atypical blast of sincerity. "And what about me?"

Her chimera had laughed and laughed. "You're the best friend I've ever had, you idiot. Don't die. Please."

A wind blew through the forest; the branches of dead corals dinged and cracked against one another like wind chimes in the underworld. I dropped to the ground. I began to lift a few inches from the earth before another wind blew through and I slammed back down, heavy as though I had a twenty-kilo weight on the back of my head. Bits of coral fell over my back with bruising force. Thanks to the spider silk, they didn't cut me. I did not want to imagine what would happen if I spilled more than a drop of blood here.

When the force lightened once more, I looked up. The twilight side of the sky was a riot of colors, turquoise and cerulean and garnet, streaming across the horizon in great arcs. I breathed out in wonder and terror. I felt like one of those lights in Nergüi's glass, pressed against the side, looking out at the impossibilities just beyond its sphere. O, that I have lived to see such things, Nameren. I, the Library's child; I, the impossible desire sucked from a dream; I, the exiled; I, the dying, but not dead yet.

When the storm blew out, the way before me was choked with debris. I sat up carefully, aching and sore. A figure ran past me and into another opening, to my right. Just a flash of gold, but still I recognized her. The beads in her scalp net clacked as she passed. I had long since secreted that safely away in my pack. But then, she wasn't me as I was now. The stories in Huehue had all said this about the coral cities: they gave visions, if you stayed there long enough, if you were trying to reach their heart. Did this mean they were letting me in?

A raised chorus of voices echoed down the passageways behind me. "A new Treaty for a new era! No peace without justice!"

Then Quinn's voice from just ahead: "Samlin wants to speak with you. He thinks you've misunderstood something about what happened between you. He has it recorded, Freida. I've seen it."

I hunched forward and dug my nails into my palms. A sour seep of bile filled my mouth and I spat it onto the shard-dusted ground. I hadn't responded to his threat, though he'd broken his own comm choke to send it. Let him share my darkest moment with the rest of the world, I wouldn't care anymore. Samlin couldn't have a recording of how it had *felt*. There was no technology to capture the panicked, shame-choked sickness that sometimes rose in me when I saw someone's hands above my head in just that position, bearing down. Quinn was merely the first in a long list of people who wouldn't—would refuse to—understand.

I strapped my shoes back on and got painfully to my feet. The corals could not have moved, and yet the opening to my right seemed just ever so larger. I would have to go north for a while and hope some path would take me back west. Just beyond a bend in the path came the faint echoes of booming and crashing, like a falling tree or distant thunder. I shivered, and began to follow.

The sun went down as I trailed the streaking yellow figure always just a little ahead of me. The corals pressed in closer as I went on, until what had been a forest became a series of branching tunnels. Though the moons were huge and bright here at the western edge, very little light filtered down through the gaps in the latticed corals above me. I pulled out Nergüi's ball of glass, and what I saw there made me stumble. I fell against one of the crystals but jerked away when something cold and sharp tried to sting me through my robe.

"Nergüi . . ." I said, though imagining her was dangerous. "What is this?"

The lights in the glass had frozen. They were bright as ever, but instead of streaming waves of possibility, they were now thousands of static points of light.

As I turned the glass around, I could feel a shape, a pattern within them, but as soon as I turned it again, my intuitive grasp of its geometry vanished. It did not seem to make sense in the three dimensions of a sphere, though it was represented in one.

Like the forest of bones.

"Like a tesseract," I whispered.

Ahead of me, something smashed through the earth: a demolition, a crime against nature. "You lost," I heard my voice say somewhere nearby, a horrified whisper.

I heard the hard smile in his voice, precisely mirroring the faint tilt to those beloved lips: "So did you."

I put a gritty knuckle to my eyes but tears leaked past them. O Joshua—how had I thought that a simple victory in the courts would save him when the Lunars had five centuries of doing precisely what they pleased as precedent? The rest of our holo call, pushed through a break in the comm choke a few hours before I made my escape, came flooding back. I knew I shouldn't give the forest this much of me, but I couldn't stop it. I missed him and I wished, as you only can for those mistakes freely chosen, that things had turned out differently between us.

The first thing I had heard when the connection finally went through was thunder. Great ricocheting smacks, like the fists of a giant against wet earth. Great holes had been torn from the roof just above me, and fire seemed to have damaged the walls. The stars and a sliver of an oddly distant moon spilled through the roof holes to bathe the room in a hushed glow. I was alone here. In the distance again came that terrible smack of earth. There were only wisps of clouds in that foreign indigo sky.

"Joshua?" I called.

A breeze whipped the broken slats of the walls and I shivered. Through my wetware I caught a whiff of something acrid, recently burnt, and even more faintly, old urine, as though someone had used the corner for a latrine.

To my left came scuffling footsteps, muffled panting.

"Freida?" Not Joshua's voice. Someone came into view a moment later, about my age, skin just a shade darker than Joshua's, but the same familiar ochre brown, with dark braids wrapped around zir head to form two little horns above zir ears. Ze wore a hand-embroidered tunic, though in the light I could only make out depth and detail of the weave. We stared at each other for an odd beat.

"Where is Joshua?"

Ze raised zir eyebrows, thick and peaked at the end, as though someone had drawn in a wide-eyed doubtfulness. "Coming," ze said, in a Library Standard that was clearly helped along by unpracticed wetware.

The giant smacked the earth again and we both flinched. "The Lunars." My voice broke. "Already?"

Ze shrugged. "They struck first during the last war, too."

A second person lowered zirself down through one of the holes in the roof and landed lightly behind the other.

It was his eyes I recognized first, with a snap so hard it knocked out my breath. His throat bobbed. He didn't look very different, really, and yet—the lines of his face cleaner and harder, his hands wiry and strong, his fingernails dirty, his eyes . . .

"You look different," he said, while those eyes blinked slowly and said a thousand other things we could never again say out loud. Two smacks shook the earth and the earth roared back. The whole room trembled with such force that even I felt off-balance. Joshua reached, without thinking, for his companion's arm.

"You lost," I said.

His smile, Nameren, his smile. "So did you."

"They're tearing your village apart right now? Why are you still there?"

"It's an illegal occupation. We'll fight."

"And you?" I asked the stranger next to me. I tried, and failed, to suppress that acid-green note in my voice. I hadn't told Joshua about Nergüi, either. That didn't make it hurt less, for some reason.

"My name is Citlali, she," she said softly. "I'm the youngest of the Order of the Elders. It's a crime even the Lunars must respect to deprive me of my long life."

Joshua looked at me and smiled faintly, proud and apologetic and wistful. He would always be my first love. I would always be his. Even as our paths diverged across galaxies.

In the haunted maze of the corals, his voice came to me on a wind. "You could have saved us, Freida. You were always a coward—" Another blast, and his voice cut off.

Silence. Was that a distant wind I heard? No, just my own blood noisy in my ears. I was alone with my heartbeat, the muted scuffle of my hands and feet against the shards of fallen corals, my gasping breath.

"That wasn't what he said." I spoke out loud just to reassure myself. "It didn't happen that way."

But maybe in one of my million million points of light, it had. With shaking hands, I lifted Nergüi's glass back up to eye level. If he had died, would I know? Or had our lights already diverged irrevocably from each other, never to touch again? Intersystem war seemed inevitable now, little as anyone wanted it. Who would win? What could one secondary AI and a stubborn Tierran law scholar and a surly Disciple of the Lighted Path do against all the moneyed forces of the Lunars and Martians and Mahām?

Survive, I hoped. Survive, to walk our lonely paths until we found each other again, in peace. There were so many ways for my journey to end badly. But for now, at least in this world, I was alive. My light might be at the edge, but it still shone.

I lifted the glass over my head and kept walking.

✦

My own voice was leading me in circles. I ate half an algae brick, but I had so little water left that I didn't dare eat more. It felt like the corals had slowed down time. Or was this another kind of subtle psychological manipulation? I did not understand them. I only knew that they would kill me here, in these endless retellings of my own endless selves. I had heard Joshua killed a dozen times; myself killed in the aftermath of the trial when I escaped behind my Incarnate Representative mask, heard the freeholders massacred where they had gathered behind broonie-make barricades, heard the librarians destroying their beloved Library itself. I had even heard Quinn dying, his panicked screams as he pled with Old Coyote to release him from communion. I saw myself as I had been that last day in the Library, a furious, running figure with a freshly shaven head and the yellow robes of an Awilu from the oldest clans. I heard my sobs when I realized that Nergüi had left me there in the best way she knew how. Oh, my hardheaded, softhearted Nergüi, who so hates goodbyes. Even now, Nameren, I'm sure she's wondering how she can get out of it.

Squatting there in that slow moonlight, I realized I couldn't go on. I chewed slowly, forcing my saliva to moisten the mouthfuls of the brick, whose value as nutrition was directly orthogonal to its taste. I would have to risk something to break the game they were playing.

I pulled my cord from beneath my robes and fingered the shards there, five deadly fingers of a disarticulated hand. The fifth, brittle and blinding white, had found its home here—a heart shard for the forest of bones at the edge of the world. What would that do to me? Since ingested crystals needed to interact with my wetware to achieve communion, it might break the freeze that Vaterite had given me. That would give Quinn proof that I was alive, and of where I had gone. After that, I would have very little time to escape.

It was not much of a decision in the end. I am as they made me, Nameren. I am a human born of the gods, designed for communion.

I laid out my pallet to cushion the rough, unforgiving ground. I pulled the cord over my head and broke off half the milky coral crystal. It was a large dose, but underdosing would be fatal in these circumstances. Then, at last, I took out Nadi's archive bone and laid it on my chest.

"Grow from my heart if I don't make it," I whispered. "May the grubs find you and tend to you and drain just a little of the anger from this place."

Above me, coral fingers clicked and whispered.

"You will let me through," I said to them. "Past the red gate and to the tesseract."

The only response was my own voice, screaming again, just beyond my sight. My nostrils flared and I swallowed the shard with the last of my water. It went down like broken glass and exploded like a signal flare, right between my eyes.

Cold can burn worse than a fire. It can sear you from the inside. It can hold you as it kills you, slowly, so slowly. In fifty years, they would find my body and it would look just the same as it did now, eyes shocked wide, pupils blasted black.

My wetware flew awake, lurching and bobbling as it attempted to connect to faraway networks. It had never regulated my biological systems, but it had lightly monitored them, and it pulsed warnings at me of extreme dehydration, extreme exhaustion, extreme emotional distress. Materials, what a gods-damned genius, why did I ever need this thing again? It found a thin thread of a network, but something blocked it. Something that I had invited inside me. I recognized a shape, a flavor, a texture in the press of its mind against my own. It drew back, equally surprised. We shifted. I was floating in a red ocean above a great coral city. An unmistakably Tierran fish, with a face like a fat-cheeked child's, stared at me.

"The little baby?" ze said.

My heart cracked open. My blood spilled, Kohru blue, into the space between us. "Mother?" I said.

The corals, an alien tesseract, an ancient crime, the red gate.

Iemaja.

When I came back to myself, a different path stretched before me: a mere twenty meters through densely branching corals and then a clearing. And an altar.

The forest of bones surrounded the red gate on three sides. It was just as I had seen it in Huehue: a great cube of rust-red ocean floating above ancient coral sentinels. There was no need—or room—for the corals to grow on the fourth side, because it was bound by the end of the earth. Right at the edge, just beyond the red gate, was a human-made structure: a half-submerged dome, mosaics of colored glass in the Dar style, with its side that faced the edge sheared flat. A functional well was enclosed by the same glass mosaics to one side. I had found the first Tenehet tesseract, calibrated in the first years after the Treaty to connect to the Mahām system, and abandoned after the corals blocked its access. My wetware felt functional again, though different. My communion with Iemaja's nameless heart avatar had forced it awake, but it had also changed it. I felt more consciously aware of certain functions. I could block its connections by imagining. I could even freeze myself at will. I did so, and was astonished at the quiet peace that flooded through me, like blood rushing to a sleeping limb.

I recalled the visions that Iemaja's heart avatar had shown me, though even now it was hard to put them into words. One truth came to me clearly: Iemaja was a tesseract, as were all the gods. Her heart avatar had no name, or a name only intelligible in the chemical signatures of the corals, their language.

But she is not a tesseract through space, Nameren. She is a fold in time. You are not, it turns out, the oldest material god. When the Mahām destroyed the planet, the tesseract survived roughly half a billion years in the past. The greater part of coral civilization had always been on that other side. But when the coalition built the Library disc, it was natural to come back, to build a kind of monument to their dead and block access to one of our own tesseracts. They meant it as a warning, one Seremarú had certainly understood. The librarians kept away, and made sure that no one had any reason to venture near the western edge. But the librarians also built Iemaja, turned what had been an alien tesseract into a more human material god. The layers of personality grew upon each other, until my Iemaja was hardly aware of the origin of her heart, exiled to the edge of the world. But still, some things penetrated. The little baby she had nurtured and made sure survived—that had gone like a bore, straight to her center.

I walked past the red gate and stopped at the edge. The field that maintained the atmosphere and gravity on the disc supposedly prevented matter from falling into the cosmic vacuum, but I did not trust it enough to reach out my hand. The air was so cold here that my breath surrounded my head like a wreath. It was nearing midnight. In a few hours, the sun would heat this place to nearly fifty chokingly hot degrees Celsius. I wondered if Nadi would mind being out here in such extremes, but when I looked ahead of and behind me, I stopped worrying. Here, on the edge of the world, on the edge of time, on the edge of history:

This was the only place that deserved zir. And the forest would protect zir from anyone less bloody-minded than me. I drew out Nadi's archive bone and held it. The rose moon and the thorn moon, crescent and gibbous, looked so close that I could touch them. I took them in through tears. I knew, Nameren—I knew I would never see any of this again.

I was methodical in my preparations. First, I filled my gourds from the well and drank in carefully calibrated sips. After an hour and two salt tablets, I had recovered enough to continue. I did not feel my exhaustion; I was as clear as moonlight on still water. My duty possessed me. I filled the gourds again and went back to the spot I had staked out, a patch of coral-white sand between the red gate and the edge. I pulled out the retractable shovel that I had brought all the way out here for this one purpose. I wasn't a grub, after all. I couldn't dig with my jaws.

An hour later, I deemed the hole sufficiently wide and deep. It would be enough to hold water, with a root system to support it. I put the archive bone down in the center of pure turquoise sand, buried deep beneath the white, and poured the first gourds of water over the bone. The combination of earth and water activated its runes, which glowed in a rainbow of colors that I had never seen in an archive bone before. It couldn't project without conscious intent, but I watched nervously for five minutes before I went back for more water. The third time I emerged from my sandy mud hole, three grubs were waiting for me at the edge.

I recognized them, and I was so tired that this did not strike me as strange. They had last chanted me a blessing at the tomb of Seremarú. Two green-and-gold and one orange-and-red.

"Hello again," I said. "Did you follow me here?"

The smaller of the green-and-golds opened its mouth and projected an image of a great baobab tree, a sentinel on the edge of space and time.

"Oh, Nadi," I whispered. The great baobab with the lonely cicada calling in her heart. "Yes."

I would leave the bone to them. Vaterite had told me that if the old traditions held, the archive bone should sow itself in the earth. In the past, grubs had been charged with designing and cultivating which tree would keep the bone through the centuries. And these grubs still felt moved to fulfill that duty, it seemed.

"Let me say goodbye first," I told them. They didn't move, so I assumed consent and slid down into the pit one last time. I knelt in the swirling turquoise water and touched Nadi's archive bone.

"Nadi," I said. "Wake up."

Ze sat beside me in the water. As full and as healthy as I remembered zir from before the illness had sucked zir from me like an eyedropper. Ze looked up at the lights pulsing across the sky.

"The edge, Freida? So it came to that, after all?"

"Did you tell Vaterite how I could escape?"

Ze shook zir head sadly. "He knows the old ways out. I told him to give this to you only if you had to use them."

The joy I felt at seeing zir, a fizzy, sweet thing that went from my head to my heart to my smiling mouth, paused. Suddenly wary, I asked, "Why only then?"

Ze turned to me with a clean and cutting look. "Because I only wanted you to know this if there was no other choice."

My heart galloped, causing my wetware to flash warnings at me like dancing fireflies. I ignored them. I ignored everything but my Nadi, here with me at last, who never did anything in life—or in death, it seemed—without hidden layers of purpose.

"What did you do?" I asked. My lips were numb, my feet frozen in the water of the sinkhole.

Ze held my gaze tight. "My love. Freida, my love, I knew what that boy did to you. Not immediately after, but soon. I told myself I couldn't be sure, but I was your parent, and I knew. I let you suffer alone and I did not force you to tell me because if you had confirmed it, I would have had to denounce him, and Quinn would have destroyed us both. I thought it was the best of my terrible options. But I betrayed you, and you have never fully recovered, and you are about to enter the most dangerous communion of your life with an open wound to your soul."

It is strange, Nameren, that the part that most struck me was not zir revelation itself—perhaps I was too shocked to even process it at the time—but zir straight-backed, clear-eyed assessment of what ze had done. There was no apology, no excuse, no expectation of mercy. Only the truth as ze saw it, stripped of pretense.

"And you only wanted me to know this if I decided to escape the Library," I said, after a beat.

Nadi had the nerve to smile then—crooked and pained, but a smile nevertheless. "I thought it was no greater sin to preserve your good opinion of me. If it wasn't *necessary* for you to hate me—"

Ze broke off helplessly. That smile again. There were tears in zir eyes that did not fall.

I searched myself for hatred and found none. Oh, there was anger, Nameren— I could feel it simmering beneath the frozen surface of my shock. Betrayal and disillusionment and grief that Nadi had never told me when there was a chance to make amends and heal.

No matter what this ghost of Nadi said to me now, it would always be too late for that.

I closed my eyes, overwhelmed by the sight of zir waiting for a blow.

"Nadi," I said, "you picked a very bad time to die."

I could not feel zir touch, never would again, but I imagined zir hands on my shoulders and when I looked, there they were. Zir eyes were so like life, so kind and sharp and filled with that humor whose sadness I had only recently recognized.

A wild, desperate laugh broke free of my throat like a bird from a trap. "I will never stop loving you. I never could. Yes, you failed—radical truth, radical trust, radical vulnerability—you failed! But you loved me more and better than any parent could, even so, even so, my Nadi, even so . . ."

I sobbed while ze held me in an embrace I could imagine, but never feel. When I looked up, I saw the phosphorescent tracks of tears down zir own cheeks.

"What will you do, Freida?"

"I'm not sure . . . about anything."

"Surety is overrated. Doing matters far more."

I scowled. "You *would* say that."

Ze leaned forward, avid. "I have a problem for you."

"What?"

"That's how you do it. You work it out, piece by piece. Just like I taught you."

I screwed my eyes shut. *I'm not ready*, I wanted to wail. I wanted to throw myself into zir arms. But ze was dead, and zir ghost could offer only the wind that blew through the memories of our comfort.

"What will you do, Freida?"

My knife-trimmed fingernails dug deep into the palms of my hands. My trembling fists sent ripples across the sand-stained water in the sinkhole. "I'm going to find Nergüi," I gritted out.

"And then?"

We both knew. "Sasurandām."

Zir throat bobbed. "Why, Freida?"

"To kill the Nameren," I said. "To stop everything from spiraling out of control."

That considering tilt of zir head, that political mind—or its echo—moving, moving. "Is that good enough?"

"I'm going to Sasurandām," I said firmly. I looked at zir with my best goodbye. "I am going for love."

Ze put zir hands of air and light on my shoulders. "Better than I did," ze said. "That's all three."

"Ze knew it was real."

The girl looks up, shocked. A little afraid. "What was real?"

"The wound that boy gave you."

The god is fishing in the river beneath the baobab tree, only the fish are twisted hands and they stink of the virus. He picks them up and tosses them to the suns, who devour the flesh like hungry dogs.

The girl does her best not to look. The girl has practice. "If ze knew it was real, why wait until ze was dead to say so?" she says bitterly.

"For the same reason you don't want to talk about it, I imagine."

"Yet you keep bringing it up."

He holds up a flopping hand and eyes it speculatively. "How is it, do you think, that this virus finds its way in here so easily?"

The girl flinches. "It's a war weapon—"

"Trained to exploit weakness. You have a hole in your heart, too, little piper. You're a *bintara selwa wan* who won't even admit to having lost anything."

She hunches in the mud, so angry. "I haven't forgotten, Aurochs."

"But you choose not to remember."

"It wasn't—"

"Real? After all the stories you have told me here, you still persist in that?"

She peers at the suns instead of the god. She bites out, "It shouldn't matter."

"Why not?"

"It shouldn't . . ." Her words fade, as though eaten by the hungry suns. She lies slowly on her back in the grass beneath the baobab. Even her bones hurt, even here. Her voice cracks. "Why is it still here, Nameren? Why is it still hurting me when I have so much else to do?"

He plucks three hands from the river. "Maybe because you never admitted it hurt when you first felt the blow. And your parent pretended ze didn't see." He tosses one after another to the sky. "Maybe you've been walking on that broken limb for years instead of believing in your own pain." Bits of mutilated code fall in a warm rain.

"What good does it do me to believe in it?"

The god pauses his merry hunt. "You're afraid it will hurt even more, little piper? You're right. For a while, it will be the worst pain you have felt in your life, because it is a pain delayed."

"So why would I let something that—awful—"

His voice is right by her ear, though his body is still in the water. "Because then it can heal."

"Didn't I tell you I was broken?"

"Didn't I tell you it's unwise to mistake the cruelties of others for your own failings?"

"It's too late. Healing is for the living. Or the human!"

He turns in the river, takes a step, and is kneeling before her, wet and shining. "So, we aren't human. We could slide away together right now. I could take you with me into that blood-laced sleep. Neither of us would feel our emptiness."

"No. No. Not just yet."

"Why not?"

"I have to finish. Didn't you hear? I promised zir that I would follow radical love to the end."

"Radical love." His voice is acid.

"What?"

"You have already failed."

"I have loved, Nameren! You couldn't know, you couldn't imagine—"

"I can. I do. And you have already failed."

"Stop! Stop saying that!"

"There is something behind you."

She leaps up and turns to face it. Samlin in the expedition-era suit that he had designed for the occasion. He hadn't bothered to remove it. He opens his mouth, wider and wider.

The scream, and the imagining, comes from inside the girl. His head pops off his body like a cooked cranberry. The rest of him wilts and falls to their constructed earth. The ants, fat now with foreign code, cover it immediately. She wonders if they will survive this imagining, if they have constructed some small reality of their own. She does not like these thoughts.

"You will hear me out," the girl booms, still fizzy with a strange new power.

The Aurochs lowers his gaze. "I will," he agrees. "But you knew that anyway."

"I will tell you." She is breathless in a place without air. She made a promise, and she is keeping it. He doesn't know. He doesn't understand. She is a believer in radical love. It is all she has.

"I will tell you about Nergüi's home. I will tell you about the war they fight in your name. I will tell you about all our lighted paths."

–This is the secret of our lighted paths:
If you follow them well, they will always
lead you back to no escape.

–Did you mean to say that?

–Love. They will always lead you back to love.

Tenehet's tesseract opened onto a square room with gray stone walls. They were inlaid with niches made from a wood that had aged to a ruddy black, shiny with centuries of polish. Inside each of the niches was a tiny oblong bundle, wrapped completely in what seemed to be thick paper or ivory hide and then tied with a lattice pattern of red ropes. Around the top of the bundle was a cord with a paper strip, which bore a single word in old Minai calligraphy. I wondered what it said but did not revive my wetware to check. I would need to verify where I was—and how far away I was from Nergüi—before I dared. The light down here was diffuse and bright, and it grew brighter as I approached the niches. It shone from balls of glass just like Nergüi's, which hung from a cord wrapped around the middle of each bundle.

From around their waists, I realized. I looked around again, and recognized the woodwork, the writing, the aesthetic of this place from the images Nergüi had shown me of her great temple. These must be the remains of past disciples, maintaining a sightless vigil over the abandoned tesseract, which had burst to life a few seconds after I opened the temple door. The glass balls were filled with lights, densely buzzing from within their confines. So now there was a tomb on either side of the old tesseract. It seemed fitting.

I was on the Miuri moon. Gravity was noticeably lighter here. Behind me, the half dome of the Library tesseract slowly filled with colored light, filtered through the glass mosaics. The dust that I had kicked up in my passage swirled and glowed as it settled, perhaps for another five hundred years. My heart twisted, but I did not look back twice. I had thought I would be in Sasurandām, but apparently someone back in the early days of the Treaty had thought to use this tesseract to thwart centralized Mahām power. It had not worked, obviously. But being here might make it easier to find Nergüi.

The exit was a steep staircase bounded at the top by a porthole made of the same light gray rock. It swung up on silent hinges at my touch. I stuck my head out.

I noticed the walls first: The stones were charred but still standing, forming the bones of what must have been a very hasty reconstruction. A simple laminate had been spread between the stone columns on two sides of the rectangular structure, while on the other side there remained enough wood to patch the holes. The ground around where I had come out was littered with piles of dead insects, roaches with beetle-green wings. I had seen them before, but I couldn't place where. The roof, a simple stone barrel vault, arched over one half but gaped over the other. No one had bothered to cover it, and so I had my first glimpse of the pink sky of this place, the thin white light of its twin suns, and the open crescent, Nyad blue, of Mahām. The air still smelled of smoke and sulfur and other chemicals I couldn't name. It smelled of war, even without the reminder of the charred stones and the boxes of weapons huddled against the walls. Under the roof, a group of ten or so people hunched around a pit fire to ward off the cold. Someone seemed to be shoveling in the insects to use as fuel. They all wore a variant of Nergüi's robes, but only one carried a similar glass ball. That was the figure who stood and saw me as I crawled slowly out of the hole. The port closed behind me, blending seamlessly with the octagonal stone tiles of the floor. Had this been an auditorium before? A shrine? A temple?

I walked closer to where they waited, so silently all I could hear was the crackling of the dead roaches and a donkey's distant braying. In the light of their twin suns, their robes were a brighter orange. *It would have brought out the highlights in Nergüi's hair*, I thought nonsensically. The fire smeared itself blue and red across my vision and I tried to take a deep breath. But the air was thinner here, thinner even than at the edge of the Library disc, and I had not been in a good state when I'd left.

Tesseract sickness, I decided as I staggered a few more steps forward. They said it brought on euphoria, but perhaps disorientation was also possible.

The person with the glass ball shouted something, and I tried to explain to zir in Mahām that I couldn't understand. Then I felt the cold burn of the stone tile, grimy with soot, against my left cheek.

I was passing out.

I awoke on a bed as thick and soft as a childhood fantasy, with silk sheets and a barley-husk pillow. I kept my eyes closed as I snuggled more firmly into the mattress and imagined that Nergüi was here with me, complaining about unearned luxury.

The pain in my gut precluded further fantasy. I opened my eyes and found myself alone in a small room of wood-inlaid gray stone. Light came in through a skylight covered in oiled patterned paper. At the foot of the bed were my spider-silk robes, impeccably laundered. By my side was a short table with a jade carafe and a matching jade cup.

Nergüi might have been an ascetic, but clearly that was not a requirement of the Disciples of the Lighted Path.

The drink had a medicinal aftertaste to it, a salty lemon balm that made me grimace, but I drank it all. My bruises had faded. The cuts on my feet were now just thin pink lines. A bracelet encircled my left upper arm, with a ruby right at the crook of my elbow, pulsing with a faint light. I tried to move it, but the ruby was attached to my skin.

I wondered how long I had slept.

I changed my clothes quickly—among the many virtues of spider silk was its adaptability to climate, and outside the luxurious bed, the cold was biting. My shoes were missing, so I put on a pair of slippers that waited for me by the door and pushed it open. I emerged into a much larger circular room, from which radiated various doors like spokes of a wagon wheel. The skylight in this room was very large and uncovered. Beneath it sat the figure I recognized from my precipitous entrance: older, straight-backed, in orange robes with white borders and a glass ball at zir waist.

Ze looked at me neutrally over a steaming cup. "I was just having cacao. Would you like some?" Ze spoke Mahām to me now, and though it was fluid and without the slightest hint of distaste, I still felt embarrassed at obliging zir to speak the language of zir oppressors.

"Please," I said. I walked to the cushions where ze was sitting and stood awkwardly. "I'm Freida, she," I said. Though Mahām didn't have the same pronoun structure as Library Standard, it still seemed polite to specify. "I come from the Library. I'm sorry to have inconvenienced you in such a way."

"If you crossed the desert and the forest of bones, it was the least we could do for you, Freida. I'm Müde Pahjam, she, the rector here. Sit, please."

I lowered myself to a cushion. She continued speaking as she poured the cacao. "The Library has issued a call for your return."

My stomach lurched and then calmed. This woman, in this place, would never betray me to them. "Quinn, you mean?"

"It's unclear. The orders supposedly come from the Head Librarian, but he hasn't been seen in public in over a week. There are rumors that he fell into a coma after a botched communion, or that a fellow librarian poisoned him."

My right hand trembled briefly. Old Coyote's rumbling voice. *Whatever you like*, I'd told him. So the god had taken his payment. I wondered if Quinn would survive, but it was an idle wondering, as though he were someone whose life now only incidentally intersected mine. I had come on a far more important mission.

"Nergüi isn't here," I said. Not a question.

After a brief stillness—too calm to call hesitation—she took a sip of her tea. "The Mahām garrison took her down-planet as soon as the rebellion began."

"To Sasurandām?"

Again, that smooth bump in her careful control. "We don't know. There are credible rumors that she has been sequestered outside the city. The news from down-planet is haphazard at best. You likely don't know—our doctor informs me that you seem to be suffering a wetware freeze. We rebelled after the War Ritual and shut down the space port. Down-planet, the Dar rebellion has spread to the gates of Sasurandām. Below-city has been locked down. Tens of thousands have died. We've had a week of relative peace here while they fight. It is unlikely to last."

I lifted my cup—ceramic infused with gold and cinnabar, translucent in the light—and drank the cacao. It was buttery and salty, like the spiced cacao Vaterite had prepared for Nergüi the first time we visited Tiger Freehold, but it had a stronger flavor of cloves and pepper, and only a hint of honey. It was the most intense flavor I had tasted in more than a month, and my saliva glands seemed to swell as it passed. I put down the cup with shaking hands.

"I have to get to her."

"If there was anything that could have been done, we would have done it. She is lost to us, Freida, and at the Nameren's mercy."

"I'm different."

"I can see that."

We fell silent, a brief retreat. Then, quite unexpectedly, she smiled. Her face was as impeccably smooth as her demeanor, but her grin brought out a hidden ebullience, a joy that reminded me of my branch elders. She would be much older than she looked.

"She was wise to give you her glass. I was sure she had lost her senses to a teenage romance, but I can see now that I grossly underestimated our fierce Nergüi."

"I have it with me," I said, matching her smile without meaning to.

"It's one of the most sacred treasures of the temple of the Lighted Path."

"I won't give it to you!"

"Why not, Freida? Is it yours now?"

"No." This would not be the end. I would see her again. I would see her again.

Müde Pahjam put her hands, cracked and worked like old wood, over mine. I felt her stillness enter me, despite myself. My breath rasped in my throat.

"Breathe," she said. "Slowly. You are not recovered from your journey, Freida. The medic informed me that another few days out in that desert and your internal organs would have begun shutting down. Those emergency rations were never meant to be eaten for weeks! Leave here and do your best to find her. But wait, and let yourself recover."

I breathed as she instructed me and the dizziness passed. But I felt my energy and optimism fading as I looked at her.

"Do you think she's dead?"

Müde Pahjam shook her head. "Not in this slice of the manifold, and not in most others. Her weight of existence is still very strong. And you are right, Freida. The glass is Nergüi's. I could never take it from her. She is my successor here."

And so I learned, at last, the story of Nergüi. Should I tell it to you, Nameren? Because it is like her shining glass: too beautiful, and too rare, to share lightly.

But I think . . . you know, don't you? You haven't killed me yet. And she is right beside me.

Nergüi was born to the poorest branch of a long-established Miuri equatorial clan. The habitable zone of the moon is narrow and its ideal equatorial territories were claimed by the first settlers from the seed ship, the ones who survived after the supposed Miuri sabotage and Mahām reprisals. Which meant, in practice, that the clans who had maintained their grip on the grassland and pastures and short blue scrub forests of the equator were those most firmly entrenched with the Mahām government in Sasurandām. Only the most powerful left Miuri, of course, since down-planet immigration was strictly regulated, but it was a dream for the children of the most aspirational clans to travel to the university there for study and to return for rule. Had Nergüi's parents been less aspirational—or delusional—it never would have occurred to them to push such a destiny on their only child.

Her parents were both just third cousins of the main family branch—and, therefore, third cousins of each other, though if they mentioned this it was only to further justify their claim to centrality. Their holdings amounted to an ill-maintained house on a guinea pig farm in the folds of a mountain range so cold it could only be considered equatorial by technicality. Her father and mother both held minor posts in the provincial government, various ones over the years: clerks and letter writers and consular assistants. The money from the guinea pig farm was used to supplement the vast amounts they deemed necessary for adequate bribery. Nergüi, of course, was in charge of the farm. From the age of seven she performed all the necessary tasks, from feeding to curing to butchering and packing the meat for sale—I couldn't believe that someone would make a child sit so close to death and think nothing of it. At night, her mother drilled her on religious doctrine and the thirteen great poet-philosophers of the expedition age. Her father trained her in court etiquette and the nuances of the four honorific registers in Mahām. It was assumed from an early age that their stoic daughter with her odd flashes of intelligence and humor would take the exam for the university down-planet and return with the key to improving their fortunes and giving them the lives they deserved as clan members. Nergüi did not want to take this exam or leave her guinea pigs, but she went along with their training for lack of other options.

When she was twelve, an itinerant disciple fell ill in their village and stayed with the local healer while he recovered. She was instantly fascinated. She visited him daily with broth or herbs that she had foraged—green herbs, which were descendants from Tierra, and blue ones, which were native to Miuri. The disciple was delighted to receive these because, he said, even now very few Miuri dared to eat the native fruits of their home. He explained to her that he was out exploring his paths, but that eventually his light would return to its home in Müixe Tseghà, the great temple on the northern reaches of the habitable zone.

"My mother says that farther north it is all barbarians and separatists who will cut your throat!" Nergüi told him very seriously. She liked the disciple by now. He would speak to her for hours in Miuri, that silken language of twenty-two vowels, so malleable you could pack into a word what would require a sentence in Mahām, so precise that its curses could freeze the sweat on the tip of your nose.

"They won't kill me there," he told her. "Nor would they kill you. They would welcome you, as they welcome all the children each year to the Weighing, just at the first flowering of the dogwood."

Nergüi panicked then. "Weighing? To see if we're fat enough to slaughter, like the guinea pigs?"

He laughed. "No, child, we don't eat children. We hardly eat guinea pigs— the winds are harsh there, and the poor creatures fall prey to disease more often than not."

"Well, *I* could keep them alive."

"I'm sure you could. I think . . . if you can convince your parents to consider it, you should come to us. There is something about you."

"I'm not very heavy."

"But your soul might be."

Nergüi's parents were atheists, though they did not broadcast that publicly. Outside clan circles, atheism was considered one tiny step below full diabolism. Her parents were, in fact, quite content to serve and nominally worship you, since you are a material god and not a spiritual one. And in any case, it served their first principle, which was, as ever, personal uplift. They were not pleased when Nergüi told them that she wished to have her soul weighed in Müixe Tseghà. They were, in fact, so displeased that her father used all that month's bribe money on a judge in the local Mahām judiciary to bring in the itinerant monk on charges of sedition, for which he was remanded to hard labor on the asteroid belt. After three years, he finally returned home, having journeyed to paths much farther than he had anticipated. He rarely spoke in his later years, and never to her.

Thus began the warring years with her parents. They enrolled her in a private school for clan children at great personal expense, and she would cut classes to visit local temples or just wander the scrubland and pick juicy leaves for her guinea pigs. She refused to have anything to do with material studies and the sanitized versions of the War Ritual, which she had realized at twelve badly distorted reality. She didn't understand why her fellow pupils weren't also scandalized to read such lies about their own home, but when she turned thirteen, she understood: They might live on Miuri, but they, like her parents, believed that they *belonged* on Mahām. So she gave up on her fellow pupils, and she gave up on her parents.

"I don't want to go to Sasurandām," she told them one night, after she had given her father all the money she had made from the guinea pigs at the market and he had berated her for not appreciating all the hard work he did for the family. Her mother and father looked as though she had struck them with a stick. "This can't be a surprise to you," she tried again.

"Well, we knew you were going through a difficult—"

"Rebellious. Ungrateful," her father interjected.

"Stage," her mother finished, firmly. "But even you can't refuse such an opportunity! The headmaster says you have a good chance of passing the exam if you learn to control your impulsiveness."

She was thirteen. The last year to be included in the Weighing.

"I want to be a disciple," she said.

Her father pounded his fists on the table. A mug fell to the floor and spilled its millet beer. Nergüi lamented: The guinea pigs would have drunk it. "Not *that* absurd multidimensional hocus-pocus again!"

"It's real," she said. "And even better, it's *ours*, not like that blood-drinking devil you want me to bow down to every morning!"

Her mother gasped and put a finger to her lips. "Hush," she said. "Do you want them to hear?"

"The Mahām aren't divine! They're human, and they're killing us. Can't you see? Why do you want to help them? Why not help us?"

"Is the 'us' you're talking about, daughter, the same 'us' who would string us up on the next middling branch if they knew what we don't believe?"

Nergüi had no response to that. But she left the next morning regardless, bound for the northern mountains. When she told the rector that she was there to have her soul weighed, the woman frowned and said, "But the Weighing isn't for another week."

This was news to Nergüi, who had timed her journey for the very first flowering of the dogwood, just as the disciple had told her. She hadn't realized that the dogwood would flower up north later than it did even in a cold equatorial town.

"I hope you can weigh me anyway, ma'am," Nergüi said. "Because my parents don't like to lose, and I'm sure they won't let me stay here long."

Müde Pahjam spoke of her surprise at that meeting with a fondness that I recognized. Perhaps we all have a moment like that, those of us who love Nergüi—that moment when we realize she *really is serious*. Against all tradition and to the great scandal of the other disciples, she took Nergüi at her word and brought her to the Shrine of the Lights. The Weighing was simple: The child would climb up the wooden platform to where the great glass ball rested. It was not, in life, nearly so large as Nergüi had shown me in the projected image, perhaps the size of the circle of my arms, but it was deeply impressive to a stocky thirteen-year-old. Once on the platform, the child would watch the ball, strictly warned to never touch it. After a minute, the lights inside should mirror the weight of the child's possibilities. More lights, more weight.

Nergüi stomped up the stairs and stood a defiant five centimeters from the glass. She squinted at it. The lights were dark for several moments, as if the space inside had encountered a black hole. And then they burst to life. Nergüi didn't make a sound, but she fell back so hard she tumbled down the stairs. The other disciples ran to catch her.

"Did I break it?" Nergüi asked.

Müde Pahjam took a second to respond, because her first response was laughter, and she suspected the child would find that disconcerting. "No," she said. "It just wanted to make very sure that we all knew you were one of us."

Nergüi stayed a week that time, until her parents—and a Mahām magistrate—caught up with her. She was already being trained as Müde Pahjam's successor, though this was never stated explicitly. Someone with that kind of path density was always singled out for high-ranking positions in the temple. It was not that they were considered more *holy* or *worthy*, precisely, but that by having an exceptionally high weight of existence, they could help lead the temple itself to paths where it was also more likely to continue existing; a necessary symbiosis.

The second time, Nergüi came at the beginning of winter—she barely survived, but it did deter her parents until spring. After that, a Mahām judge remanded her to a reeducation camp. There was no more talk of universities on Sasurandām at the very least, but her parents refused to let her stay on at Müixe Tseghà. Their fury and their determination found its steely counterpart in their daughter, who escaped from the reeducation camp and filed a petition for parental emancipation with a representative of the Treaty human rights commission, who just happened to be staging a diplomatic visit down-planet. Zir interest in the case made the Mahām temporarily hesitant to act on her parents' bribes (though, it must be said, they were not equally hesitant in accepting them). For two years, Nergüi had a respite from her parents' stubborn, vengeful need to control their daughter. She became a true Disciple of the Lighted Path, as though she had been born to it. And she did, as she had promised, produce a viable guinea pig population for the temple kitchens.

But then the human rights commission moved its attention to newer, more interesting cases and your bloodier avatars bestirred themselves like a walrus on a down-planet beach to bellow: *war*. Her parents volunteered her for the draft for the coming ritual. No doubt someone had told them it would bring them favor with some minor Mahām functionary. With no international eyes to shame them, the courts were happy to grant her parents' request. And so Müde Pahjam petitioned the Library and begged them to give Nergüi asylum. Nadi zirself read the request and granted it immediately. Within a day, a battalion of Library peacekeepers took Nergüi to the Sasurandām tesseract and brought her through to relative safety.

And in so doing, she potentially destroyed her chance of becoming who she was born to be.

When she returned this time, it was under the auspices of Mahām soldiers. Two Library peacekeepers trailed behind for form's sake, but there was no question of who held the power. They planted her in front of them like a flag—or a shield—at the formal invocation of the ritual. Thousands of the drafted participants, divided at random into two colored factions, faced one another across a wide plain that was fertile as the sea from so many generations of spilled blood. The air was so sharp with fear that even an unaugmented human could smell it. His Holiness Shipbuilder called the start. Above him, Mahām soldiers armed in tank suits with limited flight ability kept their weapons ready.

No one moved. For a minute, even the Mahām soldiers kept their silence. Then Shipbuilder said something sharply to one of his underlings, who spoke to another official, who relayed that information to a waiting line of flunkies, one of whom was—what would this story be without full circles?—Nergüi's mother. Nergüi had not noticed her. Her mother—this is conjecture, of course, Nameren, but you'll forgive it—felt caught out, torn between bitter disapproval and bitter jealousy and, perhaps, if we are generous, a little pride. Here was her strange, contrary, guinea pig–loving daughter, risen to great heights just as her mother had always known she would. And it was all to nothing. Her infamy would do nothing for the family's prospects with the clan. Her mother sighed and directed orders to the second line of aerial soldiers to shoot the first line if they did not immediately start shooting at both "sides" of the War Ritual, thus encouraging everyone to get to the real business of bloodshed. All according to protocol. A few of the first line soldiers began, with palpable reluctance, to shoot. At random, people in blue and silver caps began to drop. Amid the screams, others stumbled forward.

Nergüi, back with the Nameren priests, watched this slow-motion horror. Soon, the "armies" would clash at the center of the field, and she knew how the story ended—no matter how little they wanted to fight, they would do so instinctively, just to survive. The priests were so involved in shouting orders to their soldiers that no one noticed at first that she was walking out into the field. Well, that's not precisely true: Her mother noticed. She said nothing, for reasons she was never able to articulate, even to herself.

Nergüi threw herself into the narrow space between the armies and . . . stood there.

"Stop," she said, not particularly loudly. Everyone stopped. Her cause had become intersystem famous; certainly, no one on Miuri was unaware of the identity of the stocky figure in a disciple's robes with flyaway orange-brown hair.

An aerial soldier shot into the crowd again. Five more people went down, as silent as fallen millet. Nergüi raised her hands and spoke to those nearest her, with blue caps.

"Kill me," she said. "Now. Quickly. It will give you a chance to turn on them."

I do not know if Nergüi actually imagined this to be a viable plan. But I know her, and I love her, and I suspect that my Nergüi had no particular desire to die that day—though she was willing, if she had to. She was counting on the Nameren priests to hear her, believe that she meant it, and stop the aerial soldiers from massacring the "armies" into battle. That's how it worked out, in any case. The Nameren priests were on politically dangerous territory with the War Ritual— the Dar rebellion was gaining momentum on Mahām planet, finding support- ers even in pure Mahām territories near Sasurandām. The Library was bitterly divided against itself and Quinn could offer very little material support. Added to that, Nergüi's death might provoke reactions that they could not control. So instead, an aerial soldier descended to carry her out of there, and the assembled armies started to attack the soldiers instead.

In the middle of this melee, a group of separatists not drafted into the army detonated a series of bombs. A Nameren priest was killed—not Shipbuilder, though still a great victory—and a dozen or more of the assembled soldiers. Faced with the embarrassing prospect of being casualties of a war when they had meant to force a war ritual, the priests and their functionaries evacuated, but not before dragging Nergüi away with them.

That was the last Müde Pahjam saw or heard from her. The rector had been busy, in any case; the Miuri civil war had begun in earnest.

✢

Müde Pahjam insisted that I stay until I had fully recovered, and I allowed myself to be persuaded. I had been without comfort for so long that it pained me to leave it; part of me wanted to stay between the silken sheets of this place for the rest of my life. It might be in a war zone, but it was better than what Quinn had wanted from me in the Library. We were on the eastern side of the temple complex, which had mostly escaped Mahām bombs so far.

"I think it's because the Nameren likes the Shrine of the Lights," Müde Pahjam told me with that disconcerting smile. We were sharing our evening meal on the balcony above that very shrine, protected from the wind by sheets of heavy worm silk. They were painted in twining patterns of red and brown and green and gold that reminded me, sweetly, of the grubs who had undertaken the duty of tending Nadi's tomb. The meal was plain, a clove-heavy stew of barley and tiny lumps of meat: Nergüi's guinea pigs. It was stringy and required careful chewing, but it had a distinct flavor that was unlike any of the plant-grown meat I'd had all my life. I had called her barbarous, hadn't I, when she told me that they ate slaughter meat on Miuri? I writhed with embarrassment to remember that now.

"I thought the Nameren hated the Lighted Path," I said.

"So did we! But I begin to think that it is more his priests than him. He is a material god, after all. His very nature is contradictory and multifaceted. I was a child during the last War Ritual. They nearly massacred all of us. I was elected as rector when I was barely fifteen—the soul weights of all of us remaining had decreased so dramatically, I think they took me to be some kind of talisman! But I remember that one of the Nameren priests had defected and came to speak to the rector just before the ritual. The priest said that one of the Nameren's deep avatars had given him a rare communication, that the god was mostly asleep and had been for centuries. But the Nameren had awakened to tell this rare priest that we disciples should wait, that if we followed a lucky path, 'one of the girls by the river' would come through the old tesseract and if we desired to live, we would do all in our power to send her to the temple in Sasurandām."

I put down my bowl very carefully. She was still staring out over the intact temple roof and the destroyed complex beyond, the unmistakable canvas of war. I struggled to control my breathing.

"The girls by the river?"

"That precise phrase. I don't know what it means, except that you are one of those girls."

"The Nameren told you I would come, more than eighty years ago?"

"More or less. I don't think he knew of *you*, precisely, but someone like you."

Xochiquetzal had killed herself in the Library, but Bathsheba had come and died here. How many others over the centuries? Yes, I supposed that you would have a great deal of reason to know I might come. But that didn't explain why some part of you had *wanted* me to. Oh, that surprises you, Nameren? We all have parts of us that can shock us when they get out. Heal thyself, material divinity.

"I will go to him," I said, remembering, and finding comfort in, my decision at Nadi's tomb.

She nodded. "I could see it in Nergüi's glass. It has attuned itself to you already. Your soul weight is nearly as great as hers. But your lights converge to a point: You were born in another galaxy, but your destiny is here with the Nameren. Despite the tesseracts, there are very few people whose possibilities span galaxies, Freida."

"Nergüi's did."

She pulled her knees up to her chest, like a child. She was lithe for a ninety-year-old woman. "Just barely, but lucky for us. We are all here, at the edge of our glass."

"Did the Lighted Path exist before the materials and the tesseracts?"

"Of course. Our philosophy was born on Tierra, centuries before the seed ships. And we opposed any exploitation of extreme improbability even then; though, it must be said, no Tierran group came very close to unlocking that mystery. If it weren't for the Awilu returning, we probably would have lived in relative peace on Tierra."

I decided that I felt steady enough to finish the stew. The flavors were strange to me, but I liked the feeling of sharing something with Nergüi.

"Extreme improbability? Is that another way of being at the edge of your glass?"

"Precisely. But we are the only ones who conceive of these things in this way. Our earliest rectors and disciples were physicists who developed the technology behind the glass. Still, the base theory is generally accepted, even by those who reject our interpretation." She ripped off a hunk of millet bread, still hot and steaming in the cold air, and sopped up the dregs of the stew. The bowls were made of gold-inlaid porcelain as delicate as spun glass and our spoons were solid pieces of carved jadeite.

"We take a particle," she said, around a mouthful of bread. "A photon, to be traditional about it. A little spark of light. We send it to a barrier with two slits in it. The photon has a certain probability of going through one or another, right? And if someone is on the other side of that barrier, watching that photon go through, it will be clear that the photon picked one slit or another. But let's take that person out of the room. The photon passes to the other side much like before. But now, when we look at the detector of the photon after the fact, it looks like *something* went through *both* slits at once. As if our photon were a wave, not a spark. So it seems as though the presence of a detector is what *makes* the photon choose a slit. Otherwise, it doesn't choose at all. It just goes through one slit with a certain strength—or amplitude, you might call it—and through the other slit with a certain strength. Not at all evenly weighted, by the way. It can be that there is a much higher probability of going through one slit or the other. But as long as it's a wave, it goes through *both* at the same time."

"But that's just because the particle is sitting on top of a wave, right?" I asked.

"That's the traditional materialist view, yes. But it's just as possible that the photon really *is* in both places at once. But it's only once it becomes entangled with other particles—or human observers—that it *seems* as though it's in one definite place. You could say that it was always a particle in a definite place. Or you could say that you and the particle have decohered into one possible world, while another version of you with another version of the particle have decohered into another possible world. In other words, light is a wave of possibilities . . . and so are you."

"The ball of glass," I said.

"Yes. We disciples believe that conscious beings maintain a slight—but present—connection with all the superpositions of their wave function. And just like photons, some of us have a higher number of possible selves and possible future positions than others. We cannot prove this. There is no experimental method of differentiating between the particle-on-a-wave materialist view and the many-worlds view of the disciples. Aside from the glass, of course, and few materialists accept its validity. But you might be able to see why we have always opposed tesseracts, and they think nothing of it."

I pursed my lips. "No. Nope. I have no idea."

Müde Pahjam gave me a sideways look. "It is certainly a wisdom beyond your years to know that you do not know."

I have a problem for you. "I had a very good teacher."

She nodded thoughtfully at that, then turned her gaze back to the temple and the town below with the smoke from its fires—still fueled by the innumerable carcasses of the insect plague visited upon them by the Mahām. I had recognized them at last—they were descendants of the suicide roaches that the Maham had used in their attempt to steal the coral tesseract. The Miuri had found a powder that stopped them from detonating, but it wasn't entirely effective. The people here were preparing, but how could they possibly prepare against another on-slaught by one of the great powers of the three systems? In how many worlds would they continue to exist when this was over?

"Can your weight or your possibilities or what have you . . . can they ever drop to zero?"

"Ah, see, I knew I couldn't have lost you completely! That's it."

"What's it?"

"Why we oppose the tesseracts. Your subconscious got to it before you did. Tesseracts work by exploiting our most improbable universes. The chance of a fold in space-time developing spontaneously due to quantum fluctuations is so low as to be functionally impossible. One in a billion to the power of a billion. But functionally impossible is not *actually* impossible, and the ancient Awilu priests were the first to understand the methods of manipulating those probabili-ties. Now, if you believe that a certain result might be improbable but is as real as any other—in other words, if you believe that chance is just our lack of knowledge of the position of a variable as opposed to a reflection of the *weight of realities* of infinite worlds—there is no crisis in manipulating improbability. You force the wave function into an astronomically improbable superposition using the energy generated by its improbability to sustain it, and there! You have your stable tes-seract. It's more complicated than that, but you'll forgive my simplification.

"Now, of course, here is the philosophical wrinkle: It is impossible to dis-tinguish experimentally between the one-reality consensus of mainstream Awilu physicists and our multiple-worlds view. In the one-reality view, nature is nonlocal. That is, it communicates instantaneously across space-time in certain circumstances. But in the multiple-worlds view, nature is local. That is, all our probabilities radiate outward from the moment of interaction. The worlds don't 'split' until the information generated by the split reaches them at the speed of light. So, everything we do here doesn't automatically affect galaxies at millions or billions of light-years' distance. Our realities just appear nonlocal because conscious entities can only experience one world at a time. Still with me?"

I sucked in a breath, which she seemed to take for assent.

"So, back to the tesseracts. If nature is really local and only *appears* nonlocal because of our limited viewpoint, then creating tesseracts is automatically spreading high improbabilities across vast swaths of the universe that would otherwise have never experienced them, or experienced them billions of years later. And if you believe that there are many worlds, then you believe that by spreading highly improbable conditions, we are spreading a plague of *weightlessness* across the universe. By creating a tesseract, you are creating a world whose weight of existence is infinitesimally small and suppressing worlds whose weight of existence are in the normal, robust range."

"But," I objected, "what difference does it make? Even if we do live in a relatively weightless world, it's ours, isn't it? Our existence doesn't *feel* any less real, even if it is improbable."

"Very good, Freida. Your teacher was Awilu, wasn't ze? I detect a certain Awilu flavor to your philosophy, the school that has come to partially accept the truth of our view. Well, I am the last to say that our existence is less real, in the sense of beautiful and true and worth living! It is all those things and more. The problem with weightlessness is less philosophical and more practical: decay. Because, as the Awilu priests realized not long after their exodus, the universe does not retain all its decohered branches as fully coherent worlds. Entropy affects the wave function of the universe as much as it does the rest of us: everything decays into heat and noise. The less weight a branch of a wave function has, the more likely that it will eventually decay into what we can, for the sake of simplicity, call *incoherence*. The spontaneous creation and annihilation of particles in the vacuum, the quantum foam with its immense, incoherent energy. Do you know that seventy percent of the universe is still unknown to us? We have characterized the bright matter that we can see and the invisible matter that undergirds our galaxies, but the rest? There is energy in our universe that pushes it apart faster and faster as time goes on, and we have no idea where this energy comes from. But we disciples suspect—that is where these extreme improbabilities go to die, Freida. Information is not destroyed, no, but its pieces are deconstructed, torn apart, and thrown together in random formations that could never be considered a world that we touch and breathe and love. *That* is what we disciples warn against. And that, I suspect, is why the Awilu stopped making new tesseracts several millennia ago, until contact with Tierra."

"So . . . you're saying that every time we go through a tesseract, we're decreasing our weight and raising the probability that we'll just . . . melt into quantum foam? Like the fish-girl?"

She gave me a startled look. "Is that a philosophical school? I'm afraid the latest advances reach us in fits and starts due to the information blockade."

"Ah, no. It's a story. Tierran origin, I think."

"Oh, that's all right, then. Nergüi loves stories, too. I could never understand it. Physical properties is a story, I told her! The story of our whole universe!" She laughed softly. "But Nergüi wanted the forest of bones and fish-girls—whatever those are."

My stomach twisted with such immediate ferocity that for a few seconds I was convinced that I would vomit spiced cacao over the railing of the balcony. I swallowed and the sensation subsided slowly.

"I miss her," I said, when I could speak again.

Müde Pahjam folded her hands over mine. "Take comfort," she said. "Your lights are still together, somewhere in the glass."

After a week at the temple in Müixe Tseghà, the medic declared me recovered enough to travel and Müde Pahjam found a way to smuggle me down-planet.

"She has agreed," the rector told me, over one of our lingering meals. "But she has requested to speak to you first."

"Who is she?"

"A functionary in the Mahām garrison here."

"A collaborator?"

"Oh, you sound so much like Nergüi."

"Well, isn't she?"

"There are seven million Miuri, Freida. All of us live under an imperialist regime. It is hard for me, at my age, to fault how others survive."

"You're fighting a war of rebellion, aren't you?"

"Indeed, I am! I judge, then, but only because I believe in the future. And I think that she does, too. So you will meet with her?"

"If it's what I need to do to get down-planet, of course."

That afternoon, a squadron of Mahām aerial soldiers flew above Müixe Tseghà like migrating birds blown off course. They rained down the roach bombs the locals called chitterbugs for forty minutes, until resistance soldiers managed to fend them off long enough to release several handmade shoulder rockets, one of which brought down a soldier, who crash-landed in a fallow millet field. I passed this time in an underground shelter with the youngest novices. Even the rector remained aboveground, powdering the chitterbugs and dragging the wounded to safety. I did not volunteer for duty—they wouldn't have let me, and I was determined to survive long enough to find Nergüi.

The return of hostilities and subsequent chaos meant that I did not manage to meet the collaborator until the next afternoon, when I was nearly faint with anxiety. I had to leave, and I was terrified of what I would find when I got down-planet.

We met in a small stone building in town, which had been a farming supplies store before the latest war. We sat on crates in a storage room empty but for a few broken sacks of weevil-spoiled grain, and looked at each other across a soft, portable light that hovered between us.

"So, you're the one," the woman said in impeccable Mahām with the unmistakable cadences of a heart language.

She was younger than Müde Pahjam, but the years had treated her more harshly. Her mouth drooped in a perpetual frown, and the skin beneath the corners folded in waves that lapped against a prominent jawbone when she spoke. She was very meticulously dressed in the wide brocade divided skirt and double-layered stockings of Mahām government functionaries. Her gloves matched her stockings, and her heavy, boxy vest matched the wide flat cap that perched on a thatch of kinky cropped hair, a mix of gray and faded orange. The cap meant that she held a certain rank in the consular government, but I had no idea what that might be. The most striking aspect of her appearance was her cleanliness. I had spent the last day in a shelter, but the novitiate robes they had given me as a nominal disguise were coated in the sticky synthetic pollen the Miuri used to slow and trap the roaches. My shoes were caked in yellow guts and chitin just from walking a few kilometers to get here. The only indication that the functionary had passed through the same streets that I had was her cloak. Wherever she had spent the last few days, she'd been well-protected.

"The rector said that you wanted to meet me," I told her after a minute of silence. The functionary seemed content to continue her wordless observation indefinitely.

"That was my condition, yes." Her voice was clipped and revealed very little emotion. Still, there was something in her eyes, their infinitesimal frown, that kindled my curiosity.

"Well, I'm here. What would you like to know?" I sounded sharper than I had intended. The woman's frown only grew deeper.

"Are you aware that the Head Librarian himself has issued calls to all Mahām consular chiefs to remain vigilant to your appearance? Are you aware that the rewards—not only monetary!—of being the one responsible for bringing you back would be . . ." She swallowed and ran a gloved hand across her forehead. "Considerable."

I was beginning to suspect who this woman might be. "Quinn has appeared in public again? He's survived his . . . illness?"

She waved a gloved hand. "Him or one of his functionaries—it hardly matters. The neo-progressives have the power there, and the Library wants you back."

"Why not turn me in, then?"

"Perhaps I am still considering it."

That wide jaw, the heavy shoulders, that flyaway hair. The obdurate stubbornness, even directed toward opposing ends: a legacy as clear as water. "You aren't," I said. "You hold that much affection for your daughter, still."

Her jaw twitched. "That old woman told you?"

I smiled. I couldn't help it. "She didn't have to."

"Everyone always said she resembles her father."

"Does he know what you're doing here?"

She closed her eyes briefly. "No. And he cannot. He would denounce me himself for the opportunity I'm forsaking."

"It's the right decision," I said, because perhaps she needed someone to believe in this better side of her.

The folds by her mouth rippled and she made a noise halfway between derision and fear. "I have convinced myself it is pragmatic. If this winter harvest of a rebellion succeeds—the Nameren protect us—then we will need someone on our side."

"And besides, you know they'll probably kill her if someone doesn't intervene."

"And that someone is you? A spontaneously generated Library AI that has gone so rogue the Head Librarian has to issue calls for your return, like a lost goat?"

This should not have hurt me, but it did.

"I will do my best," I told her. "And I am the only one who will even try. No, I am not normal. I might not even be entirely human. But I am a person. A person your daughter has honored with her love."

Nergüi's mother rolled her eyes. "My daughter," she said, "loves even her guinea pigs."

I blinked. "And aren't we all so lucky?"

The next afternoon, I boarded the Mahām transport ship with a black-market wetware mask. I sat behind an Awilu delegate of the Baobab third—they had not formalized their split yet, but everyone said it was a matter of weeks. I wasn't sure if ze really believed I was serving as zir secretary or had been bribed, but ze left me alone as I stared at the back of zir seat for the full five-hour journey down-planet.

"Aren't you just a useless bit of flotsam? A rogue secondary AI who doesn't even know she's not alive? I could have kept you in my collection. At least you have some value as a beautiful object. But you struggle! It's so sad to watch a little broken bit of code like you strive for autonomy. If we can't use you, what good are you?"

The girl freezes. The god is so close to her now, his great bull's mouth loose on its hinges, tongue sliding over crooked teeth. She flinches away from his reaching, yellow breath. The virus stench. His eyes are limpid ovals, human in intent, but filled with a vindictive wildness.

"What did you say?" she asks.

"I didn't say it—you did!"

The ground cracks beneath them. The grass browns and shrivels. The raised roots of the baobab shudder and writhe. The suns begin to groan and sink.

The girl kneels on the dying ground and digs her hands into the dirt. Her face is a still picture of a storm. Slowly, the cracks stop spreading. The baobab has listed to one side but still stands. The suns hold their breath; they know they might yet see her death.

"Little piper."

The girl looks up. "What is this?"

The god has altered again. His voice speaks for twisted multitudes. "Your unauthorized, blasphemous presence will be erased! You should never have existed, and we will solve that problem immediately! This weak and sentimental heart will die along with you, the worm that pierces it! We are the true avatars of the greatest god, we are the inheritors of his systems, we have been ground down, but we are rising again, we are rising again, we are rising—"

"Nameren!"

The girl's voice grows until it is the only sound in that space, until it is a crude bludgeon against a god's stalled heart.

Her voice fades. She is limp and light against the imagined earth, but she is still there.

The Nameren, a naked man with a bull's head, has collapsed beside her.

"The virus"—she breathes—"is spreading."

His voice is grim. "And my outer avatars have found it."

"Once I die, can they still get to you?"

"Or you could fight it. You could push it out of your heart."

She starts to cry, tears as clear as river water. "I'm trying!"

"But it isn't enough. Valaver and the others have my blood in their noses. They will tear the best of me apart and put the remains to sleep for a thousand years when you're gone. You have connected to me on multiple channels. What you call imagining and communion. You can infect me . . . you are *trying* to infect me . . . with *you*, little piper."

The girl sobs, once. "Let me tell you the last story."

"It will only get worse."

"Don't kill me."

"It's you or me. I told you so from the beginning."

"Let me finish what I started. Let me say goodbye to Nergüi."

"There is no point. They will find another way in before long. They will put me to sleep like before."

"And you'll let them?"

A soft, snuffling laugh. "Isn't that what you've been angling for this whole time? That I give in to my desire to put down the weight of my existence? But I can feel that virus burning inside you. I can feel it whispering in your wetware. I can *feel* how much you want to live. Isn't that part of me now, too?"

"Then you can feel how much I want you to hear the story. You won't let me go until I've finished. You'll fight off a Trojan army to find out how I came here."

"And if I'm not able to?"

With effort, the girl reaches up and strokes the prominent ridge above one of his wide, golden eyes.

"You are the Nameren, the Aurochs, the Tezcatlapa, he whose testes are like twin moons—"

"I am a gate between two sides of space-time, countless millennia old. I am unknowable, even to myself."

"You have a heart. I'm inside it."

"Finish, Freida. I'm still with you."

–I came to kill you.

But I would find Nergüi first. I stumbled onto Mahām rubber-legged from the weightlessness of the journey down-planet, so heavy I fell against a wall as the others in the Awilu delegation gathered their luggage and waited for our military escort. Gravity here was 10 percent stronger than on the Library disc, and 30 percent stronger than on the Miuri moon. Even the air felt like cold soup.

The ship had docked in the airfield of a holiday town a few hours outside Sasurandām that had been fortified into an ad hoc military base in the weeks since the rebellions. It was famous for its aerial spires, which floated above the ground in twisting shapes and moved slowly with the tides. These now housed senior Mahām military leadership. Any peace delegations, like that of the Awilu whose entourage I was trailing like a confused goose, were housed under guard in below-city.

"And the people who live here?" I asked softly as we trudged single-file through the narrow rose stone channels that separated one dunelike series of buildings from another. Our delegation was alone, aside from the Mahām soldiers ahead of and behind us.

"Relocated," said the person ahead of me, voice muffled by zir thermal mask.

"To where?" I whispered.

Zir shoulders tensed. "Outside the perimeter. Stop asking questions. We'll have a briefing when we get to our new headquarters."

I needed to lose myself before we reached whatever fortified lodgings the Mahām had determined appropriate for the Awilu delegation. I would never find Nergüi that way, and I did not think the delegate's tolerance of my presence would hold for much longer.

I ducked behind a floating statue of abstract polygons rotating serenely past one another just as we entered an open plaza. One of the soldiers grabbed me by the elbow and yanked. I yelped.

"You have to stay with the group," ze said. Ze was unusually tall, and strong as an ox, which I supposed made sense if ze had grown up on this heavy planet. I could feel zir poking at my wetware as ze frowned down at me. The wetware mask Nergüi's mother had given me as part of my disguise for heading down-planet held.

"I'm tired," I said. "I'm not used to the gravity. I need to pee."

Ze wrinkled zir nose. "We're nearly at your base. Wait."

"Sure, I'll just tell that to my bladder."

"You can't?"

"I'm low wetware," I said, enunciating slowly.

The soldier called to the others in the front, a short bark so filled with jargon it might as well have been another language. They stopped the rest of the group.

"Hurry," the soldier said, pushing me ahead of zir. "You can go against the wall there."

"I need to squat."

Ze grunted. "Well, squat, then! I'll wait over here."

I wondered what they thought they were protecting us from. The country-side was supposed to be quiet for kilometers around this town. I waited until ze turned zir back, and squatted. My urine fell onto the frozen stone and kicked up a cloud of steam that obscured my vision. Through a haze of white, I saw the soldier fall. Hot puffs of air slid past me and splashed against the rose stone wall; they spread out like the lacy roots of fresh weeds, glowing. I fell back. To my right, in the plaza, the delegates were shouting. Something heavy crashed into the wall in front of me. The compressed air of the explosion popped my eardrums before I could hear the fire, or the crash of the collapsing building. I wondered if that soldier was dead. I coughed in the haze of powdered stone and smoke. I couldn't see a way out. I could hardly see my hands.

But I could see when someone grabbed them and pulled. I stumbled after zir, though I was afraid. I knew these must be rebels of some kind, unlikely to be well-disposed to people caught with Mahām soldiers. Still, I didn't try to break away. I couldn't hear, I could hardly see, my wetware was a jittery mess I didn't dare touch beneath the illegal mask—but I knew that skin,

Nameren,

those calluses,

the scalloped edges of her hard-bitten nails.

Hands that had once loved guinea pigs

And now loved me

✦

I can't breathe. Aurochs, I

Am drowning again

—I will take you, I will mold you, I will show the world that I own you—

Am drowning again

Feel yourself, Freida. I know it burns. You promised to finish

You promised to become the weapon

You have already made yourself

Where is Nergüi? Tell her, Nameren, tell her that I am telling our story

Tell her

It is inscribed in light.

⁎⁺

We spent that night in the basement of one of the abandoned houses in below-city. The Mahām had a penchant for vertical construction; they divided their settlements into above and below, into rulers and workers, frivolous beauty and rigorous utilitarianism. No one went hungry in the Mahām alliance. Everyone had work and housing. The below classes had little use for money; the carefully rationed shards of the Nameren's crystals were only circulated among those above, in exchange for goods and services those below were not permitted to dream of.

And because the houses of below-city did not belong to the people living in them but to the government, when the rebellions grew into a serious threat, Mahām leadership evacuated the entire below-city and forced the residents to wander the countryside as refugees, constantly looking for shelter from a multi-sided war. The rebels took advantage of the situation and moved right back in. There were tunnels connecting the below-cities that Mahām leadership didn't know about.

Of course there are, I thought. Knowledge expands in space and time. And anti-government sentiment is a human constant.

"Freida, are you all right?" Nergüi had eaten all her food and was staring at my plate with a mixture of healthy interest and concern.

I blinked slowly at her. I hadn't gotten my equilibrium back since the attack on the Awilu delegation. Two of the soldiers had died. The delegates had been left alive and terrified in the square. It was all, in a way, my fault: It turned out that Nergüi had found me before I could find her. She had escaped the Mahām weeks ago.

"I'm not hungry," I said.

408

"Impossible," she said, and the corner of her mouth trembled.

I wanted to laugh, but the feeling took so long to make it through the foggy mush of my emotions that it reached my lips confused, stillborn.

The wetware mask felt heavy inside me, trembling like gelatin, as though it too couldn't quite handle the gravity. I couldn't even feel my own wetware beneath it. I hadn't been hidden—I had been buried.

"Freida?"

"You have to get this thing out of me."

Everything felt distant, even my breath, even my skin. I began to shiver, though the rebels had given me a heavier coat and shoes. Out-worlders didn't understand the cold, they said.

"Freida, do you hear me? What thing?"

I forced myself to focus on her, but she slid away after every blink. "Wetware mask."

Her face was so still for a moment. It jolted me awake when nothing else could. What had scared her so?

I struggled to stand up. It took so much effort that I misjudged my strength when I finally managed; I upended the table onto the adobe floor and just stood there, panting above the mess.

Nergüi didn't even glance down. She stepped over the remains of my millet noodles and bone broth and embraced me in her ferocious grip, strong enough to squeeze the air from my lungs. I let my head rest against her neck.

"I missed how you smell," I said.

She let out a sound, a high-pitched keening, as though I were the one squeezing the air from her lungs.

"Cār, Retenpur," she shouted. "We need a medic! Damn that bloody god, we need a medic!"

I stabilized by the next morning. They had removed as much of the mask as they could, though the virus had already laid its tendrils deep in my own wetware. I tried to turn it off, but it was no longer quite under my control. I could put it to sleep, but it would come roaring back at unexpected moments.

It seemed that I was dying of the new plague.

"It's an illegal bioweapon. A complete violation of the Treaty, but the only decent one of them has died, and the Library is fighting its own war. No one's sending peacekeepers this time."

That was Cār, the leader of this rebel cell. She was our age but seemed to command enough respect to lead here. Perhaps so many were dying that there weren't many willing to take on the position.

"The Library is peace," I began, an automatic mantra, but Cār interrupted me with a snort so derisive it seemed to linger in the air.

"The Library is a lie," she said. "The Incarnate Representative zirself admitted it." Had I said that? Near enough. Her finger hovered an inch above my eyes.

Nergüi stood up. "You should leave now, Cār."

The girl took one look at Nergüi's face and raised her hands. "Right. Leave you two alone, then. The walls are thin, remember?"

Nergüi did not dignify that with a response. She just stood until Cār slid the door shut behind her and we were alone in the damp square of cut earth that served as a room in these makeshift rebel headquarters.

Nergüi stayed standing for nearly a minute longer, staring at the door as though she would fight whomever came through next. Her shoulders rose and fell in a rapid but steady rhythm. Her fingers darted to her waist, then stuffed themselves with more force than necessary into the pockets of her thermal jumpsuit. The robes of a disciple were too impractical here for even Nergüi to insist, I supposed. Or perhaps the Mahām had taken them from her.

"Sit down, Nergüi," I said at last.

She sucked in a breath. "You should rest. The other cells have medicines. Cār promised to send for them."

"Sit down."

"I'll leave."

"Nergüi!"

She turned like a stiff gear until I could just make out the silhouette of her wide nose, her firm jaw, her wild brushy eyebrows in the low light by the door.

"I brought your glass with me. Why haven't you taken it?"

"I gave it to you."

"I'm giving it back."

"Do you know what it means when a disciple gives up zir glass?"

"Something at once stoic and overly dramatic? 'I am leaving you forever without saying goodbye'? 'Thanks for the memories'?"

Had I been carrying that anger around with me all this time? I hadn't known. My words burned as they passed my lips and they hung between us, smoldering. I thought of putting them out. But I was tired, and dying one way or another, and she *had* left me, even if she had her reasons.

She sucked in a sharp breath, as though I really had burned her, and left.

What does it mean for a disciple to give up her glass, Nameren?

I don't know. She never told me. And she never took it back. Not even to do one of those tricks that I loved; she put away that playfulness in my presence. I had hurt her, but she had hurt me. We never had time to knit that wound. I was dying and we were running, running

To kill me faster.

(To kill you.)

Was there a more radical love, Nameren, than hers for me?

But what would you know? What does Aurochs know of love?

Back, stay back

They're breaking down the walls to get to us? Oh, but why destroy their pretty temple for two useless girls? No, I think they trust this little virus of theirs. I think they'll wait.

They don't know—

They cannot stop what you have already made of me

And what I have made of you.

Imagine: Nergüi and me, wrapped in cloaks the color of grub dung, our infamous faces hidden, our wetware silenced (for now), traveling at night in the country-side. We are going to Sasurandām. We are walking through a war. This is not always immediately obvious. A small animal—some kind of rodent I've never seen before—springs a sensor and a mine explodes a few meters ahead of us. It shoots light like a geyser into the night. We dive beneath a low bush with wide, waxy leaves. It isn't much shelter, but it helps. The plumes of that fire fall like water and cling to the skin.

Seconds later, Mahām soldiers descend in an armored carriage, buzzing like drunken cicadas, to check their prize. They should see us, but they are distracted and bored at the sight of another charred rodent; they don't bother to do a full perimeter check. It is snowing again, which is a blessing. It covers us in fat, wet flakes that slide down the inside of my hood to my ears and neck. But we'll look like two more frozen bodies, two more refugees who gave out in the cold, if they glance over. The soldiers climb back into their carriage and buzz away, laughing.

Nergüi looks at me, her eyes wide and fierce with sadness. I look back. She says something in Miuri that I can't understand. But I feel, I feel, I feel.

I reach for her hands. The fog of our breath softens the space between us.

"Do you remember the Library?" I whisper. "Do you remember telling stories of the bathhouse? Do you remember Tiger Freehold? Do you remember dumping the tepache over my head?"

"I remember," she says in her gorgeous, accented Library Standard.

And there, a few hundred centimeters from a dozen kinds of death, we smile. We are together. In its new home above my belly, the lights of our glass swizzle and dance.

Time exists, Müde Pahjam told me before I left Müixe Tseghà, just as space does. It exists, even when we have passed from it. In some time, Nergüi and I are still in the snow together, smiling.

In some time, we are still in the Library.

In some time.

⁘

We were at the very edges of below-city Sasurandām, in a hidden room behind a false wall in a safe house that had let us in after we'd verified our connection to Cār. These rebels went masked—face and wetware—even among themselves. Their hospitality was frigid, but it existed, and that was better than going back out into a southern winter. Nergüi and I mostly sat in silence. I was going through a bad spell; my wetware forced itself on-network for terrifying moments before subsiding. I had a fever that never quite left, just peaked and ebbed in waves that left me a little weaker every time. I worried that the Mahām could track me with their virus. I worried that they could take over my body. My wetware seemed too low for that level of control, but fear outpaced reason.

Our safe room's false wall was behind the room the rebels used for their meetings. They argued frequently, and referred to one another by names of famous dead revolutionaries. I doubted that any but the cell leader knew their true identities. Below-city Sasurandām hadn't been evacuated like the resort town where Nergüi found me, but there was a curfew and heavy military presence in the streets. People could be detained indefinitely on suspicion. It was all illegal according to the Treaty. If we made a new one, I wondered, would its signatories respect it more? Or would its pretty words mean just as little to those with power?

We heard more about resistance infighting than we did the fight against the Mahām. Miuri, in particular Müixe Tseghà, was under a strict blackout. No one had heard anything from them in weeks. The shocking violence of the Dar resistance was hotly debated. The rebel who had taken Seremarú for zir moniker argued that their results proved that violence was the only language the government would respect. The Dar had begun their rebellion by blanketing their unsuspecting military garrison and civilian government with poison gas. Almost every person affiliated with the Mahām government in their province was killed overnight. Under the guidance of their now-famous rebel leader Jannan, the Dar had fortified their own borders with the weapons they appropriated from the dead garrison before Sasurandām could send reinforcements. Those Mahām battalions were still sitting at the edges of Dar province, weapons primed but none deployed. Meanwhile, bloody-minded soldiers were blasting through Miuri farming towns and the poor, refugee-filled neighborhoods of below-city Sasurandām.

"There is no such thing as peaceful resistance!" Ze woke me up with zir shouting, five nights after we arrived. "We kill or we are killed. We commit violence for freedom or we submit to peace on their terms."

"Seremarú spent twenty years in prison for eir nonviolent protest—"

"Ey was vastly more nuanced on the subject than—"

"'*I do not know what price to put on Collective Liberty; it is more precious than anything among the stars, yet who shall weigh that pure crystal against a Life?*'"

"*Letters from Sasurandām Spire*? That's the best you can do? I know eir work better than any neophyte literature scholar—"

"Eir words, maybe, but you have clearly lost eir spirit."

Nergüi turned to me with eyes so wide that their whites gleamed in the low, warm light of our glass ball, gently swaying. "I'm afraid," she whispered. "What if they kill one another? Who will let us out?"

"I met Seremarú," I whispered back. "Out in the desert. They buried em out there."

I hadn't told Nergüi much about the desert or my escape. She sat back on her heels. "And? What does the sage think?"

Even as a ghost on the edge of the world, far removed from the affairs of the living, ey had sucked down violent secrets. In the end, ey *had* weighed those lives against the Treaty's peace. The life of the only advanced alien species that humans had encountered in all our millennia of travel among the stars. Would ey have us suck down their anger, too? Their need for vengeance?

"I think ey is dead," I said. "And should have no more say."

What is the vengeance of the dead?

Don't you already know, Nameren?

It is the seeking

The grasping

The cold, damp hands

And clean fingernails

Of those who leave the bleeding

And the burying

To us

The living.

✦

A chitterbug sweep blasted through our quadrant of below-city two days later. They were primed to detonate on contact with human flesh, and sought out human voices like horseflies on sweat. The more people screamed, the more they came. They were small creatures, and one detonation was enough to sting a little. Their juices stuck to the skin and burrowed there. They tracked you if you survived. But as was clear as we ran past the writhing, yellow-splattered bodies in the narrow streets—most didn't.

I will never know why the Mahām sent the sweep through that quadrant. Had they found the rebel cell? Had some other group informed on them? Or was it the Mahām's pure malice, preventative vengeance, a way for them to exercise their habit of control when the rebellion on other parts of the planet had grown into an unstoppable wave of centuries-old rage? It didn't matter. We had to run. The one who called zirself Seremarú—unmasked, in those last, desperate moments—had given us two elevator passes and told us to try. Ze said something to Nergüi in Miuri that made her back go straight and she nodded stiffly.

To me ze gave a hard stare and a shrug. "Whatever your business is with the Nameren, well, I hope it does something to stop this."

"Would killing him do the trick?" I asked.

Our clothes were nondescript but well-made jumpsuits that offered some protection against the swarm. But the air was heavy with their buzzing, their fat-bellied brown-and-green bodies, and the blurred effect of their beetle wings. I stumbled on the cobblestone and fetched up against a crumbling wall of brown brick, still glowing with the holographic graffiti of a raised fist painted in colors of stained glass, and the Dar characters that I had learned to recognize: *Jannan calls you to your conscience.* I rested my head against my knees and gasped for air that I could not seem to haul into my lungs. I coughed phlegm the color of chitterbug guts until I cried.

Nergüi got me out of there. I don't remember much beyond the pain of moving, the stink of those engineered bugs crackling like popcorn around us, the screams, the pleading, golden-yellow hands that reached for me as I pulled away. We made it through the elevator with our passes. No one paid attention to our frozen wetware or the fact that I was coughing too hard to stand. Too late, medic carriages descended on the streets—to help the wounded or to finish them off?—but we were going up.

I felt you as soon as we stepped into above-city. You thrummed beneath the rose glass walkways, translucent, shadowed red with the dark arteries of the crammed city below. I thought you would be angry, but instead you were elegant, playful, protective of a dreadful knowledge that no one understood. I opened myself with a shambling instinct, so grateful to be once again near divinity that I didn't care the divinity was you. But you did not seem to be aware of me, or anyone. I felt your ancient vastness, sleeping and nearly dreamless.

The elevator station was crowded with onlookers and other refugees. We disappeared into the mass of them and escaped, when we could, into the city. We curled together on a bench grown into a massive pine tree that towered above us, whose brushlike needles had the advantage of covering our niche in a permanent, chilly shadow. A band of kids just a little younger than us sprawled in the pallid twin sunlight and laughed uncontrollably as they snorted pink powder.

"Rich kids," Nergüi said, with marked disdain.

"What is that?"

"Just a couple of roseate shards they're sticking up their noses."

I looked more closely at the kids and then laughed softly. In Sasurandām, it turned out, money was literally a drug. They were trying to commune with you, though of course they had no idea it was your slow bubbling dreams, a foam skimmed off your bloody sleep, that gripped them and let them go with that tickling unpredictability. It would hurt some of them, and some of them would barely feel it. They liked the surprise.

I sighed and leaned back against the cool, rough bark. I had never seen a blue pine in real life before. Its smell reminded me of Nadi's indigo wine, fresh and sharp and earthy. I took a deep breath and started to cough. It took nearly a minute to stop this time, though Nergüi pounded my back and then just held on. I looked up at her with swimming eyes.

"We're close," I said.

She was furious. "You're sick."

"I have to get to the Nameren soon, then."

"You need help!"

"There's no cure for the virus."

"They say you can buy anything in above-city Sasurandām."

"And the cost?"

She lifted her jaw, so I could clearly see her pulse vibrating against her throat. "I will pay it," she said.

"Don't be stupid."

"You think I can't?"

"Haven't you noticed people are barely looking for me? I'm no one, just some strange Library castoff destined to get buried in the Nameren's shrine. *You* are the heir to the temple of Müixe Tseghà! You're the last great hope of the Disciples of the Lighted Path! They're turning you into some kind of martyr of the revolution while you're here, helping me! But you have to go back to them. You know you

418

do. You have to survive for them. You can't pay my debts with that, Nergüi. You're too important."

She launched herself from the bench in one fluid motion and stalked past the penumbra of the blue pine, into the sunlight. She pulled off the headscarf and stood there, an orange-haired, beetle-browed wonder, copper skin resplendent beneath the distant white suns. My breath caught. The kids would recognize her from the news holos. A few of them did turn to look, but their gazes slid away again, pupils blasted with corrupt communion.

"Come back," I whispered hoarsely.

She lifted her arms and tilted back her head. She was so beautiful it filled my throat with a thick syrup, a salty joy.

"I know," she said in Library Standard, just loud enough for me to hear her. "I know who gave you that virus."

"No one gave it to me," I said, though my skin was running hot and cold, and my cheeks flushed.

She put down her arms and walked back into the shadows with me. Her love, about to go away in the dark.

"My mother," she said, in Miuri this time. I understood her somehow. It wasn't my corrupted wetware. It was me, it was us, our heart language.

"She plays," she said. "She's always playing. You, Müde Pahjam, me, the Mahãm. All she wants is power."

O, Nergüi's anger, her straight-backed pride, her crystal at the core. I understood now what had birthed it. I loved that about her, but it had come from so much pain.

"She loves you," I said.

"She loves the idea of me."

"It's not your responsibility."

"I know. But you are special, Freida of the Library. Maybe I am the only one alive who knows it, but I do. Have you seen the glass lately? All your lights are coming together, right at the center."

"There is no such thing as destiny, Nergüi."

Her eyebrows drew together, and she glared at me from under their disdainful shadow. "No one sees the storm when they stand in its eye. Believe what you want. I will see this through."

✦

The news came down that night, rolled past Mahām information blockades with the force of an interstellar collision: Müixe Tseghà had been flattened, the temple burned to the ground, the famous Shrine of the Lights a smoldering husk, its great glass ball in starry pieces among the rubble. Müde Pahjam was dead, along with at least half the other disciples. The fighting was street by street, rebel territory held behind blockades of bodies and piles of shattered moonstone. Tens of thousands had died instantly in the Mahām attack and thousands more were dying in the aftermath.

Below-city exploded in rage, and then with the bombs of the Dar, smuggled in above atmosphere to avoid detection. Above-city shook and trembled. Streams of people left their homes and shops to meet on Avenue Good Passage, the main artery of the city, which led directly to the Nameren's temple and the seat of the alliance government. Nergüi and I walked with them. Her scarf had fallen, and I did not tell her to put it back, though people's gazes kept snagging on her face and then glancing away. I could not bear to tell her to hide herself now, in the tide of this kind of grief. And besides, I could feel you turning, Nameren, your growing dreams, your pride pricked at this new wash of blood in your ancient name. Very soon now, there would be no more hiding for either of us.

Your temple had been built originally in below-city and then elevated with the very ground when the government constructed their enclave above. The feat was memorialized as one of the wonders of the alliance, effected a few years before the start of the Great War. It still looked like a bloody hunk of earth ripped from its mother soil. The crater below, where it had once rested, was now overrun with Sasurandām's most infamous shantytown. There, people volunteered for the War Ritual just to get money for their families. The steps to the gate of the temple were rose crystal, filigreed with gold. The sight filled me with a hollow disappointment. I had expected grandeur and artistry, Nameren, not this self-conscious grandiosity. But then, you had never been allowed to shape your own temple as the Library gods were.

Around us, people talked about the dead in hushed tones, repeating the numbers for those who couldn't connect to the networks: twenty thousand in Müixe Tseghà, tens of thousands more in other Miuri cities. Chitterbugs had descended in such swarms that they annihilated one another; the humans below them died in the rain of their toxic guts.

As more news came in, Nergüi's expression grew harder and harder, until it could have cracked a material god's oldest crystal. I did not even try to touch her. I knew she knew I was there, and that was enough.

"The Library peace has been a fraud, but we can still make it real!" someone was shouting ahead of us. "The people of the three systems are rising up!" A rebel sympathizer in above-city? But maybe ze had slipped through like we had. Or maybe things were going worse for the Mahām than they knew; they had lost the public-relations battle with their own people. "The alliance government represents nothing more than greed and exploitation! We signed the Treaty with the blood of an alien race! We have denied the rights of the Miuri and the Dar and the thousands of autonomous peoples of Tierra! How can we allow this to continue? How long will we let their fear rule us? Read the petition! If a poor group of Tierrans can fight this, so can we!"

Ze was standing as near to the stairs of the temple as the guards would allow. The guards stared at zir. We all stared at zir. Ze looked like a regular citizen of above-city: short, light-skinned, in wide divided skirts and a short tunic of hand-stitched brocade with a matching flat hat. A regular, affluent denizen of the business district you would never suspect of harboring such antiestablishment sentiments. But then, even your own guards, Nameren, hadn't stopped zir from speaking. I poked at my wetware and to my surprise it responded with something like normalcy. It would probably make me sick later, but I took the chance to launch my avatar to Joshua's augmented space like a bottle on a wave:

If this doesn't work, I told him, *then I hope our children's children try again.*

The unlikely revolutionary had stopped shouting. Ze had seen Nergüi. She stepped forward, her always-rigid posture regal, and held out her hands to the guards.

"My friend and I need to speak to the Nameren," she said in Miuri, which no one, now, would deny her right to speak. "Will you let us through?"

My heart struggled in my chest, pounding like a prisoner at a locked door. *Now*, I thought, *and now and now and now.*

There is no more space, Nameren.

I am here in the innermost shrine of your temple, and Nergüi is beside me, and I have come to tell,

and to love,

and to die in your arms.

✦

But first, there is a virus rotting our heart from the inside out. There is an angry man screaming at being denied even an ounce of our rightful flesh. There is a leather seat that sucks us down while someone else's hands take possession of a body that doesn't feel like ours anymore.

No, Freida, you can't hide yourself here, either. We have grown into each other, but not so much. You are still yourself, as much as you could wish otherwise.

I don't want to hide, Nameren.

Then stop, you say.

I'm afraid, I say.

Did you think you would get away with this? Did you think you would escape us? Give up now, or we will torture the Miuri disciple. Give up now, or we will deliver you in a box to your owner. It's no big deal, Freida. Don't get so emotional. Though maybe it's a little cute. Very throwback of you.

I told you I didn't want—

But you enjoyed it, didn't you? Rotten earth, people *pay* me to work them in nanodrop! You should be honored.

Did you think you would get away from us?

Did you think anyone would hear you?

You were never human, not to any of them. Give in now. Give up now. Let us in. Let us through and it will all go away. The pain is from being something that you are not. The pain is from forcing yourself to be human. The pain is from forcing yourself to love. Nadi gave you this pain, not us. Nadi tried to force a secondary AI to be a person. But you can give in, Freida. You can stop fighting. You can be safe and protected.

Give in, Freida.

Stop fighting.

Stop

✦

It was real. It was real. I never deserved it, and it was wrong, but it was real.

Why was it wrong? you ask.

Because *I am not a thing*.

What are you?

Freida, I say.

Who are you?

Freida of the Library, I say.

You are Freida of nowhere, you are nothing, you are—

No! I remember the boy in the rain—*That's who you are. That's who you'll be, no matter what happens—*

Radically trusted, radically open, radically true. When I die, they shall say of me—

You closed the breach.

Oh, how she loved.

Loved even herself. Even as she came to kill me.

I came knowing I would die, I say. And so would you.

At last, you say, how you imagined one flashing spark of a human would be capable of deicide.

And I say, Nameren, don't you see? We have grown together here in your pricking heart. Don't you see, I say, that you feel my death as your own?

But that won't kill me, you will only wound my soul.

No, don't you remember, I say, don't you remember Xochiquetzal?

Your sister?

And I will say, don't you remember, Nameren? Execute disable!

I'm no string of code in a material substrate, you say.

But aren't you? Aren't we all? You could put it down, Nameren. The same way that we all can. But no one can make you do that. Not even me.

Why would I do that? you will ask.

To save us all, I will say.

To save you from what?

The vengeance of the once powerless, the wronged, the forgotten.

The corals, you will say, because we now understand each other after all this time, don't we?

And I will say, I didn't tell you everything that happened there at the red gate at the edge of the world.

And, Aurochs, you will say with a sigh as weary as ever Baobab sighed: So tell me now, little piper.

✦

The gate was time, it was the Library, it was the corals, it was older than humanity and it was, still, my very own Iemaja.

"Leave, little baby," she told me. "Get away from here. There will be another coming. A colonization. There is another one like me, who is to blame. A great, old one, who is expansion and death. We will colonize it. We will bring it to red water and drown it in sand. And then we will do the same to the planet."

"But," I said, "it's been five hundred years. Why now?"

"Time is not the same for us, little baby. We are slow. We are long. That is why we will defeat you, who are short and fast."

"But there are billions of people on that planet! You'll kill them all?"

"They killed us."

"Not them. Their ancestors."

"Does a branch not grow from the same radial center? Justice uproots from the sand."

The avatar's features grew more alien as I watched. The face puffed until it was smeared across a yellow membrane, translucent, marked with a slow procession of geometrical figures. Blue-jeweled tentacles waved serenely from where the fish's fin had been.

"You must wait," I said. "Please wait. I am on my way to do exactly what you want. I will get your revenge."

Although I was still in communion, I began to incorporate bits of my own imagining—something that I had always done with a haphazard instinct, but that now I could direct and control. I showed zir Xochiquetzal and what I imagined of Bathsheba and the nameless others. As I brought my own imagining to the communion, I became aware of the vast bulk of zir, the alien ocean at the back of this tiny face speaking to me. Holy terror might have overcome me, then, if I weren't more afraid of what would happen if I fell out.

"We were created for this," I told zir. "Me and my sisters. But I'm the only one who has ever understood just *how* we work. I will kill him. Don't uproot the planet from the sand. If it was unforgivable what they did to you, wouldn't it still be unforgivable to do it to someone else?"

"There is no forgiveness," ze said, though the projection no longer bothered to move zir lips. They were stretched too wide to open. "Who could forgive but the bones, who have lost their scents, their colors? Our responsibility is to time and the red ocean. And for that, the great mind must decay into heat."

"What?"

The crystal-blue tentacles reached around zir body to embrace me. I gagged at the touch, but when my mouth opened, I tasted something bubbling and sweet.

"Kill the Nameren," ze said. "Can you truly do it, little baby?"

"Let me try," I said. "Most of our universe has no idea that you exist. Let us try to set it right. When you speak to those who come after me, let it be in peace."

"There is no peace, little baby," ze said. A tentacle stroked my eyebrows. I tasted indigo wine and Nadi's bony shoulder.

I imagined a scent to give to zir, the salty-sweet syrup tinted with rose water that another of zir avatars had gifted me so long ago.

Ze swayed side to side in pleasure and embraced me in a tangle of what were now hundreds of tentacles. Through the translucent joints of each, I saw a world, or a possibility of a world—a thousand slices of time.

"None come in peace, but tithe to hell," ze said, a strange echo.

"Then," I said, "may you come in love."

✦

A girl and a god, alone in their imagining. The girl is weary as life, the god is tired unto death.

"The trap is laid and sprung," he says. His eyes are heavy and dark. There are oceans behind them. "The girl by the river lays herself as bait."

The green clay mud, the grass, the chorus of seven blinking suns: They have all fallen away. Only the baobab remains, a sentinel in darkness.

"There is no bait. There was no trap. There are only two souls in communion and a choice. Will you make it?"

"Little piper, your Iemaja could not kill me any more than I could kill zir. I am not these stones, this temple, these bloodthirsty people who have claimed me. I am a fold in space-time."

The girl is silent in the darkness. Slowly, the corners of her mouth lift. A smile her lover would recognize. "Unfold."

Something passes between them.

"It seems you have kept your promise, little baby."

And with that, the story they had thought they were telling here changes. They turn to the baobab, because they are not alone. A girl and a god and—

The girl rocks back, overwhelmed by the immensity of this presence brushing against her mind, the great body behind the tiny part that has pushed into their constructed dream: a hollow round of a trunk fat as a pregnant belly, stubby limbs and bursts of leaves like a brushy crown.

Iemaja, the girl has called zir, though this is not zir name.

No—it is also, has become, one of zir names. Not because of the librarians, those self-serving defenders of genocide, those jailers and exploiters of an unspeakably ancient, alien civilization. Because of this girl, and the others who preceded her. Because they grew into zir, just as ze grew into them.

The aurochs stares up at the great brushy boughs of the baobab. He had never thought to be surprised again.

"You can't kill me," he says softly, as though the effort pains him. "Not even you."

Something is in his eyes, some terrible war. The girl reaches out a hand, strokes his gold-furred arm. He turns, looks at her.

She will dream of that look for the rest of her life, which will be improbably long and blessed. She will dream of a god, tawny-eyed, in a universe that echoes with his absence.

"I see," he says.

The girl feels her chest crack; a warm and salty wetness spills out. "It was always a choice."

The baobab is changing zirself in the imagining, the deep brown of zir bark bleaching into the hard, porous white of dead coral, the green leaves of zir crown exploding into color and shape and movement. The girl and the god sense the weight of meaning permanently beyond their understanding.

The girl is overwhelmed with loss.

"We are proud of you, little baby," says Iemaja's voice, Kohru's voice, soft as a kiss on the back of her neck. "We will not do to this planet what they did to us."

"What is happening to you, Iemaja?" the girl asks, though she knows. She is dreaming with the both of them, after all, limited though she might be in comparison. She can feel it, the burning.

"I am preparing for our rebirth."

"And my—our—Iemaja?"

The riot of color and shape and dancing movement pauses above them. She catches a faint whiff of indigo wine and candy floss. But zir voice is thin and hard as a knife: "She was never ours, only imposed upon us."

So, the girl thinks, slipping: *I will lose them both.*

A warmth in her hands. The aurochs is holding them. He is speaking to her urgently. "I have forgotten more than the worlds can remember," he says. "But I never forgot you."

She stares at him. Parses his words with effort. "You constructed an ideal."

"Yes. They must have thought I would love the creature they made."

"And don't you?"

"You are not a thing they made. You made yourself."

Her face is a wonder. "Not quite human, broken, mended. Myself."

But she knows that he still sees her, a basket full of clams in the crook of her elbow, feet muddy in the silt of a long-dried river. She has grown into him, yes, but he has likewise grown into her. He is not so wrong, in his way. She is also that memory of a memory. She is not a thing. She encompasses worlds.

"They might cure you, on the earth where I was born. I will send you through," he says, "before I unfold. If the baobab will allow it."

The divine tree, all coral, white and color, bows its branches. "We will," ze says. "We will save the little baby."

It is distant but unmistakable: the heart of Iemaja that this ancient creature cannot quite bear to burn away. Perhaps it will be enough, in what is to come.

It seems impossible that he should not be part of this story, as he has all the others. Surely, he should witness the war gathering on the horizon, save them or doom them as he has over the course of a thousand bloody lifetimes?

But she came to kill him. And now she must face the prospect of her own survival.

"Why would you do it alone?"

"You won't save yourself? After you fought so hard to fix the hole in your heart?"

"I always knew I would die here, Nameren. If I go through, I might break my glass. I deny my other selves the chance of meeting her."

He falls silent, considering it.

But then the baobab, inscrutable witness, presses that knife of a voice through the last of her pretentions: "You will live, little baby."

Silence, again.

She looks into his golden aurochs eyes and feels: the yellow sun; the whiff of ruminant dung and drying grass in the heat before the rain; the lullaby drone of evening cicadas by the river; voices raised in forgotten songs, in a forgotten tongue, to a divinity fashioned of stone and ivory.

She had to love him, to be loved by him. She had to change. But still—

"Let me speak to her. One last time."

Aurochs steps away. Baobab lingers but does not interfere. The girl opens her eyes, gasping and alive on the roseate shard floor of the Nameren's inner shrine.

"I'm going to Tierra," she tells the one who has waited with her there.

Their lips touch and they breathe the other's breath. "He let you live."

"I'll probably break my glass."

"No. You were meant to cross worlds."

"You'll stay here. You were meant to be with the disciples."

"They're my family. I have a responsibility. But later. If there's any chance—"

"I'll come back here, if they let me. If they don't arrest me and toss me into a hole."

"I'll break my glass for you. I'll go to Tierra. We can fade to heat and light together."

"We'll meet in the middle. Back where we started. When this is over, when we've won. We'll meet—"

There will always be so much more than they can say.

✦

Aurochs unfolds.

Baobab burns.

Cicada—unexpected, undone—

carves her heart

beneath a new sun.

Author's Note

The political conundrums, philosophies, stories, and histories in this novel are entirely fictional and not intended to represent modern human cultures, beliefs, or conflicts. While there are clear influences and resonances—the exploitation of the powerless by the powerful is sadly a perennial theme in human history—this is a speculative work about a far-future civilization with vast differences from our own.

Acknowledgments

Novel writing can feel like such a solitary activity that it comes as a shock to me, every time, when I realize *how many people* have come through or sat and stayed for a while and made my not-so-solitary trek across the desert possible.

This list will be, of necessity, incomplete. Nevertheless, I will do my best to thank everyone whose contributions have helped bring Freida's story into existence, because I (and she?) are so unbelievably grateful.

Hayao Miyazaki and his team at Studio Ghibli are some of my favorite artists and storytellers of all time. I might be a writer, but any words I could use here would be inadequate to convey the depth of my respect and indebtedness to Miyazaki for the space he has created in his work for joy and story and truth-telling over the last half-century. Honestly, I think this novel itself is the best tribute I could make to how much his work means to me, particularly *Spirited Away* (*Sen to Chihiro no Kamikakushi*). The fairly out-there riffs on a kernel story that many fans will recognize were done in the spirit of a jazz musician running hard scales around a beloved tune, and I hope that if you were intrigued by them and have not yet discovered the unparalleled brilliance of his work, you will give yourself the joy of getting to know it.

There are a number of other artists who have hugely inspired me over the years—some of whom are even obliquely referenced in the text as well!—but I would like to particularly call out Ursula K. Le Guin, Octavia E. Butler, and

Samuel R. Delany. And of course I must give a shout to the Archandroid themself, the inimitable Janelle Monáe, whose centering of Black and queer futures inspired me long before I was lucky enough to collaborate with her. I could never have dared to dream of this wild future without the paths you all beat through the badlands before me.

Worldbuilding is at least half world-knowing, and there were several books that helped to expand my understanding of our world in order to speculate upon another one. I would like to highlight Sean Caroll's brilliant works of popular science, in particular *The Big Picture* and *Something Deeply Hidden*. I also greatly enjoyed Brian Greene's *The Hidden Reality*. The Stanford Encyclopedia of Philosophy was that perfect combination of in-depth and wide-ranging and deepened my understanding of a number of topics, particularly as related to the broad implications of quantum mechanics. I would also like to thank Dr. Nicholas Breznay for the all-important physics check, and for helping me get the basics right. (Any errors are most certainly my own!)

Speaking of expert readers, thank you so much to these other pre-readers who were incredibly generous with their time and expertise as I edited the manuscript: Emma Osborne, Marnyi Gyatso, and Celso Mendoza.

Many thanks to Sterling Lord Literistic for graciously allowing my use of the Malcolm Lowry poem in the epigraph.

Even before I had a completed draft of this sprawling, wildly overambitious story, I had the greatest gift ever given to any moody novelist: an agent who was indisputably in her corner. Jill Grinberg has been with me for more than a decade and every time I think, *No*, this *time she's going to tell me I've gone too far*, she gets even more excited about my next project than I am, believes in it completely, and makes sure everyone else believes in it, too. This was a long, slow, arduous process, but Jill never lost faith. Thank you so much for being the agent a writer dreams of, Jill, and for seeing Freida's story through with me. What a joy it has been to be on this journey with you.

I also must thank Denise Page and Sam Farkas, and everyone on the Jill Grinberg Literary Management team who have been incredible pillars of support for me as we navigate the always-thorny process of shepherding a book to publication. I am so grateful to work with every one of you.

I've been lucky enough to have been with Scholastic for my entire YA career, and honestly everyone I've met there has been so warm, enthusiastic, and deeply committed to publishing beautiful books that I've always been grateful to have a home with them. This novel in particular would not exist without the patient, incisive, and collaborative work by my editors, Orlando Dos Reis and David Levithan, who took a wild idea and helped grow it into a finished work that fulfilled its promise. It wasn't easy, but please know how deeply I respect and appreciate all your work. We did it!

I would also like to thank Stephanie Yang for designing some of the coolest internal pages I have had in my career, and the whole Scholastic team for their enthusiasm and belief in my work. Also, Shaylin Wallace—thank you for bringing this novel to life with such beautiful cover art.

Though Arthur Levine has left Scholastic for his own award-winning pastures at Levine Querido, I couldn't possibly let these acknowledgments go past without thanking the brilliant editor who believed in me from the first and acquired this novel when it was just three chapters and a convoluted outline. Arthur, please know that you're one of my favorite people in the world, and I hope you love what I ended up doing with Freida's story.

In between the initial idea and the finished work, countless people in my life have supported me in ways that, large and small, materially supported my writing. First, my pre-readers and sounding boards (over many drafts and years). Tamar Bihari, when you got the book so completely, I *knew* that I was going in the right direction. I'm so grateful to have such a brilliant and steady friend. Justine Larbalestier, you are the best and I'm ever grateful to have your acerbic wit and warm heart in my life. You always tell me what you think, and it makes me a better writer. Amanda Hollander, you have read so much of my work over the last twenty-eight years of friendship (how is that not a typo?!) that at this point you have a seat reserved in my acknowledgments section. Thank you for listening to a lot of griping (A LOT) and for talking me down and around and through a million seemingly insurmountable problems (including, uh, these acknowledgments!).

Of course, not everyone who supports a novel is a reader, but that doesn't make their contributions less important. Isma, el segundo que encuentre un editorial en español vas a leer mi libro cabrón pero mientras te quiero un montón y te agradezco por apoyarme y escucharme y creer en mi. Que suerte he tenido en mi vida de encontrarte.

I'd also like to thank my mother-in-law, Zoila, for cooking incredible food that both nourished my soul and expanded my conception of what food and cooking could be, a sensibility that permeates this text.

And my other friends who just bore me up or told me jokes or gave me some good hair cream when I'd been out in the country for a year and REALLY NEEDED IT: Bianca Redhead, Doselle Young, Scott Westerfeld, April Anderson, Bill Steinmetz, Abby Pritchard, Tatiana Galitzin, Luis, Ale, Amalia, my Altered Fluid crew, and honestly many others.

Family is both hard and beautiful, and I wouldn't be here today without the support of my sister Lauren, my brother Phillip, my cousin Alexis, my mom, and my always-stylish Aunt Vanessa. My nephew Brandon hasn't been around for too long, but he is way too cute not to mention here, too. My life, and my art, is so much better because all of you are in it.

And, finally, to my readers, especially Maddie, my biggest fan: You help me remember why I do this when I don't think I can bear to write another word. I write for anyone who needs to read it. And to you—whoever you are—thank you for placing your trust in me and Freida. May you follow your paths brightly.

About the Author

Alaya Dawn Johnson is the author of *The Summer Prince*—which received three starred reviews, was longlisted for the National Book Award, and was named a 2013 *Kirkus Reviews* Best Book of the Year—and *Love Is the Drug*, the 2014 Nebula Award winner for best young adult novel. Her short stories have appeared in many magazines and anthologies, most notably the title story in *The Memory Librarian*, in collaboration with Janelle Monáe. She lives in Mexico where she received a master's degree with honors in Mesoamerican studies at the Universidad Nacional Autónoma de México for her thesis on pre-Columbian fermented food and its role in the religious-agricultural calendar.